D0781743

the Night and its Moon

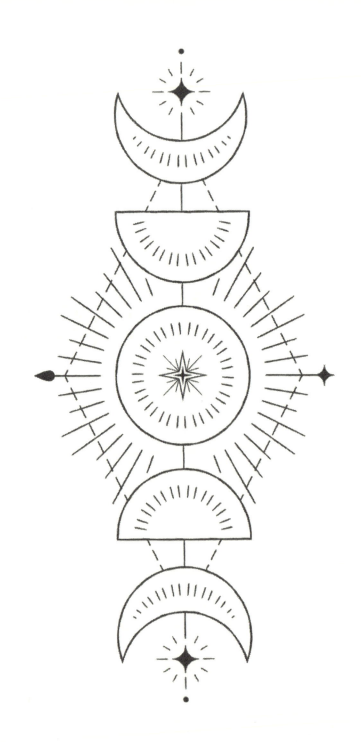

the Night and its Moon

Piper CJ

The Night and Its Moon by Piper CJ
The Night and Its Moon Series: Book One
Copyright © 2022 Piper CJ

All rights reserved® No part of this publication may be reproduced, distributed, or transmitted in any form or by any means, including photocopying, recording, or other electronic or mechanical methods, without prior written permission of the publisher, except in the case of brief quotations embodied in critical reviews and certain other noncommercial uses permitted under copyright law.

This book is a work of fiction. Names, characters, places and incidents are the product of the author's imagination and used fictitiously. Any resemblance to events, actual or imagined, including events, locales, or persons living or dead, is entirely coincidental. Any intended acknowledgements will be credited at the end.

This book is licensed for your personal enjoyment only. This book may not be re-sold. If you would like to share this with an additional party, please purchase a separate copy for each recipient. If you're reading this and did not purchase it, or it was not purchased for your use only, please purchase your own copy. Thank you for respecting the hard work of this author.

ISBN 979-8-9854544-0-6

FAWN STORYTELLING, L.L.C.
80 Broad Street,
5th floor (PMB#9987)
New York, NY 1004

pipercj.com
Orders by U.S. trade bookstores, wholesalers and all other business inquiries, please contact Piper CJ via pipercj.com/book-contact

Cover: WOLF + BEAR Co.
Editor: Katie Hamblin
Formatting: Zachary James Novels
Map: Piper CJ

NOTE: This story may not be suitable for minors and should be read and purchased with discretion. This series contains adult language, violence, and sexual situations. It is intended for sale to adults. *The Night and Its Moon* series is intended for New Adult and Adult audiences. This novel and others in the series may contain scenes and scenarios triggering to readers and should be read, purchased, and gifted with caution.

Can my dedication read:
'to buttery chardonnay, manic episodes,
and every child who wished they were a fairy'?

*No, you can't thank alcohol, mental illness,
and encourage escapism in your dedication.*

Well fine, then I don't want one.

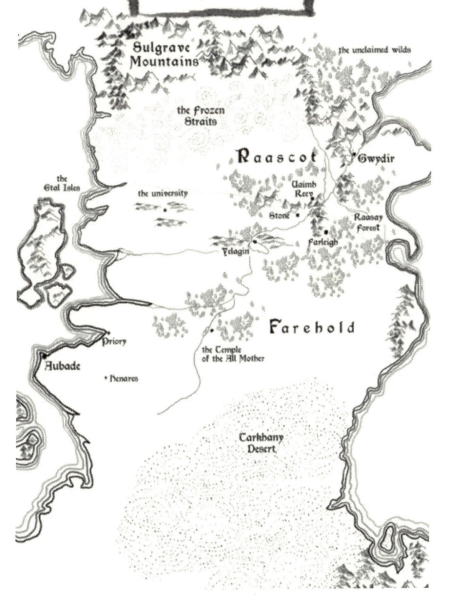

Continent of Gyrradin

"If I find in myself desires
which nothing in this world can satisfy,
the only logical explanation
is that I was made
for another world."

—*C.S. Lewis*

prologue

Cursing wasn't particularly pious behavior, but the woman couldn't keep herself from the disgruntled stream of groggy obscenities as she was jolted from her sleep.

It's seldom that a sound defines the course of history. A cannon might blast through a ship, its splintering contact declaration of the early sounds of war. A bell could ring through a city to alert its citizens to invading forces, or a king might wail into the quiet of the night at the passing of his wife as his grief began to slowly steer his kingdom. This course-altering sound was the sharp knocks against wood as they reverberated off of the stones just past midnight. The Gray Matron blinked her sleep away blearily, disoriented by the hour, grumbling her vulgarities into the pillow.

Rain tapped on the windowpanes, broken only by intermittent rumbles of thunder. Other matrons were stirring from their beds at the rhythmic pounding coming from the front door. The manor was hundreds of years old, and the noises of the storm betrayed its age. The wind whistled its haunting melody, using the staccato percussion of the rain to punctuate its music. Knocking continued as she slipped her feet into night shoes and shrugged a thick wool shawl around her shoulders. She lit a candle near her bed and held her hand to it as she hurried toward the corridor, matrons sitting up and looking on after her and she shuffled past. Matron Mabel pushed herself to the edge of the bed, her sleep-addled voice ready to be helpful.

"Should I follow?"

The woman twisted her mouth into a tight, angry line. It would not reflect well to hurl her agitated profanities at the younger matron. She was already walking out the door and didn't bother looking at her as she responded. "Go back to bed, Mabel."

"But what if it's—"

"Bed. Now."

The Gray Matron of the house left her fellow matrons behind in the gloom and continued down the hall. The matrons hadn't been the only ones in the house woken by the noise. If the storm outside hadn't bothered the children, the insistent banging certainly had. She heard the muted, sleepy noises of small voices behind the dormitory doors as she hurried down the hall. The woman felt nothing but sharp irritation that the manor's slumber was being disturbed at such an ungodly hour.

There was no excuse to wake them in the middle of the night like this. Whoever was at the door better be dying, or else she'd be the one to kill them.

A shadow moved before her, stopping her in her tracks.

It took her a moment to realize she was seeing a child. A small, bronze-skinned girl had stepped into the shadow beyond the door frame. The little girl looked up at her with dark eyes, larger than a doll's. Her fingers held the wooden frame of the doorway as she peered up at the Gray Matron.

The matron remained still. If it had been anyone else, she would have snapped at them. Instead, she frowned down at the girl. Her voice softened ever so slightly, releasing some irritation as her lips turned down at the child. "You shouldn't be out of bed, Nox. It's time to sleep."

The Gray Matron walked away without waiting to see whether the child obeyed.

Nox, no more than three and a half years to her name, didn't return to her cot. Instead, she watched with wide, coal-dark eyes as the woman disappeared down the hall with only the orange glow of her candle to betray her position.

She followed.

Curiosity pulled her forward like a physical tether, the desire to know burning hotter than the chill of the night. Her glossy hair helped to conceal her in the dark puddles of gloom. The carpet muted her footsteps as she padded along the corridor, allowing her to move soundlessly down the hall. If it hadn't been for the distracting crack of thunder and ongoing banging of the stranger at the door, the matron might have spotted her as she descended the stairs. Instead, Nox trailed the woman, unnoticed.

The girl was not just clever for her age, but had been born with a predisposition for cunning. She was always quiet, always calculating as she watched the world unfurl around her, learning its games, rules, and players. The girl was elfin small and ghostly quiet by nature, which had been an asset as she often found herself needing to remain undetected in order to observe. Her ability to slip into shadows was something she'd known intrinsically before understanding the weight of its value.

The stones were cold on her bare feet. Her knee-length nightdress didn't do much to stave back shivers. Her cleverness for shadows reassured her that she wouldn't be spotted if she crouched behind a table in the foyer. Nox remained several feet behind the Gray Matron and the buttery glow of the elder woman's candlelight. The curtain of her hair fell around her, concealing her in the shadowy puddle of her hiding place. She curled her toes into her hands to warm them as she sat in darkened silence, watching, inhaling the scent of rain and wet earth and the cold, sharp smell of late seasons.

A stranger in the middle of the night was a new player. This was a game she'd never seen before.

The matron reached the large wooden front door and lifted the iron cover to the glass spyhole carved into its middle. She peered onto whatever—or whoever— pounded on the door from their place on the landing. The matron appeared to consider her options briefly before lifting the wooden slot barricading the manor from trespassers. The knocking stopped the moment she began to pull the door open. Swirling raindrops blew over the threshold with windswept fury as if the storm itself spit in her very face. A cloaked, rain-drenched man with wild eyes leered down at the woman in her wool shawl and nightclothes. He did not step into the manor.

"Agnes, I have something you'll want to see."

The Gray Matron started to shake her head with a disgruntled sound. She began to push the door shut once more, intent on relieving herself from both the bother of the rain and the unwanted presence of the stranger.

The man flattened his palm against the door, refusing to let it close. It was clear he'd decided he'd had enough of cordial pretense.

The man ignored her non-verbal denial for entry, pushing past her as he crossed the threshold. Agnes let out an irritated protest, but he was undaunted. The stranger stopped on the landing and pulled a large, covered bundle that he'd tucked carefully under his arm. He lifted the treasure into the space between the two of them.

Water droplets dripped from the blankets that shielded the bundle onto the rug below. The matron glared, whispering something in sharp, angry tones. Nox strained her ears but couldn't discern one verbal hiss from the other. The pounding rain and angry howls of wind drowned out whatever the two were trying to say. She wished they'd shut the door. The storm was wetting the carpet and drenching the matron's nightclothes, hair and face. A few stray droplets were carried on the blustering wind and kissed her face, hands, and knees from where she hid in the shadows. She tried again to usher the man out of the hall so that she could close the door, but he disregarded her efforts entirely.

The man began to uncover the bundle. Matron Agnes shook her head again, volume growing with her anger. "I don't do that anymore."

The man's eyes seemed to sparkle with a smile, though his mouth did not curve as it should. There was a wickedness to his unsavory delight. "You mean you *didn't* do this anymore. That was before you saw what I've brought you." He peeled off the sopping wet top layer of blankets, continuing to unwrap what soon appeared to be a wicker basket. He lifted the bundle, urging Agnes to peer inside.

The Gray Matron lifted her candle close to the bundle and let out a small gasp as its glow illuminated whatever it contained. "Wait," she breathed.

The energy shift was palpable.

She hurried to the door and closed it the rest of the way, shutting out the world beyond and the storms that raged. Agnes ushered the man a few more steps inside the manor onto dry carpet. The new silence had a smothering effect. With the door latched once again, the wind, rain and thunder were muted with unnatural intensity. The silence was so pressing that Nox wondered if they could hear her little heart as it thundered with curious anticipation from the shadows behind the table.

She clutched herself more tightly, not only against the cold, but to hold herself back from the temptation to see what had caused The Gray Matron to gasp.

Agnes walked away from the man to light the hall's fixtures. She held her candle to the lanterns on either side of the door, chasing the eerie gloom from the room as their oil-soaked rags caught fire. While the lanterns filled the foyer with light, Nox's puddle of shadow remained concealed. The woman returned to the basket, her face betraying a complex array of emotions. Wariness and skepticism bubbled to the forefront as she stared down at whatever had been smuggled into her manor.

Agnes appeared to be struggling with her thoughts. Her fingers stayed against mouth, stifling her sharp inhalation. She looked up at the man's degenerate grin, scanning the strange way his eyes and mouth failed to match as he smiled. The pair kept their voices low as they spoke, tones hushed with secrecy.

Nox scrunched her face in whatever unnamed frustration burbled within her. She hated that she couldn't hear. She wanted them to share what they'd found. She needed the tether that wrapped itself fully within her chest and pulled her forward to relax its taut hold.

"Well, that does change things," Agnes painted her words with disbelief.

"What did I tell you?" he asked.

She didn't look away from the bundle.

The man pushed on, "It's just past its first birthday. It won't be needing a wet nurse. Anything in the kitchen can be mushed up right fine. It's already made it through the hardest time. I've been traveling with it for nearly two weeks and had no trouble keeping it alive."

"Two weeks?" Agnes's brows collected in the middle as calculations flitted behind her eyes. "Where did you find it? Why did you bring it here?"

"You know me," he said with too much familiarity. "I owed you one. You deserved first bid at the treasure."

Nox heard their words, but understood little of their meaning. She was too little to understand much beyond the most fundamental truth: none of them were supposed to be here. She should be in her bed. Agnes should not be consorting with strangers. Men should not be arriving with presents in the midst of a storm.

Agnes's face creased as her mind moved. She seemed to experience conflicting emotions that gathered in the twist of her mouth, the wrinkle of her forehead, and the parallel lines between her brows. She stared for a while longer before asking, "How much do you want for it?"

"Fifty crowns."

Agnes made a sound between a cough and a laugh which shocked Nox from her quiet poise in the stillness of the quiet manor. She jolted upright in a startle, but the shadows clung to her, keeping her safe from detection in their darkened pool. The matron's bark mixed with the sounds of the storm outside as the noises were equally unruly. The shadows from the lanterns made her face look animal as she prolonged her disbelieving gape.

"Fifty crowns! There isn't nothing in the good goddess's lighted earth worth fifty!" She looked over her shoulder, her gaze roving up the stairs as if she could see through the stones and into the dormitories where the children rested on their cots. "I haven't paid a penny over five silvers for half the bastards in here. I have one girl worth ten crowns on a good day, and she's the rarest of them all. Ain't no one spending fifty crowns on your stolen babe."

There was an abrupt shift in tone, though nothing had to be spoken to communicate its weight. His gaze no longer twinkled. The man's mouth tugged upward, revealing his teeth, cold smile glinting in the candlelight. The man said nothing but remained holding the basket, unmoved.

The Gray Matron balked, "I'll give you fifteen."

He remained impassively rooted to the carpet.

"Twenty, and that's the highest I'll go."

Nox knew little of money, except that it was good to have some, and that people always wanted more. She thought of the coppers, steel, and golds of the heavy coins she'd seen and what it might be like to have twenty, metal circles in her tiny hands. Instead, she continued to clutch her little toes against the cold. She wiggled them within her hands, knowing she had ten toes and ten fingers. That was twenty.

Agnes's numbers had already betrayed her. The Gray Matron

wanted whatever the stranger possessed. Be it the lateness of the hour or the unusual nature of the package, it didn't seem pertinent to conduct proper negotiations on the landing. They both knew enough of bartering and haggling to know Agnes had lost negotiations the moment they'd started. This transaction would end nearly as abruptly as it had begun.

The man tilted his head ever so slightly, raising a brow. Rain dripped off of his soaked cloak as it hung around his shoulders. Small puddles formed on the carpet around his wet boots. He pushed her for her answer. "Farleigh isn't the only mill on this side of the mountains, Agnes. It's a rainy night, and I don't particularly want to play games. I like you, and we've done business in the past, so I wanted to give you the first crack at the treasure. But you and I both know that no one's getting this pretty thing for a cent less than fifty crowns."

The woman shuffled her weight from one foot to the other for a moment. "Is it a boy?"

"It's a girl."

Agnes chewed her lip, looking conflicted. She lowered her voice when she spoke again, despite the two of them being alone on the threshold. Some things were too indecent for even the goddess to hear.

"Your stolen goods were fine when we were younger," she seemed to be arguing against herself. "We had a good thing back then. You'd take from the village. I told myself you were doing a favor to the parents, I did. You were taking away a mouth to feed. I've always preferred that parents come to me on their own, of course… I'm not that person anymore."

Nox was still listening intently as the matron spoke. None of the words made sense. It was a garble of odd language and strange words as she spoke of children, villages, and coins. Nox's eyes had adapted to the dark, but she strained them as she squinted up at the matron, hoping it might help her to understand what was happening. Agnes continued speaking, though her words were more to herself than to the man on the landing.

"I didn't feel guilty, you know? I always felt I was doing a good thing—we did a good thing. Give a poor mother a silver to feed the rest of the young ones at home. Perhaps even a few pennies to a peasant or a town whore so she could get boots for the winter or a warm blanket in exchange for the struggles of motherhood. It was a good thing, it was. Times were different then. But after..." she shook herself from her memories to meet the man's eyes. "It's not like that. People are going to come searching for this one. Look at her."

His smile fell a bit as he spoke with seriousness. The hush of his voice sent a chill through the hall. "No one is going to come looking for her."

Agnes's brows puckered, exacerbating the lines that had come from decades of frowning. She let the silence between them stretch. The window and rain beyond the closed door had a soothing, stifling effect on the room, dampening the world around them. Torches flickered, rain droplets continued to drip onto the floor from soaked clothes, thunder rumbled in the distance, and yet the matron stared.

"Will she be any trouble? With her lineage, I mean?"

"You're asking me if she's one of them?"

Agnes said nothing.

He didn't seem perturbed by the question. "Raise her however you want, and don't let her give you trouble. When the time comes, sell her for a hundred."

Agnes reached a hand in close to touch whatever was within the bundle. Her fingers stroked a slow line along the unseen package. "One hundred?"

The man's wordless stare was the only negotiation tactic he required.

"I said I was done," she repeated. Despite her words, they both knew she had already decided. Her fingers lingered on whatever, or whoever was inside the basket. Her following thoughts came out nearly as a purr, if only to herself. "Turn fifty crowns into one hundred ... Or one thousand." Agnes finally lifted her eyes to the man. She spoke with clarity and certainty. "Never again. After this, you don't come back."

He dipped his chin once in solemn acknowledgment. This would be their last meeting.

The Gray Matron sent him a final, telling look before giving him a hushed command and pattering away from the large landing room. Agnes headed up the stone stairs and down the corridor lined with doors to the children's rooms, presumably returning to her office where she kept the crowns and silvers under lock and key. A moment stretched where the man watched after her, shifting his weight on the threshold.

The tether tugged Nox once more, and she obeyed its call.

From her hiding space several paces away, the inky-haired child straightened her little legs and stepped out from where she'd been crouching. The man noticed the quiet, beautiful girl immediately. He smiled, his face a bit soft, a bit sad. For the first time that night, his expression held no wickedness. Now that the matron was absent, he was able to drop whatever hardness he'd needed for negotiations. Nox noticed how droplets of water caught in his beard and reflected in the torchlight, giving him something of a shimmer. The sparkle seemed reassuring, somehow.

The man knelt on one knee and placed the wicker basket on the floor between them.

"Do you want to see?" he asked. His voice had dropped with a paternal gentleness, though he framed his question with a conspiratorial temptation.

She did indeed. The girl had no desire to draw closer to a strange man, but the basket called to her. Nox took a few careful steps across the cold stones of the corridor onto the carpet of the threshold. Her bare feet paused on the fibers of the scratchy rug. Her eyes were too large for this world as she gazed at the man and his treasure. She'd expected him to smell of dirt or sweat, a renewed rush of rain and earth greeted her with every step she took.

He looked at her expectantly. The raven-haired child remained several cautious arm's lengths away from him. He chuckled quietly, as though he knew she wasn't permitted to be awake past bed and had no interest in getting her in trouble. This would be their secret.

He motioned her toward the basket. Nox had wanted an opening and took it. She moved forward on the tips of her toes, hands extended. She folded her fingers around the wicker edge of the basket and looked. The child stared down at the baby inside, her glossy hair creating a shadowed curtain around them while she peered. A rush of something other than rain—something more like cold and pine—drifted up from the swaddled little one. Nox found herself looking at an infant wrapped in furs, sleeping soundly despite the turmoil raging outside.

"It's a baby," she whispered. She did not look back up to the man. For all she cared, he had ceased existing. She was transfixed.

Nox had seen babies before.

The matrons let all the children play together, often with the older ones looking after the younger ones as a convenient source of unpaid labor. Infants never lasted long in the manor, sometimes for good reasons, sometimes for bad. The orphans who survived their first year of life were taken off the matron's hands more quickly than the rest of the children. They often sold the littlest ones to childless couples, or mothers who had lost their natural-born babes in birth. Babies came and went, creating a rich, playtime lore among the children, stories conceived by escapism and wishful thinking. Fairytales of being whisked away filled their imaginations.

They told tall tales of how orphans had been adopted by knights, by fae, by kings and queens, or by leagues of assassins who guarded the continent. A favorite bedtime story amongst the orphaned children at the manor had been that of a princess who came to Farleigh in the night, looking for an infant boy to match her husband's gold-brown hair. The folktale began as most did, with a dramatic pause and the insistence that it had been a dark and stormy night, as was always the case in children's richest tales. The story was that a princess had traded her daughter—one of the traitorous features of a love held outside of her marriage—for a golden-haired boy, one who would be heir to the throne. The children told it in a dream-like state, all of them hoping one day someone would sweep away their misfortune, exchanging it for a life in a castle. It was better to imagine taken children living beautiful lives than the often-cruel reality of what happened when little ones were sold. Their lives were already difficult. They didn't need to know the practical realities of what would most likely happen upon their purchase.

This babe, however, was unlike any she'd ever seen.

Nox took a small, tanned hand and brushed a silver-white strand of hair out of the baby's face. The motion revealed a tuft of white brows and thick white eyelashes. The baby stirred slightly at the movement, eyes fluttering open. It didn't cry when it looked at her. Instead, it seemed to wiggle within its blankets, blinking happily at the child who peered down at her. The infant looked up at Nox with lavender-colored eyes flecked with silver, cooing slightly before drifting back to sleep.

"She's made of snow," Nox said quietly.

"That she is."

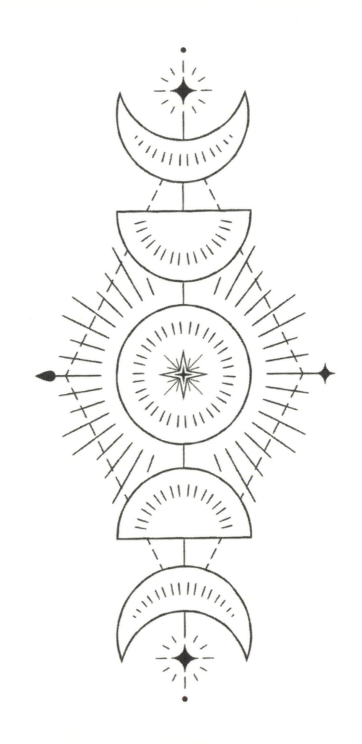

-PART ONE-

Alone, Together

Agnes brushed her peppered gray hair into a bun before pulling her aprons over her uniform. She ordered the matrons to wash and brush the children after breakfast, cleaning up any crusted porridge from the meals off their faces before the bishop arrived.

"Get going!" Agnes bit at the other matrons.

"We still have an hour until he arrives," Matron Mable attempted to sound reassuring.

"Less than an hour now that you've wasted time correcting me. You should be preparing the children."

On the first day of each month, the children were organized into clean lines wearing their pressed gray linen dresses and trousers. They would practice their letters, say their prayers to the All Mother, recite the Blessed Obediences, and listen to lessons on Queen Moirai and her lighted kingdom of Farehold, as well as its counterpart, the dark northern kingdom.

Their lessons were focused on the southern kingdom while they sat with the matrons. Their kingdom stretched from the western shores to their forested border on the edge of Farehold, only a few days from the ever-looming threat of Raascot's territory. The people referred to Farehold somewhat flippantly as the Kingdom of Light, as the coast, the fertile farmlands, and the prosperity of the All Mother seemed to shine upon it. They were permitted their murmurs about the lighted magics in the south, but any questions about darker magics in the north were met with the swift thwack of a ruler to the fingers.

Farleigh was on Farehold's northeastern border, where the seasons changed with a powerful sting, and the winters were particularly unforgiving. The manor had been standing on its property for centuries, existing long before the darker beings had been pushed back up into the mountains by the brave kings and queens of yesteryear. How a manor meant to shelter orphans had survived and remained in the custodianship of the matrons in what used to be a lawless territory remained in question. Still it, like most unexplained things, was assumed to be evidence of the All Mother and her goodness.

When a child asked about magic, they were met with lessons on math. They were sent to study their prayers, should they inquire about the fae. The orphans were a bottomless well of questions about light and dark, magic and human, Farehold and Raascot, but whatever children learned of politics or power was told through the lens of the matrons who never went anywhere nor did anything. Intelligent children learned not to ask. Any hope for tales of adventure, of demons or witches or heroes, any desire to hear of a world beyond their walls, was squashed. Curiosity was rarely rewarded.

Farleigh was a religious institution, after all and their studies should reflect it as such.

The All Mother was good. The All Mother desired order, balance, and peace. The All Mother was love, service, and humility. Her attributes stretched on, and the repetitions of her prayers were ever so tiresome, as were the visits of the men of the cloth. The orphans were even less excited about visits from the church as they were about their prayers and studies.

Each month, a bishop from the church would pass through the manor, inspecting it for standards of cleanliness, piety, and godliness. As a recipient of the church's charitable donations, Farleigh needed to remain within the church's good standing.

Everyone had a part to play in the monthly ritual.

Their actions had become a dance timed to unheard music. The matrons would bow as the bishop and his white and gold robes breezed into the manor. If there was any question as to the man and his stature, the sigil of the All Mother had been embroidered with gold stitching into his lapels. The very same symbol had been welded onto the front of Farleigh's doors, meant to drill into each and every one of them that they were one in the same.

The children were trained to answer in polite, pithy platitudes to satisfy the man of the cloth and his many questions. If a child failed to demonstrate religious devotion, he or she was taken by the matrons to be quietly punished, which usually consisted of being locked in a broom closet until they were properly repentant or writing one hundred lines of contrition. The matrons knew better than to leave a mark on the children, lest any evidence be reported to the church or devalue the merchandise on market day.

If Farleigh kept up its appearance as a religious beacon, the church would grant them sanctuary from the kingdom's taxes and would continue to fill its coffers. Surely the church had heard rumors of the child mill run within Farleigh's walls, but the bishop seemed to turn a blind eye as long as its children were clean and well-behaved. Rumors of the bishop and Agnes exchanging coin were unsubstantiated, and frankly didn't seem to matter. Nothing they said or did would change the lived experience of the orphans.

Farehold had officially outlawed mills long ago, though, stopping them with any sincerity was another matter entirely.

The church had argued that mills rewarded bastards born out of wedlock, as mothers could simply abandon their responsibilities or treat their wombs like factories, selling whatever deigned to pop out. If Farleigh were to continue receiving donations, the matrons who served it would vehemently deny all rumors of their dealings in pennies and silvers.

"Agnes?" Mable's face was lined with fret.

"I told you to get going!"

"He's just arrived. I'm so sorry. He's early!"

Agnes looked to the younger matron with withering displeasure, as though the bishop's unscheduled arrival were her fault. She hurried out of the room, barely pausing at the girl's dormitory to shout for the girl.

"Nox, he's here!"

The girl's eyes widened. He was early. "I'm coming!"

"No, now!"

Agnes hurried down the stairs to await their visitor with the dark-haired young woman on her heels. The Gray Matron barely had time to straighten her skirts and pull her shoulders back before greeting him.

"Your Excellency," Agnes bowed, letting the bishop into the manor.

He offered the barest tilt of his head in acknowledgement, fingers steepled in front of him.

The man was impeccably dressed and appeared to be in his early fifties. He would have held a stately air no matter what he wore but was always dressed in the whites and golds of his station. Agnes was of similar age and equally intimidating stature, but cunning enough to play whatever games of diplomacy were required of her.

Nox had learned more about games and how to play them from Agnes than from anyone else. The Gray Matron had the sort of wicked cleverness that allowed her to see several moves ahead of her opponent at all times. She acted accordingly. She often won the game without the competition realizing they were playing at all.

Despite the smell of the road and the horses outside, the bishop held the scent of white musk and lemons. If the perfume had possessed a color, it would have matched his robes. His choking odor was overpowering, filling the orphanage with the cloud of his presence one day each month. There was a falseness to the lemon scent that made the children's stomachs turn. The tangy smell and its link to the bishop drove the children to hate the presence of citrus if ever it was brought from the coast—a special treat that had failed to elicit the intended smiles on more than one occasion.

Nox parted her lips slightly, breathing through her mouth so that she wouldn't have to gag on the odor of fake lemons.

He did not acknowledge Nox, but she'd expected as much. He never did, no matter how many times he visited. The same frail, balding man had been their bishop for years. He knew the grounds as well as the children under her care. His familiarity with the orphanage made his visits brief—a small blessing.

Agnes accepted the man's traveling cloak and passed it off to Nox.

Nox, nearly thirteen years of age, accepted the cloak, and was happy her role in the exchange had come to an end. She knew what was expected of her each and every month. Her bronze skin was a showcase to the church of the holy nature of Farleigh and its reach beyond Farehold's borders. She served as a living advertisement of the matron's magnanimity and charity, as the deeply tanned girl differentiated herself from the pink-undertones of her peers. Agnes said, "Please hang this in my office, and be sure everything is in order."

Though the matron said 'everything', she had only one thing in mind.

Nox's expression remained neutral. She stepped forward, fully aware as to how her very presence before the bishop served as a rather insulting display of tokenism. Regardless, she didn't mind being trotted out like a show pony if it meant she could then disappear for the rest of the day. It was better than staying amidst the others and being subjected to their miserable monthly traditions. She dipped her chin slightly in obligatory respect, clutching the rich cloth before departing. The bishop made a small, approving face. He'd seen her every month for years and had come to expect her compliant servitude at each visit. It was as much acknowledgement as she'd get from the man.

Cloak draped over her arm, Nox walked down the short stone corridor and up the stairs in her soft leather shoes. She turned down that corridor and ran along the line of dormitories before pausing at the young girl's room. Her face shifted the moment she opened the door. The heaviness she carried fell from her shoulders like rainwater off of a pointed roof. Nox beamed at the white-haired girl inside, eyes glinting.

"Finally!"

"You ready, Snowflake?"

Amaris had been waiting on the bed closest to the door. She beamed the moment Nox entered the room. Her feet dangled off the edge and hands on either side of the mattress, feet twisting impatiently. The girl hopped up from the bed, her starlight hair hanging loosely down her back. Nox led the way, and she followed wordlessly into the Gray Matron's office where they hung the bishop's cloak. It was far from her first time in the office, but every visit felt like a special adventure. Forbidden spaces often seemed to carry an undue weight of importance.

Agnes's private study looked nothing like the rest of the orphanage. While Farleigh was a mundane mix of gray stone, simple linens, and cotton dresses, Agnes's office had been laminated with fleur-de-lis wallpaper and a plush carpet that existed only within the confines of her study. A gaudy painting of Farehold's royal family, an embroidered tapestry of Gyrradin, and several decorative objects were mounted on the wall. Each time they stepped into the office conjured a jarring sense of incongruity. It was a bit like traveling to a foreign land that remained hidden within the always-locked office of their very orphanage.

"Where do you think all this stuff came from?" Amaris asked, wandering around the room. "I've never seen anything new added."

Nox shrugged, "Her past life as a dragon sitting atop a treasure hoard."

"Are dragons real?"

Nox rolled her eyes at the question, though she didn't mean to tease the girl. "I don't think so, but I know Agnes is real and she's enough of a monster for the continent, don't you think?"

A large, mahogany desk rested at the study's center. On it rested a few marvelous trinkets. There were ordinary things like neat stacks of papers, rows of books, and bottles of ink. Then there were more peculiar oddities, like a crystal sphere on what appeared to be the body of a golden snail, and a pen with a long, black embellished feather quill, and an ornamental carving of a stag. While the orphanage was barren, Agnes's office was lined with armoires and shelving. Some furnishings were enclosed in glass with delicate possessions hidden behind their frosted doors. Shelves were filled with books of various sizes and states of decay. Some tomes were old, leather, dusty things. Others were small, new bright bindings with jewel-covered backs and hardly any signs of use.

"Look at this," Nox motioned Amaris over from where she had been tracing her pale finger along a map of the kingdom, finding Farleigh pinned with a star. The dry, scratchy parchment had created a dragging noise beneath her finger as she allowed her nail to trace their place in the world. Farleigh was just up and to the right of the center of the map, sitting before a sprawl of forest that was intercepted by an endless stretch of darkly shaded mountains. The dotted line that separated them from the northern kingdom loomed terribly close. Amaris stepped away from the map and came to where Nox held open one of the frosted cabinet doors. Inside, the black velvet head of a mannequin sat in the center, where a small, gilded tiara rested gently atop it, glinting with black jewels.

"Is that a crown?" Amaris's voice was one of amusement more so than fascination.

"Can you imagine Matron Agnes in such a thing? I like to think she puts it on after we've gone to bed." They stifled giggles as they shot their parting glances at the office, knowing they couldn't loiter for too much longer without getting into some sort of trouble. Perhaps next month, they'd return to the room to see what other precious secrets their matron hid.

"Put it on," Amaris goaded.

"Are you trying to get me in trouble? You're the little princess, you put it on."

"Where did she get the money for all of these things?" Amaris asked, and Nox felt a small stab that the girl hadn't yet pieced together the answer. Maybe it was a blessing to still hold on to the scraps of innocence that allowed her to be spared from the harsh realities of their mill. She didn't want to be the one to shatter the ivory girl's world.

Nox shrugged, as she did whenever she couldn't find the right words for what needed to be said.

Amaris turned away from the armoire, eyes scanning the office for a place to hide. She could always crawl under the desk, but she was rather confident they shouldn't stay in the Gray Matron's private space. "Where does she want me to go this time?"

Nox scrunched her face, "She didn't say, but I think we're safest in the kitchen. I'll stick you in with the potatoes," she smiled at her joke. "We probably shouldn't be in Agnes's room for much longer if we don't want to get caught, in case they come in here to talk business. Besides, even if the bishop visits the kitchen to see that it's clean, he never goes into the pantry."

23

"The pantry is so dirty, though!"

"Then I guess you're getting a bath tonight."

Amaris shivered preemptively at the thought of the chilly bathwater. It was challenging enough for the matrons to keep the orphans clean; heating the water between children would have been an impossible inconvenience.

"What if we hid in the clean laundry basket? It would smell much nicer."

"I bet it would," she deflected, "but the potatoes are calling." She gave Amaris a gentle push out of the office and closed the door behind them.

Most days in Farleigh blurred together with monotony. The breaks in boredom and continuity were moments like these—days of stress, fear, and trepidation. The ability to find small, private joys amid stomach-churning anxiety was a blessing.

The bishop would be gone within an hour or two. The man typically breezed through the manor in his robes, made mental notes of any new additions to the orphanage's population, inspected the premises, and dutifully inquired whether any of the small magics had manifested in any of the children.

It had been a long time since the manor had seen a faeling, as the last young boy with beautiful elfin features and a gentle disposition had one traitorous attribute betraying half of his heritage. He may not have inherited the pointed ears of the fair folk, but his forest-green irises had been nearly double the size of his human peers. If you looked at him quickly, you might miss the trait completely. Any careful student would see his large eyes as evidence of what he was.

Some of the children swore he could speak to the trees. Others insisted they'd seen him move the wind. The boy may have been utterly powerless, possessing little more than a single telltale feature of a fae lineage, but it hadn't mattered. The bishop had taken him from the manor and the boy was never spoken of by the matrons again.

Some religious folk believed both the fae and those born with the small magics to be manifestations of the goddess's power. As such, Farehold's fae were often conscripted to work by the church or put in servitude to the crown. The children told themselves in whispers that the faeling they'd known was somewhere in a house of the goddesses, living in fine robes, worshipping the All Mother and eating as much fruit as he liked. Fewer and fewer fae could be found in the southern kingdom with every generation that passed, and even the ones who did exist were almost always the mixed offspring of a romantic entanglement with a human.

Being born fae in such a world seemed like more of a curse than a blessing. Being born different in any capacity was a threat. Even Amaris, with her moonlit hair and lilac eyes, was guarded like a secret to prevent the very same fate from happening to her.

Nox didn't believe in happy endings.

She assumed that, elsewhere in the orphanage, children were being slapped on the hands with the bishop's sharp gold rod as they spoke. Nothing convinced her that the faeling boy had been sent anywhere pleasant, despite the wishful tales the others liked to tell. Children invented stories to help make sense of a chaotic world, but their hope made the world no less terrible. She'd never seen anything worthy come from the All Mother's church. This mill was one of its affiliates, after all, and what a testament to the church's goodness it was.

They avoided the front of the manor, knowing it's where the bishop monitored the students and their lessons. A set of narrow stairs connected the corridor's end directly to the kitchen before opening into the world and forest beyond. It had probably been intended for servants upon the manor's construction but had long-since served as a functional convenience for the matrons to drift from the kitchens to the chambers as they monitored the children.

The girls descended the winding steps. They followed the sizzling scents of meat and onion into the large, sweltering room. Heat from the crackling fire beneath the pot of stew hit the girls immediately as they entered. Matron Mable hadn't spotted them yet. She was the youngest matron in the house, and whenever she was on kitchen duty, it gave the children some hope for the evening meal. Mable was one of the few matrons who believed in spices and seasoning, which made her meals a blessing compared to the bland porridges and dry meats prepared by the others.

Mable, scarcely in her thirties, was an honest young woman with the kind of simple generosity that seemed to foster no dreams that reached beyond the walls of her life in Farleigh. Her hair had curled a bit against the heat of the kitchen, sweat, and steam unraveling a few loose strands from the bun she'd gathered at the nape of her neck. Her face perked at the sight of the girls as they entered from the shadows of the stairwell.

The girls smiled at the matron in her pressed gray linens and aprons, kneading dough on the wooden block table where they opened the door to the room. Not lifting her flour-covered hands, Mabel's lips tugged upward in an easy smile. She knew as well as anyone in the manor that it did no good to draw attention on days the bishop visited, so she wordlessly jutted her chin upward and to the left, motioning the girls toward the pantry. Nox offered a thankful gesture and led her friend into the dark, enclosed space, shutting the door behind them. The air was slightly cooler behind the closed door. The earthy smells of dirt and root vegetables overpowered the stew that simmered just beyond the pantry door.

Amaris ran her finger along the shelf to collect dust. She made a face at the dirt.

"Careful. You'll get a splinter," Nox cautioned.

Amaris attempted to blow the dust off of her finger, but it was caked on too heavily. She wiped it on her pants. "Goddess forbid I get a splinter. The world would end."

Nox's mouth quirked into a half-smile. "They'd blame me if you got hurt, and you know it."

Nox took a seat on the floor of the little room and reclined against a sack of flour, raising one arm so that Amaris would wriggle underneath it. The snow-white girl nestled beneath her.

"I hate the first day of the month," Amaris said.

The older of the two smiled affectionately. She pressed a kiss on the top of Amaris's head with a reassuring gentleness. "I don't think it's so bad."

While the kitchen smelled of what would undoubtedly be dinner and the pantry of roots, Amaris's hair had always smelled like juniper. It was the sweet, lingering scent of the forest and fresh, wet winter days. The girls were roughly two years apart in age, and while some days it seemed like no time at all, in these protective moments, it felt like a lifetime.

"What if we just... didn't hide? Would it be so bad if we stopped running and let the bishop see me? Or," she reached her hand up to a shelf, threatening to touch it, "what if we just cut up my hands on splinters? Let's cover me in scars!" She was smiling, but her friend didn't return the expression.

Nox's mouth turned down in a frown, knowing the many reasons it would be a very bad idea. It was useless to ask, but she couldn't blame Amaris for wanting a normal life.

Amaris was hardly the only stolen child at the manor, nor was she the only one for sale. The boys and girls alike would be presented to hopeful parents as prospective heirs, to farmers who needed labor, once or twice to a knight who needed a squire replaced for one reason or another. Occasionally a wealthy father who didn't need a dowry would come to purchase his son a young, virginal wife, or a duchess would find her way to the teenage girls and fetch a lady-in-waiting. Unlucky boys would be sold off to work under the bellies of ships once they were strong enough to hoist the sails and carry the barrels. Equally unlucky girls would be purchased for pleasure houses. The university occasionally picked up children who showed an aptitude for the small magics if the church didn't find them first, whether to study or be studied, no one knew.

While all of the children at Farleigh had a clock ticking above their heads to their eventual sale date, Amaris would be shown only to those with wallets deep enough to make it worth Matron Agnes's while. It had been pressed into the heads of the matrons that their ivory child was both a high-value asset and a target for theft should anyone lay eyes on what they wanted but could not afford. For this same reason, Agnes didn't dare risk her investment being dragged off to the church without so much as a coin in compensation. Amaris was valuable, and history had proved time and time again that the world was not always kind to its treasures.

Everything about her life was as alienating for her as it was for her peers.

"Is there anything to eat in here?" Amaris asked, scanning the shelves. She thought about how the other children weren't allowed to visit the pantry. Perhaps if they were going to hate her, she should at least find nice snacks along the way.

Nox unraveled herself from Amaris's arms and stood, scanning the shelves. "Do you like raw turnips?" She asked, mouth quirking again. Amaris didn't always appreciate her sense of humor, which she found to be quite the shame.

"Are you sure there aren't boxes of chocolates up there?"

"I'm confident Agnes is hiding sweets in her office."

"Next month? Treasure hunting for candy?"

She wrapped her finger around a rather large radish and sat down next to Amaris again, allowing them to slip into their familiar embrace. "You can close your eyes and pretend it's candy. Though raw radishes are a bit sour... and bitter... on second thought, this might be a challenging game of make-believe."

"I've never been good at pretending. Things are what they are."

Half of her tugged in a wry expression at that. The orphans may hate her, but Nox couldn't tear her heart from the feeling she'd had when she first laid eyes on the tiny snowflake. Amaris would always have one friend at the orphanage.

"That they are. Sometimes it doesn't hurt to want something more."

More often than not, it felt as though she and Amaris had been pit against the world. The other children would be thrilled if they left Farleigh for good. The matrons were neither friend nor foe. They operated with cool neutrality as one might with any business. The children needed to be well-manned, obedient, and clean to be accepted into their new homes and professions. They couldn't be bruised or beaten in a way that would mar their value or break their spirits. Education was required of the orphans—at least enough to pass in a variety of life's requirements so they'd be fit for a number of stations. More than anything, they needed to be adaptable to whatever life would hold for them beyond the manor's walls so that Agnes could turn a profit.

Nox looked at the radish in her hand, turning it over as she examined the magentas and whites of the root. She thought of Amaris's earlier question and landed on an honest, simplified answer to why they needed to continue to hide. "You're worth more than the bishop would know how to handle."

"What about you?" Amaris asked, looking up with her soft, lavender eyes.

She'd asked it innocently enough. Her tone made it sound like she didn't care too much about the response—she'd simply been talking to make conversation. There'd been nothing malicious or insensitive in Amaris's question, but Nox didn't know how to answer it. It wasn't her value that kept her away on market day, nor was it her need to avoid questions of the church that had the black-haired girl hiding in the pantry now. Agnes had favored Nox from childhood and trusted her to shield Amaris when prying eyes came to Farleigh. Perhaps being the dependable hand of the Gray Matron was her value, even if it's a title and set of duties that should have gone to one of the other matrons, not to an orphan.

Nox opened her mouth to voice her answer when a sound came from the kitchen. It didn't sound like Matron Mable. The scraping of shoes and the disorderly noise of more than one body in the space jostled beyond the door.

"Did you hear something?" Amaris whispered.

"Shh," Nox hushed her, muscles tensing with a peculiar readiness. She felt her back stiffen, her legs curling beneath her as if she were ready to run. The girls stilled as they listened to the evidence of scuffling, eyes wide.

The pantry door flung open.

The angry, defensive jolt that shocked through them was every bit as intense as a bolt of lightning.

Nox was on her feet before the others had the chance to take a single step inward. Her face tightened angrily, fists balling at her sides. Her eyes narrowed in the moment it took Amaris to understand what was happening. Of all the nightmares at Farleigh, between the chores, the matrons, and being sold off to the highest bidders, there were the fragile egos of ginger, freckle-faced Achard and his friends lording over them. Achard had been punished more times than most in the house, taking the caning, the spankings, the isolations, and punishments that would stoke the fire of his hateful heart without marring his physical value. Anytime a matron took out her anger on him, he turned around and unleashed his fists on one of his peers. Nox was no stranger to their tripping feet, their jeers, their sniggered words or their punches. Agnes's preferential treatment had been just another target on her back.

She exploded with the white-hot fire of internal rage every time he came near her.

Achard was a stereotype of an awful toad of a thirteen-year-old boy. He had picked on her and pulled her hair and then pushed his mouth against hers behind the stables after they'd crested thirteen, wanting more from her than she'd ever give. She had gagged, disgusted at his forced affection, and left him with a swollen, black eye. Her knuckles had bruised from the impact they'd made against his face and she treasured the small pain as evidence of her swift and cathartic justice. Nox would never forgive the type of person who took what they wanted, though the mentality was everywhere in Farleigh. Following the altercation behind the stables, Achard had lied to shield his pride and said he'd been kicked by one of the ponies. After that day, Achard had brewed hatred for Nox only known to unbridled youth scorned from unwanted advances in the black cauldron of his bruised, childish heart.

"Why would you come here?" Nox asked, voice angry. She knew the reason, but still struggled to understand their stupidity. Even in her darkest moments, she wouldn't have subjected a peer to the mercies of the bishop.

The way his sneering face snagged on Amaris said enough.

When the angry boys or unloved older girls of the house made fun of Nox, she was able to hold her head high. But when Amaris had become a target of their anger, it was birthed of the ugliness of their jealousy. The snow-born girl whom the matrons allow to risk hard labor, lest it mar her perfect skin, had no say in whether she chopped wood or repaired things in the house. Amaris was unable to live any sort of life, save for the gentlest of tasks, at the behest of the Gray Matrons.

The beautiful child who the mistresses fussed over and hid from the world, who was spared the terror and humiliation of market day, who was saved as a prize possession, had become the object of despise for the other children. Being universally hated by their peers was something they had in common.

"Don't do this," Nox raised a hand to stop them.

"Get up!" a boy of twelve barked, pointing with an outstretched finger at Amaris. One of Achard's sniveling friends, already a thug though not yet a teenager. What had the little wart-filled toads hoped to do with the girls? Drag them by the hair to see the bishop?

"Leave!" Nox demanded again, but she may as well have been a turnip for all the mind they paid her.

Nox took a step to put her body between herself and the boys as they pushed into the cramped food storage room. The small slit of a window at the top of the pantry showcased the dust kicked up by the scuffling of their feet as if it were smoke. Over the shoulders of the intruders, the kitchen matron was nowhere to be seen. They were alone with the boys.

"Get out, you frogs!" Nox shoved her body into the closest boy, attempting to push him out of the pantry.

"Grab her!" one commanded, shoving past Nox.

Cries of protest rose from the brawl on either side.

She could hear Amaris, but couldn't discern what was being said as they scrapped.

Perhaps it was unfair that the two girls would hide while the others did their performative duties for the church. It was certainly unfair that Matron Agnes allowed these boys out to be picked over and examined and punished time and time again while Nox and Amaris were sent to sit amidst the potatoes and carrots in the back of the kitchen. But the girls had no more control over their lives than the boys did over theirs, and Nox would be damned if she were held accountable for it.

Achard reached for a fistful of her raven hair. The fire of her rage exploded against the pain. Nox threw her entire body weight into the oldest boy in protest as he advanced. She made contact with a loud thump, sending him off of his footing. Her ears popped against the pain of impact.

"Get *out!*"

A sack of flour overturned in his backward stumble. A bottle full of cooking oil shattered to the floor as his body smacked against the shelf, eliciting a pained groan as the wood bruised his skin. Achard's immediate reaction was one of feral intensity. He kicked Nox in the side and sent her flying to the ground. Her head bounced against the stones in the floor, causing stars to spot her vision.

She scanned again for a matron—for anyone—but they were on their own. These short-sighted fools were going to wreck so much more than they could possibly realize.

Splayed in a half-crouched position, she grasped toward the destroyed oil bottle, willing to spear the boy with its jagged edges if he touched them. Her hand clapped on the ground through the flour as she wriggled her fingers toward the bottle's neck, feeling a cutting sting as a glass shard bit into her palm. A small cloud of the powder muddied her vision, but her fingers found the neck of the bottle and she rose to one knee, then was on her feet, now wielding the weapon in one hand. A paste of flour, blood and oil had smeared itself against her.

"Why!" She asked uselessly as she readied herself to hit him. There would be no response. They hadn't come to discuss the rationale of hateful idiots.

The boy slammed a fist into her sternum, knocking the wind from her chest the moment she had stood in defense. Nox absorbed the blow and bared her angry teeth up at him, fury glazing over her black eyes as she tried to catch her breath. She was poised to slash at him again when a shriek from Amaris turned her around. In the time it took to draw

Nox's attention, Achard closed the gap between them, grabbing her from behind. White flashed as Amaris was hoisted up on either side by two of the boys, one successfully knotting his grubby fists through her starlit hair.

Nox felt the internal rage boil over her edges, a flame not made of heat, but of poison and acid. She slammed the heel of her foot down into the eldest boy's instep, thrusting her elbow up into his chest. As she turned on him, winding up to kick him between the legs, watching him cower beneath her, she heard Amaris behind her once more.

It was not a shriek, or any cry of fear. Amaris was just as angry as she, and the girl had found her voice at last. She snapped with fury.

"Get off me! Let me go!"

Perhaps out of shock that she'd spoken, grimy fingers unraveled their grip on her hair and their grip on her arms slackened.

Amaris's eyes were as wide and white as saucers. Her voice, normally so soft and gentle, became shrill and desperate with her command. "Leave! *Now!*"

The commotion stopped with jarring immediacy. Feet stilled. Clutching hands released their grasp. A smothering, bewildering silence pressed down on the kitchen.

Nox blinked. She was confused, relieved, and disturbed all at once by the abruptness of their halt. Her lips parted as if to speak, but she didn't know what to say. She didn't know what to ask. They'd stopped. The fight was over.

A beetroot rolled from its place on the wooden shelf to the floor with a soft thump, the only sound of evidence of the ceased scuffle. Bewildered stillness stretched for a long moment, and then the boys did as they were told. They took one step back, then another.

Nox and Amaris exchanged looks before their eyes returned to the boys. The girls were still tense, ready to fight, prepared for whatever horrible trick or ploy their attackers were plotting.

"What?" Amaris's single word was barely a breath. Her back remained rigid, muscles flexed to run, eyes wild. She wasn't sure what she was asking. What made them attack? What made them stop? What possessed them to be such horrid, hateful pigs that they'd make another discarded orphan's life any worse than it already was?

The bullies were still creating space as they untangled themselves from the mess they'd made. They stepped wordlessly out of the pantry, feet plodding through the bag of overturned flour leaving tracks as if in the snow, toward the eldest boy. Achard looked between his companions, the half-feral Nox with the bottle still in her cut hand, and the cold face of Amaris. She glared at all three of the boys now, fists clenched at her sides.

"Go, and don't come back." Amaris's voice trembled as she called after them.

She was attempting strength, but it sounded as though she were on the verge of tears. While the other children had fostered a deep-seated hatred for her, she had only grown more resolute in protecting her peace. She had been kept in a helpless bubble for her entire life. She'd been made to feel powerless time and time again. She refused to stand by and allow herself to be dragged off. They couldn't be allowed to treat Nox like she was nothing. She couldn't allow them to be attacked without a fight. They would not get their satisfaction of having Amaris shoved into his gilded carriage, freeing the manor of its least favorite snowflake. No one would disturb their moment.

The boys left the kitchen. The eldest made bewildered declarations behind them that Nox couldn't quite discern as the door swung to a close behind them.

"What was that?" Nox blinked rapidly at Amaris.

The younger girl shook violently, fear and adrenaline rippling through her body. She'd never attempted such a bold assertion. From the tremble of her chin, it looked like the very act of standing up for herself was about to make her cry.

They weren't granted the grace of time to recover from their fight.

A yelp from the hall beyond told them that either the boys or the flour-pasted footprints had been discovered by one of the orphanage's guardians. Within seconds, Matron Mabel burst into the kitchen. Everything about the woman's body language was dripping with panic. Evidence of their brief fight littered the kitchen, spilling from the pantry to the flour-marked footprints leading out into the hall. The matron's face was bewildered. There were only seconds between understanding the severity of what had just occurred contrasted against what was about to happen.

Hardly finding the time to gather her thoughts, Mable locked eyes with Nox. Using two frantic words, she pleaded, "He's coming!"

She understood.

The fight didn't matter.

The boys were meaningless.

The bishop was coming, and he was going to see Amaris.

Nox moved wordlessly. Turning on her heels, she gave the wide-eyed Amaris a quick shove back into the pantry and closed the door behind her in one swift motion. What remained of the jagged bottle tumbled from her hand to the floor with a tinkling clatter. Barely four heartbeats had passed in the time it took for the door to click shut and the robed man to enter. The bishop stepped into the space accompanied by Agnes. Nox leaned her back against the pantry door, attempting a face of contrition.

Agnes's face flashed from confusion, to anger, to horror. A three-act play painted itself across the woman's face as she regarded the disaster that had befallen the kitchen, the way the young, dark-haired girl stood alone as the sole object of blame, and the realization that the bishop was there to witness everything.

The kitchen suddenly felt entirely too cramped. The way the

bishop filled the doorway made Nox feel terribly small. The women, the child, the shards of glass, puddles of oil, and flour were strewn throughout the kitchen. The permeating smell of homey foods and the happy crackling of the fire felt as though it mocked the grim occasion. Nox's linen clothes were covered in flour with splotches of cooking oil pressed into her knees where she'd been kneeling only moments prior, her arm covered in paste from where she'd grabbed the jagged bottle. Droplets of blood continued to leak from her palm, dripping off of her fingertips and joining the mess on the flour. Her dark eyes remained fixed on her shoes, unwilling to meet the judge and jury of the adults around her.

The holy man's eyebrows had arched with painful disapproval.

The Gray Matron spoke first, her words raspy and hurried. "What happened?"

What had happened, indeed?

Nox scarcely knew, though she had been present for all of it. Agnes wasn't really asking, as the answer didn't matter. Nox was at the epicenter of this disaster, and that's all the bishop would be permitted to see. Agnes's voice caught in the question as though it had been filtered through a sieve. Even as it left her lips, she'd known Nox wouldn't be able to respond. The Gray Matron understood precisely what treasure lay behind the closed pantry door, just as she knew why the Nox now leaned against it, concealing what needed to remain hidden.

The bishop turned to Agnes, his lip pulled up in a sneer. "Is this the kind of home you run for children?"

Agnes was shaking her head, reigning in the emotions and willing her face into a quilted stillness. "No. Certainly not."

"And how will this be punished?"

The bishop's face portrayed little emotion. He sounded nothing more than curious as he examined Matron Agnes, looking down at her over the length of his nose. He struck a pose that was perhaps meant to emulate a vision of piety and patience.

Mable looked between Agnes and the young girl as if she might protest. Her face twisted to hold back whatever it was she suppressed. Her hands went to her apron, fists balling against the fabric to smother her urge to defend Nox.

Everyone in the house knew that their silence was worth the fifty crowns hidden amongst the burlap sacks, dried foods, jars of pickled vegetables, and dust. Amaris's sale would line every matron's pocket with three years' worth of coin. Nox's silence as she guarded the door was for an entirely different reason. She couldn't have cared less about whatever monetary value had been ascribed to the girl. She'd known it from the moment she laid eyes on the vulnerable infant in the wicker basket that she'd never let anyone hurt her. If she had to betray the church and cut every matron in the house with the shards of the oil bottle, she'd do without a second thought. Amaris was the only friend, the only family, the only person in the world who mattered to her.

They would have to leave the kitchen to draw the bishop's attention away from the pantry.

Voice strained, Agnes gave a curt command. "Nox, come."

Nox pushed away from the door and leveled her chin, keeping her face blank. Her inky braid was in slight disarray, strands tugged out during the brawl floating around her as she moved. The cold drench of adrenaline pumped through her veins. Her heart rate increased in an arrhythmic thunder as she readied herself for punishment.

She was old enough to understand the severity of what she faced.

Nox followed Agnes and the bishop out of the kitchen. She resisted the urge to look over her shoulder, praying Amaris would stay put. It would do her no good to risk drawing attention by casting a glance to the pantry. Her feet carried her through the corridor, past the dining hall, and over the threshold. Nerves rose up her throat as a sickening bile that threatened to escape as they stepped into the courtyard in front of the manor.

She could hear the patter of feet behind her but didn't see who'd joined them until they were in full view of the orphanage's exterior. They reached the center of the courtyard and turned to see the house. Mable had followed, shaking her head in a worthless, silent plea.

She thought the weather was rather mild, considering it was the end of the world.

The clouds overhead were a flat, depthless shade of gray. Wind moved the bishop's robes as he grazed the courtyard with speculative eyes. They landed on Head Matron Agnes, curiously examining her inaction. Her mouth was pinched, clearly fighting the urge to speak. His cool curiosity wandered to the still-shaking head of Matron Mable. The only sound in the courtyard was that of the leaves rubbing together and the fine, loose gravel that wiggled against the stones. He scanned Nox, from her disheveled hair to the flour smudges on her hands and clothes. She wondered if the others could hear her heart and its thunder, or if it were only loud to her as her blood buzzed in her ears.

"Where is your whip?" asked the bishop.

Agnes balked. Whipping had never been a punishment she'd allowed, though abstaining from corporal punishment had nothing to do with benevolence. The Gray Matron would never hurt her children in a way that would leave scars. She wouldn't risk their market value by marring them. Agnes was not a virtuous woman, but she was a shrewd merchant.

The bishop arched an expectant eyebrow. There was a cold curiosity to the way he examined her.

"Your Grace, I thought perhaps public repentance would suffice. The girl will kneel here for the peers to see until this time tomorrow morning," the matron said woodenly. Agnes was not a woman easily won over by pity or begging, and this would be no different. "With the cold of the night and the long hours, it's a fitting, miserable punishment."

"This child destroyed property, did she not?"

The matron inhaled slowly, "She did, but—"

"Property that belongs not only to the bellies of orphans, but to the All Mother herself, does it not?"

"Yes, but you see—"

"And she was out of bounds, in direct disobedience of the safety and virtues required of the children, was she not? Or are your children allowed to wander the private kitchens, to desecrate items meant for service to the All Mother, to rummage through the pantries, and to vandalize spaces forbidden to them?"

"No, Your Excellency." Her answer was as stiff as her back. Tension stretched from the pepper of her bun, to her very feet as they planted on the cobblestones.

He closed his eyes while reciting a text from the Blessed Obediences. "Though I've known suffering, I make all things new. In the absence of mercy, I create goodness. It is through my pain that I can rightly see."

They'd all heard the text. While many matrons and devotees interpreted this passage as a call for clemency, empathy, and building benevolence in the presence of cruelty, men of the cloth had used this verse to justify correction for centuries.

"Pain is purifying, is it not? To punish this disobedient child is to cleanse, so that she might rightly see, to be made new, and to create goodness." His fingers were still steepled before him. The indifference in his voice seemed crueler, somehow, than if he'd been angry. He wished to see a child suffer for little more than semantic appeasement.

"Many interpret 'the absence of mercy' to mean that the All Mother is *calling* for mercy..." Mable's words flitted away on the breeze at the sharp, cutting glare from both Agnes and the bishop

40

Nox knew that Agnes's feelings mattered little against an important, more pressing truth: one should not bite the hands that feed them. Farleigh needed the church's provisions more than it needed to protect the innocence of the children within it.

Nox hadn't looked into any of their faces after exiting the manor. She didn't want to see Agnes's expression or witness the woman's unwillingness to stand up for her. She didn't want to see the pain in Mable's eyes, as she didn't have the space to be sympathetic for another adult's failure to protect her. She most certainly would not meet the taciturn face of the stoic judge who had already decided her fate.

A detachment called to her, and she answered. Nox responded to the lure of the void and felt herself retreat into a small, protective space within the walls of her mind. Her body was in the courtyard, yes, but she was no longer present for what the powerful chose to do to the girl who stood before them.

She disassociated into the way the branches moved gently in the forest surrounding Farleigh. She absently watched a ladybug crawl in the grassy space where vegetation sprouted up between the cobblestones. Some part of her was conscious of the curious faces of the children who had ceased practicing their letters or reciting their prayers in order to press their faces against the windows of the manor. There were other bodies in her field of vision. Other people. Other things. A few other matrons clutched nervously at the front door, fretting as they watched after the commotion in the courtyard.

Agnes gestured for Mable to go around back to where the manor's lone whip hung in the stable for the few times animals had needed correcting. After all, what were the sinful to the church other than animals in need of correction.

"Kneel, girl," the bishop said.

Girl. He hadn't bothered to learn the name of the child he intended to harm. Her identity meant nothing. She was a pawn in the game for

41

control as men in power demonstrated their ability to do whatever they wanted.

This was the game of men, the game of religion, and the game of power. She had no moves. She had no chance at victory. Her defeat had been a foregone conclusion.

Nox felt herself kneel obediently, though her mind remained drifting with the sparrows that fluttered somewhere near the roof. She faced the children and matrons of Farleigh with glazed, unseeing eyes. She'd stay with the leaves, the birds, the beetles.

Though she remained as far from her body as the clouds in the sky, she was distantly aware that the Gray Matron was touching her. It was with trembling hands that the matron untied the topcoat of Nox's dress and left her white underclothes exposed.

Her spirit found somewhere new, somewhere darker, somewhere further. She would not remain with the rustling leaves or the free things of the earth and sky. Instead, she fixated on emptiness. The doors to the orphanage had remained open, revealing a blackened mouth of a monster made of stone and mortar. She lost herself into the indistinguishable void as she detached.

In her peripherals, the Nox witnessed the single, acknowledging dip of the chin from the bishop as he pressed for her correction to begin.

Her teeth set with readiness as she stared into the shadows until she was one with them. She was numb to the high-pitched crack that echoed through the courtyard. She was dead to the gasps, the blood, the twisted faces of the children and matrons. She fixed her eyes so tightly on the dark space between worlds that reality fractured, breaking free as it drifted into the emptiness, like a star into the night sky. She barely heard the whip crack as it broke through her dress, her skin, her back, over and over again.

2

There is a word for the space between moments. It's a term for the breath between heartbeats, for the emptiness that exists betwixt things, though its name is one that's been forgotten. The nothingness is much like the gap while one sleeps—how time seems to pause and resume between your last moment of consciousness and your first moment awake. This space can be minutes or hours or months that stretch into years, everything blurring together as if nothing happened at all. The word is for the time that passes when no time is passing at all, and yet everything changes.

"I'm ready."

"You don't have to be ready," Nox said, maybe as much for herself as for her snowflake, "We can wait."

"Wait for what? I'm as ready as I'm going to be."

It was the fourth time Amaris had reassured her that morning while Nox worked on her hair. It was spring market day, and Nox was thinly veiling that she had more anxiety over the day's arrival than Amaris. Nox had brushed and plaited the girl's pearly hair into a knot so that half of her white tendrils spilled down her back, and the other half bloomed in a rose atop her head. She was now tall and slender, with the early hourglass shape of a young woman. She wasn't old enough to have switched into the dresses that Nox was now forced to wear. If Amaris was lucky, she'd probably spend another year in the unisex britches and tunics worn by all children before their teenage years. After young girls crested maidenhood they transitioned into linens, skirts, and aprons, not unlike the muted dresses worn by the matrons. Where once a snowy baby had rested on her threshold in a basket, now stood a young woman in a white tunic. At least, the tunic was white on most of the children.

On Amaris, the purity of her hair and lashes made the shirt appear rather dull and yellowed.

The years had come and gone and Agnes was ready to call in the axe of a life-debt that had hung over Amaris's head for thirteen years. This eventuality had loomed from the moment the babe had been "gifted to them by the goddess", as the matrons liked to cleverly word her unorthodox delivery.

Farleigh's children were spoken for at slower and slower rates as time marched on, which was one of the many reasons that Amaris could no longer remain set aside on market day. She had been trotted out only twice in her thirteen years in Farleigh. Once to a lordling and his wife as a prospective adopted daughter— a meeting that had ended disastrously. And another time to a duchess seeking a proper lady-in-waiting. The duchess had been genuinely offended that she had been presented with someone who would outshine her in her own court.

There were a few catalysts for the lack of consistent profits that the mill now faced. The first was the Gray Matron's own reluctance to replenish the beds as they emptied, as she found herself less and less willing to purchase incoming children as she aged. The other cause of their ever-thinning purses was a result of Farleigh's increase in runners. After three young boys with promising fetching prices had escaped the mill after an altercation in the kitchen many years ago, more orphans were emboldened to try their hands at braving the forests rather than take their chances with the market.

While it was now time for Amaris to make herself presentable for buyers, she remained hidden once a month whenever a representative from the church would inspect the manor, lest she be whisked off to serve in the temples. Amaris shuddered at the thought of a life spent in proximity to men like the bishop.

While they had once spent the first day of the month in smiles and conspiratorial whispers as they hid, the bishop's visits were now accompanied by ritualistic silence. Nox and Amaris had an unspoken agreement to never discuss the traumatic day the bishop had forced Nox to kneel, or the atrocities that had been committed at his command. Instead, it served as a somber monthly reminder of how powerless they were at the hands of those who oversaw them.

The nights that had followed her punishment had been the longest nights of Nox's life. She neither slept, nor spoke. She'd tumbled so deeply into the detached void within herself that it had taken a long time to return. By some small mercy, Nox had been allowed her monastic silence. No one forced her to rise, or eat, or participate in lessons for more than a week. Agnes had shooed the other children and matrons away from the healing young woman in her own show of remorse, aside from Matron Flora, the nurse who was allowed in and out to change Nox's bandages and oversee her healing. While the Gray Matron hadn't wanted to perform such an inhumane punishment, intentions were dust in the face of action, and Agnes had whipped her bloodied.

The bishop had gotten into the white and gold carriage that matched his robes and been carried down the road, away from the orphanage. The matrons had wrung their hands over what to do, some fraught with guilt, others worried about the implications such a travesty might have on their income. Nox was no longer perfect. She'd be forever scarred by the atrocities that had been committed in that courtyard.

For the rest of that cruel day and the painful ones that followed, Amaris had knelt wordlessly at Nox's bedside. She'd been the only one permitted to stay near Nox in those solemn hours, curling up beside her in sleep, and holding her hand during the daylight.

"Let me do your hair, now." Amaris insisted. Nox obliged, sitting on the bed so the younger girl could weave her fingers through her friend's loose, night-dark locks. Just above the back collar of Nox's dress peeked a tiny, white mark. She knew that, beneath the cover of Nox's dress, the mark stretched down her back in a clean, thin cut.

Angry, ripping scars had been expected. They'd whispered speculatively about torn, raised skin, discolored welts, and the jagged intersections that would forever mark her with the evidence of the church's intervention. Instead, Nox's wounds had healed somewhat miraculously. Where maiming had been expected, only a few nearly imperceptible lines remained. There were scars, though. Not all wounds could be seen on one's surface. A hardness had been born in the darkness that day that never fully dissipated. The shadows had built a home within Nox, one that wrapped themselves around her heart, pushing out anyone and everyone who wasn't Amaris.

The ivory girl's loneliness stretched into her lessons as she buried herself in books, in calligraphy, in sketching and song. The Gray Matron had already invested so much in her purchase, it only strengthened Agnes's resolve to ensure that Amaris could pass any social or proprietary test put forth and prove she was worth any asking price. Nox served as her tutorial counterpart, learning alongside her so she could drill the ivory girl as their education progressed. Her lessons intensified as her years stretched on, her studies more thorough than most anyone at the orphanage. Agnes seemed to grow more and more determined to foster Amaris's value with every day that passed. The monetary fate of the mill rested on her moonlit shoulders.

All children were obligated into the basics of education. It molded them into a state of competence, should they serve as the hands of shopkeepers in need of basic maths, or purchased as young penmen for wordsmith's whose fingers had tired with arthritis. While Farleigh was not the most pious orphanage in Farehold, it was, however, the most determined for financial success.

"Are you done?"

"I'm not as good at braiding as you are! Let me try again."

Nox combed her hair out with her fingers, allowing her glossy hair to cover any evidence of the small mark that had shown itself from her dress. She smiled, "It's fine. I think it looks better unbound."

"Then why did you braid mine!"

"So they can see that pretty face of yours." She said.

Amaris made a face to express her displeasure. They drifted past the dorm's cots to peer over the balcony onto the landing where prospective buyers were already filtering into the manor. The girls stood beneath one of the few decorations in the orphanage: a gaudy portrait of the royal family. A similar painting hung in the Gray Matron's office. She wondered if such displays of fealty garnered them any additional favors when bishops and patrons came calling.

She'd seen this oil painting in its ugly, fake-gold frame for thirteen years. Amaris studied the overly-regal portrait of the king, queen and princess. She knew this must be a very old painting, as it hadn't truly represented those in Farehold's seats of power for a long time. The portrait contained the king, queen, and princess—at least, he would have been their king, and she would have been their princess. Farehold's king had left the earth to be with the All Mother nearly twenty years before Amaris's birth. The golden-haired Princess Daphne had also passed rather tragically after giving the kingdom its crowned prince, presumably during childbirth, though she'd never cared to ask. Maybe one day Matron Agnes would update her oil painting to reflect Queen Moirai and the young prince. Perhaps she'd wait until Moirai departed and the prince took his rightful title as king. Perhaps she'd never change it at all.

Her eyes left the portrait, returning to the view overlooking the balcony. "What's expected of us?"

"Nothing," Nox shrugged. She'd only been present for a few market days, herself. Most of the markets had been spent at Amaris's side. "We stay visible, I guess. It doesn't matter where we go as long as we don't leave the manor. Want to stay here and watch? See if anyone gets swept off their feet by a handsome lord?"

"Does that happen often?" Amaris asked.

"Does what happen?"

"Being bought for marriage," she responded.

Nox looked away. Yes, of course it happened, though she didn't know how much of life's misfortunes she should put in Amaris's head. It was clear from the matron's grooming that they were specifically preparing Amaris for the sorts of social circles that might allow for her to be wed into upscale society. There might be worse fates than being married off to a lordling. There were probably better ones as well.

Nox glanced up to the painting of the royal family, then back to Amaris. "Maybe the crowned prince will find himself in need of a particularly pretty bride. Then Agnes can update her portraits to reflect Farleigh's favorite snowflake."

"No, Farehold's favorite snowflake." She retorted humorlessly. Her tone made it clear she neither believed, nor entertained such an idea.

They'd barely relaxed against their perch on the balcony before a captain smelling of brine picked out a boy near sixteen. The seafaring man toted him away just as soon as the doors to Farleigh had opened. The orphanage was nowhere near any sea, and it remained something of a mystery how the man's clothes had been so saturated with salt and fish that the ocean's odors hadn't abandoned him no matter how far he'd traveled. Nox hadn't minded the boy, and stared after him wondering what a life at sea would be like. His whole world was about to change from the stone walls of the orphanage to the open, endless expanse of the blue horizon. It was a world she couldn't fathom.

Spring market tended to be the busy time for ranchers needing helping hands in the field in calving season, so the boys were under a bit more pressure than the girls. A farmer, hands knees still covered in dirt from his freshly tilled soil, had arrived to inquire as to whether any of the children had shown an aptitude for growing things. The matrons had chastised him for pursuing the use of magic and attempted to get the man to settle on a young farmhand, but the man wasn't interested in any of the orphanage's human children.

"Can you imagine yourself as a farmer?" Amaris had whispered to Nox from where they watched the play unfold beneath them as patrons entered the mill, leaving empty-handed more often than not.

"I'm too pretty to get dirty," Nox had whispered back.

"Would you prefer to have gone with the sailor?"

Nox attempted to twist her face into a look of revulsion, but her eyes sparkled as she answered, "I already said I was too pretty to get dirty! Now you want to hide me in the hull of a ship? Honestly, Snowflake, it's insulting. What about you? Where would you like to go?"

She saw her answer.

A girl of about four with a muddy brown halo of ringlets was plucked up by a plump woman and a docile-looking husband who followed along in his wife's wake. The woman had a permanent blush about her cheeks and joy in her eyes that made the unselected girls bite back snarls of jealousy. What sort of happy life was the mousy-haired girl about to go live with her new jolly mother and father. What sort of pies and toys and dresses awaited her? Only the small children had a hope of finding families and being raised as natural-born heirs. After a certain age, only horrors awaited.

"With them," Amaris had said, eyes watching the newly stitched-together family of three. "She looks like she'd make a good mother."

They weren't the only children who had gathered near the balcony. Over their shoulder, two freckled girls, one around Nox's age and the other several years Amaris's junior, were making similar comments as they watched the movements in the foyer below. The ginger sisters had come to Farleigh together long ago and created nearly as reclusive of a two-person bubble as Nox and Amaris.

The pair of strawberry-haired siblings had been dropped off together so many years ago in the filthiest of rags. Their arrival had not been a clandestine event in the middle of the night, but a very public, humiliating mid-day display while the children of Farleigh looked on from their seats in the dining hall. The girls' bedraggled mother had been desperate to give them a roof over their head and something to eat other than the cold water and the scraps from pitying strangers.

The peasant woman had stood in the foyer with smudged hands cupped to receive the coin for which she'd traded her only children. Agnes had paid her well, perhaps better than the girls had been worth, not only to compensate for the loss of the girls, but also as a quiet charity for the woman to find a place to sleep for the night and a hot bath. Moments like that are ones that everyone in the manor tried to forget. Memories of being impoverished, discarded, and sold were best left for nightmares. Their mother had never returned, nor had they expected her to. Some things were better off in the past.

"What about you?" Amaris asked the sisters who stood near them.

One raised her coppery brows as if she was surprised she'd been spoken to. They'd made little attempt to integrate into Farleigh's general population in their years, which was something the sisters had always had in common with Nox and Amaris. The girls were occasionally assigned the same chores and tasks around the orphanage, which always resulted in friendly pleasantries, but they did very little speaking beyond their little worlds of two. "Where would I like to live?"

"Yes," she prodded, "don't you two talk about it?"

The siblings exchanged a telling look. They didn't want to go anywhere.

On market day the children often muttered about what it would be like to run away, as Achard and his friends had done so many moons ago. The freckled family members had more than likely been among those exchanging such whispers. Had those boys found nice homes in warm cottages where their bellies were always full of breads, meats and pies? Had they been swept up by the fae of the forest, or trained to be warriors of the shadows, hunting in the spaces between things? Those were some of the favorite tales the children told amongst themselves, that of Achard the Shadow Warrior, an invention born of the boredom, wanderlust and hope of their little minds.

"Good luck," the elder of the two said quietly as they departed. The ginger sisters left to wait out the market day sitting on the low cots in the dormitories.

She didn't blame the siblings for dreaming of running away. Rumors and wishes flitted amongst the residents of Farleigh, but Nox knew that happy endings were not for people like them. More than likely, the boys the orphans had turned into folk heroes had made it twenty steps into the forest before being torn to shreds by wolves or pulled under the earth by the twisted hands of the wicked creatures of the night. She'd sooner believe she'd find their polished skeletons than hope to see his stupid, freckled face gathering straw outside of a farmer's cottage one day.

Families, merchants, and prospective buyers of all sorts were given free-reign of the orphanage's grounds on market day while children stayed within its walls. Unfamiliar faces with odd clothes and off-kilter accents wandered in and out of their rooms, examining the merchandise. Some adults would ask questions of the orphans. Some would sit a child on their lap, some would tower above, barking down with breath stinking of sour ale as they examined the young charges. Usually a few children were purchased by the end of every showing and Agnes's pocket was lined with enough silvers to sustain the house until the following solstice's market.

"I'm going to be honest," Amaris said quietly, still perched on the balcony, "I thought market day would be more exciting." She relaxed her back against the cool stones, enjoying her precarious seat overhanging the foyer.

"Exciting?" Nox was amused. She leaned her elbows on the balcony and propped her face in her chin, eyeing her silvery counterpart. "I'm sorry there was no handsome prince this time around."

"Yes, well, I've never been allowed to attend. I assumed there would be more structure. More buyers and families and movement. I don't know! And I thought at least someone would look at me."

Nox sighed at the very thought, looking deeply into the lilac eyes that stared back at her. "Count yourself lucky, Snowflake. You made it through your first market without being dragged off to live in the belly of a ship."

Reds and oranges glowed through the open door and the polished windows of the manor as the sun began to set. The spring day had nearly drawn to a close. She'd nearly released a sigh of relief over making it through their first successful market day unscathed when a glossy, black carriage pulled by two chestnut horses pulled up in front of the manor. Most of the buyers had come on broken-in quarter horses with flat-bed wagons. Some of the farmers had come on foot. It was a rare sight to see a fully covered carriage at Farleigh, save for the bishop and his visits. The arrival of this dark coach and its owner was as much a source of curiosity as it was something vaguely ominous.

Nox couldn't explain the coal she felt in her stomach as she watched the carriage. It was illogical. She had no reason to feel any emotion toward the stranger.

"We should go," Nox warned.

"Why?" Amaris whispered back. "I want to see who owns such a carriage!"

She wanted to grab Amaris's hand and drag her away but couldn't summon the power to do so. The coal in her belly was spreading, creating a lead in her feet that weighed her to the ground.

There was no explanation for why the lovely, decorated stranger filled her with inexplicable dread.

The carriage belonged to a woman in her late thirties. She was dressed in deep blue finery with green, jeweled accents, resembling the noblest aspects of a peacock. Her attire contrasted starkly against the black gloss of her carriage. Her curled yellow hair had been elaborately pinned atop her head. The season was still chilled enough that she had a black fur around her shoulders held together with a gem-covered clasp, and long, dark gloves stretching up beyond her elbows. The stranger glided over the courtyard without looking around. She passed over the threshold of Farleigh and immediately began tutting under her breath, waiting for a matron to attend to her.

"Have you seen her before?"

"No, I'm always with you on market day," Nox muttered, a chill snaking down her spine as she eyed the peacock. She couldn't describe the feeling, but she felt distinctly like a doe who'd caught sight of a mountain cat amidst the rocks and trees. "Please, let's go."

"Who do you think she is?" Amaris ignored her.

The matrons greeted her with some familiarity. Whoever she was, she'd visited before. The lavish outfit was absurd when contrasted against the gray and white cottons of the matrons and the children.

The moment she entered, the matrons began ushering her to the various rooms in the girl's wing of the manor, specifically tailoring her tour of Farleigh to the older girls. She was ready to leave nearly as soon as she'd arrived. In under thirty minutes, she was in the foyer once more exchanging a purse full of coins with Matron Agnes. She'd returned to the landing with two young women in tow. Nox felt her tightened chest relax slightly as it was clear the danger was passing. The woman was leaving. The girls she was leading out of the orphanage shifted their weight uncomfortably behind her, clutching their own arms in sorrowful attempts to self-soothe. It was plain on their faces: their futures were changing before their eyes.

One girl, nearly seventeen, had short-cropped hair and a waifish build. The other was the freckled girl who'd stood beside them on the balcony not thirty minutes before. She was a full-breasted, strawberry-haired girl of about sixteen, freckles extending from her face down her bosom, stretching beyond the places on her hands and arm that her dress hadn't covered. Their names had been Cici and Emily. Perhaps their names would no longer matter in Farleigh and would become as forgotten as the stones beneath them. Once they left, who would remember them?

Emily's face twisted in fear as she raised her chin, scanning. She was looking up the stairs at the vacant space beyond Nox and Amaris. Emily's stress was both unmissable and tragic. Something about the strange woman's opulence made the way Emily shrank behind her seem all the more intimidating. Amaris's eyes widened at Nox in a silent question, but she only shook her head. She had no answers. They continued peering over the balcony to ogle the strange woman's beautiful dress, speculating on where Cici and Emily might be taken.

"Always a pleasure, Madame Millicent." Agnes was saying as she escorted the stranger out of the mill. The woman called Millicent responded something indiscernible in a preening voice that was appropriate for her bird-like features. The two exchanged niceties until it seemed clear that Millicent was ready to depart. She angled her body toward the door, ushering the silhouettes of the two girls into the salmons and yellows of the setting sun of the courtyard. The woman urged the girls in front of her as they headed toward the horses, clutching one another by the arm.

"Em!" The identically freckled younger sister had called from upstairs somewhere down the hall. Her only blood relative bounded down the corridor after her, screaming through her distress.

The younger sister pushed past Nox and Amaris and ran down the stairs to hug her only family in this world. She crashed into Emily with an intensity that nearly knocked the elder sister to her feet. The child's thin, dotted arms wrapped around her sister's hips as she cried. Hot tears were spilling over her face, clinging to her jaw and smudging against her sibling's dress. Her cries were heartbreaking.

"Please," she begged, "You can't leave me!"

Emily scooped her up, shushing her. She wiped at the tears spilling over her sister's face, willing herself to find a sense of calm. She played the reassuring role of comfort and confidence despite the turmoil that had been painted on her face only moments prior. She didn't want her baby sister to see her afraid. "Be good now, you hear? You listen. You mind your manners." She kissed the young girl atop her head, muttering the love into her pale reddish hair. "You'll go to a good home someday. I'll write to you when I get the chance. I love you. You hear me?" She scanned her sibling's face, waiting for a nod in acknowledgement. She kissed her again. "I'll always love you."

Millicent had turned in response to the commotion and her gaze had roved up the stairs to watch the younger sibling run down. Her peacock eyes had frozen at what she'd seen. Millicent ignored their embrace, seemingly unbothered by the display unfolding beside her. She acted as though the emotionally charged family exchange had been invisible, imperceptible as her predatory gaze snagged on the balcony. Something far more interesting twinkled in her line of vision.

An unintended byproduct of the younger sister's display of affection had been the wake of evidence she'd left of the children who'd gone unnoticed. On the floor above, just out of Matron Agnes's eyesight, Nox and Amaris had been glued to the balcony, watching.

Millicent did a full-faced turn, no longer interested in departure. "And what have we here?"

Agnes shifted her body to follow the jeweled woman's gaze up the stairs where the sibling had come from, her eyes floating over to the railing. It seemed a lifetime of emotions flashed in the Gray Matron's face, from surprise, to anger, to opportunity. Agnes cleared her throat.

"Yes, yes, Madame. I have several beauties they're still kept in the younger girl's quarters, as neither of them have bled."

This wasn't entirely true. Nox had her first blood several years prior. Whether guilt, love, or some perversion of the two, the girl's stranglehold on Agnes's heart had kept the matron from admitting anything to the contrary. It wasn't believable to anyone that Nox wasn't yet a young woman, but the lie hung between them as her true query was on the white-haired girl. Amaris was just shy of claiming womanhood, though perhaps within the next year she'd be both blessed and cursed with the advancement of her years.

The peacock took one step forward, then another, eyes locked onto the girls.

Amaris felt herself freeze. Spring had shifted into the deepest, coldest day of winter within her. She wanted to look at Nox, but couldn't even summon the courage to move her head. Her feet felt stuck. Her lilac eyes were as wide as teacups as her heart thundered. The woman was coming for her.

A commanding presence, Millicent used two fingers of her gloved hand to usher the head matron to stand behind her as she took careful steps, high heels clacking on the stone stairway. Millicent sauntered up the stairs where the two girls were stuck on the landing atop the stairs. Agnes followed hurriedly behind her. Millicent paused for the matron to explain herself.

A cloud of vanilla preceded her arrival. It wafted up the stairs, strangling the girls as Millicent settled on the balcony. Her eyes were growing hungrier with the second.

Nox opened her mouth to say something, but had no idea what to do.

"Nox is my personal servant girl. Come here, Nox." Agnes waved her hand quickly, ushering the young woman to stand behind her and away from the prying inspection of the Madame. The dark-haired girl hesitated, looking into the eyes of her panicked snowflake. She felt every bit as feral as the freckled sisters must have felt. She wanted to drag Amaris away, to throw her arms around her protectively, but she didn't know what to do. She didn't know how to intervene. Nox held Amaris's gaze, urging a sense of calm and reassurance onto her. She wished she could tell her that she was here for her, but there was nothing to be said. They had no agency.

"But this one," Millicent stretched out a hand to touch Amaris's face, cooing absently as she drew her fingers over her features. "My, what a pretty shade of purple. Milk and cream and moonlight, you are…. Such angelic features, this one."

"Have you ever seen anything like her?" Agnes prodded.

"Truly, I haven't," the woman purred. She stared into Amaris's lavender eyes for a long moment. "Come," she commanded. Millicent herded Amaris into the dorm room behind her with a shooing sound. Other children had been waiting in the dorms, but Millicent banished them with a bark. The lavish woman was as commanding as if she were the true matron of the house, clearing the other children from the room and its many cots. Two other younger girls who had been chatting on their cots scattered, leaving their things in disarray as they hurried from the space.

"Shut the door," Millicent said curtly to no one in particular.

Nox and Agnes trailed behind Millicent's formidable presence. Agnes complied, closing the door to the dorm room.

"Disrobe," Millicent commanded. Her face was cold as she watched Amaris impatiently.

Amaris gaped, looking from the peacock woman to Agnes. Her pale mouth was parted in appalled speechlessness. Her pale hands clutched at the edges of her tunic as she looked to the matron, eyes desperate for help.

"What?" Amaris could barely croak out the word.

"I need to see if you are unmarked." Millicent's tone was slightly annoyed, as if Amaris's idiotic question were holding up due process. The woman's voice was not kind.

Agnes nodded in acknowledgement.

Nox started toward Amaris in silent protest, but the Gray Matron lifted a hand in a gesture meant to keep Nox standing behind her, shielded from advancing to intervene. The Gray Matron addressed the Madame directly, saying, "We have taken extreme precautions," Agnes's voice was tense. It was an unusual emotion to hear in the matron. "She's a rarity. She's been spared from any activities that would mark her."

Millicent didn't look at Agnes. Her beady, bird-like eyes remained fixed on the young moonbeam. "Forgive me if I'm unwilling to take your word for it. Disrobe, girl."

Her hands did the opposite. Her ivory arms crossed before her, covering herself in front of her shirt. She continued looking at the others with a mixture of horror and confusion.

"Nox?" She looked helplessly at her friend, speaking her name as a single, pathetic plea for help.

It was the single, worst moment of Nox's life. Amaris looked to her for help, and she failed. She was powerless. She burned with anger, with helplessness. She felt as though her ankles had been shackled by steel manacles. She wanted to put herself between Millicent and Amaris. She wanted to push Agnes to the side and grab Amaris's hand. Instead, she stood there, abandoning her in her truest moment of need.

Nox wasn't sure if she would cry or vomit, but her head began to spin as the world unfolded in slow motion.

When it became clear she would not be rescued, Amaris began the quiet, humiliating process of taking off her clothes. She moved with glacial slowness, slipping her tunic off, shuffling her pants down around her ankles. One arm draped over her small breasts with the other hand hid her womanhood. Millicent pulled her hands away, looking positively delighted at what she saw. She put her hands lightly on the fair girl's shoulders, spinning her slightly to ensure there were no scars or deformities anywhere on her perfect, ivory body.

Nox had turned her face away, skin reddening with anger as she stared at the wall, battling the heat of shame-filled tears.

"She is starlight personified, isn't she," Millicent mused to herself.

Agnes's energy was vibrating. Her confidence had grown with every passing moment. "We have many inquiries about this one."

The lie had come out quickly and believably. No one had offered to purchase Amaris, only as no one's pockets had been deep enough to have afforded her.

Agnes continued, "Lords have stopped by to see this rare beauty for their sons. The church has examined her as an excellent ambassador for the All Mother for the sacred temple. She truly is brimming with opportunity."

"I assume she is also intact?"

The question was as soulless and as abhorrent as the woman asking it.

"She's never been touched by a man. We've kept her very protected—set apart from the others. Nox has been something of a personal attendant to assure she was always escorted by a female peer for safekeeping. We know what a treasure we have in her."

Agnes had never considered that a pleasure house would be the one to purchase her moonbeam. Imagining the small fortune men might pay to take the maidenhood of winter in its human form made it clear she'd been missing opportunities by the bucketful. One could almost hear the tinkling sounds of crowns rubbing together as they tumbled into her purse.

"Mmm," Millicent continued turning Amaris around with the evaluating eye of a rancher buying cattle. She brought her hand to Amaris's mouth. "Let me see your teeth?"

"Like I said," Agnes reiterated, stopping the process. "She hasn't bled. She is too young to leave our guardianship now. But if you put down a deposit, I'd be willing to hold her for you and send word to The Selkie once she reaches her womanhood."

The women ignored her as they began discussing business.

Amaris redressed, pulling on her pants first and then the tunic over her head. Her face was hot with shame. She'd refused to cry, but silver tears were rimming her eyes. Nox was horrified to stand there helplessly, watching Amaris be debased in such a way. She felt her temper prick, and as if Agnes could sense the dark-haired girl behind her, she reached a hand back and placed it in front of Nox's path once more. Nox felt like an antagonized bull pinned behind a gate.

Millicent clucked her tongue, "Many of my clients would be thrilled that she hasn't bled. There is quite the market for—"

Amaris found her voice. She choked out a single, humiliated word. "No."

The women in the room turned to her, giving her their attention. Millicent tilted her head curiously.

Amaris swallowed, feeling as though dry bread were caught in her throat. She couldn't swallow the obstruction as emotion threatened her. Still refusing to cry, she leveled her voice. "Matron Agnes has already said she will send word when I'm ready. Today, I'm not going anywhere."

A flood of tension came into the room in a defiant wave. Like the ocean's tide, it rushed in, and rushed back out, leaving a strangled sense of nothingness behind it. Agnes was rigid, perhaps worried that Amaris's disregard for authority would ruin her business dealings. She didn't stop Nox as the young woman finally bypassed her to go to

Amaris's side. She helped her tie the back of her tunic behind her hair. Nox murmured a stream of somethings that may have been rushed, quiet apologies, hands shaking as she tied the knots once more. Her trembling, burble of words was unintelligible to any of them.

Millicent seemed to consider the two for a long while before dipping her chin slightly in acknowledgement. "Fine," she said with cold amusement. "I will respect your spirit, girl."

It was over.

Millicent turned to Agnes, leaving the girls behind her as she went out the door, discussing something about timelines and the crowns in deposit. They headed down the corridor, their footsteps quieting as they walked away. Talks of coin and crowns faded into the distance. The two were left alone in the dorm. Tears she'd battled began to spill. Hot salt water tumbled freely down her cheeks.

"I'm so sorry." Nox gripped both of her shoulders. She wanted to shake the terror and pain away from the girl, but could do little more than pull her into a crushing hug. She stroked Amaris's hair in a frenzied attempt at comfort. She hadn't protected Amaris when she'd needed it most. Nox's heart had cracked under the weight of her failure.

"I'm not going with her," Amaris's voice quivered.

"I know," Nox was wavering with impending tears, "I know."

"No," Amaris clarified, hiccuping against her suppressed sobs. "I'll never go with that woman. I'll never go with her."

Nox held her, and the charge between them was something more profound than the ties of family. They weren't sisters. Their connection was all-encompassing. There was a ferocity and bond between the girls that held no logic, no reason. She knew with a primal sense of protection that she would never let Amaris go with that woman. She'd fight, she'd die, she'd kill until no one stood before she let Amaris go with that woman. Nox squeezed her more tightly before loosening her hold. She took Amaris's face in her hands, dark eyes burning with intensity as she begged Amaris to see her grave sincerity.

"And I will never let her take you," she swore, her words a solemn oath.

Nox's life had never meant much to her or anyone around her. The girl was glad she couldn't recall being sold to the orphanage the way that Emily and her sister must remember it. Nox couldn't imagine what her own mother had been like, though there had always been a sickening pity that the matrons had when they looked at Nox that made her feel like her arrival had not been the tear-filled loving regret of a mother making the right choice for their child.

Still, in her twisted upbringing in Farleigh, she had found a purpose. It had been planted as a tiny silver seed. It sprouted into starlight connection with the ivory baby whom the other children hated with their jealousy. Amaris had loved her back, and their moonlit plant grew into a metallic wildflower with roots so deep that they bore themselves into her very core. For years she had called it friendship, and for years, that had been what it was. The two stayed cast off from the others, defending their inseparable bond. They were each other's everything.

As she held Amaris's face in her hands, guilt gnawed in her gut. What she felt was an intimate love that she couldn't bring herself to understand. Maybe she didn't need to understand it. It didn't make it any less real.

"What just happened—"

"It will never happen again. I'm so sorry." Her voice broke with the pain of helplessness, of regret, of anger. Nox vowed, "I promise with my life: you won't go with her."

The rumors started spreading at dinner. Whether it was the matrons or the other orphan's spreading them, who was to tell. The friends of the boys sold to farmers and sailors chatted briefly of their lost companions, but Farleigh was aflutter with their fixation on Amaris's fetching price. Some whispered twenty crowns had been put down as deposit, others claimed they'd heard it was a song to the tune of fifty. One matron was caught cursing quietly that one hundred crowns were counted in the head office just to hold the white-haired girl until her time had come.

It had never felt so suffocating to be surrounded by people. Children were on all sides of them as they spoke and chatted excitedly on the long benches of the dining room table. The girls shrank into silence, allowing the talking and scraping of forks and knives to become a white noise around them. Between bites of roast chicken and dark brown bread, the voices stayed animated in the hall as they discussed a successful market day, one that surely no one would forget. Everyone was murmuring save for a ghostly silent Amaris and Nox whose food was pushed around their plates, tasting like ash in their mouths.

"Are you awake?"

"I'm looking at you, aren't I?" Nox whispered back, voice so low it was nearly inaudible. Amaris crouched beside her cot in her nightdress while the girls around them slept. She'd waited until the tossing and turning of the others in the dorm had relaxed into the steady breathing of deep sleep before she'd left her cot and crossed the hall. Nox had been moved into the older girls' dormitory two years prior. Night was the only time they were truly separated.

"Can we go?"

Nox was out from beneath her covers before Amaris had finished her question. It was a warm enough spring day that she didn't bother with night shoes or sweaters. Her thin nightdress clung to her, betraying evidence of chill as they crept out of the orphanage.

The girls took a rare trip outside of the walls of Farleigh. It was dangerous to get caught sneaking out after bedtime. The matrons wouldn't scar the children, but there were plenty of closets one could be locked in, darkened spaces in which one could be shut, and the forced skipping meals that wouldn't leave lasting marks. Sneaking out was rarely worth the risk of being shoved into someplace small and terrible, deprived of food, just to leave the grounds past bedtime.

Nox and Amaris slipped into the hall and tip-toed down the stairs. The door seemed to be in on their plan, as it made no noise, its well-oiled hinges opening and closing behind them. Fresh air and privacy awaited them beyond the listening walls of the manor. They carefully picked their way in the darkness without the aid of candles in the full light of the moon.

The girls headed for the stables on bare feet, hurrying forward should anyone happen to look out a window. The sooner they could round the corner, the safer they'd be. The sound of a horse whinnying within the stable alerted them that the animals had been disturbed by their presence, but no loud braying had given them away.

Amaris slipped around the corner first, Nox close on her heels.

They placed the wooden walls of the stables between themselves and the windows of Farleigh, sandwiching themselves between the wooded structure and the looming shadows of the forest that encircled the property. The silver moonlight bathed them, illuminating the pair where they stood.

"Goddess dammit!" Amaris was aghast, panting through her anger. Nox had never heard her curse before this. "How could this happen! How could this be my fate!"

Nox slumped to the ground with her back to the stable wall, eyes glazed as she faced the dark forest beyond. It had been hours, and she still had no words for what had occurred. The shock she felt had seeped into her like wet socks freezing within one's boots, chilling her in an all-consuming way.

Amaris hadn't sat down. She was pacing in tight, anxious repetitions, looking at nothing in particular while she worked through her energy. The moon painted curves and lines against her lithe figure, her hair, the tilt of her nose, her hips, her legs. It was hard to tell where the silky white of her nightdress ended and her skin began, as her entire body was painted from the same shade of dipped silver.

Nox made herself look away, keeping her coal-dark eyes to Amaris's face and hair alone. Her friend was in pain, and it would be a fate deserving of death if her mind wandered to anywhere other than support. She allowed the girl her space, not interrupting her rhythmic march. Her dark eyes traced the path, watching the way the moonlight reflected off of a girl so white, she could have been carved from chips of its surface. Nox felt her chest tighten with a deep, terrible pain.

"I've been kept away for years for what—to be sold to a pleasure house?" Amaris demanded, incredulous. She kept her voice low enough to prevent suspicion, but her words were harried. Her question had been rhetorical, but Nox answered anyway.

"Their pockets must be far deeper than the matrons had ever considered."

Amaris was furious. Her hands flew upward, reflecting white in the moonlight. "What am I supposed to do?"

Nox shrugged her shoulders. Her tone did not match the intensity of the situation, but that was for the simple reason that she did not feel afraid. She felt only calm defiance. Her sentences were resolute. "The world is big. We will leave."

Amaris didn't stop walking, turning tightly as she took seven steps to the left, spun, then seven steps to the right. Her arms were wrapped in front of her chest with her thumb and forefinger pinching her chin anxiously. "Where will we go? What will we do?"

Nox's dark eyes continued to calmly follow the pacing. She wished Amaris would sit beside her. She felt like she needed comfort and reassurance just as much as the girl born of snow. Amaris was to be sold, but Nox would be just as robbed of her life as her friend if Amaris was taken from her. Her heart fractured at the thought.

"Do you want to go for a walk?"

Amaris paused her steps and looked to the trees. "I can't sit still, but I don't know if it's a good idea..."

"The worst has already happened. Is being eaten by a monster so much more frightening than Millicent?"

Nox lifted herself to her feet, desiring the closeness. She just wanted to stand beside her, whether or not they went anywhere. If Amaris wouldn't sit, she'd go to her.

"We're barefoot."

"You have a lot of nervous energy. We don't have to go," Nox took a step nearer.

"No," Amaris eyed her, "I want to."

Nox wished she could discern more of Amaris's face in the obscured shadows of the moonlight, but her expression was unreadable.

They angled for the forest line. Their hands brushed as they walked. Nox's face flushed, and she cursed herself at the feeling as her heart caught, stuttering in its pattern as if it had been jolted by lightning. She was sure it had been an accidental touch and cursed herself all the more. She was grateful for the night's darkness so the blush of her face wouldn't give her away. Amaris was walking off her anxious energy, she told herself. She needed to focus on the walk. She was to listen. This night was about nothing more than listening and support.

They had just made it to the edge of the woods when a rustle made them stop.

"Did you hear that?"

Nox didn't respond. She stared into the darkness, her eyes rapidly adjusting to distinguish the shapes and shadows before her. She scanned but couldn't see any movement.

Amaris spoke again, her voice barely a whisper, "What do you think are in these woods at night?"

Nox took a step backward. "I'm sure it's just an animal." Something told her the rustle was not the noise of a rabbit. She began to hear her heartbeat over the hush of the night. Amaris wrapped her fingers around Nox's arm and the girl's heart rate increased, this time having nothing to do with the shuffling in the underbrush. Their bravery had been a bluff. They hadn't needed to take a walk. They hadn't required the looming darkness of the trees. All they'd really wanted was to leave the four walls of Farleigh.

"I want to run," Amaris said. She wasn't talking about the animal in the woods. She continued to stare into the shadows, hands tightening around Nox's arm.

"We will," Nox promised. "And we'll do it soon."

Amaris turned toward her, slipping her hands down to grab her hands. "Both of us, right?"

Nox almost choked on a laugh at the absurdity of the question. She squeezed the hands clasped in hers, "As if you could get rid of me."

Nox was sure she didn't imagine it as she slipped her arms around Amaris. There was a glow so palpable it almost had a shape, a color. She could feel the blue glimmer of life and soul and love between them as she clutched her snowflake against her. She would have to be pried apart from Amaris. She'd never willingly be separated from her.

If they were going to make it more than twenty steps into the forest before being picked clean by demons, they needed to be smart.

She slipped her arm around Amaris and began to steer them away from the forest. Tonight had just been an effort to escape the oppression of the manor. They'd needed to state their proclamation to leave. They needed to accomplish what the freckled sisters hadn't in their plans to run.

If they were going to escape, they would need to be careful. They would plan, they would wait, and they would prepare until there would be no question as to their success. Amaris would not go with Millicent to the place the woman had called The Selkie. The girls would not follow whatever fate she was sure had befallen Achard and his cronies, cleanly picked bones lining the forest floor, blowing leaves burying them unceremoniously as their forgotten bodies joined the earth.

🌙🌙🌙🌘🌕🌖🌗🌗🌘

Time passed as it did. Lessons, shams of church processionals whenever the bishop visited, prayers to the All Mother, reading, cleaning, chores, and so forth filled their days. The girls found ways to ask the matrons questions outside of their lessons and spent their time cherry-picking knowledge of geography, terrain, and the sorts of animals that roamed the forest near Farleigh. Every day was a new opportunity for covert reconnaissance. If they kept their questions spread out between the matrons and dispersed over time, no one thought to ask why Nox and Amaris were collecting mental layouts of their surroundings, of foods that grew naturally in the forest, of poisons or animals or towns.

No one would question when things went missing as long as it happened gradually, with the plausibility of time and forgetfulness of others. A spare sock here, a clean tunic there, a blanket, a hat, all became stashed in places that could be easily retrieved in their moment of need without being discovered by prying eyes.

Mable proved to be the chattiest when they could catch her in a good mood, though they'd expected as much from the friendly matron. She was from a village two day's ride from Farleigh called Stone. While the children had been led to believe that Farleigh was on the northmost edge of the kingdom, it seemed Stone was so-named as it was backed up against a cliff so sheer that it drew a firm, unquestionable barrier between the kingdoms. She missed Stone, she said, but she was happy to be of use to the All Mother.

When Mable was sixteen, her deeply religious parents had

dedicated her to servitude at Farleigh so that she could be a steward of the goddess and help disenfranchised children. Mable had left it unsaid that Farleigh turned out to be neither religious nor helping children, though her faith in the goddess hadn't permitted her to leave. Perhaps it was the mill's very immorality that pressed her to stay. The All Mother needed her small light of goodness here in the depravity of a mill more than at a truly pious institution.

Nox had asked why anyone would live in Stone when it was so close to the dark kingdom, and Mable had waxed poetic about a league of guardians in the mountain who served neither the north nor the south. Nox and Amaris had exchanged looks at that, confident that Mable was more naïve than they'd initially thought. It would be a lovely tale and a pretty upbringing to allow a child to imagine guardians watching them in their poor peasant village. Certainly, such a legend would prove a useful story for parents of frightened children to keep the night terrors away when signs of demons came down from the mountains, particularly when backed against the shadows of the northern kingdom.

Mable was distracted enough as she'd busied herself skinning vegetables and discarding the peels that she hadn't paid much mind as to why the girls cared. She was happy for the company. Potato peeling could get rather monotonous, she'd said.

Nox kept her questions focused on the warmth of the southwestern coast.

"You've asked about the south a lot, little Nox. Do you have big dreams of living in the southern part of the kingdom?" Her hands continued working on the potato, thumb edging the knife deftly around its skin while she made eye contact with the dark-haired girl.

"I've always dreamt of the sea," Nox claimed. "It would be lovely to work for someone along the coast. I've thought about the water even more after the sailor visited on the last market day. Have you ever been? To the sea, I mean?"

70

The lie was pretty enough that Mable was happy to tell them about a time when she and a few of the devout matrons had taken their horses on pilgrimage to the Temple of the All Mother. From there, they'd gone onward another day to Priory. The coastal town was just outside the royal City of Aubade where Her Majesty resided. It had been more than two weeks of hard travel, Mable said. Still, it remained a joyous memory as she had been able to worship with other matrons who had come from surrounding territories throughout the southern kingdom, all sharing in the sacred pilgrimage to visit the All Mother in her earthly form. Her stories of the temple were otherworldly, surely colored by a combination of time and wishful thinking. It had been the only time she'd been able to celebrate in community with other women who truly loved and served the goddess, Mable had told them.

She seemed lost in her thoughts at that, fingers working absently on her chore as her eyes glazed over at vivid memories. Perhaps her mind drifted to the holier path her parents had wanted from her, and the thinly veiled slave trade masquerading as a church-run orphanage her life had become.

"You'll get to see it, though, little Amaris." Mable's voice was distant, her eyes still unfocused while her hands busied themselves with dough.

Amaris cocked her head at that.

She nodded to herself, not really speaking to either of them. "You'll have to make the trek to light a candle for me at the Temple someday when you go off to live in Priory."

She continued discarding skins into one bin and placing the peeled potatoes into a pot as the girls left the kitchen. She'd bid them a rather absent goodnight, presumably still lost to her memories. She'd unwittingly shared where the Madame was to be taking her. The menagerie of exotic women, of special treasures from around the world, was just outside of the royal city. Her virtue, her body, her life was to be sold in the seaside town of Priory.

71

4

Something was wrong.

Pain lanced through her side. A light sweat clung to her brow. Amaris jolted awake, curling into herself as she brought her knees to her chest with a gasp. She couldn't fully stretch herself into a seated position as she moved her legs over the edge of the bed, bare feet chilling against the cold floor.

The summer's heat had cooled to autumn. Early winter began to nip at their heels as leaves tumbled to the ground in shades of brown, yellow, and orange somewhere beyond the darkened windows. No moonlight filtered in to illuminate her bent shape, leaving her alone in the dark with a swirling, gripping pain.

Cold continued to work its way from her feet up her calves as she stumbled out of the dormitory, down the hall and toward the bathing room. She'd known her way past the other cots in the dorms well enough that she didn't need to light a candle, though she had bumped into a bed on accident as she gripped at her abdomen, waking someone. One of the other girls stirred in her beds and called softly out after her, but she ignored the other girl and let the cold of the night rouse her fully from her sleep.

Amaris was almost to the bathing room when she doubled over, a fresh pain twisting its fist deep within her gut. She muffled the sound that threatened to tear from her mouth and kept herself from crying out, not wanting to alert the matrons. She had been sick before from food, or when a bout of flu had swept through the house and stricken nearly all of its residents, but this felt like a hot, angry twist in her lowermost belly. It was a terrible brand of nauseating pain she'd never felt before.

Amaris made it to the bathing room and wished she'd brought a candle, gripping at her nightdress for the source of her pain. It felt as though she'd wet herself, which caused a renewed panic to stir within her. How sick must she be if she'd wet the bed? She dabbed at the mess with the towels on the wall, barely seeing through the gray-black gloom of the window. From the next room, a sharp yelp cut through the night. Amaris clutched her abdomen and padded back down the hall to see who was in trouble, only to find a candle had been lit in her dorm. Two of the younger girls looked up at her.

"Amaris is hurt!" one of them cried.

Nox had been relocated to the dorm of the eldest girls just across the hall nearly two years prior, but she'd balanced between insomnia and light sleeping her entire life. She was a creature of the night, and her eyes had shot open the second she'd heard a sound. She'd undoubtedly stirred from her sleep the moment the door to the younger dormitory had opened. The raven was through the door in a heartbeat, shushing the girls frantically. Her eyes were wide with an alarm Amaris couldn't comprehend. Nox wasn't looking at her. She was focusing on the crying girls. Her tone was low and hurried with her commands.

"Shut up! Shut *up*! Go back to bed!" Her voice was strangled with its urgency.

The youngest of them had taken to crying some pitiful sob.

"Stop it! Be quiet!" Nox was urging in a panicked hush, sounding like she might cry, herself.

The other young girls were stirring now, lighting the candles by their own beds. All the girls in the middle dorm were between the ages ten and thirteen, with Amaris nearly old enough to be moved to the eldest dorm. The younger ten- and eleven-year-olds were fussing louder and louder, and the more Nox urged them to quiet, the more distressed their murmurs became.

As the candles lit, one of the girls closest to the door pointed at Amaris, face paling with terror. "She's dying!"

Of course, Nox had known exactly what had happened the moment she'd entered the room. It had proven impossible to silence the idiot children with no education about their bodies. Amaris was the oldest in their room, and as such, was the first time they'd bared witness to the curse of womanhood. While her exact birthday was unknown, the moonlit girl was between her fourteenth and fifteenth year. Her curse had been blessedly belated, as these things went. While some of the women and girls suffered relatively little during their moon time, this had been an especially crimson sight. This horror was appropriate, as this was the moment that officially marked her as a sacrificial lamb. Her time had come.

Surely, the matrons would make the time to talk to the childish residents of this dorm after tonight's events regarding women's health in the morning. The bed linens would be scrubbed and boiled of the tell-tale blood. Amaris's nightdress would be soaked, salted and washed until it shined once more as if this gruesome event had never happened. The talks and education would do nothing for them once the letters had been sent and the Madame had been alerted. Her first blood had come, and it was too late to hide it.

Amaris looked at Nox and shook her head slightly, and she knew what it meant.

She was not going.

No matter what.

It had taken them months for their plan to take shape. This had been the final sign that they had to leave. They were out of time. They had the physical provisions stored throughout the manor. They had knowledge of the continent, where to go, and how to survive. They knew from Mable's tales of travel that Priory was at least two weeks of hard travel—assuming they'd find access to horses. They were so close to freedom.

It took three days to finalize the execution of their plan.

"What do you need to get?" Nox asked in a whisper as they walked from the dorms to their lessons.

"I have changes of clothes for each of us," Amaris recounted the sets of boy's clothes she'd stolen, stuffing away britches and tunics for each of them. "I have one blanket. I need to find cloaks, and a second blanket. It's an unusually cold autumn. We won't make it far if we freeze. I'm meant to be on laundry duty tomorrow."

"Can you find mittens?"

"I can try."

"What about you?"

They began descending the stairs, "I'm scheduled to help Mable the day after tomorrow in the kitchens. I'll get as much food as I can carry."

"Two days?"

"Two days." Nox reached out to her, giving her hand a quick squeeze as they parted ways for their separate chores. They'd reunite again after lunch for the typical lessons and tutelage, though learning seemed a bit irrelevant now that they knew Amaris was not being groomed for a lordling or life in the courts. Classes would require their greatest skills in acting, as it was essential that they maintained the same bored, disinterested expressions, lest the matrons grow suspicions.

There would be no opportunity for planning again until after dinner.

While neither girl had stepped foot beyond the grounds of Farleigh, they knew enough of the land to know that if they headed North, they'd reach the forests at the base of the mountains. Raascot wasn't just the kingdom of dark fae. It wasn't just the birthplace of monster lore. It was also terribly cold, densely wooded, and filled with icy, treacherous terrain. All hushed manners of things mentioned about the mountains filled their veins with enough ice that they knew their safest bet was to angle themselves southwest toward the coast. Even if they were to end up unloved and homeless, it was a fate best served in conditions that wouldn't chew their fingers and toes with its frostbite.

Nox was old enough to find gainful employment as a seamstress or in any variety of shop as an assistant. She'd even spent enough time in the kitchens to feel confident she could bluff her way into a bakery if someone would give her the time of day to allow her to plead her case. She was sure she could find work quickly and support them both the moment they reached the sea. She'd helped Matron Agnes for many years and was sure she'd be an asset to any mistress. Amaris would be a little more challenging, as she stuck out like a ray of sunlight on a moonless midnight.

It would only take one villager to lay eyes on Amaris and word of their travels would spread. The girls would have no chance of escaping if they couldn't stay hidden.

Their only hope was that of disguise. They'd seen the matrons bleach, dye and color fabrics in boiling hot water in the Farleigh's basement, and were confident they could attempt as much with Amaris's hair. The moment they reached a village, they'd prioritize whatever needed to be done to conceal her. The tailors and seamstresses with hot vats of dye were sure to have what they needed. A batch of red, black, or even a normal shade of yellow—goddess be damned—would be better than her giveaway silver hair. She could smear it into her eyebrows and lashes, concealing her most noticeable traits. She'd plaster her locks with the goddess damned mud if it would do the trick. The lavender eyes would be impossible to hide, but if she wore her hooded cloak low and kept her sight to her feet, they'd be able to put enough distance between themselves and the house that they wouldn't be caught.

Amaris's chores in the laundry the day before had gone well, though she'd only found one cloak, and wasn't sure that their thin, leather shoes would be warm enough for their travels. She promised she'd continue looking.

"Mable had said that Priory was more than two weeks away," Nox did her best to reassure her, knowing that Millicent was coming up from the coast. They had time.

Amaris was resolute, "It has to be tonight."

"It doesn't," Nox cautioned, "Even if she left The Selkie the very moment she received the crow, there'd still be two weeks of travel ahead of her. That was one week ago. It's a large continent. We have seven days. If we aren't ready…"

"We're ready. It must be tonight. We go after your shift in the kitchens."

Nox bit her lip as she eyed the unwavering intensity in Amaris's stare. In practical terms, it didn't have to be tonight. Yet she recognized the look of a trapped animal, and knew that if they stayed for a moment longer, Amaris would chew her leg off like the proverbial fox in a snare.

"Okay," she conceded. "Go see what you can do about a second cloak. I'll get us what we need. We'll leave tonight."

Her shifts in the kitchen had always been pleasant. It was Nox's favorite chore, as it meant the ability to spend time with Mable. Being amidst food and the friendliest matron had always been more fun than scrubbing the floors, pressing linens, or doing yard work. Tonight, she was brimming with a tense anxiety that she desperately hoped couldn't be sensed by the cook. She'd need to be able to sweet talk Mable if she hoped to have any time alone with the foods.

Nox had always possessed an aura of likability. It was the quality that had drawn Agnes to singling her out as Amaris's chaperone, it was what soothed the staff into giving her things like mugs of warm milk before bed or a pastry when she wanted to sneak dessert, and what had kept her out of the worst chores or punishments Farleigh had to offer—save for one. Her charm, like most things, had infuriated the other children. Life wasn't fair. It wasn't fair to her, or to Amaris, or to any of the discarded orphans. That didn't change her urgency to leave, or the need to use whatever charms or skills she possessed to facilitate their escape. They didn't have the leisure of considering what was fair.

"Matron Mable?"

"Hmm? Yes, little Nox?"

Nox hadn't been little for more than ten years, but it was an adjective of endearment Mable seemed to tack onto all their names. She smiled up from where she'd begun to wash up from dinner.

"Are there extra apples? I'd love to be able to bring one to the horses. It makes them so happy to get a treat."

Mable was charmed at that, as had been the intent. "Remember to keep your palms flat! Don't be getting your fingers nibbled off."

"Yes, of course," she smiled with what she hoped was her most innocent, disarming show of appreciative affection as she was allowed to rummage around in the pantry. While Nox pillaged the kitchens, Amaris's task had been to go through the laundry and find the mittens and second cloak she hadn't been able to locate the day prior.

If they were both successful with their endeavors, they'd be able to leave as soon as everyone in the house had fallen asleep.

She'd never traveled, but she knew enough of food to understand what would spoil and what would keep. She reached for things that would last them long enough to get to a village and plan their next steps.

Nox stuffed as much hard cheese, dried meat and bread into the pockets and folds of her clothes that could possibly conceal and then emerged from the pantry with an armful of apples. The armfuls of hard fruit seemed to excuse her awkward angles and lumps. Mable laughed dismissively and shooed her away, eyes lost in distracted amusement.

Nox hurried up to the dorms while the rest of the children were eating dinner. She stripped her pillow and used a pillowcase to create a makeshift satchel. It wasn't the best time of the year to be running from the grounds, as late fall was just starting to threaten them with frost. She eyed her bed wondering at the cold and whether or not she could risk taking the entire scratchy comforter from her cot without being detected, and how long it might take them to get far enough south for the climate to become milder. Perhaps they could convince a traveler to let them ride with them. Surely, people used the regency's road to venture to the royal city all the time. They could be on a cart and bound for warmer weather before they knew it.

Nox held her food-stuffed pillowcase by the corner when something jarring shook her from her train of thought.

The manor erupted into a confused flurry as the sounds of banging, followed by the commotion of an argument floated up from the foyer. Nox looked over her shoulder to ensure no one had spotted her. Her heart caught in her throat, somehow convinced she'd been thwarted. She shoved the pillowcase full of food under her bed, tucking evidence of her plan for escape out of eyesight, and sidled around the corner to peer over the balcony and see what was causing the excitement.

She blinked against the sight, struggling to comprehend something so unusual in the walls of the orphanage… It was a man.

The sight of him was as jarring as if there had been a troll on the landing. She felt an odd confusion ripple through her as if her eyes were betraying her. There were never visitors to Farleigh. The only people who came and went were the bishop, the sellers, and the buyers. This man was unaccompanied, and it didn't look as though he were here to purchase.

Nox blinked rapidly as she absorbed the alarming shift in events. She felt her breath catch, unsure as to what the sudden change might mean for her plans.

The stranger was the size of a mountain and covered to the gills with more weapons than even the heroes in stories. He spoke with a loud frustration to a defensive Matron Agnes. She was making no secret of her loud displeasure as she confronted him. Other children could be seen peeking their heads from the dining room, dorms, and over the balcony, all drawn by curiosity to witness the unusual disturbance. The front door to the manor remained wide open as if it had been flung on its hinges and left where it stuck itself to the innermost wall, letting in the cold autumn air. The night behind him pressed in with the lanterns and fires in the manor barely making a dent in the gloom beyond.

"You can't stay here," Agnes raised her hands to herd him out as if he were a feral animal who had wandered in. There was no kindness in her voice as she motioned to push the man out of the manor.

The grizzly, dark-haired man took a half-step back, but made no move to leave. The steel of his weapons jangled against his armor with the movement, drawing further attention to just how outfitted for danger the stranger was. Nox scanned him with intense curiosity, from the hilt of his swords to the hardened leather of his armor. Her eyes locked onto where he was clutching at his abdomen. The man was injured. "Your temple has the sign of the All Mother out front."

The stranger's gravely voice was referring to the iron that had been welded to the doors of the manor. The goddess's sigil consisted of only three, simple components. Two straight, vertical lines, and one half-circle. The bishop had it embroidered onto his finery and painted onto his carriage. Farleigh used the symbol to continue its sham of affiliation with the church so that their donations might line the mill's pockets.

"This is no temple," she shook her head, still pushing him backward.

"I am in need of a healer." His tone was firm, but there was an underlying hint of something in it. His gravelly statement was not one of desperation. Rather, he spoke with something akin to resignation. The bearded man had a fatherliness to his features, belying his years. His face and neck were etched with the pink lines of battle. He had a rugged aged handsomeness about him, but the markings were unmistakable despite his stubble.

Agnes held no compassion as she said, "The closest healer is in Stone. That's about a two days ride. We wish you well."

From somewhere behind the commotion, Mable's quiet voice bubbled, "Matron Flora was trained as a nurse under a healer."

Agnes shot a fuming look over her shoulder at the meek matron whose face immediately betrayed her regret for speaking. Mable would be heartily punished later. Perhaps no marks could be left on the children, but the same was not true of the matrons who stepped out of line.

Agnes was feral, "This is a haven for children. No weaponry is permitted on these in this house."

The stranger seemed to ground himself. He looked neither angry nor threatening. His voice was steady and deep as he answered, "Any establishment with the sign of the All Mother is bound to the Law of Sanctuary. I call on that law now, and seek sanctuary in your establishment. I will leave my weapons in your care, and give you whatever price in coin you wish for your shelter, as well as pay for any tonics you may have. Please show me to Matron Flora for bandaging. Thank you."

His negotiation tactic was one Nox would have to remember. The firm way he offered no alternative while still providing the matron with something she wanted and making it sound like a win for all parties involved. Agnes was no holy woman, and the Law of Sanctuary was probably as important to her as any other prayer she faked or formality she navigated. Coin, however, was a language she knew how to speak.

Agnes looked like she might fight him, but the man motioned to move more deeply into Farleigh. Children clutched at the door frames all around him and she noticed him scanning their faces. He should have been terrifying. He was enormous, bearded, armed, and one of the only adult men Nox had ever seen, save for the bishop and the buyers. Yet something about him didn't seem frightening. She found herself feeling somewhat pleased that he'd bested Agnes in her argument.

Clearly displeased, Agnes turned and began leading the man to her office where she would presumably lock up his weapons and accept his compensation for lodging. Nox needed to make herself scarce before the Gray Matron took any special heed of her whereabouts. The girl slipped into the doorway as the two passed, watching the blood on the man's side spread, amazed at the small, ruddy droplets that dropped onto the stones as he walked down the corridor. The moment the door to the office closed, she took off into the hall.

She needed to find Amaris.

The din of chatter and sounds of eating resumed, perhaps with more excitement as the children pressed each other about the stranger in the manor. The sounds from the floor below drifted up and reminded her that dinner was almost over. They'd soon lose their distracted opportunity to gather supplies.

The girls were almost ready—if only she could track down her silver counterpart.

Maybe the chaos of this man's arrival would provide additional diversions, securing their escape from the orphanage. Nox pricked with an idea as her eyes floated over her shoulder and down the hall to where she knew Agnes's office would be locked. The stranger had been relieved of his weapons. Perhaps she could steal a knife or two. If the man had paid the Gray Matron, his coin purse may very well be sitting on her office floor amidst his pile of blades. Nox's mind was buzzing with the ideas as her thoughts began to slow. A fear-filled doubt crept in to replace her excitement.

What had injured him? Was whatever caused the wound still out there?

Nox pressed herself into another dormitory doorway just in time for one of the matrons to move quickly past.

Matron Flora padded past the entrance to the dorm, headed hastily down the corridor. It sounded as though the man was being helped down the servant's stairs in the back to be kept on the kitchen level overnight. It made sense that the matrons wouldn't want him slumbering near the children.

Nox popped into the younger girls' dorm and saw her friend immediately. Amaris had her back to the door. She was standing on a chair, collecting her stolen items from where they'd been hidden out of the line of sight on top of a tall cabinet in the dorm. She quickly got down off the chair, blanket bundled under her arms. They both turned their heads from their respective places in the dorm. Two of the matrons could be heard hissing instructions just outside the hall.

Nox made a stilling motion as they both angled to listen to the women.

"We're to take guard in shifts," one said, her tone urgent.

"Do we just roam the halls? Do we not get to sleep?"

"We shouldn't be alone. Two matrons at a time need to be everywhere, to protect the children, and guard the office. Matron Agnes is very wary of having any man under our roof, let alone an assassin. This is meant to be a holy place."

One of them laughed, "It's no more a holy place with or without an assassin."

An assassin.

Nox tasted the word. She rolled it around on her tongue. Assassin. She made eye contact with Amaris and knew she'd heard it too. Nox noiselessly returned the chair to where it belonged and then moved to where Amaris was finding her other stashed items from around the dormitory. She'd procured mittens, wool socks, and was on her belly to pull a rolled cotton tunic from beneath a cot when Nox knelt beside her.

She kept her voice hushed as she spoke. "The one night we chose to escape is the night all the matrons will be patrolling in shifts and an armed killer is just down the hall."

Amaris attempted humor, "Well, technically I think he's unarmed and in the basement."

Amaris got up off her belly and they sat together on the bed. Their eyes touched, dissolving into a long, sad look. Nox put her arm up in that familiar way, and Amaris nestled in. Nox wondered if it comforted Amaris as much as it did her.

"This can't be happening," Amaris finally said.

So much had changed, but some things—things like this—she knew never could.

Their precise birthdays were as unknowable as the change in weather or shifts in Agnes's tempers, but the ivory girl was almost fifteen now, and the raven-haired counterpart in her seventeenth year. Amaris's white hair had never lost the scent of junipers, and Nox breathed it in, feeling a hitch in her chest like she might cry. She swallowed it down. The bond between them, stronger than anything comprehensible, would not be severed by Matron Agnes, or Madame Millicent, by bloodied assassins or the demons of whatever entities of the dark kingdom may slither under the dead earth beyond of Farehold's borders.

What she felt was electric, vibrant, and petrifying. She felt that very terror course through her, heat squeezing as she leaned into Amaris. She was scared. She was afraid of the road ahead. She feared escaping the orphanage unharmed and without being caught. But there was something far more nerve-wracking than running, than assassins or demons or cold, dark autumn forests.

They were going to run away together, and Nox was terrified.

"I—" Nox was caught in the middle of her words. Her mind raced, matching the hummingbird's pace of her heart. She had to say it. She needed Amaris to know. She screwed up her courage like a tightly wound cork, allowing the seal to pop as she said the words.

Amaris relaxed against her, seemingly unaware of the bottled emotions raging within her.

"I love you," Nox breathed into the silver tufts. A jolt of electricity spiked through her as the words escaped her, tightening her squeeze. She felt the threat of tears, but they were not tears of sadness. It was cowardice at the fear of rejection, and dread that her Snowflake wouldn't feel the same.

"I love you more," Amaris replied, enveloping herself more fully into the hug.

Nox pulled back a bit and shook her head slightly, but couldn't get out what she needed to say, nor was now the time to say it. There were so many names and faces to love, and this was not the time to tear off the mask. It stuck within her like dry medicine swallowed without water. It burned in the center of her throat, refusing to dissipate. She'd dreaded this moment, feeling its ache as it had already gone awry. The dismay at sharing what she needed to say, and knowing it hadn't been conveyed or understood the way she'd intended was a nauseating twist in her gut.

She couldn't do it.

She wouldn't do it.

Not now.

Not tonight.

Tonight was about escape. Her stomach was wrung tight with the nerves of her adrenaline. She had wanted to speak her heart for so long, but never known how. Nox was glad that Amaris no longer leaned against her chest so that she couldn't hear the way her traitorous heart thundered. She pressed her eyes closed and allowed herself the coward's out. It was the assassin that she feared. It was getting caught. It was the commotion. That is what she would say. That is what she would claim.

Amaris had the slightest knit between her white eyebrows, a gentle question on her lavender eyes.

Nox felt like she was going to start letting tears spill down her face if she dug too deeply into herself, so instead she stood, stifled her tears, and asked, "Tomorrow?"

Amaris's eyes widened. Even in the dark of the night, her purple irises still caught on the moonlight filtering in through the windows. She made a dismayed, choked sound as she asked, "Not tonight?"

"Farleigh is more guarded tonight than has ever been before or will ever be again. I'm so sorry, Snowflake. There has never been a worse night to try to run."

She bit her lips and closed her eyes, and Nox recognized the face the girl was trying to conceal. It was the same caged animal expression she'd seen before. Amaris needed to run. But she would not do it without Nox.

"Amaris, I'm sorry…"

"You're right," she looked away.

Nox felt as though she were failing spectacularly once more. The pain, the heart's utter crack was transparent through Amaris's every subtle expression, from the slump of her shoulders to the wilt of her face.

She parted her lips just enough to exhale slowly, calming herself. Her frosted white lashes fluttered open as she looked up into Nox's coal dark eyes and agreed with one final parting word. "Tomorrow."

The girls separated. Amaris hugged her pillow, staring at the colorless shadows of the wall. Nox didn't blink as her eyes remained glued to the ceiling. Eventually, despite their racing minds and the crushing disappointment in their hearts, they fell asleep slowly in their respective cots. They remained on either side of the hall, too plagued with questions and plans of the escape to a better life together. The thoughts of escape, of reprieve, of success filled their waking restless minds.

Tomorrow, they would run.

Tomorrow, at long last, they would be together.

Mable was shaking Amaris awake just as dawn broke. It was an hour too early for even the chattering of birds, but the purple-gray light of morning was coloring the room. She saw the silhouettes of the other children in their beds, unmoving. The other girls in the dorm were still asleep.

"Wake up, little one," the matron whispered, jostling a single shoulder gently from where it rested beneath the covers.

Mable smiled down at her, a cup of tea in her hand. Amaris rubbed at her eyes, uncomprehending. The matron extended the warm teacup to the girl who sat up slowly, looking around the graying morning light of the room, wondering why she was here.

No one had ever brought her tea in bed.

"Today is your big day."

Amaris accepted the cup of tea. It was hot in her hands, but felt nice against the cool morning air. She was still too groggy to understand what was being said. She blinked repeatedly at Mable, willing something about the matron's words to click into place. Her head shook slowly in confusion, loose, white hair moving in a cloud around her ears.

"You get to move on to your next adventure today!" Mable continued in feigned cheerfulness, keeping her voice low so as not to wake the other children. Her words were bright, but her face was tightly controlled against the pity she failed to conceal. Even in the shadows of the early morning, thinly veiled sadness was plain on her face. "We were so lucky to have you in Farleigh for so long, little Starlight. The Madame is downstairs in the dining room. She and Matron Agnes are having tea as we speak. The Madame would like to share breakfast with you before you leave. It's a long journey to the coast, my dear. Get dressed and wash your face. I'll see you downstairs soon."

"Mable—" Amaris's voice was a spark of fear.

"Yes, little one?"

She was wide awake now. Her breathing came out in rapid, shallow questions. "How can she be here? How can she be here already? Priory is two weeks away." Amaris's eyes were as wide as the very cup she held.

Mable made a sympathetic face. "She must have been close by when she received the raven, little one. Go, wash your face. Enjoy your tea. I'll see you downstairs in a moment."

No. This was impossible.

It had scarcely been one week since the raven had gone out. There had barely been enough time for the bird to reach Priory, let alone for a carriage to make the trek this far north. This couldn't be happening. It wasn't even first light. Nox wouldn't have woken yet. They were going to leave tonight. They had planned to run. Now she was being told they'd never have the chance to flee.

Amaris swallowed, working through her dread. She set her tea to the side, leaving it untouched. She needed to get up, but she couldn't stand while her head was spinning. She closed her eyes and forced herself to breathe in slowly through her nose, then exhale slowly through her mouth. The air felt unusually cold in the dorm. Amaris extended her inhalations and exhalations longer and longer, knowing she wouldn't be able to think if she let the dread cloud her mind. She would not be a helpless damsel. She would be strong. She would be capable. She would not be taken.

Affirmations aside, she had no contingency plans. She had one one plan only, and that had been to escape, regardless of its cost.

Her feet were quickly against the cold stone, and she savored the feeling. The discomfort helped to shake her awake, chasing the drowsiness from her mind. The cobwebs of sleep fell away as she planned her next steps.

Fetch supplies. Wake Nox. Run.

She dressed in pants and gathered the bundle of the boys' clothes she'd stolen from the laundry so that the dark-haired girl wouldn't have to run through the trees in her dress. The matrons who had been protectively patrolling the hall must be in the neighboring wing surveying the male children, as the elder women were nowhere to be seen.

Amaris carried her bundles with her as she snuck past the children's cots. She crept across the corridor to the elder girls' dorm and opened the door as quietly as she could manage. Before she even reached Nox's bed, she noticed her friends' coal-dark eyes were wide open. They didn't need to exchange a sound. Somehow, Nox seemed ready for the information. Amaris said nothing. Nox began wordlessly dressing into the offered tunic and pants without a moment's hesitation. A girl in a neighboring cot rolled over in her bed, but no one stirred from slumber as she gathered the sheet filled with food for the road and held her shoes in one hand, lest the soft leather soles make noise on the stones. It had been mere minutes since Mable had awoken her with tea, and they were already well on their way, ready to make it out into the chilled, early purples of dawn.

The girls began to creep toward the back stairs that would allow them to escape through the kitchen when Nox paused outside of Agnes's office.

"Why are we stopping?" Amaris was as silent as she could be while still conveying the tremor of urgency. She looked over her shoulder and down the hall, staring into the shadowed gloom of the empty hall. Any second, children could begin to wake.

"Trust me," Nox began to fish in her hair for a pin. Her fingers clasped successfully around the object, and she began to carefully pick the lock.

Nox had been Agnes's chore girl for years and had learned how to slip in and out of the office early in her teens, even if just to read books, comb through hidden treasures, or steal a piece of freedom knowing she was doing something all in the manor were strictly forbidden to do. She hadn't realized those skills had been culminating to this moment.

Nox knew exactly what she was looking for.

Disrupting the typical stateliness of Agnes's office, the assassin's weapons were strewn about the space. A long sword rested unceremoniously on the floor, a crossbow and accompanying quiver beside it. Amidst the blades, daggers and arrows, she found the man's bloodied cloak. Nox plunged her hands into the fabric, patting it for the bulges of pockets.

Her fingers hit something hard and bulky. There it was. The man's coin purse.

Nox wrapped her fingers around the small bag and stood in the dark of the office. She had never hoped to escape with money. They couldn't have dreamed of such good fortune as they'd planned their run. Matron Agnes had kept her silvers and crowns locked up, but in the confusion of the assassin's arrival, this had been more than they could have hoped.

Fortune smiled upon them.

Nox grabbed a thin knife from the man's numerous weapons and slipped it into the band of her pants. She palmed the second one and handed it off to Amaris who had been waiting impatiently just outside of the office, keeping lookout. Her eyes flared when she took the blade from Nox, but asked no questions. She may have been too fragile to learn much by way of self defense, but she'd need all the help she could get on the road.

"Here," Nox passed her the coin purse.

"You found money?" Amaris breathed appreciatively at its weight, hearing the gentle scrape of metal as pennies, crowns and silvers rubbed against one another in the pouch.

"Hide it," Nox commanded in a whisper.

The night-haired girl twisted the lock from the inside of the office and quietly pulled it closed once more with a gentle click. Amaris tucked the extra weapon inside her shirt and draped the winter cloak she'd grabbed from the laundry over her arm.

They were ready.

It was a tight corner from the office at the end of the corridor to the back staircase that would wind them into the kitchen. They could slip out the back entrance before anyone came looking for Amaris. The girls began their quiet descent down the manor's back stairs. They picked their careful steps by feeling the curvature of the stones when they were brought to an abrupt halt. An unfamiliar figure blocked their path. It took everything in them to remain silent as they skidded to a stop.

Amaris inhaled sharply, but resisted the impulse to cry out in surprise.

The man's eyebrows raised in surprise, but the stranger wasn't looking to chat.

"Ladies," he acknowledged. His voice wasn't loud, but the deep male grumble still startled them in the stillness of the morning light.

Amaris began backpedaling immediately. She took a step up the stairs, practically shoving against Nox in the tight hall. "I'm sorry, we—"

"Amaris!" a woman's voice called from the hallway.

"Shit," Nox's curse was both panic and a tragedy.

Clearly a matron had been alerted by the brief exchange. The sound of their detection was the single most horrible noise in the world. Amaris's stomach fell to her feet. Her vision swam. The matrons must have come looking to see what was taking her so long to get to the dining room.

The man grunted something akin to annoyance, but she didn't have time to manage his emotions. Perhaps he'd also been hoping to get up to the office and gather his things without being seen. She could hear feet coming down the hallway. Amaris handed the rest of the belongings over to Nox with a shove.

"Go!" She pleaded. "Wait for me out back."

"Amaris—" Nox clutched the cloaks and items to her chest.

"Tell me later!" Amaris's face twisted with desperation. She would deal with this setback and meet her in a few moments. Nox could not risk getting caught with her now if they had any hope of escape. First, she would do what she must in order to rid herself of Millicent. Then they would run.

Nox squinted against her conflicted pain before tearing from Amaris. Her dark eyes searched the man who raised a curious eyebrow for any sign he might betray them, but he politely side-stepped. He allowed her to push past him in a cloud of inky shadowy hair as she ran down the stairs toward the kitchen. Whatever was happening, it was none of his business.

Amaris felt her chest tighten, struggling to remain calm. She began walking up the stairs, returning to the landing. The staircase had been dark, but the early morning light illuminated enough of the corridor to reveal that Amaris was not alone. Mable's face was painted with fear and surprise as she spotted the girl and the assassin ascending the shadowy stairs together.

Mable was bewildered. "What on earth are the two of you—"

"I was just going down to meet the Madame in the kitchen," her words came out in a rushed, dry apology. "I ran into him on his way up. I'm sorry, Matron."

The man shrugged in agreement, further emphasizing his unwillingness to intervene in whatever the girls had been doing. He went from the staircase directly to the office, avoiding addressing them altogether.

Mable didn't know which issue to deal with first, eyes flitting between the stranger and the girl. Her eyes remained trained on the assassin, though her words addressed the thin, ivory young woman. "I said we were to meet in the dining room, Amaris. Not the kitchen."

"Oh," she attempted what she'd hoped was an apologetic smile. She moved past Mable toward the primary staircase that descended from the front of the manor toward the dining room, forcing her feet to walk at a normal, unbothered pace.

"What ever are you wearing?" Mable called after her, horrified as the pants and tunic unbecoming of a lady colored her vision. As a young woman, she'd been expected to be presentable in the dresses for maidens, not the children's attire she wore.

"Traveling clothes—for the road!" Amaris attempted to sound cheerful, throwing the response over her shoulder. Her stomach filled with rocks and her knees felt wobbly as she continued her forward steps. She could hear Matron Mable exchanging words with the man and then the distinct noise of unsuccessful twisting of a doorknob. He jangled the knob in his attempt to get at his cloak and weapons as she disappeared down the stairs. She was glad they'd remembered to lock it as they left. It seemed everyone was ready to make a hasty departure from this place.

She descended the stairs. Her foot hit the final stone on the landing with the resounding toll of a funeral bell. Amaris entered the dining room, heart so frenzied that she wasn't sure the organ had much interest in keeping her conscious.

This meeting was never supposed to happen. She had intended to be long gone before this day had ever arrived. Amaris had firmly believed that by the time Madame Millicent arrived in Farleigh, she'd be a week's travel from this goddess forsaken place. She made no attempt to show any respect as she took in the sight of the Madame, perched near the window on the far side of the dining table. She wasn't alone. Millicent had company for her breakfast tea.

Matron Agnes's worn features etched into deep disapproval upon seeing the girl. She was selling a prized possession. The least the girl could do was look the part. Agnes didn't have time to object to her appearance. The Gray Matron had barely opened her mouth to address Amaris's entrance when Mable hurried into the dining room, bending to whisper something into Agnes's ear. Agnes's frown deepened the carved lines of her age and she excused herself from the table, presumably to address the man's need to access his belongings in the first hours of dawn. While Agnes had been a vision of displeasure, Millicent's expression was the picture of delight. She radiated her cat-like joy as she eyed Amaris, the little mouse who'd wandered in to play.

Her voice was bright, like the ringing of a silver bell. It was too pleasant, too musical for such a dark woman. "My, what a flawless treasure you are. I'd nearly forgotten just how radiant. Come, dear, sit down." Millicent motioned for the girl to join her across the table, sweeping a gloved hand in a graceful gesture.

Amaris made no move to sit, but her refusal didn't seem to faze the Madame. She shrugged as if it didn't bother her in the slightest, sipping on her tea with proper, delicate movements. She acted as though she were performing for court rather than drinking out of an orphanage's cup.

Today Millicent was in a deep amethyst dress with black gems, her golden hair pinned half up in elaborate curls. Her elbow-length gloves stayed on while she used a fork to pick at her breakfast with bird-like delicacy. Her lips had been painted a shade of night to match her dark jewels, careful not to make contact with the food lest her blackened mouth smear. Although Amaris had never seen one, something in her gut distinctly shouted to her that this woman looked like a witch.

Perhaps it was numbness, but Amaris had no emotion when she spoke. "How did you get here so fast? It's supposed to be at least two week's travel to Priory."

Millicent eyed Amaris's position from across the room. Her feline smile grew even more wicked. She said, presumably to herself, "Oh, it is fun when they have spirit."

Amaris looked over her shoulder as if the Madame had been addressing someone else, but they were alone. She took a single step closer to the table, but would not sit down. "What is your plan for me?"

The Madame let a flicker of a frown cross her features. Millicent chose her words carefully, gesturing again for Amaris to sit, though the gesture was fruitless for both of them. She didn't have time to play Millicent's coy game of pleasantries. She needed to leave. Amaris wondered how much time had passed. How much longer would Agnes be upstairs? Was Nox already waiting outside? Would Millicent chase her if she turned on her heel and attempted to flee?

"You are a rare beauty," Millicent said finally.

"And if I weren't beautiful?"

Millicent clucked her tongue, "What's the point of such a useless question? The truth remains: you are. Short of being mauled by a beast, you're still the most marvelous diamond I've seen in my ages. You'd be amazed what men will pay to possess something unique, even if only for a moment. Everyone wants a piece of something special. Now, to be the first to have you… well, that will be worth your weight in crowns, my dear."

The Madame rose to her feet and began making her way slowly

around the table. Amaris matched her steps, backing away in the opposite direction, keeping the space between them equidistant. She was deeply uneasy that the woman had stood, intimidated by how she attempted physical proximity.

A voice within her screamed at her to run. The internal voice was so distant, so drowned by the hum of her own fear.

"Your friends are already in Priory waiting for you. They're very excited to see you," Millicent lied. Amaris knew she was referring to Cici and Emily, but she hadn't been friends with either of them. She wasn't friends with anyone. No one would be happy to see her at the pleasure house, aside from the hungry faces of patrons and the greedy coin purse of its Madame.

"They're both quite lovely." Amaris remarked flatly of the girls who'd been taken before her.

"Oh yes, they are," Millicent agreed, but her voice was not kind. She used a bored tone as she recalled the others, sinking her weight into one hip as she looked off into the distance. "They have the common, virginal beauty that fetches a high enough price on their first night, and then the steadfast price of a workhorse from then on. But you, Amaris, are no work horse. The life that awaits you is quite spectacular indeed. The matrons tell me your name means 'gift from the goddess'. Believe me when I tell you that you will be marketed as such. You are a treasure. You can have a very pleasant life if you allow us to work as a team, dear. I'd like that very much."

Millicent took another step toward her. The clack of the Madame's heels on the stones mingled with the commotion of the matrons coming down the stairs with the male stranger. The man's footsteps were heavy enough to indicate he had redressed in his armor, intent on departure. Amaris dared to take her eyes off the Madame long enough to glance over her shoulder, peering beyond the dining room into the foyer. She saw the matrons clucking after him like chickens after a fox in their hen house as he sauntered out after his horse. His dark hair had been slicked back a bit from a morning wash, and he no longer seemed to be clutching his stomach. She hadn't been able to catch more in the brief moments her eyes grazed the stranger. Perhaps his wounds had been shallow enough that the nurse was able to stop the bleeding with bandages, if not for the manor's limited supply of tonics. It would doubtlessly be another scar to add to his collection.

Millicent made another move toward her, snapping her attention away from the man and the matrons.

"Stop," Amaris cautioned, and Millicent stilled in her steps. As she stared at her options, she was struck with inspiration. Amaris reached into her shirt and wrapped her hand around the hilt of the small dagger Nox had handed her.

The Madame let out a sharp, dark laugh, shaking her golden curls slightly to emphasize her surprised delight. Her black lips peeled back into a predatory smile, teeth glinting in the early morning light. "You mean to hurt me, girl? Oh, my, I wish you would try."

As the Madame began to peel off her gloves, Amaris shook her head. Her voice was stronger than she'd ever heard it before as she spoke her resolution.

"No," and her words did not waiver as she finished, "I mean to hurt me."

Amaris struck fast and hard with the dagger, closing her eyes and jerking her face up and to the side as she slashed the knife down in countering motion. Millicent let out a blood-curdling shriek as the merchandise before her mutilated itself, dragging a deep line from her forehead, across her brow bone, and down her left cheek. The acute pain was a sharp, sweet sensation of relief as she knew her dagger hit its mark. A hot rain of her own blood spilled over her face, soaking her tunic.

She was no longer perfect.

The Madame's horrified screams sounded as though she was the one who'd been stabbed. The sound, the pain, the blood—it had set Amaris free. She was no longer glued to the floor. She felt as though a millstone had been removed from her neck as she began to run.

Millicent ran for her but Amaris was already out of the dining room, over the threshold and out the door. She ran into the open, spinning amid the bright, clear, indigo morning of the courtyard to see how close the Madame was on her heels. It was not the clean break for which she'd hoped. The courtyard was crowded with matrons and the assassin. Her back was to the man and his horse with the matrons watching in utter terror as the Madame advanced on her.

Amaris held her dagger aloft and she swung again, this time slashing down cutting a line from her collar bone down nearly across her right breast, shredding and bloodying the tunic she wore. The matrons were realizing precisely what transpired as the crimson evidence poured down around their starlight girl. Agnes made a lunging move for her, but Amaris prayed to the goddess on the only wild card in the courtyard. She ran to the assassin. The man had already mounted his horse and had begun to nudge it out of the premises when the pandemonium had spilled from the manor into the courtyard.

"Please, take me with you!" She pleaded up at him, reaching his horse.

The women were still advancing around her as if cornering a wild animal, approaching Amaris from where she was triangulated between the Gray Matron, the Madame, and the assassin's horse.

The assassin was speechless.

Amaris wondered if it was one of the few times the world-weary man had a true face of shock plastered across his features. This probably wasn't how he foresaw his morning going. He began to shake his head. She pressed her body into the mount, her blood staining its slick coat.

He'd barely spit out a bewildered stammer, "I—"

Her back was to the women as she made eye contact intense with the stranger. Amaris pulled a familiar coin purse from her shirt and swung around so it was firmly behind her back, where he could see it and it could remain hidden from the matrons and Madame alike.

She was presenting him with his own coin purse as bribery.

The stranger wasn't sure if he was impressed or irritated, but he tried to keep the amusement from his voice. The scene before him was bizarre, to say the least. A white-haired bloodied girl was attacking herself with a dagger—*his* dagger, he was quite certain—and offering his own coin to him. He didn't know a lot about women, but he knew these matrons had been no holy servants of the church. However awful the matrons had been, the Madame in purple might be a sore sight worse.

"Take me with you," she said again, her void a desperate beg.

He loosed a sigh tinged with conflicting emotions.

"I'll buy her off you," he finally said. His gravelly voice had an upsetting effect on the women in the courtyard, like snakes disturbed into writhing.

Millicent was horrified. "There was a down payment made!"

He nodded, "I will reimburse whatever down payment. I'm in need of a…" he searched for a word before settling on, "squire."

Millicent shook her head so hard that it appeared her curls might release themselves from the elaborate pins. Every step she took brought her further from the open door of the manor and closer to the man and his horse. Her voice was shrill and cruel as her fist raised, "I own you, girl!"

If they did nothing, Millicent would be at her side in fewer than ten paces. The Madame began once more to yank at the black fabric on her forearms and stopped just short of pulling off her gloves.

They had an audience.

The moon faces of children waking up for the day were pressed into the glasses of the dorms up above. The matrons were gaping, horrified at the mutilated young girl in the courtyard, fresh blood soaking her hair and tunic, plastering it to her body. A crowd had gathered both within and without Farleigh to witness the bedlam caused by the girl who would rather disfigure herself than go with this woman.

"Amaris—" Agnes said her name sadly from where she'd remained equidistant from the girl. Her expression was confusing, as she truly did look sorry. Amaris's choice to slice her face and body rather than be sold to the Madame had broken something in Agnes that had hardened so long ago.

"You can't make me go," she said with a feral intensity. Her back was pressed against the tall, dappled horse with the man's leg ending at her hip.

With a prayer to the All Mother, she reached her hand up and—praise be to the goddess—the man gripped her elbow, swinging her up behind him. She passed him the pouch in a seamless exchange and the man tossed his coin purse to Matron Agnes. He instructed her to keep the change before urging his horse into a trot out of the courtyard, down the road.

They may have been departing, but the pandemonium had just begun. The clatter of hooves against the road mixed with the cacophony of angry shouts, shrill accusations, clustering children, and the incongruously happy chirping of early morning birds.

Amaris looked over her shoulder one last time and said a prayer that Nox had made it out safely, hoping she was well on her way to the coast to start a new life. She prayed that the All Mother saw fit to bless their journeys, and that they would be together again soon.

5

Amaris didn't know what to do with her hands.

She had never so much as been alone with a man, let alone touched one. Now she was supposed to wrap her arms around a stranger as their horse plodded onward. She was quite sure that she was only seated behind him since he'd already been in the saddle when she'd been swung to her rescue, and wasn't sure if that made things more or less uncomfortable between them. It required her to use entirely too much muscle power in her thighs as she clutched the horse with her legs. It would probably make things easier for both of them if she used the stranger for balance. Too many thoughts clashed against each other like mismatched music, angry sounds, and the counter-harmonies of voices. She couldn't focus on any of the sounds as they lapped over one another. Amaris was strangely aware of the chill as autumn wind cooled the blood that dried against her shirt and skin.

They hadn't spoken since they'd left Farleigh behind.

The morning had given way to a quiet, awkward afternoon before they'd finally dismounted for mealtime. The dapple-gray horse was tethered to a tree and the man set to work building a fire, not forcing

Amaris to speak. He allowed her to sit in her blood and thoughts, clearly numb from the events of the day. Eventually, a mid-day campfire was crackling between them. It was still the late afternoon of daylight, but the fire's glow felt nice against the crisp bite of autumn. Amaris stared into the flames, watching them twist and pop and dance in a mesmerizing tangle of reds, oranges, yellows and blues. The sparks and embers helped her mind to detach fully, lost to her silence. The smell of smoke, dying leaves, and the chill of oncoming winter would have been pleasant under any other occasion. She could hear what she thought might be an owl, though it seemed too early in the afternoon for the great, nocturnal birds to hoot.

She raised her eyes to the trees to search for the bird. She didn't care about the owl, or the temperature, or the fire. Her world was spinning, and she had no idea what to do.

The man wordlessly disappeared into the woods, and Amaris didn't bother to watch him leave. She wouldn't have known how much time had passed had it not been for the elongating shadows. He'd been absent for nearly an hour before reappearing with a rabbit. The bearded stranger sat across from her and began to quietly skin the creature.

Her eyes continued to stare into the fire, feeling her pupils burn against the prolonged exposure to light. Her peripherals could see the man and how he occasionally looked to her with what may have been concern. She wasn't sure if she was using her peripheral vision to study him in order to assess whether he was a threat, or only for something to do to occupy her mind. Though she didn't look at him directly, she absorbed his dark beard, thick brows, broad shoulders, and that the man appeared to be in his fifth decade of life. His hair had remained slicked back from his morning wash, and hung roughly as long as his cropped beard down the back of his neck. He appeared as though he would be an intimidating foe in battle, to be sure, but the man did not seem threatening in a way that had stirred her to run as she had from

Millicent.

After he'd discarded the hare's bloodied fur, he skewered the rabbit and stuck it across the campfire to cook. While the meat roasted, he offered her a flask of his water.

"No, thank you." She was surprised at how her voice croaked. She hadn't used it since she'd cried out in desperation that morning.

"It's for your face," he said. They were the first words he'd spoken since their exchange in the courtyard.

She blinked rapidly, wondering what she must look like through his eyes. A distant part of her felt quite certain he felt he was staring at the gore of a girl's reanimated corpse. She took the canteen. The man tore a length of clean cloth from inside his satchel that seemed to be for just this purpose. He was no stranger to being injured on the road.

"Clean your cuts as best as you can, and I'll give you a healing tonic. I'll bill you later."

She wasn't sure if he was trying to be funny, or if he genuinely wanted payment. Amaris was almost positive he'd purchased healing tonics from the orphanage, and that whatever money he'd used to buy the tonics had been stolen by Nox and regifted by the ivory girl in exchange for whatever her life was worth.

It had been quite the deal. He'd received shelter for the night, healing tonics, bandaging by Matron Flora, and the life of a particularly valuable girl for one coin purse.

Amaris had no money, and no way to pay him. As the hours wore on, she was growing increasingly lucid as to the weight of her decisions and the consequences that may result from her choice to follow an assassin into the woods. Amaris shifted uncomfortably, feeling herself begin to wonder about the wisdom of her path. She had spent no time around men. There had been the boy at the manor—both cruel and stupid. There had been the bishop—pious and crooked. She knew little of men, save for the certainty that the lesser sex had never given her a reason to trust them.

When she didn't respond, he tried again, "There's a village not too far from here. It's not big but I need to meet a bishop about settling a debt. You should be able to catch a ride from there."

"A bishop?" She felt her face go bloodless. The fear in her voice must have been clear.

"It's not about you, girl." His thick brows furrowed, curiosity about her peculiar reaction clear. "We help the kingdoms with... Well, I suppose it doesn't matter. When I speak with him, feel free to find yourself a ride. I'll make sure you're safely on the road to wherever you're going before I leave you."

"Wherever I'm going?" She hadn't considered it. She had never planned to travel alone. She didn't know if she could brave the roads without Nox.

The man's frown deepened, "Where are your people?"

She shook her head slowly, "I don't have any people."

He considered this. "And the woman at the orphanage?"

"She was buying me for her brothel," Amaris kept her eyes on the fire, her tone quiet and monotonous as if she didn't dare attach feeling to her words.

He seemed lost for words at this bit of information. He had known he wasn't in a holy place, but this news was a bit more than he'd been prepared to receive. "Is there anywhere you'd like to go?"

Her frosted lashes fluttered to a close as mind wandered to the only plans she and her friend—her sister, her family, her partner, her lone person in this world—had ever made. She thought of the blue expanse of the sea and how it was said to meet the horizon in an endless, salty sense of openness. "I suppose I want to go to the southern coast, where it's warm."

He nodded at that. They didn't attempt further conversation.

Amaris took the time to wash the blood from her face as best as she could. She used the clean cloth as a compression against the gash that had skipped her eye, but had otherwise marred her from her forehead to her cheek. Once she began washing the wound, she found even the simple tug of the cloth had reopened it to a fresh flow of blood.

"Good, now that it's clean, press some of the tonic directly into the wound."

"But it's bleeding."

"That's a good thing. It's more effective without the risk of dirt or infection."

Amaris dipped her finger into the bottle and watched her pale finger come up with a sticky, brown liquid. It matched the color of the bottle that held it. She felt along her face for the gash, smearing the tonic into her wound.

She thought of the times she or her peers had fallen ill in the orphanage and how Matron Flora had busied herself with the small brown bottles, but she'd never had use for any that hadn't been administered to her. "Do I drink what's left?"

He nodded, "That you do. It helps knit your insides and outsides."

"It's magic?"

He considered that, "It's an old magic. Tonics like that are one of the first inventions healers and manufacturers came together to create. Tonics have been around since... well... long before you or I were born."

Amaris didn't understand half of what he'd said. She didn't know what a manufacturer was, or what he'd meant by old magic. Regardless, she drank half of the bottle. She dipped her finger into the bottle once more to wet it with the brown, honey-stick liquid as she attempted to rub the tonic over the gashes on her face and across her chest with what remained, wincing against the sting.

She stared intently into its crackling flames while the man finished cooking the rabbit. He tore into it and stretched himself over the fire, offering her half. She accepted the gift of food from the man and chewed on it sullenly, thinking of Nox and the meal of hard cheese and bread that her friend was sure to be having somewhere in the forest. Had they run in the same direction? How far would she be now? That was, of course, unless she'd gone back inside to live among the matrons. Amaris hadn't considered the possibility that Nox might want to stay in Farleigh without her.

The stranger kicked out the fire and began to untether the horse.

"Shall we?"

"We're going?"

"Like I said, I have a bishop to meet with."

She stood and considered the scarred, fatherly assassin from a ways off. He'd fed her, offered her healing tonics, allowed her silence, and most importantly, he'd aided her escape from a life of unimaginable horrors. She hadn't even asked him who he was.

Amaris felt a stab of shame at her ingratitude as she asked, "What's your name?"

He didn't look up from his horse, continuing to repack the satchel and prepare for departure. He offered his name and nothing more. "Odrin."

It was a nice name. A friendly name. She hoped he was kind.

"I'm Amaris."

He chuckled slightly at that. "That makes sense."

"Come here, Amaris" Odrin said, gesturing for the horse. "You can take the saddle this time. It'll be easier on those jelly legs of yours." He helped her up with ease before swinging himself into the space behind her.

"Why do you say that?" She asked.

"About your jelly legs?" He did his best not to look patronizing. "It's clear you're no rider. You'll need the saddle's help more than I do."

"No," her brows furrowed from where she sat in front of him, but he couldn't see her perplexed facial expression. "Why do you say that about my name?"

He clicked his tongue to urge the horse forward. The dappled mount began moving with unhurried steps away from the campfire as Odrin asked, "Do you know what it means? Your name, that is?"

She nodded. She did know. "The matrons gave it to me. Since I was a gift left on their doorstep, they said it meant 'gift from the goddess'."

He nudged the horse forward and considered it. "Did they now?" He chewed on that for a moment. "Perhaps in a dialect deeper in the south of the continent it means something to that effect. But that's not what people in the north will hear."

"What does it mean in the north?"

He smiled, looking over his shoulder at her silvery features. "Child of the moon."

The two unlikely travel companions were in a small village by the last coppery lights of sundown. At least, Amaris assumed it was a village. She'd never been anywhere, and had no basis for comparison.

The horse plodded down the grassy center of the village, carrying them deeper into the collection of homes and shops. Amaris wasn't sure if there were establishments or cottages behind trees or around bends out of view, but the village seemed to have fewer than ten buildings.

The structure at the heart of the village looked like how she'd imagined an inn might. A few thatch-roofed homes were scattered about. A steepled church with the iron sign of the All Mother decorating its cathedral sat directly across from the inn.

They dismounted and Odrin waved her away, instructing her to ask around to see if anyone in town were headed to the coast while he chatted with the village's bishop. Odrin disappeared inside one of the only homes with clay shingles in an otherwise thatch-roofed village. Amaris idled nervously about the horse for a minute. She was nearly fifteen, but her whole life had consisted of the grounds of Farleigh. The world felt too big. Every face was new and strange. Every building was crushingly unfamiliar. Given that two strangers, one a towering man and the other a girl bloodied beyond recognition, had entered the quiet town, they were drawing some stares. It didn't help her ever-growing sense of crushing discomfort. Amaris fidgeted before heading nervously toward the inn.

She stopped short of the door, unsure whether or not she was supposed to knock. Visitors and sellers at the doors of Farleigh always knocked. Buyers entered freely on market day. After a long moment, she decided that she was more of a buyer than a seller, and eased the door open with more trepidation than she could rationalize.

The woman within—whether a barmaid or the innkeeper herself—nearly dropped her pitcher of ale when Amaris walked in.

Amaris stopped on the landing, unsure if she'd done something terribly wrong. Warmth and the sour smells of beer, sourdough and smoke hit her, freezing her to the doorway. She felt herself shrink, not knowing if she should retreat. Perhaps she should have knocked. This was one of the first decisions she'd ever had to make for herself, and clearly, she'd done it wrong.

"Oh my, dear." The friendly-faced woman approached, creased with worry. The ivory girl had scarcely crossed the threshold onto the wooden floors before she was met by maternal hands. The woman gaped at her injuries.

"It's not that bad," Amaris lifted a hand self-consciously to the wound on her face. She nearly pressed her back into the door, flinching away from the woman's advances.

The middle-aged woman put her hands on her hip, one still clutching the dirty rag that she'd been using to wipe the tables around her. "Do you have coin?"

"How much do you need?" Amaris looked around, not even sure

what service she required.

The woman shook her head, tugging Amaris forward, "I won't charge a thing like you more than two pennies. Come now."

Amaris blinked. Of course, she would need money. Her mind flitted to the coin pouch she'd exchanged with Odrin. She chewed her lip with uncertainty as she allowed herself to be tugged into the tavern. "I think my traveling partner might—"

The woman clucked her tongue and continued to usher the girl into the back. Soon closed doors separated them from the tavern beyond for privacy as they sat beside a wash basin. The woman helped her scrub off the wound on her chest and bandaged it properly, blinding Amaris completely in one eye with bandages, covering half of her face with gauze. The other straps of clean cloth wrapped around where Amaris had nearly mutilated one of her small breasts, tightly binding half of her chest to her shoulder in a criss-cross of bandaging. While bandaging her, the woman marveled how she'd managed to keep so much blood on her face given how old the wounds had been.

Amaris intended to correct that it had happened nearly this morning, when she caught the scarcely scabbed, grimy-looking wounds in the mirror above the wash basin. They did indeed look two weeks old. Matron Flora had administered medicine in brown bottles, but she hadn't educated the children as to what was being done. Amaris had never truly heard of a healing tonic before she had drunk the one Odrin had given her.

The woman filled the wash basin with warm, soapy water. She had Amaris flip her blood-stained hair into the basin. The woman scrubbed at Amaris's scalp, freeing the crusted, crimson stains from her hair.

Once the dried blood was cleaned from her strands and the woman had fitted her with a fresh tunic, the elder woman was finally able to see how truly strange the girl was. She could no longer hide behind the excuse of wounds or blood or dirty clothes. The silver-haired young girl was a moonlit anomaly with eyes as purple as the fresh, fragrant lilacs in spring.

"So," the woman started, attempting to sound casual while Amaris looked at her bandages in the mirror, "Was it your mother or your father?"

"Excuse me?" Amaris lifted her lavender eyes to the middle-aged woman, which further underscored the innkeeper's conviction.

She pressed, "Who was fae? Was it your mother?"

Amaris shook her head, comprehension eluding her. Her white brows pinched in the center as she waited for the woman to explain.

The woman scoffed, "This village may be small, but we're not so backwater that we don't get our share of the fair folk from time to time, at least, some with distant lineage... Though I will say, it's been ages... I do know how to spot a faeling. I'll be damned, I've never seen one who looked like you..." Her voice trailed off with each peculiar sentence, growing quieter with each passing word.

Amaris wasn't sure what to make of the stranger's speech, feeling particularly disconcerted with how disconnected the woman's thoughts had seemed. She'd involuntarily begun with honesty, finding herself responding before she thought better of it. "I never knew my parents. I grew up in—" she stopped herself from saying Farleigh.

Amaris blinked away how stunned she was at her own stupidity. She didn't want to risk word getting back to the orphanage of which direction she'd headed in. The girl didn't know how far Millicent's talons reached. Amaris pursed her pale lips to silence herself and offered a sad shrug. The gesture would have to suffice.

"No family, then?" The woman frowned apologetically. "Come, let's get you something to drink. You look pale. Well—pale, even for your complexion."

She led them out of the bathing room and busied herself with fetching a glass of water from behind the bar. They'd re-entered the tavern so the barmaid could resume filling pitchers. She set a glass of water down in front of the girl before tending to her other customers. Amaris looked around nervously and took in the two dark patrons skulking in the corner. A conciliatory hand went to her hair.

"Say," Amaris twisted her lips, prepared to ask the favor. "Since I'm already buying the tunic from you, would you also be able to find me a scarf, for my hair?"

The innkeeper's eyes flitted from Amaris's hair to her face as she nodded. "I'll do that, and it might help a bit, but you'll want to be keeping your cloak on and hood up if you want any hope of people not catching those eyes of yours. They are..." she allowed her eyes to roam with more concern than Amaris understood, "They're really unlike anything I've seen."

Amaris knew her features were rare, but she hadn't understood just how unusual looked until this stranger had cast her evaluating gaze upon her. She'd been kept away from prying eyes for years. Aside from the children raised as her peers, desensitized to her appearance, she'd had very little exposure to how an outsider might respond to her features.

As the woman returned with a scarf, Amaris caught a glimpse of Odrin through the window. "Oh! One moment, let me grab your payment."

Before the barmaid could stop her, she was heading out the door, twisting her hair into a scarf. She ran up to the assassin and as the man reached his horse. The gray mount chuffed as it stepped to the side, wary of her rapid approach.

Her inquiry was rushed, "May I steal two pennies off of you?"

"Haven't you already stolen enough of my money?" Was his way of greeting as he saddled the horse.

"I stole it back from Agnes, so technically she was paid twice with the same coin."

111

"That she was, but my purse is still empty nonetheless."

"Didn't your bishop—"

He fished two pennies from a pouch in his vest. "I hope you found a ride, girl."

"Don't leave the village without me!" She yelled as she took off.

She dashed inside the inn and hugged the woman, bewilderment clear on the woman's face. Amaris wouldn't forget this act of kindness, even if it had been in exchange for compensation. In a heartbeat she was out the door and jogging down the village to catch up to where Odrin and his horse were plodding away. He hadn't left the village. He also hadn't been willing to stand still.

"I want to come with you!"

He kept the horse at a walk, not bothering to look at the pale teenager who was already breathless from keeping pace. "No, you don't."

Dauntless, Amaris kept her up jogging. "I know nothing of the world. I don't know anything about the villages. I don't know about people, about money, about customs. I don't know the first thing about getting to the coast. If I had known how to fight, I could have defended myself today."

The horse flicked its ears in irritation as it continued its forward motion. The beast was clearly uncomfortable with the girl invading its space.

"We all have to grow up sometime, kid. Why not start a new life here? Ask the inn if they're hiring."

She shook her head, short of breath. "Will you teach me how to fight?"

Odrin laughed from where he sat in his saddle and looked down at her then. "Girls don't train where I'm from."

Amaris's tone was cheerful, if not breathless, "Well, that's rather sexist. Sounds like they had to grow up sometime."

He chuckled again at how she'd turned his words on him. Odrin shook his head, but she cut him off. He looked set to argue once more.

Amaris was resolute, "Look, I've never had a father. But if you'd have me, I promise I won't be a burden."

He pulled the horse to a stop then and she stopped running, panting slightly at the exertion. The sun had set. Only the flickers of torches on buildings cast light and shadows against the sincerity of her plea. She knew her words had hit a chord with him. Something tugged his vision into the middle distance, a memory pulling his focus. Odrin breathed out a long, slow breath, and shook his head as if his body were willing him to say no, but instead he looked her in the eye.

"I don't think you'll like what you're getting yourself into."

She put her hands on her hips, the inhalations coming in more easily now. "I won't like what? Getting strong? Learning how to defend myself? Take me with you."

He looked back at the town. It was clear from his face that part of him wanted her to leave, to start her new life. Amaris stared intently at Odrin for his response. She didn't recognize the emotion at the time as a second, long dead part of him listened to the memory of a woman singing, the gurgles of a happy baby in her arms. She studied his features as he seemed to shake off whatever had invaded his thoughts. Odrin blinked away whatever the reverie had challenged him before it resurfaced. He stared at her for a long moment.

The horse huffed impatiently as if urging them to make up their minds.

With a look that informed her he fully understood he was making a mistake, he extended his arm to her, and swung her up behind him.

Her tailbone had never felt such pain.

Amaris wanted to whine, but she knew she had to do everything within her power to prevent Odrin from regretting his decision to bring her with him. His reluctance had been clear, and if she griped about the ache of her legs or bruise of her lowermost spine, she was worried he'd make her walk back to Farleigh.

No one had told her that riding could be so grueling. Her legs throbbed painfully from gripping the saddle. All her muscles were screaming at her as the pair dismounted for the night. She was so stiff; she wasn't sure if she remembered how to walk.

Odrin hadn't permitted them to start a fire that night. When she asked why, he explained that fires were fine during the day for cooking, but there were plenty of reasons a pair of humans—or a human and whatever she was—would not want to draw the attention of the things that lived in the dark.

Amaris curled on her side, listening to Odrin move about as he prepared himself for sleep. He'd disappeared into the forest, which wasn't unusual for their short time together. He'd gone to get rabbits and wood and taken care of goddess knows what whenever they'd stopped. This time he did not return empty handed.

"Amaris," he said her name, extending her something.

She sat up and looked at what was being offered to her. He'd cut a large bough of a soft conifer. Her brows puckered as she accepted the tree branch, staring at him with mixed confusion.

"Most of your body heat is lost through the ground. You shouldn't sleep directly on the earth, even with your cloak." He set down a few cut branches of his own and pulled his cloak up over his body, grunting what could have been a goodnight.

Amaris felt her heart tug at the thoughtful gesture. She copied his actions, placing the branch beneath her to create a thin barrier between herself and the earth as she balled up for sleep. She curled her knees against her chest as she huddled into a space so small, she thought she might disappear. It hadn't even been the fully cycle of a day. That very morning, she'd been with Nox. It was in the violet lights of dawn that Nox's dark eyes had opened and silently dressed as she prepared to run with her. Between Millicent, the dagger, the matrons and the escape, it felt as though a lifetime had passed.

Sleeping on the forest floor, tucked into a tight ball under her cloak was the coldest, most miserable night of her young life. She couldn't imagine how much colder she might have been if this cut of evergreen was keeping her warmer than the alternative. Amaris's mind thought of the frozen meats that were stored in the boxes chipped from ice in the winter and rested in the snowbanks beyond Farleigh's doors. She was willing to bet that her thighs resembled the frost-bitten slabs of beef that had been thawed and cooked in their kitchens. Except, she had yet to defrost if someone wanted to eat her.

Between the dull throb of her healing wounds, the burn of her muscles, the maddening hurt of her tailbone, and the deeply bone-chilling temperatures, Amaris was quite certain she was in the most pathetic, wretched state she'd ever been.

She didn't hear owls this time. Every so often, the moonlight revealed something as glossy shapes reflected against its silver beams. She would have sworn the yellow orbs of eyes stared right back at her.

She was afraid. She was cold. She was in pain.

None of it mattered. She welcomed the pain like a new friend. She invited the chill to invade her muscles, her blood, her bones. Amaris didn't doubt her decision. She would rather freeze to death or be eaten by whatever unholy monster looked at her between the gaps in trees than have left with the jewel-toned Madame in her glossy, black carriage. Not a single stab of pain, twinge of fear or dread of the future as she lay on the forest floor made her wish she were in Millicent's possession.

Somehow, she slept.

It hadn't been a long sleep, nor was it a restful one. However cold she'd been in the late hours of night was nothing compared to frigid, immobility of early morning. Her fingers were stiff. Her ears burned with the red of early frostbite before she began chafing her cloak against them to get the blood flowing. An hour or two of slumber was enough for them to stir at the first signs of gray and begin moving again before the sun came up. Her eyes had opened with a feeling of surprise that they'd managed to close in the first place.

She hadn't frozen to death. She hadn't bled out. She wasn't in Farleigh. She wasn't with Millicent. She was alive. From one morning to the next, everything in her life had been made new.

Odrin wasn't chatty as they mounted the horse, and she didn't mind. She didn't feel like talking, either. The only sound was the mount's hooves on the brittle, fallen leaves.

The gradient was beautiful as the sky turned from grays and blues to lavenders, peaches and eventually a vibrant orange. Amaris was still freezing, she no longer feared touching the strange assassin. He'd given her the saddle again as he sat in the back, which offered her some reprieve of his body heat. The trees thinned, giving way to great, rolling hills. Deep green, ruddy orange, and thick brown foliage that may have been mosses and lichens clung to huge stones spotting the hills. Now that the forest was no longer blocking the horizon, she was able to see the deeply violet mountains in the distance.

"Are we headed north?" She asked quietly.

"That we are. Well, northeast."

"To the Dark Kingdom?"

He laughed, "Who educated you girl, folklorists? Only superstitious villagers call it such things. Call the northern kingdom by its right and proper name."

She felt a surge of bile rise in the back of her throat and tried the question again. "Are you taking me to Raascot?"

He seemed satisfied with her question this time around, but shook his head. "No, girl, we're bound for the border, just past the village of Stone."

She perked, however dully, at the familiar name. She fixated on the

116

violet mountains on the horizon as she summoned a memory. "One of the matrons was from Stone. She was nice, if a bit naïve about the world. She said guardians lived in the cliff protecting their village."

He smiled at that, which was rare for the man. He'd had the lines and crinkles that vouched for a life of easy smiles, but his time with Amaris had remained guarded. Warmth now colored his voice as he answered her. "That is a bit naïve, I suppose. I don't think anyone outside of Stone would call us guardians."

He was one of them.

She sat on the horse with one of the very assassins Mable had referenced so fondly. She felt her body shrank away from the man, clutching them into the sleeves of her cloak. Amaris didn't mean to show cowardice, but she felt herself speak with a hollow, empty response.

"You're one of the assassins, aren't you?" It wasn't a question.

"We've generally preferred to be called reevers."

With that, Amaris realized who she was with, and that if Mable's fairytales were to be believed, they were headed into the mountain itself.

There was a small pond behind Farleigh that would freeze in the winters. If you stepped on it too early, it would fracture into ten thousand clear slices. Though the water might appear clear and flowing beneath, the truth of its brokenness was plain on the surface. Nox thought of that pond as her hand went to her heart, clutching her palm against her chest as if to hold it together from crumbling.

She had shattered. She held herself together with the only fragments she could grab with weak, fragile fingers.

Nox stared out of the window of the glossy black carriage as it bounced dully down the road, pulled by its two chestnut horses. Her fingers hadn't left the pain in her chest in hours as she clutched her organ together through the barrier of her rib cage. Millicent attempted to talk to her many times after getting the girl into the carriage, but had long since given up, muttering something about how Nox wouldn't be very good at her job if she didn't know how to make conversation.

They were only a few hours into their journey, but everything out the window looked the same. Every naked, autumnal tree was the same tree. Every gray, broken rock was the same. The wind shuffled the branches around slightly overhead, blowing the same dead, brown leaves around the same stretch of bumpy road. The sounds of the hooves were the same, the too-sweet vanilla smell of the woman's perfume was choking her in cloud after cloud of sameness, her breathing was the same, but her heart... it had never been truly broken before.

Wait for me, Amaris had said.

And so Nox had. She'd gripped the pillowcase of dried foods and the spare cloak close to her body. She'd tensed, ready to run out the back door beyond the kitchen in the late autumn morning as the minutes grew achingly long. She'd waited until she heard a shriek coming from the front of the manor. She'd wanted to run, to see what was happening, but her feet were frozen to the ground. She didn't want to face the world without Amaris.

Wait for me.

She'd waited.

She could have fled without Amaris beside her, but her heart would not allow it. She wouldn't escape into the trees unless ivory fingers were interlaced against the bronze of her own. She couldn't go. Not willingly.

She'd known something had gone horribly wrong. It had torn through her as if she'd been made of little more than paper. Her body was in a carriage plodding toward the southwestern coast, but her mind had stayed behind Farleigh, listening to the screams that permeated her memories. Her heart was somewhere far stranger as it continued to travel further and further from her. Nox had heard muffled cries, a protest, the whinnying of a horse, and then the angry screams of women from somewhere beyond the courtyard. She had felt them then—the hot tears that erupted from her carving salted lines down her cheeks. She hadn't known she was going to cry until it was already happening. Her face had contorted, her chest tightened, and she felt like she couldn't breathe.

Nox didn't understand how she knew it to be true, but Amaris was gone.

She'd felt the absence as if it were a dark, shadowy presence. The separation was a physical void, its presence a pressing, angry companion. It poured into her, filling her the moment Amaris had left as if she'd been little more than an empty glass before its black waters consumed her. She didn't need to see the evidence to know its truth. She was alone.

Nox had willed her knees to bend, willed her feet to carry her somewhere. She begged her feet to take her into the woods, to bring away from the mill. She was a three-minute run from the trees that lined the orphanage. She could be between the browns and grays of their trunks and hidden within the underbrush in moments. She had the supplies she needed. She had the food, the clothes, and the provisions to run. She could do it. She could leave.

She pleaded with herself, begged herself, commanded her body to do *anything*. It could carry her back into her house, return her to her bed, sprint for the forest, it could do anything other than stand like a statue. It could transport her into the kitchen for seventeen loaves of fresh bread. It could drown her in the cold waters of an early-winter river where the waves would wash her away, carry her on their icy rapids until she drifted into nothingness, her lovely corpse making it to the coast she had dreamed of one day seeing. How poetic would it be, to drift into the sea. Instead, she would bring the sea to her, as all the salt in her body poured out from its bottomless well in her eyes.

Hands were on her. Nox hadn't even heard a door open. She hadn't been aware of feet or noticed a second body. She was jolted from where she'd transformed into a living sculpture, frozen just outside of the kitchen door to Farleigh.

"Nox!" hands were at her shoulders, shaking her.

Her eyes snapped to see that it was Flora who had found her. The matron was looking her over for wounds, trying to find the source of her tears. She found nothing.

Flora's face transformed from concern to anger in an instant. She grabbed Nox, dragging her into the manor. One hand flattened on her back, the other was wrapped firmly on her wrist as she restrained the girl against the ability to bolt.

Nox had balked, heels dug into the ground, but eventually her body obeyed, rattled from its frozen state. Flora grabbed the pillowcase of food and goods from her arms, lofting them in her own hand as evidence of the pending crime. It seemed quite clear that the girl had been ready to escape. Between her changes of clothes and bag of food, there was no hiding her intention. She'd been caught in a botched attempt at flight, making it no further than the back door to the orphanage.

The moments following Flora's discovery passed in a blur.

After wiping up her tears, Flora led the dark-haired husk of a girl, cheeks and nose red from tears, down the hall and out the main door. The sounds of breakfast were just starting up in the dining room from the other orphans and attending matrons. The smell of eggs wafted from the kitchen. She knew with some certainty she would not be joining her peers for breakfast.

They'd floated through the orphanage, Nox vaguely aware of her body's movements as the nurse had dragged her forward. She was being taken to Agnes. She was in trouble. She knew it to be true, but couldn't come into her body long enough to react. She belonged to the dark, fractured nothingness of the space between stars. She was empty. The void had called to her before, and she'd answered. The dark was her friend. The shadows were a comforting companion. She welcomed them as they took her. Things beyond her were surely happening. People were speaking. Life occurred around her, but she retreated further and further into the small space within herself.

Agnes registered Nox's disheveled state, and immediately began to gesture for them to turn and leave.

Flora started, "I caught her—"

The Gray Matron was not alone. Nox had been dragged into the courtyard to face not just the matrons for her punishment, but the Madame.

Millicent cut Flora off, waving a hand. The Madame's temper seemed to stave slightly as the Nox fully entered her line of sight. She nodded with cool examination.

Agnes shook her head with a strange intensity. Nox wasn't quite present enough to comprehend Agnes's expression, though she knew it wasn't right. It didn't fit. There was a panic behind her eyes as if she were begging Flora to return her to the house, as if Agnes denied the possibility of their presence in the courtyard. Her wrinkles disappeared as her face tightened in an unknowable emotion.

Nox said nothing. She was nothing.

"What have we here?"

"Oh, Madame Millicent, no, this girl—" Agnes's voice began in dismay.

Millicent used her hand like a sword, slicing the sentence short with a single, quick gesture. "I won't be robbed of my down payment, Matron. But this substitute, albeit a disappointing consolation prize, will do."

Agnes made a strangled sound. She brought her hands to her mouth. She was fighting a peculiar, internal battle as the Madame made her determining proclamation.

"Millicent, she–"

"She is acceptable. Be grateful I don't pursue further action against your negligence and robbery."

Nox felt as though she watched the exchange from beyond herself. She registered that Agnes was acting quite unlike herself. The woman should have been glad for a sale, rather than being asked for a reimbursement. It was interesting, but that was all. It was not stirring. It was not moving. It was vaguely curious.

The Gray Matron wanted to protest, but it was clear she had no right to do so. A debt remained to be settled. Nox looked uselessly from the Gray Matron to the Madame, then to the black carriage. She hadn't needed to inquire as to what was happening. She'd understood it the moment the dark void of a companion had filled her heart. Amaris was gone, and Millicent required someone to go in her stead.

Nox had promised Amaris that she would sooner die than let Millicent take her, and the All Mother was prepared to test that oath. The goddess offered Nox and her solemn vow on a silver platter.

Nox reached for an emotion, but felt nothing. Invisible fingers grabbed for a hook within her body, trying to pull herself back in, but she was too numb for emotions to touch her. She listened rather absently as the Matron and Madame exchanged whatever parting words remained between them. She was aware of Agnes's fretful gaze, but she did not bother to make parting eye contact. The door to the carriage was held open and Nox was ushered in as if climbing into a black coffin in her own funeral procession. She remembered entering, but little else. She couldn't recall what had been said between the women. None of it mattered. She saw and heard and felt and smelled only same after same after same.

The Madame sighed loudly enough that Nox felt something within her stir, eyes drifting to a glazed attention. How long had she been on the road? She would need to face her reality: she was in the carriage bound for Priory.

Millicent allowed her to despondently refuse food at first, but by their second meal on the road, the woman forced her to eat. When Nox finally drank the water offered to her, she noticed her tongue had become a texture not dissimilar to sand. She hadn't realized how dehydrated she'd become. Awareness of her thirst brought her more sharply into herself, though the darkness stood nearby, ready for her retreat. Nox clutched the cup with two hands. She gulped the water down, and soon after heard a ringing in her ears. The ringing grew louder and louder into a deafening, constant sound. The Madame's smile seemed to drift further and further away until Nox was asleep.

When she opened her eyes, the sameness had… ceased.

She blinked her eyes rapidly, straightening her stiff body as she pressed into the window.

Things were greener, somehow. The autumn had not consumed the land so fully here. How long had she been asleep?

"There she is," Millicent cooed.

Nox looked out the window and stared in open-mouthed awe at the city looming before them. The trees were unfamiliar. She saw tall, bare drunks, with leaves existing only in a collection at the very top. She brought her face closer to the window of the carriage to peer at the buildings and colors beyond the glass. They appeared to be less than a mile away from polished white buildings, tall cathedrals and bustling life. She could smell the city. The people, the animals, and something like salt, heat and fish soaked the air.

They were near the sea.

Nox went from scarcely stirring to instant alertness. The young woman gaped at the Madame, shaking her head skeptically. "Priory is two week's travel by horse."

Millicent curved her black-painted lips into a smile. "She speaks."

Nox stiffened, fully aware of her body, the carriage, the horse, the Madame. The darkness vanished, her dissociative companion spooked as she was jarred to a state of full presence. Nox felt a new confusion prick through her. "We haven't been traveling for two weeks."

"Well observed, girl." Millicent seemed bored with the conversation, disappointed that her lip-locked travel companion had loosed her words over something so mundane. Instead, she fancied herself to look out her window at her home town, excited to have returned.

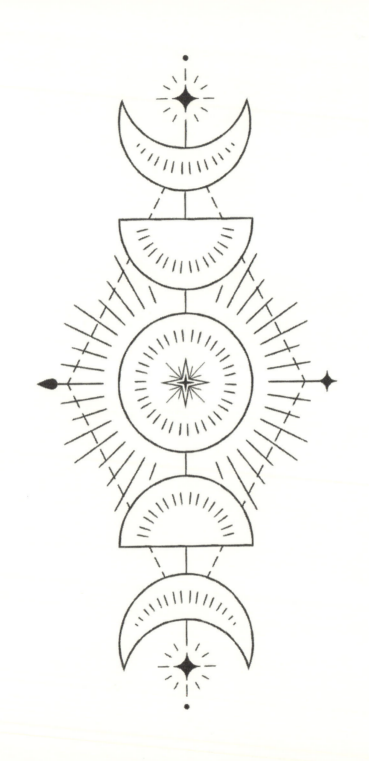

-PART TWO-

Ownership

7

They stopped in the town of Stone, so named for both the suffocating presence of the mountain that loomed over it, and the litter of discarded granite boulders its bluffs had released into the village below. Stone clung to the perimeter of a sheer, vertical cliff. This limited the entrances and exits to the primary road that emerged from the forest. It took Amaris roughly four minutes of shrinking against the long-cast shadows of the mountain to decide that she hated being in Stone and hoped never to return.

"How can people live here?" She cringed as she eyed the town.

"What's wrong with it?" Odrin asked, confused by her tone.

"The mountain! They're stuck against the mountain! How do they not feel like they're about to be crushed! I've never been anywhere that's made me feel so… claustrophobic."

He chuckled a little too heartily for the occasion.

"What?"

"Are you sure you want to become a reever?"

"Does becoming a reever mean being crushed by stones?"

His throaty laugh came again. "If you have some trouble with mountains, you may want to reconsider your choices." These were the first times she'd heard him laugh. She wondered if it was the first time she'd ever heard any man laugh. There had been the giggles of boys and smiles of orphans, but the hearty, honest sound of Odrin's joy at whatever it was he found so amusing about her statement came from somewhere deeper in his belly than any she'd encountered before.

Odrin dismounted the horse and helped Amaris down. He pursed his lips to hide his expression at how stiff her muscles were and how rigidly she moved away from the horse.

"Keep yourself busy for a bit. Don't go far," he instructed.

She didn't intend to wander away from her only means of escape from this wretched town. The sooner they could leave Stone and its ominous cliff, the better.

Odrin had stopped at what seemed to be a rather ordinary shopkeeper's stall and made idle chatter while refilling his waterskins, talking to the vendor as if he was an old friend. Odrin and his blades, bows and armor weren't met with suspicion. The scarred, grizzly man drew no particular stares from the citizens. She wondered how often Odrin and his league of assassins made the trek to visit this village to have imprinted such a sense of ease in his presence. They hadn't been received nearly so openly at their last village, and his appearance at Farleigh had caused outright bedlam.

She needed to find a way to keep herself busy so as not to bother Odrin.

Amaris looked for signs of familiarity in the faces of its citizens as the people milled about the town square that seemed to make up their market. She was curious if she would recognize Mable's family if she happened upon them in their hometown. Just yesterday morning she'd looked into the gentle eyes of the matron who'd handed her a cup of tea in the warmth of her bed. Now, she peered into the features of the woman selling goats, the man with crates overflowing with ears of corn, or in the girl hanging scarves in the fabric stall, searching their qualities for the same slope of the nose, dimples, or qualities that had been one of the few rays of kindness in Farleigh.

Odrin had told her not to wander, but she supposed a little nearby exploring wouldn't hurt.

There was a honeyed smell of something brewing that drifted out from Stone's inn that Amaris felt required closer investigation. Her nose followed the sugar-sweet scent to the window. The inn in this small town was perhaps three times the size of the inn she had seen in the tiny village only one day prior. Merry sounds of a fiddle drifted through its open windows, an unfamiliar jig on its weathered strings. Aged, hearty voices were talking and laughing within its walls. Honest, plump faces, loud, belly laughs, thumping boots of uneven dancers too drunk to care about the tune or its steps colored the view beyond the glass. They seemed so happy. Their lives looked so easy.

Amaris idled by the window, but didn't enter. She couldn't feel the joy that the tavern's music intended to elicit. It had nothing to do with the traumatic changes she'd undergone in the past night and day. Those feelings were something she'd shoved into a small, wooden box deep within her. It was an airless, impenetrable thing that she refused to touch. She couldn't function if she allowed herself to take them out, playing with them like toys from a treasure chest. Instead, her emotions needed to remain under lock and key so that she could do what needed to be done.

No, her wariness had nothing to do with yesterday's tragedies. This particular brand of joylessness was entirely the fault of the mountain and its ever-present shadow.

How did the people of Stone not wallow in their the same claustrophobia Amaris presently felt with something large enough to smite their existence looming overhead? If the peak decided one day that it had become too tired to uphold its cliff, surely one tremble would be all it would take for the goat herder, the corn farmer, the seamstress, the fiddler and all of the town's laughing residents to be buried under its rubble.

The pale girl busied herself studying the features of the village while Odrin finished conversing with the shopkeeper, a man who'd happily prattled on about this and that with his acquaintance. She gave them their privacy, her feet carrying her around the nearby storefronts.

"Hey!" A child's voice floated above the sound of the fiddle.

A leather-stretched ball made from the skin of a deer hide rolled from the pressed muddy space between two homes and into the square, stopping just a few arms lengths from Amaris. She bent to pick it up as two children, no older than seven, ran out from the alley after their toy. A third had stopped at the entrance to the alley, anxious to restart their game. He paused when he saw Amaris holding it. The boy looked at her curiously, but he did not appear afraid. He tilted his head, undoubtedly waiting for her to toss it back.

"Well," he asked, somewhat impatiently, "are you going to throw it back or what?"

"Sorry," she blinked rapidly at the jarring normalcy of the exchange.

A taller child behind him was a matted-haired boy with dirty hands and mud-caked knees. His disheveled appearance seemed like one born out of a day's hard play rather than that of poverty, given his healthy round face and the way he smiled at the others. He outstretched his arms for the ball and Amaris tossed it gently into the air, satisfied when he caught it. He spun away, their interaction completed as if interacting with strangers was an everyday occurrence. They ran off in the direction they'd come, shouting some directions about their little sport. She marveled at what life must be like to grow up with friends, free to run, to roll in the wet earth, to see new faces, to live without fear of scrapes and scratches. She had nearly lost herself in a fantasy of what-ifs, forgetting to keep an eye on her companion.

She blinked in dismay when Odrin wasn't where she'd left him. It had been one single heartbeat of panic, convinced she'd been abandoned, before she spotted him a few feet away.

He had not left her. She was not alone.

Amaris jogged quickly after him to ensure he didn't change his mind and leave her altogether.

"Odrin!"

"I told you not to go far," he shrugged, not looking at her.

"I was right there!"

"I saw."

Odrin was leading his steed away from the shop stall to the stable at the side of the inn. A large stone tub rested near the edge of the stables, filled nearly to the brim with somewhat brackish-looking water. She'd never seen such a large object of solid stone before. She idly wondered if this had been one of the many uses for the boulders that had tumbled from the cliff and given the village its namesake. Rather than break the rocks down or roll the large boulders away, the citizens had chipped and chiseled them into functional fixtures throughout the town. While it had been innovative of the villagers to find so many ways to use the chips that tumbled to their soil, their presence disconcerted her. Amaris wondered how often the cliff sloughed off its unwanted boulders onto the town below and felt an eagerness to get going.

"Are we leaving after this?"

"You wouldn't be so eager to get going if you knew what awaited you."

If she didn't stop thinking about the mountain, she was going to drive herself mad. Instead, she turned her attention to Odrin and his mount. Amaris rested a hand on its dappled neck, stroking it gently beneath her fingertips while it drank its fill.

"What do you call your horse?" She asked, changing the subject.

His eyebrows raised as he made a face to indicate this wasn't something that had crossed his mind. He gave the horse two quick pats on its side while he examined it. "I don't rightly know. I took him as payment about four weeks back when a bishop couldn't settle his contribution."

"He owed you a debt? Are you a mercenary?"

Odrin laughed, "Hardly. We aren't swords for hire, girl. You'll learn soon enough."

"So, this is not your horse?"

A smile still crinkled the lines of his face as he continued petting the beast. "Well he is now, isn't he?"

She continued to stroke the docile gelding's neck. It didn't seem to notice her existence while it kept its nose close to the water, lips gently parted while it drank. "Shouldn't we give your creature a name? Aren't horses meant to be like family?"

Odrin entertained the idea. "What would you call it?"

She frowned, considering. She patted at the mount, surveying it from its sides. "He's not particularly noble, is he? He's a gentle boy. With his gray and white spotting, he looks a little bit like the moments before dawn, do you know which ones I'm talking about?" She briefly glanced up at Odrin's expression, somewhere between amusement and boredom as he allowed her to entertain herself with the process. "Maybe Cloud would suit him. Or Skyfall."

"Those are terrible names for a horse," Odrin dismissed, getting ready to leave. He began adjusting the saddle, letting the beast know they'd be moving soon. Water dripped from its nose as it raised its head from the trough.

She shook her head and continued stroking the creature. "You're right, they don't suit him. He's not majestic enough to be a Twilight. I feel like Whisper would displease him."

"Does he have feelings about the process?" Odrin asked somewhat dryly.

As if in answer, the horse flared its nostrils.

Amaris inclined her head at that, listening to the horse. "Are you a Ghost? A First Snow? What shall we call you and your gray dots, my friend?"

"I had a dog named Cobb growing up. He was a rambunctious little mongrel. After he died I named the stray cat near our house Cobb too. I think it's a good name for a beast."

"Are you serious?"

Odrin mounted the horse and swung the girl up with his scarred hand, giving his steed a small kick. He urged, "Come on, Cobb."

And so Amaris, Odrin, and Cobb had plodded straight for the face of the mountain.

Matron Mable had once called the reevers a league of guardians who lived in the mountains. With this in mind, she had anticipated the open maw of a cave. She'd braced herself against entering the dark and horrible mountain she'd hated so much in Stone, silently chanting that she was no coward—whether or not she believed the repetitious voice in her head was irrelevant.

They were only two hours from Stone before the last lights of the day faded to purple. She continued waiting for them to be swallowed by some cavern, but perhaps the sun would abandon them long before they were lost beneath the rock. The moon was already out, despite the day clinging to the final lavenders of sunset. The moon was nearly full, its silver light washing the space ahead of them before the sun had fully set.

Odrin, Amaris and Cobb rounded corner after corner, following the foot of the mountain. Cobb carried them forward at a leisurely pace, hugging the base of the cliff until a thin trail began to rise. It had been so narrow that it was imperceptible until they were upon it. The jagged pathway switched back and forth as it climbed. When the trail became particularly tight, Odrin pulled back on the reins and had the two of them dismount. He led the way, handing the reins to Amaris so that she could lead the horse as they carried onward. Odrin said that, while he trusted that most beasts would be sure-footed enough to find their purchase on the rocks, he didn't want to risk it after dusk.

Unlike the pressing shadows of the forest, they were totally exposed to both prying eyes and the elements on the cliff. As evening's final grays abandoned them, the moon was given its chance to truly shine, splendid in its brightly waxing state. Its metallic beams glinted off the rock. While it wasn't quite the clarity of broad daylight, she was astounded at how hard the moon was working to light the world around them. The cliff seemed to reflect the pearly light, illuminating everything around them with more intensity than any normal night. It gave the very air a shimmery, iridescent quality.

Her legs burned from the ride. Her feet throbbed from walking. Her arms were as limp as wet pasta noodles fresh from the pot. She opened her mouth to comment on her misery, but thought better of it.

Amaris had learned that Odrin wasn't much for talking, and felt satisfied whenever she did get the man to exchange a few words with her. She didn't mind the silence. She wasn't interested in dealing with her thoughts or reflecting on the recent events, but the quiet gave her an opportunity to release her tension, focusing on nothing but the way the stars burned, the sound of Cobb's steady breath, and the feeling of the pebbles that poked their way through her thin, leather shoes.

They walked in silence for most of the night, absorbing the star-soaked sky above them, and quite intentionally avoiding looking at anything that belonged to the dark, sheer plummets below them.

She opened her mouth and closed it repeatedly as the hours passed, fighting the urge to complain, or to comment on the pretty pearly quality of the light, or the fresh smell of pine and crisp mountain air. She thought to comment on how high up they were. Then, she wanted to ask how much longer their trip would be. She thought to inquire as to how often he made the trip. Instead, she only asked one question.

"If I fell off this trail, would I die? Or would I just be mangled and *wish* I had died?"

His silhouette pressed forward. "I was wondering when you were going to spit out your thoughts, back there. You've been making gaping noises like a trout out of the pond."

"Well?" She pressed, "What would happen?"

He'd chuckled softly without turning toward her. His shoulders had shrugged ever so slightly while he continued down the trail. "Are you planning on finding out?"

"No."

"Then, I suppose it doesn't matter." He didn't seem annoyed by her question, but he'd also made it clear he preferred the quiet.

Sharp rocks bit into her soft leather shoes. Amaris felt the passage of time rather acutely as blisters formed and popped within her shows, scraping her raw. She fought the need to limp, to mount Cobb, to sit down in the middle of the path and take off her shoes until the pain subsided. Stronger and louder than any of those needs was a single, potent desire: the girl made of moonlight didn't want to be treated like a special treasure, hidden away only for special occasions, she wanted acceptance.

She was on the trail to become an assassin, she told herself. She didn't have the luxury of whining about her shoes or the blood that filled them. That being said, whenever she was sure Odrin couldn't see her, she allowed herself the grimaces, winces, and secret flinches of pain.

Amaris learned something new about herself. She did not care for heights.

No one but the goddess should ever be so high. The birds scarcely dared to fly this far beyond the lines of trees. In the dark of the night, they were more daring than the bats and as lofted as clouds that scraped the mountain's granite peaks.

Whenever she did dare a glance over the sheer drop-off, it was to note that the trees and homes dotting the countryside below were smudges no bigger than her thumb. The mountain had curved in such ways that the residence of Stone would have had to have swung miles and miles wide and then dipped into a valley between mountains to see where they were headed, though the assassin, the girl and their horse looked like no more than pebbles themselves from their height, no doubt.

At some point, they'd have to run out of mountain. Surely, this path had to end. Her legs burned as they continued their never-ending upward climb. She'd lost track of time, but her flare for the dramatic tended to count the passage of time a little differently. It had been hours, she was certain. Then she felt as though it had been days. At some point, she knew in her soul that she had been climbing this cliff for her entire life. She had been born on this trail, and it was on this very trail that she'd grow old and die.

If she wasn't mistaken, the moon had moved low enough on the horizon to let her know it wouldn't be night much longer. Given the lateness of autumn, and despite her penchant for exaggeration, she was rather confident the sun had been down for at least twelve hours.

They walked and walked and walked and then, they didn't.

Odrin stopped in his tracks. He took the reins from her, urging her alongside him as there was now space on the trial for two.

"Is this it?" she whispered.

"Few more steps, unless you'd rather stay on the mountain."

Amaris felt her feet glue themselves briefly to the ground as the path dropped off on either side. The cliff had finally come to an end. They had reached a stone bridge connecting the gap between two, terribly steep mountains of other-worldly sharpness and height. The singular stone bridge united the adjoining cliffs over the dramatic plummet of the valley below with what seemed to be little more than wishes and prayers. She squinted her eyes to the dizzying depths of the valley where the moonlight caught a tiny silver thread. The ribbon was that of a river—presumably the very one that had cut its path between these mountains so many lifetimes ago.

"Is it safe?"

"The bridge? Probably not."

"But—"

"Like I said, you can also stay on the mountain."

She wasn't ready. Her fear of heights had been a gnawing throb. The potent stab of arrival was a new, sharp terror. Odrin began to move forward with Cobb, but she wasn't sure if she was ready to follow. It wasn't just the crossing of some bridge straight out of nightmares that daunted her, but the strange, obscure gloomy shape that awaited them once they crossed.

It would have been difficult to understand what she was seeing in the sheer light of day even under the high noon sun. By moonlight, it was damn near impossible. Just across the bridge, a few small lights seemed to have embedded themselves into the mountain itself, as if a few orange fragments of starlight had chipped from the heavens and landed on the side of a mountain.

Amaris strained her eyes and as they shifted into focus. The orange flickers of light were illuminating rectangles—candlelight in windows, she realized. Something rounded and smooth like columns or pillars loomed up ahead. A deeper, darker gloom seemed to cast an arch above the triangular roof of the structure, space between its ceilings and the rock above. She was staring at a fortress. This was no fortress built on a mountain, but *into* it. Carved within the very cliff itself was an entire castle.

"It's in the mountain," she breathed.

She could see his appreciative nod, "I told you, if you were bothered by Stone, this might not be the place for you."

When her muscles had ached, she'd wanted her travels to end. When her feet had rubbed themselves raw within her leather shoes, she'd silently pleaded with the goddess to allow her to stop walking. Now they'd arrived, and she would have traded anything for another twelve hours to prepare for what she might face. They crossed the final length of the bridge, leaving the dizzying valley below as they reached the last remaining steps of their journey. The bridge came to an end at a great door. Her heart was pounding in a way that made her quite aware that she'd never be ready. The door before her was made not of stone or wood, but of iron.

Odrin banged on it a few times, presumably waiting for someone to answer within. Turning back to her, he broke his long traveler's silence. "This is Uaimh Reev."

8

In theory, the next few days should have been tumultuous, nerve-wracking, and terrifying. In practice, they were exceptionally boring.

The fortress had been in an uproar about Amaris's arrival. As a result, she'd been sequestered to solitary quarters until they could decide what to do with her. She wasn't a prisoner, as she was free to wander back the mountain and return to the villages below should she please, but she'd also been strongly advised to stay put if she hoped to win any favor.

Women did not live or train at Uaimh Reev. Whether it was an issue of allowance, tradition, or coincidence was part of the three-day feud happening within the keep. The disputes, she was told, covered most of the subjects one might expect. Some arguments took on a medical or anatomical nature: women couldn't keep up in sparring, a woman's presence would slow them down the pack on runs, women had special health needs that the keep was not equipped to meet. Others bore a more misogynistic tone: women were too tender for the hardships of a reever's lifestyle, women required coddling and there was no place for pussy-footing in the ring, a woman couldn't be guaranteed safety in a castle filled with men. These were the rather unfortunate messages that were relayed, anyway, when Odrin had visited Amaris where she was confined in her rooms.

"I'm to stay here by myself?" Amaris didn't fully understand her anxiety as he showed her to her rooms the first night, but the idea of being left alone was gripping her with icy fingers.

"You're safe here. I'll come visit and let you know what's being said."

"I wouldn't be safe out there?" It was all she could do not to beg him to take her with him. Her fear of abandonment was a terrible, strangling thing.

Odrin frowned, "Let's just say that a few more conversations need to happen before you should be roaming about the keep."

"So they hate me," Her tone was matter-of-fact.

"They don't hate you. They might hate the idea of you, but they don't hate you."

"I'm sorry, is that better?"

After arriving at the keep, she had been shown almost immediately to a chamber with an adjoining bathing room, a shelf full of old books, a bed full of linens and furs, and more or less shut inside while the men of the keep debated what to do with her. The bathing room contained a large, deep tub. The rug, the duvet, and the curtains were not particularly fine, but they were all clean and quite comfortable. Her room had even been decorated with a tapestry of a rather unfortunate-looking crow, hung to watch over her as she slept like her personal guardian angel.

It had taken her a full day to absorb the crushing isolation of being in a room alone.

She had never had a bedchamber to herself before. Her life had been spent in the dormitories, relying on the comfortable circadian rhythms of dozens of small bodies with their chests rising and falling in sleep. Her chores were with peers at the orphanage. Her free time was spent with Nox. She wasn't sure that she'd ever spent more than ten minutes alone in her life. Now as she paced the granite stones of the room, examining its nooks, crannies and secrets, she wasn't sure whether or not she enjoyed the solitude. This room was nicer than her dorm, and its bed far more comfortable than her cot, a renewed desolation crushed her. The silence tempted her to open the box in which she'd tightly stored her unpleasant emotions. If she didn't find a way to distract herself, the lid would slip to the side and everything she'd delayed feeling would spill into her chest cavity.

There was a quick, light knock in the door, a pause to the count of five, and then the door eased open as it had three times each day. After enduring the suffocation of loneliness, she'd been so excited to have a new visitor in her room. Despite her enthusiasm at his arrival, the boy had quickly made it clear that they would not be speaking.

A slender boy several years her junior had stopped by morning, noon and night with her meals. She'd attempted time and time again to engage him in conversation, but he'd been unwilling to respond as he dropped off her food. The boy's eyes would graze hers, offering the barest of nods before exiting, and closing the door behind himself. Three times a day he'd enter, and thrice daily she'd try to ask the child his name, ask of the weather, ask about the food, ask his favorite color, but he'd been resolute in his polite silence. Every time the small boy came and vanished, she felt as if she had been abandoned a second, then a third, then a fourth time.

One thing she could do to entertain herself was eat.

Amaris always had an appetite, but she stretched her meals throughout the day, making each dish last for hours, just to give her something to do. The food was quite different from the porridges and stews commonly served at Farleigh, but so far everything she'd been served had been enjoyable. If she ate her split barley, corn cakes, meat pies, stewed apples, mushrooms, or whatever else he'd delivered too quickly, she'd have nothing else to entertain herself.

Amaris brought a small, coarse loaf of brown bread onto her bed and stretched on the fur, slowly picking at the loaf while she paged through one of the dustier books. This one was a particularly dry text of histories of the continent's battles, heavily focusing on names of the deceased and locations of the conflicts. A few illustrations of weapons decorated the pages from time to time as a special treat.

The books, like the meals, were something with which she'd forced herself to pace her consumption. If she devoured everything too quickly, she'd be alone with nothing to read. Her first book had been a much more interesting choice, though poorly written and sickly sweet. It was some four hundred page ballad about a king of the night and the princess of the sun and the romance that had divided the world in its misguided attempt at unity. Their love story had been a tragedy, ending in murder. The sister of the slain princess had been offered as a replacement in marriage before the continent had fallen into chaos. It was both sloppy prose and dreadfully unbelievable, but it was better than staring at the stones of an empty bedroom. Amaris vastly preferred the romantic nonsense to a list of the names of dead warriors and had already read their love tale three times.

Each night was spent in the bathtub in her en suite bathing room until her pale fingers shriveled into prunes, trying to see how far she could flick beads of water and making a competition with herself to see if any of the droplets would land on the ceiling. She had little to do, and too much time to do it. When she'd first arrived, she'd been road-weary, covered in blisters, and in desperate need of soap. Cleaning the first night had been essential, but every night that followed served as yet another stretched-out activity to pass minutes as they became hours, which turned into days.

She wrote, "I'm bored," six hundred and fifty-two times on a single piece of paper late into her second night. She was just beginning to write it for the six hundred and fifty-third time when a louder thud sounded at her door. The only two knocks were that of the small boy at mealtime, and the heavy fists of her lone ally. She perked as Odrin eased open the door.

"Anything?"

He nodded, dark brows lowered in seriousness, "They're going to meet with you."

Her heart skipped. "Tonight?"

He eyed her paper and how she'd perched against the desk, but decided not to ask her about her very important written masterpiece. "No, not yet. It's taken this long just to agree to give you an audience."

"When?"

He hadn't fully entered the room, which made it clear to her that he didn't intend to stay. He was merely passing information. "Sometime tomorrow," he said. "Get some sleep. Keep your chin up.

Odrin closed the door behind him.

She was left staring up at the desk, wishing she'd cursed him out for the crushing case of unnecessary anxiety. Amaris wished he hadn't said anything. It served her no good to know if there was nothing she could do about it.

She got almost no sleep that night. She preferred staring at the ceiling with crippling anxiety, envisioning her life as a dirty, penniless street urchin scavenging the alleys of Stone. Maybe the children who had kicked the leather ball would let her join their group of friends, though she supposed it would mean she'd have to learn how to play their sport, and she'd never been interested in kicking a ball. She kept a small fire going to keep her warm throughout the night, and the shadows that danced on the walls seemed to play out the pictures of her dark, hopeless future.

Amaris probably slept an hour or two, though if one had asked her, she would have sworn she hadn't gotten a wink. She was awake by the time the sky beyond turned to a shade of dull gray. Amaris tugged the fur from her bed and bundled it over her shoulders to stare out the window. The view was stunning, though its drop was too perilous a drop for her to look out beyond its panes for long before her stomach began to twist with the odd sensation of falling. She noticed that as she stared into the valley, the birds flew several hundred feet below. How high must they be in their fortress that even the hawks and crows wouldn't alight the windowsills of this keep.

She had thought she'd been bored the first two days, but the third day passed with excruciating slowness. Every minute took an hour to transpire. The sun seemed to be taunting her with how lethargically it crossed the sky. If there had been a clock in her room, she was positive it would have been moving in slow motion. Breakfast came and went as she studied another boring text about herbs with medicinal properties. If they didn't make a decision soon, she'd stay in these rooms forever and become the single most educated person on the names of dead warriors and the recitation of naturally growing healing plants.

Amaris had scrunched her face in distaste as she looked through yet another book. This tome was a gruesome, anatomical text illustrating the inherent differences in a fae body and that of a human, from their enhanced hearing and vision and regenerative cells to the predatory, deadly lure of their beauty. It had been morbidly fascinating, but the ghastly trail of scholarship had led the text's creator to recount every detail, whether for good or for evil. She called the morality of its author into serious question based on the nature of several of his entries.

Odrin's authoritative knock came at her door and her heart stopped. This was the sound she'd been waiting on bated breath to hear. Now that it had come, she wasn't sure if she was ready. It was a similar feeling to walking for riding for two days and then climbing a mountain for twelve hours only to find herself unprepared as she stood outside the door.

Maybe no one ever truly felt ready when important moments arrived.

Odrin eased the door open and slid inside. The man gave an apologetic smile as he closed the door behind him.

"I can't imagine this is easy for you," he offered by way of greeting.

Amaris shrugged, "I wouldn't say life has been easy, as a whole."

Her statement was neither entirely true, nor entirely false. She imagined the other children at Farleigh would shake with fury to hear her call her cushioned life anything but easy. She held a small, smug smile in her heart at the matron's years of effort protecting her delicate features, all shattered like a glass dropped to the bottom of the valley below with the single downward slash of a dagger. She'd like to see what had become of her face in a mirror..

"Are they going to kick me out?" Amaris asked. She didn't know how it was possible, but her voice held no emotion with the question. Her future would not change whether she worried, pleaded, or fretted. What would be, would be.

Odrin neither reassured nor confirmed her fear. He did his best to keep his message free of feeling, even if there were underlying notes of sympathy in his words. "They want to hear from you directly, but we knew as much. You'll need to plead your case. You'll need to convince them that you deserve to be here."

"Is it the leader? Or a council? Or... what is your government here?"

He smiled at that, though it was not a particularly warm expression. "Perhaps I should have prepared you more for what you should expect—no, I definitely should have prepared you. I am sorry for that. This is no kingdom, girl. The reevers are as much of an orphanage as your shoddy home. We don't have a true hierarchy here, though Samael is as close to a leader as we have, as he's been here the longest. We tend to give him final say." He muttered the next part to himself, "Longest may be an understatement. He disseminates dispatches and... well, I suppose it doesn't matter just yet." Odrin straightened before opening the door and making a sweeping gesture. "I'm to take you to meet with them. Just... be yourself. You convinced me, didn't you?"

He was trying to be encouraging. Amaris hadn't been sure that she could experience new levels of anxiety after he'd set her on edge with the previous night's update, but she had been wrong. Her blood pressure spiked. "Right now?"

She'd had a night and a day to prepare herself, and yet.

Maybe she should have been readying a speech or researching their laws—though with what resources, she hadn't the slightest idea.

"Should I tie up my hair?" She felt stupid for asking the moment the question parted her lips. It was a rather feminine worry for such a masculine fortress. She kicked herself, hoping he wouldn't repeat it to the others.

Instead, he responded, "Many of the men have uncut hair. They wear it tied back or unbound. Tying it is an issue of function, which you'll need to do if you spar. For now, your hair is of little concern. Though, it is white. That may be a point of curiosity, but there isn't much you can do about that."

She tried to smile, as she knew he was attempting to be comforting. He wasn't very good at it.

Amaris felt the heavy, stickiness of nerves gluing her to her chair. She checked her fingers and toes for paralysis by forcing her hands to continue to flip through the text of various autopsies. Odrin watched her, waiting for her to stand and follow him. She landed on an image of something that might have been a man. It was a bipedal creature with arms, a torso, fingers and toes, but where humans had nails, the creature had talons. Where she had shoulder blades, it had membranous, bat-like wings. Its lips were pulled back to reveal its elongated canines, and irises double the size of a human's. A faint memory of a boy with too-large irises flitted somewhere between her ears, and then the memory was gone.

She looked up from the book, heart in her throat. "I guess whatever's waiting for me in the dining room can't be too much worse than what's waiting for us in the woods."

"We can hope."

She left the page open as she stood, the leather-bound book displaying the unmistakable image of a demon.

In nearly fifteen years of life, Amaris had seen only three dining rooms. The first, of course, was that of Farleigh. It had been a well-lit room with a long wooden table and high, arching windows to let in the sunlight. The table had been simple, lined with wooden benches and no décor to its name, save for a modest table runner that was easy to clean in the laundry. The youngest and eldest children had taken their meals in separate shifts to ensure space for everyone at the table, along with the matrons supervising their assigned age groups of the orphans. For most of her life, this had been Amaris's only exposure to food for breakfast, lunch, or dinner.

The second dining room had been her brief visit inside of the tavern of a nameless village the day before Stone, where the middle-aged woman had bandaged her wounds and found a scarf for her hair—a scarf she had worn until she had made it to her chamber at the keep. The tavern had a low ceiling, several wooden beams to support its structure, and something like eight to ten rectangular tables on one side of the bar. The tavern's dining room had been lined with preserved foods, spices and glass bottles on the other.

The third dining room was the one she stood in now.

She took one slow step into the room, then another, Odrin at her side.

Roughly one dozen men of various sizes and ages sat at an oblong table carved from the mountain itself, though she couldn't bring herself to truly absorb any of their features. Looking directly at them would either intimidate or distract her, and she could risk neither. Amaris was unable to recognize which one of them had opened the iron door on her first night, though she scanned for a spark of familiarity in their faces before averting her gaze. She opted to keep her eyes from their faces. She knew that obvious signs of hostility might further thwart her efforts for their acceptance, and the cards appeared to have already been stacked against her. She wouldn't require any additional obstacles in garnering their acceptance as she slowly walked into the space.

Odrin placed a fatherly hand on her back as he urged Amaris forward to the end of the table closest to the door. He left her to take a seat at one end of the table amidst the others.

Her attention went to the table itself. Its legs did not end, but rather melted into the stone below it. It appeared as though this piece of granite had never moved from its place in the mountain's heart, but simply been reshaped for a flat, polished surface. The table had then curved inward so that the legs of the men who sat at this table would find space beneath its lip before it rejoined the immovable rock below. She was unfamiliar with dining rooms, but even as someone with little exposure to the world, she knew she was looking at something peculiar.

Though she hadn't been permitted to wander the keep, she'd had a good sense as Odrin had led her down the corridors that she was going deeper into the mountain. As an innermost room in the fortress, there were no windows in this dining room. A fireplace three times the size of the one in her room and rows of torches on either side running the length of the room chased away any shadows, eliminating the need for the white light of day and replacing it with the reds, oranges and yellows of fire. The ceiling was high and vaulted, sparkling slate curving upward as if they were in a large, stone bell. She couldn't tell if she found this dining room beautiful or terrible. Perhaps her feelings toward the room would be contingent on the result of this meeting.

Her eyes flitted to Odrin as he took his place at the table close to the opposite end. Amaris wasn't sure if she liked him in her line of vision, or if she'd preferred that he stand beside her, holding her hand. Of course, that hadn't been a real option, and she knew it wouldn't win her any favors for bravery if she needed to be coddled.

The room was full, yet she felt completely alone.

Several empty spaces ran on either side of her, isolating her at the far side of the stone table that was meant to sit thirty or forty, rather than the dozen or so before her. She wished she could have remained standing for the sake of her own comfort, but she knew enough of politics and courtliness to know it would win her no favors toward acceptance if she remained poised to run. Amaris needed to prove herself strong enough to be in their presence. Surely, the first test would be their initial impressions of having a young woman at their dinner table.

She wasn't sure if they would speak first, or if she was meant to, but the silence must have been as uncomfortable for the men as it was for.

In the spirit of first impressions, she could only imagine what a sight she was to take in. Not only was a young female in their keep, but a silver-haired, purple-eyed anomaly with the scabbing slash marring her otherwise stark-white face. Her clean tunic covered most of what she'd done to her chest, but the top of the wound she'd inflicted on her collarbone undoubtedly protruded above the neckline of her shirt. She was no ordinary child of the fair kingdom.

On the far end of the table directly across from her, sat a too-beautiful man in his late twenties. He was a dark-haired man with the handsome, tactful face of a diplomat. She was surprised to see someone so young in the most prominent seat. Amaris was unfamiliar with men, but irrespective of her lack of exposure, this person did not seem like any natural-born male. Something was strange, striking, and intimidating about his face all at once. Though she'd opted to look at none of them directly, she avoided his face in particular.

The seconds continued to stretch. No time had passed, while still allowing her the ability to take in her surroundings. Her eyes grazed the room to try to guess which one was Samael. A disheveled man with an unkempt beard in thick fighting leathers looked to be pushing sixty years of age. He had the thick chest and broad shoulders of someone who looked like he could command a room. Odrin had said that Samael had been here the longest. If she were a betting woman, she'd guess him to be the oldest.

The sensation of slowed time that often came with shock could not last forever. The acceptable moment for pause had come and gone, and it was time to speak.

The present snapped into reality. The deeply human rainbow of golds, reds, browns and blacks tilted toward her as hair and eyes shifted expectantly in her direction. The men stared at her, presumably waiting for her to state her piece. She'd never been alone in a room with men, but she couldn't allow herself to think about that. The enormous fire popped and crackled, providing enough white noise to prevent the room from being as stifling quiet as it might have otherwise. She was twinged with the recurrent sensation of unbelonging and willed the fire to warm her from the chilly fear that had settled in her stomach.

She urged herself to begin. She begged herself to speak.

Goddess damn it all, she needed herself to say something, *anything*!

The matrons had wanted to raise a well-spoken girl—one who could fit in if she had been purchased to live in the courts. They'd prepared her for a variety of positions, staking their time and combined intellects for their eventual return on investment upon her sale. The silver girl had no idea if the assassin's coin purse had held anything close to the crowns they'd spent those years cultivating, nor did she care. Regardless, she was thankful for training in oration as she pleaded with those skills now, rallying her courage to introduce herself. She couldn't be afraid. She couldn't be self-conscious. She couldn't think of consequences, or danger, or anything but the words she had to spit out.

"I am Amaris, of Farleigh, though I do not call it my home."

Her treacherous heart thundered, but her voice did not shake.

The varied collection of men watched her attentively. The twenty-something man at the end of the table had one arm on the side of his chair, resting his chin on his hand. His face was impressively blank, though he paid close attention to every word.

Amaris's face had flushed when she'd absorbed how truly beautiful the stranger was. His skin was a golden brown as her friend's had been and hair, tied behind him, was a rich, glossy black. Both of these features reminded her too much of Nox. She shook the beautiful girl from her memories, afraid that if she allowed herself to think of her friend for too long, she'd lose her resolve. She wasn't sure that she found this man attractive—rather, he was beautiful in a way that was both disconcerting and distracting. Her eyes glided from the man to the table before them like droplets of water sliding off of a glass surface. In the moments before she'd dropped her gaze, she'd taken note of the slender points of his ears.

He was fae.

Time had felt as though it had slowed once more while she'd taken in the features of the others. She had grazed the faces, postures and ages of the dozen or so assassins before her. While many were in the second half of their life, there appeared to be more than a few men in their teens and twenties at the table. Her eyes snagged once more on the arch of fae ears as she looked away from a young, coppery man who may very well have been her age. There was more than one fae at the table.

She shouldn't have looked at him. It had been a distraction, and she found herself stammering to pull her thoughts together.

Somehow, starting to speak and then stopping again was so much worse than if she hadn't said anything at all. She was butchering her first impression, and she knew it. Amaris didn't have the luxury of sounding like a child. She swallowed and willed authority into her voice as she spoke. She didn't truly know what she was saying, but spoke from her heart, scarcely examining the words that left her lips. She hoped she sounded intelligent.

"I have no people," she restated, voice wavering slightly. Insecurity would get her nowhere. If she didn't feel particularly bold, she'd need to fake it to survive. Her words swelled to a false confidence as she spoke, faking a sense of resolve, "but if you'll have me, you will be my people. You're worried I'm a woman? I have no interest in being a damsel. I want to train, to learn, and to fight alongside you. I know what you must see when you look at me. I don't blame you for your skepticism. Yes, today I am soft, but I wouldn't ask for softness. Treat me as you would any boy of my age who arrived at your doorstep. Put me through the same trials. If I fail, I will fail as an assassin, not as a woman."

"A reever," the fae at the end of the table corrected.

"I—" she stammered at the amendment, not sure if she should apologize to the man. "If I fail, I fail as a reever."

Or, was he a man? Is that what she should call him? His voice was almost as lovely as his face, though there was no question as to its strength. She'd caught on the correction, feeling her courage unravel. She'd been so close to a rallying speech and tripped at the finish line.

The eldest man grunted his disapproval, not looking at her as he spoke. "There's a reason we don't have women here. I won't be making lighter armor, making smaller weapons, creating dainty—"

"Grem," a golden young man in his early twenties cut off the elder. So, the eldest man was not Samael. The bearded one called Grem stopped and glared, his bovine qualities exacerbated when set against the muscular young man who opposed him. The one with the blond mop of hair continued speaking, "Her size is no different from the boys in their teens. She wouldn't require new armor, clothing or weapons. By the time she'd be ready for a real sword, she'd be strong enough to hold one."

"This is no place for your grandstanding, Malik—"

Was the golden young man arguing on her behalf, or just against the bearded elder?

"Women were allowed to train and fight for hundreds of years before your borders," the fae at the end said with matter-of-fact delivery. "Human and fae fought and lived side by side, male, female, and anyone in between. Uaimh Reev has acted as the sword arm of the All Mother for centuries. This reev was a keep for the honorable who believed in the protection of all peoples against magical imbalance long before it became today's band of society's discards." He looked to the bearded man, eyes tightening slightly with disapproval as he chastised the grumble the man was emitting. "You know very well I served under a general who slew any enemy she met in battle for a century three lifetimes before you were born."

Amaris felt herself blink slowly at the words the lovely man had spoken. She attempted to process the information as it was offered to her. This bronze-skinned man seated at the opposite end of the table was hundreds of years old. He didn't just have the delicate ears and beauty of some distant fae lineage, she was looking into the face of a full-blooded fae.

"That was then," Grem pushed back. "Women-folk were different in your time, Samael. She's not a warrior at our doorstep. She's a stray cat who followed Odrin and his soft heart home. Escort her back into Stone and be done with it."

Odrin spoke, tone both defensive and resolute as he said, "She's not a warrior by training, but she has the heart of one. She has no fear of the fight. See for yourself. Look at her face."

They did once more, considering her wounds more carefully. Odrin hadn't spoken the truth, whether or not he realized he was telling a lie. He hadn't witnessed what had occurred in the dining room at the mill. Amaris had accomplished what she had done at Farleigh not out of bravery, but out of fear. She had been more terrified of a life with Millicent than of anything that could be found in an assassin's keep. The stolen knife—Odrin's knife—had been the quickest way to provide an exit. She would not be the pure, unmarked treasure, set aside like a delicate teacup for the finest of guests. She would take her life into her own hands. If she had gone with the Madame, she would have been bound and clipped, her spirit broken. With the kingdoms of men, she at least had a chance to become something more. She would sell her body to the fight of her own volition rather than to the highest bidder against her will.

"Shall we vote?" Grem pushed the men.

"No," she objected, surprised at herself for speaking. Her voice was a mixture of confusion and impatience at their unwillingness to hear her story. She didn't have any follow-up plan, except that this hadn't been fair. They shouldn't be able to vote yet. They didn't understand. They didn't know what she'd been through. They didn't understand how far she was willing to go.

The reevers seemed jarred by the firmness of the word. There was a tension, unsettled by how she'd disrupted Grem's petition for a decision.

Amaris shifted in her chair. She felt confident that if it were put to a vote, the scowling faces would outnumber the open-minded ones significantly. The energy was not in her favor. Rather than allowing her feelings of discomfort to take root, she felt herself transition into anger. She would not have escaped Farleigh and cut her way out of the claws of Millicent just to be turned away by men and their prejudice. She had not slashed into her flesh for rejection at the feet of sexist males. She did not leave Nox—the only person who had *ever* cared for her— just to be cast back into the world alone. She would not have begged an assassin to take her in, ridden for days, suffered mangled feet, aching muscles, bruised tailbones and bright pink scars only to be told her womanhood forbade her from training.

Her body moved before her mind understood what she was doing. She was on her feet, slamming a fist onto the table. It was a childish outburst, and the flimsy impact of her balled fist made little to no sound on the stone table. Still, the confidence and command that surged out of her hit its mark. She looked the men in the eye without a drop of doubt. The tumultuous curl of her fury burst out in a single demand. "You *will* let me stay, and you *will* let me train!"

Her lavender eyes sparkled with her eruption. Her fire burned into them for a moment until, in the quiet that followed, she realized what she'd done.

She blinked, horrified.

This had been far worse than not talking at all. Regret surged like bile in her throat.

Her lips parted as if to apologize, but shut quickly before she spoke another word. She'd done enough damage. Her body remained rigid as the anger ebbed. Amaris wasn't sure what had come over her, but she'd undoubtedly done more harm than good. She felt so foolish standing before them, hand still planted against the stone table. A spasm of embarrassment clenched in her stomach.

The events that followed were… bizarre.

A hushing wave pressed down on the reevers as their faces drifted from an amalgamation of confusion, to something accepting and contemplative as the men murmured among themselves. They appeared to be quietly nodding to each other.

The fae, Samael, glittered with near-wicked amusement. He lifted his head from where it had been resting, bored on his chin, and steepled his fingers together in a triangle.

"My, isn't that a talent."

Shame pushed her back down in her seat. She wished she could melt into the rock below her like the legs of the table. Amaris refused to meet the eyes of any of the men. She tuned out the reevers and their mutters, horrified at what they must be saying about her.

He ignored the others, looking directly to Amaris. "It appears it won't affect myself, or Ash, for the most part," he gestured to the coppery teenage boy, "but I do applaud you. It's quite unlike any skill I've seen. Honestly, I'm quite relieved I'm spared from the onslaught of such a gift. Well done, Amaris."

Amaris lifted her eyes. Despite her crushing humiliation, a confusion tugged her back to Samael's face. Her eyebrows pinched. "What?"

The others continued speaking to each other as if the conversation across the table weren't happening at all. Their mouths moved in quiet exchange as they discussed the situation at hand.

Samael sat up straighter, something like realization dancing amongst the entertained expression on his face. He pressed his fingers into the table, maintaining an interested eye contact for a moment. The fae then stood and addressed the others.

"Well," he looked to the reevers, "since it's clear you've all decided she's to stay and train, let's call this meeting adjourned." Samael made a sweeping gesture with his hands, and with no objection, the men began to push themselves away from the table. They rose from their seats and continued their chattering as they headed for the door. Samael continued, "Do carry on with your day. I need to have a word with our newest reever-in-training."

The disorientation was jarring.

Amaris felt her face twist as if she were waiting for a slap that never came. Her brows lowered deeply. Her lips remained parted in an unclear objection. She looked to Odrin, but he appeared to be smiling with their success. She raised her eyes to meet Samael, and felt her whole body flinch at the realization that he was staring fully at her. His gaze was nothing predatory, nor was it perverse by any interpretation, but it was definitely intimidating.

She had the disjointed sensation that she might be dreaming.

What had happened? After her tantrum, Samael had adjourned the meeting? Could this be some cruel form of sarcasm? If it wasn't a joke, what had he meant by, 'since they'd all decided'? She had been certain they were about to vote her out.

The men pushed their chairs away from the stone table. The scraping sounds of wood against granite offered a brief, grating distraction while she watched the reevers depart. They filtered out of the dining hall, leaving a bewildered, moonlit girl in their wake. She recognized a few of the faces and hair colors mentioned in the meeting, from the rather friendly-faced young man with golden hair, to the red-headed faeling.

Amaris stood as well, feeling too awkward to sit as they walked on either side of her to shuffle out of the dining room. Odrin clapped her on the shoulder as he passed and while his smile was relatively warm, hers was still a mask of confusion. It took fewer than three minutes for the room to clear out and the boy to take the abandoned pints from the stone table. What on the All Mother's lighted earth had just happened?

She and the fae were alone.

He was still standing, backlit by the flames of their large fireplace. He made a sweeping motion as he returned to his chair, reclining in a way that was meant to be disarming.

"Amaris of No Home and No People, come take a seat by me, won't you?"

158

She twisted her mouth into discomfort, but had few options. Odrin was gone. She hadn't understood the meeting's outcome. She didn't know whether or not she trusted this man and his gestures, but she obediently left her chair on the far side and walked closer to the fireplace where Samael had been sitting. The idea of sitting directly beside him made her uneasy, so she allowed an empty chair to remain between the two of them, taking a seat slightly off to his left.

The fae turned from where he had reclined to face her more fully. He waited on her for a time with impressive patience.

She was quite sure he wouldn't have spoken if it hadn't been for the inarticulate, near-strangled sound she made as she shook her head. Amaris had intended to ask a question, but failed spectacularly. She was too confused to compose words.

He perked, "Are you to tell me you don't know of your gift?"

She stared at him stupidly, no recognition of his meaning lighting her eyes.

Samael frowned, "You do know you aren't fully human, correct?"

"I…" her hand touched her ears. There were no points to them. What use had her years of schooling been if she was too unintelligent to find words when it mattered most? "It has been suggested that perhaps I was part something-or-other. But other than my hair, and my eyes, I've never shown any traits…" She trailed off.

He smiled, though, not unkindly. His irises were the too-large circles of the pure fae—eyes she'd seen only once in an unfortunate faeling who hadn't lasted long in Farleigh. There was a gentle consideration in them as he studied her. "Your hair and your eyes should have been giveaway enough. You won't find lavender eyes on either side of the border. You aren't human."

She recoiled at the implication, even if she couldn't fully fathom its weight.

"Do you truly not know of your ability?" He pressed.

She shook her head. Not only did she not know of gifts, but she didn't even understand the nature of his question.

He relaxed again, the same amused expression returned to his face. His elbow rested on the arm of his chair as it had in the meeting. He rested his chin in his hand as he had before, an entertained smile tugging at the corners of his mouth. "What would you say happened just now? In the meeting?"

"I honestly don't know," she answered, puzzlement coloring her words.

He nodded with slow consideration. "How interesting, Amaris of No People." His eyes turned to hers, but with the gentleness of a teacher. He didn't seem to be chastising or agitated, merely instructional. "Persuasion is a rare and dangerous gift. In my many centuries, I, myself, have never met one who demonstrated it–though those with the silver fabled tongue have been hunted and killed by humans for millennia. While other fae might find you compelling and charming, it's nothing like the absolute obedience you'll find when you give a command to a human. Do you know of persuasion? Any such tales?"

"Persuasion?" She repeated uselessly.

He didn't sigh as she might have expected. The matrons had never attempted to conceal disappointment if Amaris hadn't been ready with answers. This fae had the unruffled feathers of one who'd weathered lifetimes. She'd never met a true fae, but she could see it in his eyes. She could sense it in the relaxed confidence of his posture. His soul was old.

"Yes, persuasion." He continued, "You could tell a human man who you fancy to leave his wife and marry you. You could tell a queen to hand over her crown. You could tell a mother to drown her newborn babe."

She twitched in rejection. Her brows lowered. She shook her head against the absurdity of his words, but his face remained smooth. He was so impassive, so unrelenting, that she found herself willing to believe the conviction of this absolute stranger. The men had shifted like the ocean's tide, their decision whirring with her outburst. Had she truly done that?

Horror seeped into her features. What kind of monster did he think she was? What kind of witch would have such a horrible power? She shook her head more violently, rejecting the information. It was ridiculous. It was blasphemous.

"What are you saying?" Amaris's voice had escaped as a scratchy rasp without her realizing how dry her mouth had become.

"This can't be your first instance of exercising your gift, Amaris. Perhaps it's the first time you've been made aware of your ability, but do me a favor. Think of a time—any time—where you've had an effect on those around you. Think of a time where you made a demand, and your will was adhered to. Does anything come to mind?"

Even as her heart pushed against the information, a door in her mind opened to a memory. Something did come to mind. That day in the pantry, when the wretched, freckle-faced Achard and his friends had pushed through Nox and tried to drag her to see the bishop, she had told the boys to leave. They had. They had left the pantry. They had left the kitchen. They had left Farleigh, never to be heard from again. Had that been because of her? Because of one command ordering them to go? A gross, sickening understanding hit her, twisting her stomach into a pained knot.

He asked with a careful, quiet voice, "Did you ask Odrin to take you with him, or did you tell him to bring you?"

Repugnance filled her as she recalled their conversation.

Samael seemed to understand her recognition as she worked through her past. "While it has no impact on my feelings toward whether or not a woman trains in the reev, I do see its value on our team. Your gift is an asset." He waved a hand toward where the redhead with arched ears had been sitting during their meeting. "Ash will also have a bit more of a resistance to your charm as a halfling, so it'd be pertinent to pair you two together. Don't mistake my words, he'll find any command you give to be immensely influential, but it won't be met with the same compulsory response, as he's only half-blooded. Gifts meant to work on the mind generally affect humans and halflings more acutely than the fae, though I acknowledge there are some powers of the mind to which even fae are utterly susceptible. That being said, I can't very well have you winning your fights by telling your opponents to drop their swords—at least, not while training. Your ability may be exceptionally useful in mortal battle, what good will that do you if you come across a beseul?"

She knit her brows, but was able to ascertain from context that a beseul was perhaps a creature that she did not want to stumble upon without the knowledge of how to wield her sword.

"It's evil," she said.

"The beseul? People think so, yes, but many of the dark creatures—"

"This power," she corrected, "it's evil."

The fae reever stood then, seemingly finished with their conversation. "A gift is no more good or evil than the one wielding it."

She stood with him.

"I think we've had enough of the dining room, don't you?"

Amaris nodded, though she wasn't sure why. She would have been fine remaining in the dining room. Anywhere other than her rooms had been a treat, and she wasn't entirely convinced she was in the frame of mind to see or do much more.

"Shall we tour the reev?" The fae motioned her to follow him, and she did.

He introduced himself finally, fully, as Samael, though she had gathered as much. Even if the men hadn't said it in the meeting, his age and authoritative energy had revealed him to be their leader. He disclosed that he had been living and serving at Uaimh Reev since before the kingdoms had drawn their jagged borders and divided the world. She couldn't call on any such dates that made sense to her. The borders between Raascot and Farehold had been drawn, disbanded, and redrawn nearly one thousand years before her birth. Surely, that hadn't been what he'd meant.

The reev—an old word for fortress in some fae dialect—was chosen for its neutralized location, and hewn from the very mountain by someone with the magic to wield stone. The mountain had obeyed him, and the labor of love, Uaimh Reev was ready. In those days, fae and humans found honor in defending the lands below from magical imbalance. Reevers would be dispatched not just for the dark creatures from the Unclaimed Wilds, but to unravel concentrations of unnatural power that might upset the harmony of the continent and its kingdoms. They were the goddess's sword arm, fighting for no monarch, but working in the shadows for the peace and stabilization of their world against the forces that warred men and fae alike, irrespective of territories or rulers or borders.

Every few lifetimes, a king or queen would rally his or her people for a territorial invasion, and as long as the battles were fought fairly and the magics untouched, the reevers would leave the ways of men to themselves. If magics were wielded that could level the lands or if the unnatural powers of blood magic were bound, the reevers would dispatch to intervene. Being a reever had been an honorable profession for centuries. Over the last two hundred years, the need for reevers had grown lesser and lesser in the public eye. Magic quieted as it had been slowly bred out of the southern kingdom, and the creatures of the land were content to roam their own territories. The fae populace in the northern kingdom of Raascot had asked little of the reevers. The Farehold's fae were far fewer, Samael had said, but they'd lived peaceably among humans for some time.

She wasn't sure why it was the first question that came to mind, but Amaris tilted her chin as she looked to Samael and asked, "What was Odrin doing near Farleigh?"

A nod, "There have been several tales of beasts in Farehold that haven't been reported south of the Unclaimed Wilds for centuries. There's no reason for so many unnatural monsters to have free reign of the continent. The church called to us, and Odrin went to investigate the claims by a small town near—what did you say your home's name was? Farleigh?—and it seems he found a thing or two that the reevers will be discussing further."

She changed her topic then, her eyes flitting back to his pointed ears. "How many fae are left?"

He looked at her briefly with his overly large, dark irises before his eyes fixed on the wall behind her. Samael's face was distinctly sad for a moment. They continued their tour of the keep, this being her first opportunity to truly see the grounds. The fortress had the combined sense of decay and vitality. The structure was immobile, never to wither as it had been made from the seamless pieces of the mountain. Other aspects of the keep revealed the centuries of their age. It was unnecessary to mind her step, as the floor was composed of the same clean, seamless granite she'd seen throughout the fortress, no threat of tripping or stumbling underfoot. Later elements composed by the handiworks and masonry of men and fae in the centuries that had followed would require slightly more upkeep than the unbreakable structure of the reev.

Samael continued to lead Amaris down a long, straight corridor lined with windows that showcased the plunge below lighting one side. He continued contemplating her question as they carried themselves down the hall. She didn't feel ignored, but rather that her words had a heaviness she hadn't anticipated. They emerged on the far side of the keep and looked at what appeared to be something of a coliseum—she'd never seen one in person, but the rounded shape fit the descriptions from her books. Samael continued walking as he spoke.

"You were born at a time where the fae are almost a memory in the southern lands. Farehold is not a kind kingdom to the fae—it's not a kind kingdom to any human that doesn't display their pink undertones and colorless hair, to be honest. It's no place I'd want to live, nor do I envy you for your upbringing. The fae are rather numerous in the north, though they haven't dared to set foot in Farehold for nearly two decades. This is just speaking of Gyrradin, mind you. Your whole life has been limited to a rather narrow strip of Farehold. I suppose if you were to leave the continent behind, you would find magic still plentiful in the warmth of the Etal Isles. If you were to cross The Frozen Straits, where humans haven't stepped foot in a millennium, the Sulgrave Mountains are a place where you won't find a rounded ear in sight. I've never had the privilege of crossing the Straits. The descriptions of Sulgrave fae don't quite fit your coloration, but if you're going to find a fae people who resemble you, I suppose it would be there, as I've never seen such features on this side of the ice." He studied her, dragging his eyes with a scholarly question from the silvery tip of her hair down to her lilac eyes. There was a frown on his face as he considered her. "That being said, those from Sulgrave might be horrified if they saw your poor, small ears on such a starlit face. I'm sorry you weren't able to inherit our hearing... Though with those eyes, I'd love to see what gifts of sight you possess. You're not like any fae I've met, and I've been around for... some time."

Amaris didn't know what to say. He'd more or less welcomed her into the reev, and she'd remained mute. She felt like this was their first lesson and she was already falling short.

With their brief introduction to history at a close, he gestured to the training arena beneath them. "Amaris, our newest reever, you've decided to stay and train, and so you shall. You'll arrive here each morning at first light. As Odrin has brought you to us, he's responsible for you. I'll inform Odrin that Ash is to be your sparring partner."

Amaris's mouth opened as if to speak, but she had no words.

Samael turned to leave and then, over his shoulder, said, "Oh, and if I catch you using your persuasion again while in the reev, it will be your last night in this fortress. Is that understood?"

She almost choked on her nod, appalled with herself for the manipulation she'd wielded amidst the men. Samael wandered off, disappearing into the keep. Amaris had spent so long locked up in her rooms that she had no interest in hurrying back to her chambers. She continued along the path he'd led them, surrounded by the circular shape of their granite training arena. It had no roof and was fully exposed to the autumnal weather that rushed in from overhead. The air was cold both from the lateness of the season, and from their elevation. The wind chafed her face and hands. The chill didn't bother her nearly as much as the idea of returning to her bedroom, so she stayed. Amaris picked her footing carefully down the stairs, sinking into the lower levels of the training ring.

The fresh air was a relief from the jarring meeting. She needed the crisp, bracing wind to shake her mind free of the cobwebs that had gathered, connecting her mind to her tongue as she'd remained more or less speechless throughout the bewildering events of the day. Even if she hadn't just had a life-changing experience, the clean mountain air was a nice break from the days spent in her room, and she was in no hurry to return.

This was to be where she would train.

The entire arena was littered with objects meant for instruction, education and honing one's craft. Wooden beams ran along one side. Spheres and disks of stone and iron intended for weight training were scattered on the opposite side near a rack of swords. Some blades were made of true steel, others composed of wood. A quiver of arrows hung from the rows of weapons. Hole-punched targets on the far end of the arena, demonstrating the evidence of the archery she was sure took place every day. She ran a cold, chilled finger along the blade of a sword on its stand and was surprised to see it draw blood. She'd expected practice weapons to be dulled.

"Don't you reckon you have enough scars?"

Amaris whirled and found a coppery boy of about sixteen, just barely older than herself, leaning against the opening to a dug-out pit in the arena. She wiped the droplet of blood on her pants. She blinked at the young man and shrugged, unsure of what to say. She recognized him from the meeting as the faeling Samael had mentioned. In a single afternoon she was to meet not one, but two of the fair folk.

He approached with a crooked smile, extending a hand. "I'm Ash."

She eyed his hand skeptically for a brief moment, then took it. His hand was warm and calloused in all of the places that might indicate familiarity with a blade and its hilt.

"That was quite the performance back there."

She responded on instinct, attempting levity. "What can I say? I'm prone to theatrics."

He laughed at that. His teeth weren't pointed like that of the full fae, but his amber eyes, a swirl of honey, gold and chipped bronze on their outermost lines were slightly too large to belong to a human. His ears betrayed the fae half of his lineage. "Won't the men be pleased to hear all their thoughts of women have been correct."

"Which thought, exactly? That women are dramatic? Or is it that we're remarkably persuasive?"

He seemed to be good-natured with his jest. "A little of this, a little of that. I think a few of us are just excited to watch how much you'll irritate Grem."

"He does seem like a joy to be around."

Ash grinned, "He's not so bad. At least, I don't think so. Malik doesn't like him—you'll meet him later, though I guess you got a fine enough impression for him in the meeting. He's a good egg–Malik, that is. Don't be surprised if Grem doesn't warm up to you anytime soon. He's not known for his jovial character."

"What is he known for?"

Ash arched a brow, "He's our bladesmith. You can't be in Uaimh Reev without being useful." He looked her up and down. "Clearly, Samael thinks you'll be useful. Though, you don't look like you're about to give Grem a run for his money in metalworking."

Amaris brushed it off, fully unwilling to engage in his line of questioning. Why Samael found her an asset to the team was a secret that would die with her and their fae leader. She eyed her would-be sparring partner. "Samael said we're supposed to train together."

He nodded, "I figured as much. I have fifty pounds on you, but better me than a warrior with thirty years of experience. I guess you could also fight Brel, but his training is pretty limited to the kitchen at this point. He'll get there, he's just a bit young to go through the rite."

She almost repeated the name as a question, but through process of elimination, there was only one child in the keep younger than either Amaris or Ash. Brel must have been the child who had been responsible for delivering her meals. She made a note to use his name the next time the boy visited.

Ash's reddish hair was the color of dark embers just as the fire died. His eyes were golden, ringed with the brown of the earth, and the tanned skin that reminded her of Nox, though perhaps she'd find a way for all things to remind her of Nox . He had an easy likability about him. Amaris's guards were up, cautious as they spoke, but she didn't feel threatened. He looked—and smelled, if she wasn't mistaken—distinctly of autumn. There was a spice about his relaxed energy.

"You're fae." It wasn't a question. She had been told as much by Samael.

"Part fae."

"And part human."

"As are you, Snowflake."

"Please, don't call me that." The pain in her heart hit suddenly, surprising her with its intensity. Had it merely been a week since she'd seen her friend? Her only family? Her tether to this world? Between the last few days locked in the keep and a number of days on the road, the math added up, though it felt as though she'd been away for several lifetimes.

Nox had gripped her arms only one week ago. The black, bottomless eyes had quietly looked into her lilac ones, dressed, gathered their food, and been ready to escape with her in the twilight hours. She'd held her in the pantry. Studied with her. Laughed with her. Grown with her. Plotted, shared, danced, and lived side by side with her throughout every moment of her life. The night-haired girl had taken an unspeakable beating from Agnes at the behest of the bishop to protect Amaris from the church's discovery. It had been the sort of memory that belonged in her tightly sealed box, too horrible for Amaris to unpack.

They'd been meant to run away together. Instead, Amaris left her alone.

The morning Millicent came, Amaris had told Nox to…

Oh, goddess, no.

The sensation of a dagger pierced her gut, twisting deep within her. Goddess be damned, she understood the disgusting, treacherous moment all at once. Calling on the death of a one thousand All Mothers, the sickening fear tore through her.

She had told Nox to wait for her.

At the time, it had been the hushed urgency of a girl who wanted them to run away together. Now, she saw it for what it was: a persuasion. A command, given and received. Her dreams of Nox running toward the coast were shattered. She pictured the dark-haired girl with her feet glued to the back of the manor. She wasn't sure if she was about to cry or be sick.

"Hey, I'm sorry." The boy looked confused. "Your coloration... I just thought–white, snow..." He was clearly flustered. Ash searched uselessly for a defense, still unsure as to his misstep, "I wasn't..."

"Oh," Amaris shook her head, using the back of her hand to wipe away one treacherous tear before he could see it tumble. Of course, the first day they allowed a girl in the keep, she would blubber in the training ring. "It's nothing. It was someone... it's nothing. It's not just not a nickname I like to be called."

Ash offered one quick nod, making an apparent mental note. She wished she hadn't made him uncomfortable. She would have to find better ways to seal off her emotions if she were going to succeed as a reever.

Amaris couldn't think of Nox right now. She pictured her emotion as the kraken of lore, battling it into a shell of space within her chest cavity. She tackled the beast and locked it in a cage, forbidding it and its feelings for the raven-haired girl to sweep its treacherous tentacles toward her. The cage would be slapped with a lock, then wrapped in chains, then shoved into the same seamless chest where all traumatic feelings were kept.

She had told Nox to wait. That meant her friend would still be in Farleigh, undoubtedly carrying on her chores as Agnes's favorite assistant. Amaris made a vow to herself. She would spend her life making it up to Nox that she'd abandoned her behind to survive the orphanage alone. She would not let her rot in that mill.

As soon as she had the skill, Amaris would return to Farleigh and liberate Nox from the matrons. Perhaps she could earn enough to buy out Nox's debt from Agnes, though after years as the favored attendant, she knew Agnes would be reluctant to part with the dark-haired girl.

Besides, seeing Amaris set free would surely only enrage the Gray Matron. She shook the thought from her head, slamming the box on the kraken into place, and resolved to train, to learn, and to one day rescue the friend who had spent so much of their childhood saving her.

She had to stop thinking of Nox or she'd find herself given over to her emotions. Instead, she refocused on the faeling in front of her. Attempting conversation, she ventured a question.

"Did they buy you to fight?"

Ash blinked at the implication. "What?"

Amaris gestured to the coliseum and the hewn keep around them. "The reevers—did they buy you for their cause?"

The offense was plain on his face, though Amaris wasn't sure what had provoked him. "What kind of question is that?"

She wasn't sure how she had managed to do so many things wrong in such a short amount of time. Her mouth pinched to prevent herself from speaking further, hands clasping in front of her. Everything she said, everything she did seemed to betray her ignorance of the world. What was the use of the books she'd read and the lessons she'd endured when everyone beyond the walls Farleigh reacted to her as if she were a cave child?

Her face was a mixture of apology and defense as she pressed, "Some of the boys at the orphanage went to farmers, or sailors, but sometimes a knight would purchase them. It's not common. I just thought…" she let her words trail off, eyes on her shoes.

It took a few moments for her meaning to absorb. The red-haired young man softened a bit, sympathy creeping up on him as he grew to understand the implication of her question.

She hated that pity in his eyes, and hated what he had to say even more.

"I didn't realize," he said, his voice less playful than it had been before. "I'm sorry about your childhood. In much of the world, slavery is illegal. It's easy to forget about the mills. And no, no one brought me here. My father serves the keep, and it was my mother's wish that I followed in his footsteps. She was human, and passed away a few years ago from a common sickness. I didn't know much about healing then. It's not my gift. But when she left the earth, I had nothing left keeping me in her village."

"We weren't—"

Amaris stopped herself. She wasn't sure how to respond. She knew she was meant to feel empathy for what Ash had shared, but she had caught on the word he had used. Slavery? No, that couldn't be what the children were. How had she never considered that their purchase price had made them the merchandise they were, devoid of the agency offered humanity? Regardless of how she'd gotten here, a boy was in front of her now, offering his life story. He had chosen to be here. And now that she thought of it, so had she.

Once more, she had to change the subject. She had to deflect. Her box of emotions was growing too full for one day. She'd need time and space to expand its edges so it could contain new pains, new contents. For now, if she had any hope of maintaining a sense of normalcy, she'd need to convince the other reevers that she wasn't a wreck. Amaris shivered against the autumn chill, holding her arms to herself as she searched for a new question. She couldn't let him leave with this feeble impression of her.

"Does your father live?"

Ash nodded, seemingly unbothered by the weather. "Yes, I believe as much, though I haven't seen him in nearly ten years. He's still in service to the reevers. His work has taken him somewhere into the northernmost parts of Raascot. I'm sure the northern kingdom is in as much need of management as Farehold."

She didn't know what to say. Everything she'd heard of the northern kingdom had made it sound like a goddessless hell. She opened her mouth to say she was sorry, but closed her lips instead. The cold pressed down on her further. If she had known she would spend so much time in an uncovered part of the keep, she would have brought her cloak.

It seemed as though his father was a topic he didn't much like to discuss. Ash either hadn't noticed her growing physical discomfort, or hadn't cared. Still entertained by the presence of the reev's newest member, he asked, "Do you have a nickname?"

She blinked, coming back into her body, out of her thoughts. Her hands chafed against her arm. "No, not really."

"Come on," he pressed, "Everyone's friends give them a nickname."

"I didn't really have friends where I was." And she definitely wasn't going to win any this way. Her awkward answers were garnering her no favors, despite the olive branch he was extending her. She wished she could relax, but every gust of wind and chill of the weather only underlined how poor she was at communication. She couldn't even stand up for herself enough to tell her soon-to-be sparring partner that she was freezing. Amaris caught a glance at her fingers long enough to see the shades of red and pinks they were turning around the tips and knuckles.

Ash wasn't truly looking at her. He seemed to be eyeing the late autumn sky as he chewed on an idea, unfazed. "Well, Amaris is a bit of a mouthful, but give me enough time and I'll think of something to shout at you while I'm crushing you in the ring."

"Ash?"

"Mmm?" He perked at the use of his name.

"If we keep talking out here much longer, you'll win all of our fights, because I'm about to lose my limbs. I'm freezing."

His smile sparkled at her frankness as he jerked his head toward the corridor. She returned the smile, and he seemed pleased that his attempt at friendliness had been well-received. The heat flooded into her the moment the door closed behind them. They parted ways as soon as they'd eased into the door to the keep, but she knew she wouldn't feel truly warm again until she had the chance to soak her bones in the hot bath of her quarters.

It took a while for her to find her way through the corridors, but Amaris returned to her rooms and took her dinner by the boy, whose name she'd learned to be Brel, in her chamber. Presumably, she would one day join the men where they ate, but she was grateful for the chance to be alone with her thoughts. She flipped through the books on her shelf and found one that was nothing but a genealogy of kings and their heirs, and began to scratch in her own history with strokes of a quill. She wrote her name, and an arrow from her to Nox, connecting them with a parallel line. She wrote the names she had learned from the reevers. Samael, Odrin, Ash, Malik, Grem, and somewhere below them she wrote Brel's name as well. She made a column for the matrons, one for her peers at the orphanage, one for Queen Moirai, and then, with a big black 'x' to the side, she wrote Madame Millicent.

9

Torture took on a new name, and that name was training.

The road to becoming a reever was agonizing.

Every pain she thought she'd felt, every muscle ache, every embarrassment she'd experienced leading up to this moment had been a grain of sand on a frothy beach compared to the endless desert of daily misery that was exercise and practice with the reevers. True to her testimony, they would not offer her any special treatment. She was given no grace as she was thrown into the ring.

Amaris woke at dawn for her first morning of training and trailed behind the others as they walked up and over the many-tiered training ring to a trail she hadn't noticed on her tour the day before. It was just as thin as the one that had led up from Stone, though this particular pathway wound its way down the opposite mountain. The men took off in a pack and her eyes widened.

"We're meant to run down?" She hadn't meant for it to come out as a gasp, but it didn't seem safe to sprint down such a steep trail.

The one with the golden hair had patted her once on the back as he passed, responding with cheery levity. "And back up again!" He began his run and she watched after the men as they began what would be a daily exercise in suffering.

For weeks, Amaris was so far behind the men on runs up and down the mountain that most of them would reach the base of the mountain, turn around, and pass her on their ascent before she'd even completed her initial descent. If it weren't miserable enough to feel every muscle in one's body scream in protest, the added humiliation of needing to avoid their eyes as they surpassed her was an entirely separate layer of excruciation. Even Grem, for his advanced age, never missed the morning run. The daily runs fostered community and maintained stamina essential to their survival on the job, or, so the men had claimed.

The run took place every morning, and was completed well before lunch. The particularly agile reevers could finish the exercise in two hours. Others required three or four for their round trip. Amaris was lucky if she could finish her run in six.

The reevers kept this particular mountain to themselves. It belonged to no one but the Uaimh Reev, the marmots, and the bighorn sheep. It would have been terrifying enough to slowly, carefully walk up and down the trail, particularly if you startled a ram perched on the jagged boulders of the mountainside. Instead, the speed expected of them as they pounded up and down the steep route made it feel like a daily practice in learning to manage your adrenaline. Precipitous trail running was as much about psychological torment and learning to control your fear and channel your adrenaline as it was a practice in stamina.

The steep switchbacks offered no forgiveness if a single foot slipped out of place.

It was not an entirely gray, lifeless run. The trail, like the keep, was dotted with tenacious little plants, including some scraggly trees that hung out of fissures in the stones had found a way to survive high up in the mountains. Amaris had no time for sightseeing. She was too busy ensuring that she didn't make a wrong step, lest she tumble to her death and spare the reevers from the tribulations of having to raise a girl in their keep.

Running was the tip of the iceberg with these men.

After lunch came daily combat training, including weapons sparring, archery, and hand-to-hand fighting.

When it came to weaponry, not only could Amaris not swing a metal sword, she could barely hold one. Her arms would have been too weak for the blade even before her runs, but the taxing exercise had turned her body into gelatin. They'd permitted Amaris the use of the wooden training swords intended for children, which, thank the All Mother, she still technically was. When she wasn't wielding her wooden weapon, much to her ever-growing humiliation, young Brel would lunge, slash and advance on invisible opponents with triple the grace that she possessed.

Amaris was proving herself both disappointing and abysmal as a new recruit, particularly as nothing came naturally to her. The singular quality she possessed was tenacity. If the goddess was good, an unwillingness to quit might just be enough to justify her presence.

The kindest reevers kept their comments to themselves. Others didn't attempt to conceal their irritated groans, eyerolls, and overall displeasure as they continued to watch her flounder at each and every task. At least with running she spent the majority of the time by herself. Sparring came with the shame of an audience.

She failed to parry time after time. Amaris received blow after blow to the ribs, to the face, to the legs. She would limp to bed covered in purpling bruises from neck to navel, refusing to whimper in front of the men, having never landed a single hit to Ash. Each night she'd test her bones for breaks in the bath and seemed to single-handedly be depleting the keep's supply of healing tonics, desperate to stay on top of her injuries.

Ash was always kind, but seemed relentlessly disappointed that his partner didn't put up more of a fight. Not only did it dampen his morale to so thoroughly pummel his opponent each day, but it also meant he had to spend extra hours in the ring with Malik—the blond in his twenties who had spoken up for her during the meeting—just to get in proper competition. Ash and Malik were a far better match, and she hated herself for holding Ash back in his training.

Malik had his own sparring partner of equal skill, but didn't seem bothered by the additional opportunities for swordplay, shooting, and hand-to-hand melee. When he finished his own regime, he'd hang back and wait until Ash was ready to start their combat all over again. Fortunately, the golden young man was eminently good-natured, whose kind smiles and dismissive shrugs had disarmed the apologies Amaris had offered each time he'd had to train for extra hours.

"Move your feet, Ayla!" Ash had shouted as he stood over her, cursing her in the southern dialect, settling on insulting her as an oak tree. He'd knocked her to her back once again, just as he always did in swordplay. The shortened, similar variation of her name—Ayla, the word for oak—had become his nickname for her. It was less of a mouthful than Amaris, and a more accurate representation of how her clumsy feet seemed to be rooted to the earth—her moves so slow and timbering that she might as well have been carved from wood. She didn't mind the nickname. Frankly, she deserved to be called far worse.

Much to the chagrin of her and everyone around her, she did not seem to be improving.

The colder the winter grew, the harder it was for her to move. Her hands were red and chapped with the season. The extra weight of the warmer leathers and elbow-length fur cloak seemed to hinder her movements all the more. Was it possible that she was getting progressively worse? Between her beaten-down spirit, broken body, and the All Mother forsaken weather on the mountain, it seemed she was truly growing less and less impressive with every day that passed. Perhaps she truly was nothing more than an oak tree in a girl's body.

Still, she pressed on.

Wake up. Run. Train. Spar. Eat. Study. Sleep. Repeat.

After their lunches, most of the men went free for the day. Odrin, however, was responsible for teaching her about poisons, tonics and the basics of being one's own combat medic. Reevers usually took on tasks throughout the kingdoms alone, independently dispatched on their patrol of the territories. Should Amaris ever show a will to survive or the ability to hold her own in battle, she'd need to be able to avoid sabotage, spot healing plants, and know how to patch a wound. Odrin had her tying tourniquets, practicing the art of starting fires with nothing but a stone and one's weapon, and sniffing goblets of wine or water for signs of tampering. When they finished studying together, he sent her to her rooms each night with a stack of books up to her hip on what plants and creatures were safe to eat, and which ones would paralyze, blind, or boil you from the intestines out.

"Isn't there a magic item or something I could use to do this for me?" She grumbled, pushing away her book on poisons and remedies.

"Probably," Odrin had agreed, shoving the book back to her to force her to continue her studies, "but spelled objects are exceptionally difficult to make and even harder to come by. If you find one, hang on to it. In the meantime, why don't you focus on your studies rather than hoping you become the luckiest reever."

Time passed, and she did not give up.

As winter melted into spring, she learned she could wound a vageth with a blade and use its blood to coat her weapons, as her opponents would be defenseless against the resulting infection. She studied the lore of the sustron, and how one could steal its scent to hide in the shadows. Odrin taught her of djinn, who could grant three favors to any who held it, but that unless you were ready to recapture the beast, it would have your heart in its talons after your final wish. She skimmed over the more fictional beasts of lore like the icy aboriou or the collection of what were most certainly wishful sailor's tales of sirens and merfolk. She learned beseuls actively avoided the pain of sunlight, and that if you met the ag'drurath alone in the forest, you best make your peace with the All Mother, as no method had been recorded to subdue or defeat the winged dragon.

Demons, she'd learned, couldn't truly be killed. The knowledge had horrified her, but Odrin had reassured her that anything could be bested if you cut it into small enough pieces, whether or not those separated parts stayed alive.

"And if we don't?"

"If we don't what?" He looked up from his bestiary tome to see what needed clarification.

"If we don't cut them into smaller pieces?"

Odrin nodded, "Many things can reattach, given enough time. Bury the head separately and you'll be fine. We include a spade in your saddlebags to help with the digging."

"Oh, joy."

It didn't sound like she'd be fine, but he said it with such nonchalance that it made her believe he'd dealt with such things a time or two.

Odrin was gentle but firm with his lessons. The man was more than a little glad to find her a quick study. His relief had been no secret when he discovered her wit to be sharp, with an iron-clad memory. If he was going to break tradition and bring a young woman into the castle, at least he'd brought a girl with a warrior's heart and a fox's mind.

Every few weeks, Samael would intercept her as she left training and educate her on politics, history, and strategy. She'd had numerous questions about the fae, and he'd been a willing vessel for her inquiries.

Perhaps some part of him felt an obligation in his bones to help lost fair folk find their place in this world. Occasionally Ash would join them, sweat still clinging to his copper brows from the morning's practice and listen while Samael spoke on Raascot or the Sulgrave Mountains. The elder had smiled when he'd heard the girl called Ayla, but hadn't expressly said why. He'd kept a knowing twinkle behind his eye, teaching them of the empires. While kings and queens were titles in Gyrradin's kingdoms, Imperator had been the term amongst Sulgrave's fae until they'd dissolved to self-govern under a Comte for each of their seven territories. There had been no Imperator in the mountain kingdom beyond the Straits for a thousand years, though on the other side of the world, the Etal Isles still had a long-beloved Imperatress sitting upon the fae throne.

"You said you've never been to Sulgrave, right?" Amaris had asked Samael.

"That's correct. It's a challenging pilgrimage, to say the least."

"How do we know, then? How do we know how their government is run and things like that?"

"I said it's challenging to visit. I didn't say it was impossible. Fae do cross The Frozen Straits, though usually only in one direction or the other, as it's often too difficult to make the trek twice. It's rare, but visitors and ambassadors will come from Sulgrave once every few hundred years."

"And the Etal Isles?"

He'd made something of a shrugging gesture at that and carried on with his lessons. It would take her years to learn all of the things she should already know, but she was determined to make up for lost time.

The kingdoms of Raascot and Farehold were the only known regions where human and fae lived together rather peacefully. While Farehold held the human majority, the few remaining fae could still live full, prosperous lives in the southern kingdom. If the southern fae proved themselves more of a help than a harm, they were assets to their community, often in respected positions throughout their villages and cities. In this way, the fae had found prominence and room for advancement on the human continent in ways that they may have been overlooked as ordinary or mundane in their own lands. It wasn't uncommon for fae with powers that humans found useful to move from Raascot to Farehold for specifically such reasons.

As the human lifetimes went on, many had intermarried with the fae, bringing generations of minor power to the continent. The blood grew thinner and thinner as the years stretched and fae failed to repopulate themselves at the speed at which the humans could reproduce, particularly throughout Farehold. Their numbers dwindled, and between the years and distance from exposure, the humans began to struggle to discern fact from fiction when regarding their kind. As the north and south had split into its kingdoms, the south had grown especially distrustful of non-humans. The reever presence in Farehold had felt eminently important to Samael, lest the people have nothing but insidious rumors on the fae and magic to educate themselves. The past fifty years had been particularly hard, Samael had said. He felt uninspired to leave Uaimh Reev, preferring instead to dispatch his men from the fortress where he could best keep the continent safe.

The more Amaris learned about reevers and the function they served in maintaining magical balance, the more astonished and offended she felt that she'd never even heard of this league of assassins before encountering Odrin.

On several occasions over her first few weeks in the keep Amaris had tried, and failed, to speak to Brel. Odrin caught her talking to the boy one day as he dropped her meal in her rooms, and as the child left, her surrogate father-figure explained why the boy never spoke. She'd been horrified as he told one of the most terrible tales she'd ever heard.

As a babe, Brel had been discovered as someone with one of the small magics. He possessed the power to speak to fire. Some of Brel's first words aside from "mama" and "papa" had been the sort of magic that had caused the hearth in the home springing to life under his crackling flame whenever he was hungry or cold. Brel's village had been superstitious, with little knowledge of the magics or how they manifested in human bloodlines. On the advice of their church, his human parents had cut out his tongue to keep him from casting spells on the town.

When magic chose humans, she learned, it always seemed to reveal itself in unexpected ways. The small magics did not appear to pass through bloodlines and heritages the way that height and eye color would, but emerged in long, thin bloodlines with distant magical lineage whenever the goddess saw fit. There had been no way for his parents to have expected a small magic in their ordinary child, and they'd punished him for it in an act so cruel and inhumane that Amaris wasn't sure she'd ever fully recover from knowing such callousness existed in the world.

It had been a coincidence that Brel was discovered by a member of Uaimh Reev when he'd been on dispatch in the little boy's village. A reever had brought the boy home to live in the keep, though he'd been scarcely older than four at the time. Brel busied himself between lessons by helping in the kitchens. In the sanctuary of the reev, he could still train and grow in a place where his magic would be accepted, even if he would never again speak.

When Odrin had finished his story, Amaris had answered with the low, nauseated whisper that the world was a terrible place. Even as she said it, she couldn't bring herself to fully believe it.

This world was a hard and treacherous place to be sure. She'd been bought and sold and passed around like cattle. She'd seen cruelty and mockery and foolishness. Humans and fae alike could be born into ignorance, traits which often manifested in greed, fear or betrayal. But in the midst of pain, there was good. While there was dishonesty and jealousy and agony, there was also strength, beauty, and power. She had seen this goodness every day in Nox, and she saw it now amidst the men of Uaimh Reev.

Brel's parents had been afraid. His villagers had been ignorant. The man who had saved a mutilated child from a life of misunderstanding on society's fringes had certainly been good. She wanted to see goodness in herself as well.

It happened so slowly that she had no way to mark its progress.

Over the months, Amaris proved herself to be a sponge. She absorbed knowledge, tactics and skills each and every day. She would learn any skill, craft, trade or technique from anyone at the reev would give her the time of day. Even Grem begrudgingly let her into his forge a time or two to show her how he hammered out their weapons and made their blades from molten steel. She could have sworn she caught him smiling as he pounded away at the red hot unformed blade, but he stopped himself as soon as she saw the curvature of his lips. He chased her out of his workrooms, remembering some old belief that blacksmithing—like Uaimh Reev—was not for women.

For months she was trailing behind, too proud to let herself stop no matter how pathetic her stride or how feeble her limping steps. Then one day, she found she was keeping pace with Grem. The elder reever had been the slowest of the group, and it was to his extreme displeasure that she began to stay within arm's reach of him for their morning run. The day after she surpassed him, he found a reason to excuse himself to an errand in the foothills and wouldn't return to the reev for a very long time.

☽ ☽ ☽ ☽ ● ☾ ☾ ☾ ☾

By her third year at Uaimh Reev, her muscles had hardened beneath her pants and under her tunic, turning her soft arms and legs into taut, sinewy appendages able to throw the iron balls on the field and hoist the discs above her head. As the months had stretched into seasons, she'd felt the sword become such a familiar part of her that she ceased to notice its weight, switching between left and right hands until neither could be encumbered by the blade. The steel was now an extension of her body.

The softness of her cheeks had ebbed into the features of a woman. Any fat from her childhood was gone after her first winter in the fortress. She had acquired a few new scars from the ring. Perhaps the largest scar in her collection, apart from her self-inflicted dagger wounds, was a nasty scrape of skin from a time she had sprinted past Malik and Ash on the mountain in an attempt to show off and twisted her ankle on a loose rock, tumbling an arena's length down a drop-off before her bloodied arm and leg and caused enough friction to stop her fall. Odrin had watched over her as she washed and bandaged the wounds to ensure she wouldn't catch infection, eyeing the tonics she chose for her health, but he hadn't needed to intervene or correct her.

By the time Amaris was eighteen, she was ready to take the oath as a full-fledged reever.

10

"Is it always at sunset?" She whispered to Odrin as they exited the keep to stand in the red light of dusk, joining the eleven other men. Everyone in the reev, save for Brel, was accounted for. The night was warm, with the lightest breeze to move the loose dust and sand of the ring in small swirls at their feet. The open-air fighting arena served many purposes, though this was the first time she'd seen it used for ritual. This was only the second swearing-in ceremony to take place since her arrival, but she hadn't been permitted to attend Ash's rite, as she had not yet been a reever.

"It's tradition," Odrin whispered back, "plus, oaths require a certain sense of drama, don't you think?"

Torches flickered around the ring, joining the blazing oranges and crimsons of the dying light overhead. The smell of oil and smoke joined the otherwise crisp mountain air where they convened. The other men had gathered near the steps, sitting and chatting in a variety of positions. They pushed themselves to their feet, standing in a rough semi-circle as Amaris approached.

"Ready to add to your collection of scars?" Odrin asked as he left her side to stand by the men.

She didn't know what he meant by that, but she was ready.

Samael clapped his hands together, dramatically silhouetted against the sunset. He began, "We're not much for liturgy, Amaris. Repeat the oath, and then shake hands with your brothers. Shall we?"

She nodded. They hadn't told her what to expect. She wasn't sure why, but she felt a surge of nerves as the late hour seemed to set the sky on fire. The men looked at her expectantly as Samael began. He held a dagger loosely in one hand and looked to her as she repeated her vow.

"I am the sword of the All Mother. I will answer to no king, join no armies, and seek for myself neither power nor glory. I stand between magic and its imbalance as its sentry in this world. I will not flee, fail or falter. I am a reever."

Samael finished as Amaris echoed his words. He raised the dagger to one hand, squeezing the blade to create a cut in his palm before passing it to Grem, who did the same. Odrin traced a deep scar in his palm with the blade, exchanging the knife with the next man, then the next, until droplets of blood dangled from the fingertips of every man around her. Finally, the dagger was given to Amaris.

She took it with nerves, anticipation and pride, cutting into her flesh to seal her vow.

Samael was the first to offer his hand, their blood exchanged in a solemn grasp. Odrin took her hand in a shake, but clapped her opposite shoulder with pride, a smile on his face as she completed her ritual. The blood of every reever would pump through their veins, uniting them as brothers, sharing blood with the first true family she'd ever known. The process repeated with shakes, smiles, clasps, a wink from Ash, and a hug from Malik until she stood before them, pride, honor and valor radiating from the legacy that pumped through her veins as the thirteenth reever.

Ash leaned his body weight to the side, drinking deeply from a waterskin while Malik and Amaris sparred in the ring. He occasionally found himself shouting encouragements to her as the clang of metal reverberated. They were long past dulled, wooden swords. The summer heat had them dressing lighter with every passing day, which freed their movements and enabled the reevers to navigate training in barely more than a tunic and pants.

"It's always your feet! Watch your feet, Ayla!"

"Shut it!" She chirped back without looking at him, "I know what I'm doing."

The redhead grinned at her while she danced. Malik was nearly a foot taller and markedly stronger, but the little ivory reever was giving him a run for his money. A drenching of sweat had begun to cause his shirt to cling to his hardened body, betraying his exertion as he brought his sword up once more.

The other reevers finished up their morning routines and found themselves joining Ash, watching as Malik and Amaris exchanged blades. A large bead of sweat trickled down Malik's brow. His features were normally relaxed in a smile, but his face was trained in concentration. His golden hair had been tied back in a knot, though a few stray curls had unraveled themselves as he moved. He lunged and she successfully blocked his blow and retreated, sword in the defensive position.

They were both breathing hard from the effort of sparring, but it was clear that Malik was wearing down faster. Amaris's face was red from the spar, but she kept her shoulders steady. Though she pulled at the air, she was not panting like he was. She wet her lips, tasting the salt and heat and dust of the ring and the fight.

"When did you get this good!"

"I think you're just getting old!" She sparkled.

He swung high and hard, but her spin had both of her hands

gripping simultaneously at her hilt, holding it with the rigid strength of both outstretched arms as she blocked again. She grunted from her belly as her weapon absorbed the hit. She took his blow and spun, swinging for his legs with another high sound. Amaris had hoped that his weight would slow him, but she should have known better than to catch him off guard.

Despite his size, Malik was quick. He leapt backward, successfully avoiding her sweep. His side-step may have helped him to dodge her initial swing but it left his right side wide open. She faked to the left and came in hard for his right. His green eyes went wide with surprise as he registered her movements. Amaris barely had the time to twist her sword and strike him with the broad side, sending him to the ground with a blow to his pride rather than a pierce through his ribs.

He groaned from where he'd fallen. She grinned, thinking she'd won.

Dust kicked up between them as the golden-haired man bared his teeth, on his feet before she could advance fully. Malik had some fight in him yet. He twisted his full body weight into a swing, whirling from one side to the other, but what the white-hair girl lacked in size and strength she made up for in deft, nimble speed. Her ground roll put her behind him before he could blink, now smiling with the thrill of the fight. She was on her feet with instantaneous grace before he could turn. With a hard kick, she shoved her foot into his back and had him on the ground. In one more leap, Amaris was atop him, beaming from ear to ear.

"Fuck!" He gasped from where he stared up at the sky.

The elder reevers made some commotion between cheers and boos as they watched.

Malik was momentarily conflicted between feeling proud of his friend and embarrassed at his own defeat, but he shoved her off of him while she beamed her glee. The men around the camp barked their approving laughs. Malik dusted off both his tunic and his pride while Amaris made a show of bowing in faux humility.

"Fighting you is like battling a rabbit with a sword! You're so damn agile!"

"Yes," she panted happily, unbothered by his comparison, "I've always fancied myself a bunny with a blade. Thanks for that."

He clapped her on the back and grinned, heading for the water.

Ash stepped up, "Do you have another round in you?"

Malik took a break from the water he'd been guzzling. "Not fair," he gasped between swallows. "If you beat her, it will be because I wore her down."

Amaris jutted her chin slightly, arching a brow at the challenge. "And if I beat him even after you've worn me down, all the better I'll be proven."

Most of her hair remained tied in a single braid down her back. Her white strands were slick with sweat, though loose pieces around her face coiled with the salt and heat of the day. Normally as pale as the snow, it was a bit amusing for the men to see Amaris in such a strawberry shade of red as the heat of early summer scorched her neck, hands and cheeks. She could feel the burn against her skin as though she'd set her face on a skillet and knew she'd need to rub tonic all over her body once she left the ring to prevent sunburn.

Odrin had been sitting off to the side, something like paternal pride on his face as he watched his tomato-colored rabbit with a sword. The bloodied, soft child he'd brought to the door of the keep—the girl who had been kept so gentle and safe— had a warrior's heart indeed, and now a warrior's skills to match.

Ash took a few steps toward her, allowing the tension to build before entering the sandy space reserved for sparring. She'd remained baking in the heat, still tasting the chalky cloud of dust from her fight with Malik and how it had scattered the fine, powdery grime into the air on their hot, windless day. Amaris suppressed the urge to shake out her limbs. She didn't want to appear as though she needed any extra effort in staying limber, even if she was feeling a bit tight after winning her scuffle with Malik.

Ash's red hair was fully tied up, not in a braid like Amaris's, but in a knot on top of his head in the same fashion as Malik's. They were already sweaty from their morning run, but as he glided by her, she was reminded once more of his distinct sweet smell of autumn's dying leaves. If anything, the sweat only accentuated his unique scent. She'd always wondered if it was a fae quality—the lure of scent—though now wasn't the best time to ponder such attributes. She was quite confident she smelled of dirt and sweat and like she was in need of a bath.

Ash was grinning a fox's smile, unable to keep the thrill from his eyes. She'd become increasingly fun to spar as the years had worn on. By now, Amaris was a rather formidable force. Her small size offered a lithe agility that none of the men could hope to master. The pair began circling each other, his blade hanging at his side, hers already in front guard.

"Ready, Ayla?"

She took the first swing. Ash saw the opportunity in her haste. The copper reever made a move as if to trip her, but she leapt out of his foot's path, turning the force from her failed swing into a smooth whirl until she was on her feet once more, creating space between them. His teeth flashed his amusement. What a long way she had come. She could have sworn she heard Odrin clap once from where he'd gathered on the sidelines, then hold his hands together as he leaned forward to watch them spar. Her avoidance had been textbook.

"My feet haven't been rooted in a long time, Ash!" She goaded him forward. "Though I suppose imagining me as an oak tree will only make it easier for me to best you. You know as well as I do that underestimating your opponent will get you killed."

She waited for Ash to make the next move, circling him like a predator. He was hopeful that her pride would keep her on the offensive in order to prove herself, but she was too smart to fall for the same mistake twice. When Ash surged for her, they crossed blades in a flurry of thrusts, each twist of the wrist slashing to the opposite side hoping to catch the opponent with a flank unprotected. The high, loud metallic clang as steel clashed was louder than the scraping of their shoes on the sand or the grunts of exertion.

"I know exactly how you fight," he swept and missed. "I taught you half of what you know!"

She laughed at that.

Amaris was as adept on her left as she was on her right, blocking and counter striking blow after blow. Ash retreated, opening up space between them to resume their slow, daring circles. The remaining reevers had all finished their morning exercises now and were lined around the ring, exchanging impressed sounds and murmurs each time a death blow was blocked. The white noise of their conversation seemed like a mixture of admiration and the placement of bets.

"Come on, you can take me out." Amaris taunted. "I'm already worn down, aren't I?"

He was huffing from the effort, but his teeth flashed in a crooked half-smile. "When did your roots grow wings?"

She swung from the top, but her blow came with too much force. When he countered her strike, he thrust both hands up and back, loosening her grip on her hilt. It slipped from her hands and he outstretched his own to catch it. His feet went back into the defensive position, a sword in each hand.

He shrugged, breathing heavily. He'd won her blade. "Shall we call it a match?"

She drew her right foot behind her left and lifted her fists.

"Why?" Her eyebrow arched, "Afraid to hit a girl?"

Odrin started to shout something as the reevers burst into their cheers as if at a sporting match. Ash shrugged a loose shoulder smirking behind the blades. The cackles and amusement that erupted from the surrounding reevers egged her on. She returned the smile, starlight twinkling behind her lavender eyes. Ash tossed the swords to the side and slowly raised his own fists. He tilted his head to one side.

"Fine. Dance with me," he tempted.

She unleashed the first blow—a kick to his chest. He caught her foot as it made purchase and twisted her leg, spinning her into the air. She stayed true to form as she swiveled, not fighting the movement. She flowed with the rotation and landed on both of her feet like a cat, one hand to the earth to balance her. Her land was graceful and as feline as every other element of her battle strategy.

Staying low, Amaris made a sweep for his shins that rolled into an uppercut. The red-haired faeling jumped over her sweep but her fist made contact with his jaw. She felt the impact ripple through her arm, hurting her knuckles slightly as a slip of air escaped her lips against the pain.

She could see Ash's vision danced as stars clouded his amber eyes, taking him a moment to blink them away. The ivory girl didn't give him the time he needed to catch his breath. She was close enough to him to use her elbow to drive into his midsection. The blow sent him back two steps and created just enough distance for her to bring up her knee and land a kick. She planted on her left foot and pivoted on its ball while she sent the power of her right foot into his sternum. The kick aimed for his chest once more, but rather than fall to the ground, Ash dropped back and to one knee, opening up his side so her second kick found air. He grabbed her leg from beneath and had her on the ground, facing the wrong direction. She was quick to her feet in the cloud of dust, but from his advantageous position, he was quicker.

She attempted to grunt in a twist, voice pitched against impending panic, but he had her in a lock.

It took half a heartbeat for his arms to grip her. Holding her from behind in a split second, he had one arm around her neck in the crease between his bicep and forearm, the hand from his other arm grasping the elbow into the sleeper hold.

Her eyes went wild for the second it took for her to realize she was being choked out, and in a frenzied final attempt to free herself, she moved her hips to the side just enough to thrust the heel of her hand into his manhood. Ash gasped and released his grip in pain and shock. The watching male crowd either laughed or barked at the cheap shot as she kneed him again, sending him to the ground. She didn't waste a second as she crossed to him, kneeling over her kill.

Her knee stayed on his throat as he stared up at her from his place on his back.

She leaned in close, her mouth close to his so the others couldn't hear. "Sorry about hurting your favorite part."

He put both hands on either side of her knee to hold the pressure off his windpipe, but had accepted defeat. "I'm sure you'll find a way to make it up to me later."

Amaris was up on her feet then, helping her sparring partner up with an outstretched hand. The reevers had loved the show. The men clapped her on the back with heavy, happy, calloused hands. At least two of them continued to cry foul about her cheap shot, but the others agreed that he'd need to keep his vulnerable places guarded in battle to anticipate the enemy. She was the undisputed victor.

The time had come for pork, summer fruits, and ale. It was a little early in the day for the beer to flow as freely as it did, but between the dramatic retellings of the match one would think that they hadn't all just been present at the same event. The men kept filling her mug, teasing Ash for leaving his manhood exposed to the enemy. Malik defended him, pink in the face as the men ruffled his golden hair. The dining hall was thick with the smell of their sweat, their dirt, and their day. The food was hot, the laughs came easily, and their hearts were light. Here at the keep, Amaris knew she was with her blood, her family.

11

The man was both young and handsome in the rakish sort of way one rarely saw in Priory. Nox has spotted him as soon as he'd entered the salon and kept her dark eyes trained loosely on the man while he made his way through the incense-laden haze of the lounge. Elegant tufts and silks lined the room, a few pillows with patrons already lounging on them as young women listened intently, feigning interest about the crop yields and or the investments or the politics they spieled. Aside from the boring chatter of patrons and the women who pretended to be enthralled, their in-house musician was a rather pretty woman whose fingers moved deftly and softly over her lute. She always knew what songs to play, picking up the tune when she read the room to encourage excitement, and selecting slow, sad ballads if the women needed to pander to emotional connections. Presently, the lutist seemed to be plucking the pleasant cords of a song with no name, continuously creating ambiance for the patrons and girls working the floor alike.

The room was thick with the same strong vanilla perfume she'd first detected on Millicent, accompanied by notes of sandalwood and lush, smoky burn of the sticks themselves. Every time she entered the salon, the scented haze triggered the part of her mind that readied her for the hunt. The lush smell acted like a signal, tingling some imaginary talons.

Tonight was different. This target was of particular importance, and everyone under The Selkie's roof knew it.

She'd kept to a shadow behind a pillar, sizing up her prey. She wasn't ready for him to see her yet, as first impressions were vital. He'd need to swallow a gulp or two of burning liquor, relaxing into the salon and its music before she revealed herself. If she played the game correctly, he'd convince himself that he'd been the one who first spotted her—and she always won the game.

The duke made his way directly to the bar and ordered a drink, not bothering to look at any of The Selkie's girls. He had the arrogance of a lordling who was familiar with getting whatever he wanted. It was obvious from his cocky strut across the room to the presumptuous way he'd cut in front of other patrons for his drink. The bartender's eyes had flitted briefly to Nox where she idled, then slid the man his two fingers of whiskey.

Once he had his glass in hand, he turned to open himself up to the room, elbows behind him on the counter. This duke was making it abundantly clear that he was unimpressed. It was evident he'd been to brothels, and his expression declared to the world that The Selkie would be nothing new. His golden-brown eyes began scanning for whatever life-changing encounter he'd heard whispers about, face slack with boredom. The young lordling took one, slow sip of his whiskey, then another.

Nox felt her lips twitch in anticipation, but she fought down the smile. It would do no good to gloat before the victory. Her dark eyes wandered to where the Madame had remained engaged in conversation with a patron, though she'd kept her peripherals trained on Nox and the duke the entire time. She was a shrewd businesswoman, magnanimous host, and an excellent multitasker.

It was time.

With a nod of confirmation from Millicent, the beautiful raven was ready to make herself seen. The lutist across the salon knew the game as well as anyone else in the lounge. She transitioned her song into the soft melodies of a love ballad. In a paper-thin silk dress that clung to her curves and a neckline so plunging she may as well have been naked, she allowed her eyes to touch the duke's brown-gold gaze from across the lounge. Once he saw her, the cacophony of the salon faded away, subdued to white noise in the background.

They made it too easy, she thought. Even from across the room, she knew he'd felt the world shift beneath him. The smug boredom had dissipated from his expression. He continued to hold his glass of whiskey, but he wasn't moving as he watched her.

The act of unintentionally brushing gazes while making herself seen was merely her opening move. She looked away—not shyly, but as though she had more important things to do. She waited for his counter movement, predicting the duke to shuffle a pawn through the invitation of prolonged eye contact.

Nox made a show of dangling the bait around the lounge for a few minutes. It was time for her to move her knight in their game of chess. This display of intrigue required her to chat with another girl, stroking a slow, idle hand down the bare skin of the girl's exposed back while casting sidelong looks at the lordling at the bar, heightening his anticipation with every moment that passed.

He'd counter with one of two moves. Either he'd remain passive and continue to push his pawns forward through hopeful looks, or he'd make a power move by buying her a drink.

The duke responded with the equivalent of his bishop.

He raked a hand through his loose, brown hair, eyes still trained on her. His body rotated toward the bartender, who'd been waiting for exactly such an event. The lordling had ordered Nox a glass of red wine and held it aloft, beckoning her to him with the offer of the floral, gilded wine glass. It was bold, without being too daring—the perfect secondary play.

The next step was the most important. The opening positions had been performed flawlessly, but she still had to reel him in. The duke would need to feel as though he were in charge of the match, confident in his victory even before she needed to use her queen.

With something of a wry smirk, Nox finally approached the bar and leaned into the space beside him as if she were the one who needed convincing. This was a stalling move—her second knight. She rested her elbow on the bar, arching a brow as she eyed the wine. Her curtain of dark hair tumbled over her shoulders. A common mistake was showing too much enthusiasm, which could be avoided by refusing to be the one to speak first. The highest-earning girls prompted the men to do all of the talking. And so, she waited. The duke lapped up the chase, eager to catch her attention with each word that passed over the threshold of his lips.

"Would you do me the honor of having a drink with me?"

Her lips twitched upward, revealing a hint of teeth. She could see the rush of endorphins flow through the man as he believed himself to be making progress. She idly wondered what piece he thought he'd played and how far alone he thought himself to be. Was this his rook? She extended her hand for the stemware, accepting it. She smelled the wine, but didn't drink.

"What's your name?" He asked.

"I'm Nox," she smiled, face relaxed in a posture meant to disarm the opponent.

"Aren't you going to ask mine?" He cocked a brow again, exercising the arch of his brow more often than one should.

"We'll see," she said, finally lifting the wine. She paused before drinking.

Her response had won her all the more favors. They toasted the air before drinking. She smiled fully then, white teeth glinting at the lordling. He was a fish on the line–an opponent who didn't realize how greatly he'd misjudged his competition. The man didn't look away from the depth of her dark, mesmerizing eyes—he made no effort to conceal that she had already won. His pretense had dropped. The man was utterly enraptured.

Yet, there were still moves to be made. Her eyes wandered away from the duke, landing on the lutist. She didn't need to signal the musician for the woman to understand her cue. She picked an up-tempo drinking song. Priory was a coastal city, and there were a number of sea shanties to choose from that would excite the crowd. Many of the more intoxicated patrons began to sing along, which brought the perfect level of too-loud rowdiness to the salon. Every time the lutist began the chorus, the clients would take over with jovial energy.

Meanwhile, the duke's compliments burbled out like water breaking over stones. After scarcely sipping half of her glass, Nox had heard enough. She tilted her head, as if struggling to listen to him speak over the happy chorus.

"It's a bit difficult to hear down here, don't you think?"

He agreed wholeheartedly that, yes, it was entirely too loud in the lounge. The duke was practically glued to her as she led him away from the bar, far from the haze of vanilla and sandalwood, and beckoned him to follow her up the stairs, distancing themselves from the tufts and silks and prying eyes of patrons. Nox didn't look at the others, but she knew that if she'd met Millicent's gaze, the Madame would have been concealing a thin smirk.

There was something childlike about the way the duke smiled while he looked at her, his eyes wide and expectant as they'd entered a private room with a four-post bed. The click of the lock behind them had been heavy with implication. The lordling's eyes matched his hair, both golden brown and glittering with excitement. Nox smiled back through dark, lowered lashes, though it was an evocative, conciliatory smile. She knew enough of male eagerness to understand she'd have to temper his haste. She also knew enough of her own thirst to know she'd have to proceed carefully if she wanted to keep him alive. While greedy impatience colored his face, her returning gaze was positively bloodthirsty.

She gestured for him to find his way to the bed while she stepped behind an ornately carved wooden screen, the gaps in its pictures barely obscuring his view of her near-nakedness. He hungrily eyed her as she stripped off her black silk dress and let it dangle it over the carved separation. The lordling hadn't realized how long ago he'd lost the game. The duke crawled onto the bed eagerly, watching her as she stepped out in a thigh-short, practically sheer dressing gown with nothing underneath.

Check.

The room, the bed, the silks, the scents, the girl all screamed of sex. This was not the quick, back-tavern draining of one's balls, or the chaste lovemaking of the marital bed, but the silks and perfumes and energy of wild, passionate affairs. The room did not smell of the lounge and its incense. There was no evidence of haze, smoke, vanilla or sandalwood common to the salon here. This was Nox's room, and it radiated her scent. The air was thick with plums and dark spices. His senses were overloaded with pleasure before they'd even begun. She watched his eyes for the tell-tale, dizzying glaze that betrayed his hunger over the prospect of their entanglement alone.

She'd heard the report of his reluctance in the debriefing. She knew the duke had been entirely sure that The Selkie would be yet another event in his life that was over-promised and under-delivered. She hadn't been worried. Getting him in the door had been the hard part. The exchange downstairs had been executed with textbook precision. Seeing his expression now, she knew she'd won the match. She still had one move left to play.

"Tell me why you want me," she purred.

His animated eyes widened a bit. She was finished with playing coy. It was time for power. She knew enough of his reputation to understand the bashful maiden would not impress him. She knew enough of men to know what would thrill him. He saw her not just as a bronzed beauty, but as an absolute force of nature, unlike any woman, or man, he'd come across. He'd been said to have experienced more than enough dalliances in his reckless thirst for life that she knew she'd have to bring out her best closing moves to count him amongst her stable.

"You're the most beautiful thing I've ever seen. Your hair, your eyes, your incredible body… what I can see of it, that is." His words were heavy with implication. He wanted to see more. "You could be the goddess herself."

She enjoyed the answer, circling him a bit as her bare feet moved her slowly toward the bed. He laid on the tufted comforter, watching her very casually walk around the four-post bed to one side. The light was sensually low, but not so low that he couldn't make out every detail of her mouth, her full breasts, her hips and the way the sheer fabric left little to the imagination. She was nearly close enough to touch. The duke leaned forward, extending an eager hand to close the space between them.

Nox tutted her tongue in a playful, authoritative correction. She took a seat on the end of the bed, the weight of her hips compressing the duvet in a way that made him long for her to rest her weight on him. She slid her dressing gown to the side in such a way so as to expose only her shoulder. Her eyes sparkled and the lordling felt her energy course through him from across the room.

The cost of a night with her set expectations exceptionally high, and she could see the longing in his boyish eyes as he was ready to sink his teeth into the experience his money had bought. Her price had been a small fortune of the inheritance left for him, but she would be worth it. She dragged her eyes over him with a feline intensity, and every tremble in his face, from the throb of his jaw, the tension in his eyes, to the twitch of his eager fingers conveyed this was lust more potent than he'd encountered before. She felt rather smug, knowing full well that the man before her would have paid the price three times over.

The Duke of Henares had become consumed by the numbing boredom experienced only by those who lacked nothing and wanted everything. He'd tasted, seen, purchased, traveled, and taken the world by its very balls.

In his twenty-three years of drinking and whoring and falling asleep in the opium dens of his lands in Henares to the Queen's walled city of Aubade, the women, the men, the gambling and drinks had grown so dull. The ale, the pleasure houses, the frilly proper society ladies who feigned their walks through the gardens in Henares just to catch his eye tired him. There was no drink, drug or depravity that brought him thrill any longer. He'd highly considered throwing daggers at moving house cats just to feel something. If something didn't pique his interest soon, he'd try his hand at throwing knives and live bait.

His father had been a relatively fair man, and hadn't the faintest clue how he'd raised such a lecherous miscreant. He'd failed his son terribly, and didn't know what he could possibly do to make it better.

The young duke's father had pushed opportunity after opportunity into his lap, desperate for something to force the little lordling mature and grow into his father's shoes, particularly as his own health had started to fail. The harder the elderly man pressed, the more the degenerate young lordling had grown in his demonstrations of rebellion. When the older man had fallen terminally ill, he called for his son to hear his deathbed wishes, but the boy had been ruining the virtue of some merchant's daughter, making himself unreachable.

His father passed unceremoniously in the night, surrounded by the kind servants of Henares. When the power had passed to the new duke, he had no more idea how to handle his newfound title than a child thrown into a pond would know how to swim.

So he did what he knew best: he indulged.

Counselors and advisors had urged the young man to sit down and take his title seriously. They'd begged him with the threat of reporting his neglect to the regency, compelling him to make plans to take charge of Henares. All he wanted to do was yank life by its tits and enjoy what was left of the short, miserable existence one had in the All Mother's lighted kingdom.

He hadn't been difficult to track down.

The Duke of Henares had been drowning the memory of his father in the rowdiest tavern in his city. A woman who seemed to be composed entirely of freckles approached the bar, feigning nonchalance. He'd scarcely looked her way, loosely interested in her large bosom and ginger hair. She slid in from the side, ordering a drink as if disinterested in his presence. He shook her off before she had a chance to open her mouth.

"Not tonight, my dear," he drawled, "though I'm sure whatever you have under that bodice is spectacular."

He was a few pints in, and the girl offered to get him another. She spoke loudly, her sweet voice lilting above the sound of the fiddle and the roar of the card games being played near where he sat at the bar. Her freckles did lightly tickle his curiosity, as he'd never seen someone so speckled in his life. He wondered how far down along her neckline they traced.

She grinned dismissively, her eyes barely touching his. She seemed unbothered by the hobby, sour scent of ale that undoubtedly emanated from him. "Oh, I'm not looking for companionship. I've already had the best there is."

The young Duke of Henares raised a half-amused, half-annoyed eyebrow, "Trying to make me jealous? I'm glad a man keeps your bed mussed up. May we all be so lucky as to find someone to fuck until our days are done. Here, here."

He raised his mug to his own insincere cheer and she laughed lightly, turning her body away from him as she murmured her own musings to the crowd. "I don't much care for the company of men."

Now this piqued his interest, and he allowed the gentle pucker of his lips and movement of his brow to say as much. Women with such proclivities were never so bold as to be open about their preferences in public. He admitted to himself he did enjoy the pleasure of any sex that would tumble with him in the bedroom, and was quite curious about what could have been so enticing as to bring her to speak freely of her predilections. He eyed the strawberry-haired girl more carefully, allowing himself to one again picture how far down those freckles extended against her tight corset and the pillowing parts that tumbled out. He envisioned a second woman's soft hands, and softer chest pressed into hers.

The ginger nodded absently, bringing the ale to her lips, acting somewhat lost to her memories.

The duke urged her on, adjusting his posture so that he was fully engaged. "Well, do share with a poor lad. Make my night a bit better, would you."

The freckled girl laughed, "Normally I'd say a lady shouldn't kiss and tell but this... this changed my life. Have you been to Priory?"

He shook his head, leaning toward her further. "Your beloved is in Priory?"

"Oh, to call her mine." She drank deeply, gasping against the refreshing, bright pops of the bubbles in her ale. The sounds of the rowdy Henares alehouse drown their thoughts for a moment, exacerbating the pleasant memories that stole her away. "This goddess belongs to no one. She is mine as much as she's anyone who can afford her, if only for a moment. Though, I'll be damned, it's a once in a lifetime price to pay. I will say, there aren't words for the night we shared. It ruined all men for me. And to think! I was once engaged to a merchant's son."

She laughed and motioned to the barmaid as if to pay her tab. The duke felt his interest wane once more, waving the freckled girl away.

"I've had whores," he said dismissively.

"I'm sure you have," she began to stand, gulping deeply at her drink as she paid her tab. "And when you tire of your whores—as all earthly things become tiresome—and if you find yourself seeking something transcendent, look for The Selkie."

That had been all.

The stranger was gone nearly as soon as she'd arrived.

She'd left with her ale practically half full. He finished his own and set out to walk back to the family estate. The young duke spent the walk trying to clear his head, but he couldn't shake her words. It gnawed at him for hours, then days, then weeks, constantly chewing at the back of his mind. The nagging sensation grew more tempting, more undeniable, consuming his thoughts as he sat through the dull droning of meetings and magistrates. Responsibilities and boring women and flirtatious knights and irksome letters came for him day in and day out until finally, he found himself on the threshold of a stately townhouse in the center of Priory with a waifish mermaid's silhouette emblazoned on the door.

She nearly had him.

"Nox?" He repeated her name reverently.

"Mmm," she agreed, watching him with something that might have been curiosity. The duke unbuttoned his shirt a bit hastily as he watched her now and the glossy-haired beauty chastised him with a wicked smile. Nox hiked her dressing gown up over her thigh and began to move toward him. Rather than mount him as he'd hoped, she slid into the space behind him, resting his own golden brown head on her soft chest and rubbing his neck and arms with her gentle hands. It was a bit more predictable of a first move than he'd expected. She could see this disappointment on his face, and it was all she could do to keep from rolling her eyes. Predictable. Surely, he'd entered her rooms expecting whips, wax and knife play, but instead found himself getting a massage.

He'd have to be patient.

She couldn't pull her finishing move. Not yet.

"My Lord, you carry so much tension. I can't imagine the pressure you're under."

He agreed with her assessment, attempting to shake off his annoyance, "You don't know the half of it."

The banter in the lounge had been charming, but his eagerness would undo them if she couldn't keep him focused. He licked his lips and attempted to turn his body to make a move, but she held him to her, forcing him to stay in the massage. The man was ready to touch her, taste her, see for himself if there was something exceptional about the stunning creature behind him. Of course, he believed he'd spent enough days talking with counselors and advisors about his role in the kingdom. He'd come to The Selkie to drink deeply of her sweetness and forget.

She concurred, her voice a low, erotic drip of honey as each word stuck to the one before it. "And I'm so glad I don't have to! The kind of responsibilities a lord of your stature must have... it's understandably too much to handle."

She ran a hand along his arm, her nails tracing soothing lines down his veins.

"I didn't say that it was too much," his protest came hastily, torn between focusing on the tingling trail of sensation she left on his arm and his desire to argue against her implication. "I just don't see the point in it all. What does it matter what the queen wants to do with my men, or how much we owe the crown? Whatever Moirai wants, she gets. She can take them for all I care."

Nox reached a hand into his shirt, her fingers moving in lines along his chest. She could feel the steady thud of his heart as she carved a path between the demarcation of his pectorals. His skin was too soft, almost as if it had been waxed and oiled himself before he'd arrived. "I agree," she soothed. "I wouldn't have the sense about me to deal with troops, either."

He struggled to find his words as he emphasized his point. The duke flushed with irritation once more, "I have plenty of sense. I just don't bother myself with her wars. I don't see why she needs me to strategize if she's on a witch hunt to find where Raascot has infiltrated. She clearly knows exactly where they're hiding, so why bother me at all if she's requesting a dispatch to Yelagin? Moirai knows I can't say a damned thing to the contrary, or I'm a traitor to the crown. So explain to me why I must have these consultations with ambassadors and feign my say in it when she's going to take however many she wants, wherever she wants."

Yelagin. There it was.

Their game of chess had come to a close. She was ready to finish the match.

Nox withdrew her hand and pulled herself on top of him, straddling the young man, enjoying the view of his gold-brown hair and gleam of his eyes as they admired her. She did love the way they looked at her. She was art, and they worshiped her as such. His excitement was contagious. She was excited, herself, though for very different reasons. She was just past twenty-one, now with the full-figured body of a woman and the ethereal youth of something a bit more predatory than an angel. Her womanly hips opened up for him. She appreciated the music of his moan as he watched her.

"By the All Mother you are exquisite," he reached to cup her breast, but she stopped his hand, pressing it to her lips and kissing it gently. The duke made a slightly frustrated face once more, but paused obediently. This was her game. He was here to play by her rules. Reaching under the pillow behind him, her breasts dangled dangerously near his mouth beneath the dressing gown that hid them. When she sat back up, she'd pulled out a long band of silk and grinned wickedly.

"If it pleases you, my lord, I'd like to please my lord."

He beamed the tawdry, open smile of the foolhardy at her play on words. His manhood throbbed, aching to be touched by her. "Goddess, yes."

Nox winked through her black eyelashes and began to bind his right wrist to the bedpost, and then his left, watching the man tense in anticipation. Once his hands were secured, she approached him like a mountain cat from below, crawling toward him, drowning him in the plums and cinnamon and nutmegs and spices of her scent. She tugged on his britches, pulling them down over his hips and unleashing him from the constrictive cage of his pants. The duke wriggled like a child at playtime, absolutely delighted at her dominance.

The raven-haired beauty began to lower her painted mouth, taunting him with her hot breath before she pulled back up and made a sound meant to say *not so fast*. The tension heightened his thrill. He wanted her so badly, his desperation had a flavor. It was a tangy, sticky want—no, a need. Goddess, she was lucky she'd tied his hands, or he'd have leapt for her. His reckless lust glinted wildly in his eyes.

"Tell me how badly you want me," she murmured. Nox moved to her knees, hovering slightly above him. He arched his hips to meet her but it wasn't enough to bridge the gap. He was unable to make contact with the angel above him.

"I want you so badly."

"What would you do to have me?" She slid her dressing robe off the rest of the way, naked beneath the gauzy, silken scrap of clothing. Her body was lean, her breasts were supple. Her skin was flushed with the heat of their arousal.

"I'd do anything."

She bit her lip, following his gaze as he soaked her in. "Would you bring me to your estate?"

"And fuck you every day," he answered confidently, ever the cocky bastard.

"Would you give me a duchess's title?" She pushed her hands into his chest, her breasts pressed together to accentuate their fullness with the motion. She dug her fingers slightly into the muscles of his chest, and he made a sound at the small hurt at her sharp nails.

His words blurred together, hurried with his eagerness. "I'd make the people worship you like I do."

She licked her palm and lowered her wetted hand to him, teasing him with the touch of her fingers. She encircled his shaft, allowing his appreciative moan to fill her as she made him slick and ready for her. "Would you give me your lands?"

He groaned against her touch, closing his eyes as he answered, "All of them."

"And your men?"

"They're yours to command."

"And your soul?"

"It belongs to you," he whispered.

Checkmate.

Her hand remained upon his shaft, dangling his tip just at her entrance. She guided his length in as she eased herself down ever so slowly. She slid the duke inside of her and watched the twinkle in his eye as every inch of him became soaked in the starlight and glitter and oceans that knit the very fabric of the universe. Nox moaned a true, wild sound of delight as the sensation within her exploded, the vibrancy of his life force coursing through him.

She inhaled sharply at the intense, perfect lightning that bound them.

Oxytocin flowed into her, a dam of the chemical erupting from the lake of the lordling's life force, now a river flowing from him to her. She arched her back, opening her mouth in a gasp, the delicious drug filling her veins, her capillaries, her lungs. Her hips thrust with the electricity, draining the river, sucking it dry. The hard, thick rod of dopamine and serotonin and heart and soul throbbed within her as she moved. She felt herself begin to increase her speed, her desire swelling as endorphins bubbled within her. Her back relaxed from his groan of ecstasy, and she saw the light in his eyes begin to dim. The lordling's body went limp as she rode him. His eyes remained open; his mouth slackened. She looked at him and frowned, doing little to conceal her disappointment. Controlling this part was more art than science. Her euphoria had felt a bit like a feeding frenzy each time she consumed the oxytocin, but she was learning to tame it.

"Goddess damn you, you're not even going to let me finish?" She looked at him, frustrated over the climax she'd been denied. Nox took several stilling breaths and forced herself to stop. She wanted to continue. She wanted to consume him. She wanted to feel the release of climax and lust and desire as she swam with orgasmic delight. She wanted to drink deeply from this well until nothing was left, but she rarely got what she wanted. This mission was too important for her wants.

The duke looked back, unseeing.

"Well, you didn't last near as long as you promised. I thought I was supposed to be pleasured all night." She was half-amused, still pulsing with the cocktail of drugs made solely of pleasure, hunger, and chemistry. Her head vibrated pleasurably, but she'd need to clear her thoughts if she had any hope of getting things done tonight. It was better than three bottles of fine wine. More dizzying than the numbing tonics healers often used. Better than presents or first kisses or breakfast in bed. It was the best fucking thing in the world, and she'd need to tear herself from it.

"Come on," she slapped him a few times on the face, then checked his pulse, the dying duke's semi-stiff manhood still inside her. He wasn't dead, but he was close.

Perhaps she had gone a bit too far, as was easy to do when she found herself drunk on the power. This part had gotten easier with time, but she still struggled. She needed him alive if her ownership was to mean anything. Even without the young duke, she'd still make her way to Yelagin, but it would be so much easier to have a puppet title-holder carving a path for her. She needed to steady herself and think rationally. As much as she wanted to cling to every drop, it was worth sparing a spark or two for the mission.

She slipped him out of the wet grip within her, but her legs remained planted on each side of his hips in a straddle.

Nox leaned down to the young lord's mouth, planting her lips gently on his. She breathed a droplet of life back into the duke and watched the faintest spark of candlelight reignite behind his otherwise listless, caramel eyes.

"There you are," she purred, satisfied.

She dismounted and made her way to the bedpost to begin untying his wrists. Dazed, he was whispering something about how sensational she was, and she agreed with the low murmurs of a lover. His compliments continued spilling over his lips. She was even more beautiful, even more magnificent than ever before. She sat him up and re-buttoned his shirt for him. Nox pulled the translucent piece of fabric around her shoulders and tied it at the waist as she leaned into the duke.

"I need you to listen to what I'm about to tell you."

He nodded, entranced. "Anything you say."

How long had it been since Nox had seen her first corpse?

Of course, tonight the reanimation process had been as simple as breathing, quite literally. She hadn't always been so lucky. The faces of the dead did haunt her.

Her first brush with death had been as a child.

A flu had once swept through Farleigh's dorms, gripping so many of the orphans with the spindly fingers of illness. This influenza hadn't discriminated against its victims, shaking matrons and children alike. Amaris was one of the many who'd fallen terribly ill. Nox had never been so afraid in her life as she was while she watched her friend sweat and shake. The ivory girl had been so hot, her pale forehead blistering to the touch, despite how she'd shivered as if she'd been left to suffer in the snow. Nox had held her through the night until her fever broke. It had been the first time Nox had prayed. She'd begged the All Mother to let Amaris live.

Nox had been one of the fortunate few who managed to never get sick. She'd been kissed by good health, avoiding the colds, swollen tonsils, runny noses, and mysterious ailments of the blood that took without mercy. While her health remained vibrant, other children had not been so lucky. They lost three young ones that icy winter, their bodies covered with sheets by the matrons. The ground had been frozen, but Matron Mable—ever the beacon of faith in that faithless house—had worked for two days to dig their graves, chipping away at the arctic soil as if chiseling stone. Nox hadn't seen the faces of the children after they'd passed on to be with the All Mother, so she was left with her memories of them playing, laughing and pink-cheeked.

The first time she'd seen the lifeless face of a man had been at The Selkie.

She arrived in Priory to work, but not on the salon floor with the others. Her first year in service to Madame Millicent had been behind the bar, mixing drinks and taking the patron's coins. She tried mulberry gin with the clients, learned the names and vintages of fine wines, could anticipate who needed another pint of ale before they asked, and had thrown back fiery whiskey with establishment's frequenters who enjoyed the faces she made as it burned her throat.

Though the Madame had intended to put her right to work, the woman and her elaborately pinned hair had taken a liking to her new, prized acquisition. They'd scarcely entered the vanilla-scented lounge on their first tour when Millicent had announced rather suddenly that Nox should begin her servitude behind the bar. The dark-haired girl had possessed a rather charming effect on adults throughout her life, and felt exceedingly fortunate that her gift had extended to Millicent. Though she hadn't understood the Madame's decision, Nox wasn't foolish enough to look a gift horse in the mouth. She milked her time as a barmaid, happy to run Millicent's errands, clean the rooms after the girls had finished with their clients, and flirt with the regulars who returned night after night as long as it meant avoiding the salon and the duties of the private rooms.

Then, she met Theo.

Theo, All Mother rest his soul, had been a man of thirty with the clean, soft hands and babyface of someone who had never known labor. He was a barrister, which meant his entire life revolved around the paperwork and litigation of common law—all profoundly boring, in Nox's opinion. He had come to The Selkie four months prior, intent on finding a woman to take his long-overdue virginity. He'd paid a girl handsomely, his coins damp with sweat due to the nerves of his clammy hands. Once he'd gotten up to her room, his nerves had overwhelmed him. He'd stammered a few things about what was decent and proper. He urged her to put her robe back on and insisted they talk about their childhoods. Despite feeling terribly awkward, the poor girl had politely obliged, fully clothed. She'd sat with Theo for his two prepaid hours while he asked her invasive questions about her siblings, her food allergies, her faith, and what had resulted in her life in a whorehouse. When his time was up, she'd firmly requested that Millicent pair him with another girl the next time he visited. Something about his shame had made her feel sullied, and she wouldn't allow the humiliation into her heart if she had any hope of continuing her line of work at the brothel.

Theo had come back the next night and tried to catch the same girl's eye, but she had pointedly avoided him. Nox dutifully poured him a chilled pint and chatted with the disheartened man. He finished his drink and he thanked her for her company and for listening to his woes on life and women.

Night after night Theo returned, usually guilting Nox into joining him for a glass of blackberry wine that she would cordially sip throughout the evening. Before long, she knew she was looking into the doe-eyed glaze of a man who fancied himself in love. While he did indeed ask her about herself, he preferred to do most of the talking, as was common with all of The Selkie's patrons. She listened, nodded, smiled, and always knew how to ask the correct, polite follow-up questions in order to keep him drinking, tipping, and returning. As long as his coin flowed and beverages for the clients were poured, lubricating their moods and the wallets for the girls working the floor, Millicent appeared more than happy with her performance as a barkeep.

Soon, Theo was spending every evening at The Selkie. He had no family, he'd said, as his parents had passed, and he'd never married. He told Nox that she was his only family. It had given her a distinctly disquieting feeling, though she'd done her best to smile. Theo did have something of a knack for making women uncomfortable.

Before approaching Millicent, he asked Nox directly if she was available for The Selkie's private rooms. The expression he'd made when she said she'd never worked on the salon floor made his face shine like the sun itself. He glowed with the romanticism as he painted a fanciful picture of the two of them, their bodies intertwined, deflowering one another in the most beautiful union. Meanwhile, Nox did her best to find excuses to spend more of her time on the opposite sides of the bar, putting as much physical distance between the ever-growing feeling of distress that his awkward presence brought. Other patrons chuckled at Theo's pitiful advances, often tipping Nox more generously than they usually would help ease her obvious discomfort. At the very least, the love-lorn virgin provided amusement for the other men who preferred their drinks in the company of beautiful women.

When Theo asked Millicent for Nox's hand in marriage, she'd calmly quoted him a bride price that was just astronomical enough to buy Queen Moirai's crown directly from atop her head, and he'd settled on inquiring about the cost of her maidenhood. Theo's frequent visits had given the Madame plenty of time to investigate his estate, and she knew exactly how much the man could afford before it broke him. She asked that number plus a single crown more.

The flicker in his eyes between panic, desperation, lust and love had amused the Madame greatly, but she knew all about the foolishness of men in love. The fortune Theo would pay to be the first to have Nox in his bed was more than enough to cover her long-forgotten hopes of having a silver-haired girl in The Selkie. She informed Nox rather unceremoniously that the girl would not be bartending that night. The freckled Emily took her shift serving drinks. The strawberry girl offered a sympathetic smile and comforting touch to Nox as she moved from behind the bar and walked numbly up the stairs. Nox was shown directly to one of the smaller rooms in the townhouse.

It would be her first night working, and she felt sick.

She'd numbly bathed, perfumed, and sat upon the bed in waiting for the rotund man so deeply in love with her while she fought feelings of disgust and nausea. She couldn't care less what he looked like. She'd grown to hate him for his refusal to see things for what they were. He'd painted a romanticized narrative onto Nox, viewing her as a concept of affection rather than a human. She couldn't bring herself to feel anything but annoyed and physically ill at the knowledge that he was to be her first.

Theo entered the room with nervous energy, hanging his hat and coat beside the door. He headed to sit beside her on the bed, then thought better of it and took off his shoes, too. They finally sat beside one another, both dreadfully uncomfortable. Still, Theo's sweet, misguided love for her emboldened him to make the first move. Doing her best to focus on the fact that he was a relatively good man—a sweet, misguided man—helped her abstain from the urge to cringe as he touched her. He hadn't known what to do with his tongue when he kissed her, and it felt terribly like a worm as it pried her lips open. It had been her first kiss.

"You taste like rich, ripe plums," he'd said with a poet's conviction.

She'd been told as much throughout her life, as even Amaris had commented a time or two on how her very skin had shimmered with the scent of plum. How pleasant for him, she thought. She resisted the urge to respond by telling him that he tasted like stewed turnips.

Attempting a picture of heroism, he fumbled an attempt to scoop her onto her back. He failed, and she wriggled somewhat awkwardly backward on her elbows to position herself toward the center of the bed. He kissed her on the mouth far too many times, which she found particularly repugnant, and desperately wished he'd go ahead and get whatever was supposed to happen over with. She let her eyes shut, which he took as a sign of endearment, but she had every intention to use this as an opportunity to visit the detached void where she could float when she couldn't exist within herself. She'd gone there while suffering the bishop's wrath. She'd gone there when she'd been left on the landing outside of the kitchen. And she would go there now.

Theo kissed the soft parts of her body gently. Perhaps if it had been someone else, the sensations might have been pleasant. She tried to imagine what it would have been like if someone she loved were against her shoulder, her neck, her stomach.

She squeezed her eyes tightly and thought of another mouth, of other lips. She was glad his face was too distracted with burrowing himself against her flesh to see how intently she scrunched her face and eyes to block out his movements. She needed to relax if she was going to succeed at drifting off into the dark, shadowed nothingness.

She breathed out slowly through her nose and felt the darkness behind her eyes deepen. This was what she needed.

Her mind left her body as she forced herself to think of something—anything—pleasant. She pictured a delicate, female touch. Her mind wandered to the scent of juniper and wet winter days, envisioning the girl she loved so deeply as the one touching her neck, her arms, her inner thighs, the very center of her. Nox had resisted every time her fantasies had wandered to these desires, but in this moment, there was only one person she wanted to share the bed with. Her first kiss, her first sensual touches had been reserved for someone so special. At least in the escapism of her mind, they could stay that way.

No, she never let herself think of Amaris in this way. She loved her deeply, but she didn't permit herself these fantasies. She didn't let herself want these things unless she knew that Amaris might want them too. But for now. Just for tonight. Just for this experience, behind the dark void of her floating emptiness, she needed to believe they were together.

When she was entered, she held onto the single, tender thought of someone she loved, hoping she was safe, hoping she was happy. Nox meditated on that love, holding it close to her heart, letting it fill her.

Her reverie was shattered as an instant as a thundering weight came down on her, pinning her to the bed.

She gasped, then yelped. She nearly suffocated on the flesh of some part of his body that had pressed against her mouth involuntarily. Her eyes had flashed open in surprise, shattering her quiet escapism. Theo had fully collapsed. She was pinned beneath the unsupported weight of his limp naked body.

"Theo!" Nox gasped angrily once more, trying to shove him off of her. "Theo, get off! Get up!"

Panic began to rise in her as she realized he was unresponsive, and she was still trapped with him inside of her. The air was being forced out of her lungs by the sheer compression of his weight. She let out a scream and scrambled to get out from underneath the collapsed man, thrashing and twisting until she managed to remove herself from the crushing position. It was an effort that required more strength than she'd thought she possessed, as the dead weight of a lifeless body had smothered her. She cried out again, jerking and shoving as he'd proved heavier than she could handle.

Nox could only imagine what it must sound like, but she was scarcely able to free herself and didn't care how many grunts of effort it took to writhe out from beneath a corpse.

"Nox?" Millicent's voice was painted as professionalism, thinly veiling whatever underlying emotion she'd felt as she rushed to the girl's door. Her screams must have been heard throughout The Selkie of the Madame had come running. Nox had finally clambered off the bed and opened the door, heaving for breath, tears spilling over her eyes.

Nox had no air in her lungs as she stood naked and trembling, clutching the brass doorknob. Her jaw was slackened. Her dark eyes were confused and wild.

"Did he hurt you?"

She shook her head wordlessly, still shaking. She covered her breasts with her arms as she melted into the wall, sinking slowly into a seated fetal position on the floor.

Millicent took one look at the naked girl, then over her shoulder to the man who remained face-down on the bed. The Madame pushed into the room and shut the door behind her. Millicent crossed over to Theo and rolled him onto his side through a grunt of gargantuan effort. She lowered her ear to his mouth, checking for the tell-tale heat, sound or moisture of breathing. The Madame lifted a hand to feel for the artery on his throat.

She shrugged slightly. "Don't worry, dear, he paid in advance. You can take the rest of the night off, of course. I'll handle things here."

Nox's eyes bulged like she was a fish who'd been taken from the water as the calloused Madame brushed her hands, sniffing dismissively.

"He's dead," Nox choked. "He's dead."

Millicent motioned as if to leave when she caught the girl's eyes again. The look of shock that flashed across the Madame's face was an expression Nox had never seen. The woman looked as if she'd seen a true phantom, jaw dropping and eyes practically doubling as they widened. She remained frozen near the bed for a moment, the same shock stuck to her face.

Nox raised a hand to her face to see if perhaps there'd been blood or something horrible on her that she hadn't noticed, patting at her hair and cheeks before looking back at the Madame in confusion.

Millicent closed the space between them. She knelt on the ground in front of the young woman. The Madame grabbed Nox by the chin and tilted it up, peering down into her eyes at an unknown revelation.

At first, she shook her head in amazement. Then, a slow, delectable smile spread across Millicent's lips.

"Well, well, well. What have we here?"

12

To her credit, Millicent had handled the nightmarish events swiftly, quietly and efficiently. The woman knew exactly which men of disrepute to call to discard something like the corpse of a middle-class barrister with no family or title. A perk of being the city's most elite Madame was doubtless the blackmail she had been able to compile on its patrons in an infinitely growing record of their darkest deeds. The things she knew could topple kingdoms, and when she needed to call in favors, they were done without question.

"I killed him," Nox was still caught in a state somewhere between her conscious attempt to detach and the numb horror of the corpse in her bed. "He's dead. I killed him. I killed him."

"Hush, dear." Millicent didn't have time to deal with Nox's feelings at the moment. She was busy orchestrating extraction and disposal.

"Will the constabulary come for me?" She managed to ask.

Millicent had laughed at that and proceeded to ignore the girl. Her response had only one meaning. Nox ascertained from the Madame's utter lack of concern that the law would bother getting involved, considering half of the constabulary frequented The Selkie.

In a vile act that flew in the face of the All Mother's goodness, the men stinking of booze and piss who had removed the body had simply feigned Theo to have been too drunk to stand. They'd splashed a strong liquor on his clothes so that the scent rolled off of him, laughing away the limp legs of their supposedly unconscious friend as they walked him out of the establishment through the front door, his hat low and feet dragging behind him. The patrons hadn't batted an eye as the round-faced regular had been taken from its grounds.

He'd been given no dignity in death.

Nox was a wreck. She'd risen from her fetal position on the floor and had begun pacing the room, clutching her hands to her upper arms in a hug in an attempt to self-soothe. She had been a barmaid at a brothel, this had been true. A regular had fallen for her and paid to take her maidenhood, this had been true. He had been inside her when he—

She shuddered again and felt her stomach roil as her dinner came up. She was going to vomit. Nox caught most of the acid and liquid in her hand as she spun for the chamber pot that the women had kept in the rooms in case a patron had been too tipsy amidst his session to make it to the bathing room to piss. There were a number of contingencies for the disgusting tendencies of men. This pot was blissfully clean— goddess be praised—before she vomited the remaining contents of her stomach into it. Between the nightmarish events, the disgust with herself, and the texture of the half-digested food in her throat, her stomach churned again and again, forcing her to empty any last drop until she was merely dry-heaving.

Her fingers clutched the cool edges of the chamber pot as her back continued to flex and convulse with the heaves.

Emily entered with a glass of water and a damp towel.

The freckled, ginger girl who had also grown up in Farleigh had been taken to The Selkie roughly six months before Nox's arrival. She remembered Emily's purchase vividly, as it had been the same day

Millicent had set her sights on Amaris. Given the dark-haired girl's year behind the bar, Emily had eighteen months of experience with patrons under her belt, or rather, atop her.

"It gets easier," Emily said, rubbing her back lightly in soft, circular motions.

"Has anyone ever died while inside you?" Nox spat into the pot, not lifting her eyes. She took a drink of the water, swirled it into her mouth, and spat again.

Emily kept her voice soft and compassionate, hands still moving in comforting circles. "Me? No, I can't say I'm so fortunate."

Nox glared up from where she clutched the pot at the gentle joke.

Emily continued rubbing her back. She let her eyes drift toward the wall as she looked into a memory. "When I was first here, a girl did tell me about an elderly gentleman who had dropped dead from the sight of her tits!" She smiled sadly, as it was one of their favorite stories to tell in their hellhole. "I do think she may have been embellishing, as he had been years overdue to go home to be with the goddess. His children were quite embarrassed to collect their father's body from a brothel."

Cautiously certain she had nothing left to vomit, she took another small sip of water and shifted her weight to the wall, her back pressed against it. She used the damp towel to wipe her mouth and clean her hands before returning the soiled rag to Emily.

"Do you want me to stay with you?"

Nox eyed her freckled colleague. They hadn't been friends at Farleigh, though they hadn't been enemies, either. Their time under the same roof in Priory had bonded them. Emily had always had her sister to keep her company until the day she was torn from her younger sibling's arms. Nox had considered Amaris so much more than a sister, but the rip that happened when they were separated on that late autumn day might be something she and Emily had in common. Nox shook her head.

"No," she felt the void call to her like an old friend, her voice detaching from her body as she allowed a numbness to drift in and out of her heart and mind. It comforted her when life was too unbearable to handle. She allowed the darkness to answer for her, voice flat. "I'm sure the Madame will want to speak with me."

"Okay," Emily agreed, still quiet. She left her hand on Nox's back for a minute longer, "Please call on me, though. If you want to talk, or want company, or…" she didn't finish her thought. Slowly, she rose to her feet and left Nox to where she remained near the pot. "I'll be right back," she promised.

Emily had left the cup of water beside her reluctantly deflowered friend and disappeared for a few moments. She reappeared with Nox's nightgown, a pair of socks, and a robe made for warmth rather than the gauzy scrap of fabric intended for seduction. Nox gave what might have been a smile, and Emily departed, leaving her alone in the room with the ghost of a dead man.

She closed the lid on the chamber pot. The night was disgusting enough without the smell of bile filling the room.

It took Nox a long time to find her way to her feet, but once she stood and changed into her nightclothes, she began to feel a bit better. She opened her window a crack to allow fresh air to move into the space. The night was cool and damp, and always tinged with the coastal presence of salt. It was a welcomed distraction.

Staying as far away from the bed as possible, she opted for tucking her knees to her chest on a chair in the corner of the room.

If she was honest, it was her heart and mind that writhed at the events of the night far more than any physicality. Her sense of goodness and morality had been the one commanding her stomach to upturn. As she checked in with her body, she felt a levity akin to several glasses of wine. It wasn't in her head the way alcohol blurred one's thoughts, but rather, in her tendons and her muscles, humming slightly in her limbs.

She stretched her fingers out and looked at them, almost expecting to see a change of some peculiar nature.

Nox continued to clutch the glass of water that Emily had left behind for her, fingers wrapped tightly around the cup as she sipped. She had nearly finished her glass of water and was feeling far better than was logical when Millicent entered the room.

"Well, you certainly managed to make your first night eventful."

She shook her head, dread and regret bubbling from her stomach into her words. "I'm sorry, Madame. I have no idea—"

"How were you feeding before?"

"Excuse me?"

Millicent gestured for Nox to follow her. She didn't wait as the young woman unraveled her legs from the chair and stood, slowly exiting the room. They made their way down the now-empty townhouse toward the Madame's office. It was as ornate and gaudy as one might expect from a woman who wore jewel-toned gowns and black fur shawls, someone so vain that she never took her elbow-length gloves off, lest she dirty her hands or expose them to sunspots. The woman covered nearly every inch of her walls with art, including a lavish oil portrait of herself commissioned in a rather flattering light. Statuettes, jewels, and even the taxidermied body of a snowcat with its exotic, speckled face forever frozen in a threatening snarl. The office would have been ridiculous had it belonged to anyone else. Millicent, however, fit right in like a dragon atop her hoard of treasure.

Nox wasn't sure what to do or why she was here. Still feeling the aching need to hold her knees to her chest, sat down in a chair near the desk and curled into a ball while Millicent scanned her shelves.

"Ah, here we are." The woman pulled a black-bound book embossed with gilded symbols from the wall. The Madame's elaborate ringlets bounced slightly as she sat down in her high-backed chair across the desk from Nox and flipped through the pages until she found what she was looking for. Eyes twinkling triumphantly, she turned the book over and pushed it toward the young woman.

Nox looked at the woman's smile, then down at the page. Her face twisted in confusion and she returned her eyes to the jewel-toned woman across the desk, uncomprehending. She untangled her legs once more so she could straighten her back, leaning closer to the book.

"What is this?"

Millicent shook her head. "I think the question is, dear, what are *you?*"

Nox pulled the book closer to herself and read the entry in earnest. The passage started with a simple term, a definition, a territory, a list of powers, and ended with runes and wards for protection against and methods of defeat. Below that was a horrid illustration of a woman straddling a man, black wings outstretched, talons dug into his helpless flesh of the human male below as the creature was arched in pleasure. The unmistakable drawing of ghostly tendrils of his soul left his mouth as they were sucked by the creature. It was a foul drawing.

"I'm not *this!*" She said finally, pointing at the horrid image.

Millicent rolled her eyes slightly, "Yes, the old tomes have a flare for the dramatic, don't they. However, I'm rather pleased to be the one to tell you: yes, you are."

Nox straightened further, closing the book with a slam. Her eyes flashed with anger and disgust. "That's not possible. I've never shown a single inclination toward this evil, this demonic—"

"Please, dear. Demon is such a pejorative term. The dark fae have been misunderstood for far too long. Don't let your ignorance betray you."

Nox's face twisted in disgust. Millicent couldn't be serious. This was absurd. It was appalling. It was blasphemous.

"You do know you're Raascot fae, yes?"

"I—"

"Do you possess a mirror, or did you think that you had the same pink, colorless cheeks of all of the other discarded orphans in Farehold?"

Nox blinked rapidly. She had known that she hadn't been fully southern. Matron Agnes had treated her deeply tanned skin tone as a token, parading her around the bishop as a living testimony to the borderless magnanimity of her orphanage. Agnes's showmanship had always been transparent, and hadn't bothered her any more than everything else about Farleigh and its amoral existence.

"Dark fae?"

"Call it by its right name. The northern kingdom and its fae are of Raascot, dear. My, my, how poor *was* your education?"

Nox felt as though the air had been sucked from the room.

Millicent repeated her earlier question. "How were you feeding before tonight? I've been thinking it over while the men disposed of your handiwork with that sop. I have a theory or two, dear. Here at the house, I've considered the validation and adoration of the men may have been sustaining you, however remedially. Their praise and affections, even from behind the bar, may have kept you going, though at a fraction of your potential. Even *I* didn't know why I found you so likable. I do wonder how much my own favoritism fed into your nourishment. Here I thought I'd just found a suitable protégée—not to say, dear, that you wouldn't make a splendid protégée, perhaps now more than ever."

Nox felt sick again. Just like before, it was a sickness of the heart manifesting in her stomach. Her physical body still hummed, insisting upon its contentment. Despite having just consumed a large glass of water, her mouth felt dry. "I don't understand."

Millicent sighed rather impatiently. "At Farleigh, you didn't have men fawning over you, did you? In the orphanage, you didn't enjoy some puppy love with any such fellow? I'm just dreadfully curious how you've managed to stay in the shadows as a damned virgin! Think of it, a goddess damned succubus under my own roof, the roof of a brothel no less, already twenty-one, and still a *virgin*! I don't know if I've ever heard anything so comical! Such a peculiar accomplishment, yours is, my dear."

Nox was shaking her head against the cruelties Millicent was saying. The ornate walls of the office swam. What sort of horrible lies were these to tell her in the wake of such trauma? What had she ever done to deserve this brand of emotional turmoil?

"I'm part demon?"

"Well, are you part demon or are you part stupid? I've never known you to be daft. I'm asking you a question, dear. Try to keep up."

The girl didn't want to speak. Though she didn't feel the urge to respond, her mouth moved of its own accord. She answered, "I guess the matrons always favored me? I was set apart from the others while the Gray Matron kept me for her personal errands? Is that what you mean?"

Millicent accepted the answer but seemed profoundly dissatisfied. "You have an inherent ability to make people fall in love with you, Nox. Now that I think about it, even your name makes more sense. Who was it that called you 'Night'? Was it the matrons?"

"No," she shook her glossy, black hair. It moved against her chin, her shoulders, down the middle of her back like a thick, silken curtain. She looked like the shadows themselves. "I'm told it was the only thing my mother had ever given me. It was her parting gift before she abandoned me."

"Well, I don't suppose she would have known what to do with you. A fae wouldn't have dropped you in Farehold, which means your father must have been the fae. If she was a human woman, and she must be, by the sight of your round ears. It's lucky, really. You've been able to hide in plain sight. You would have been sired by a dark fae—"

"A demon."

"Pish posh, dear. You'll come to find the world isn't so black and white. Whatever it was that kept you nourished, I'm glad for whatever love in your life sustained you for the seventeen years before meeting me. I don't know if the matrons could truly have achieved such a feat, but you kept yourself alive long enough to bring you here to me. Though, truly you've been running at a tenth of your potential. Now that we know what you are and what you're capable of… oh, the world is just opening up for you, dear."

Nox swirled within herself, fingers gripping like oil against metal, unable to firmly grasp any sense of truth. She could neither dissociate, nor could accept what was being said. She was caught in an airless, terrible middle. Nothing about Millicent's office was grounding. The colors and sparkles and sheen on the woman's gilded possessions only added to the kaleidoscope she felt. She felt as though the floor were rocking, as if she'd been stashed in the belly of a ship without her knowledge or consent. She didn't know what to do, what to think, what to feel.

If the earth was unsteady at The Selkie, she could leave. She could run away.

She ran a quick mental inventory of what such a feat might require. Nox didn't have much for belongings, but girls had run before. She had some experience in preparing for escape, though her earliest attempt had been fruitless. Of course, very few of the women who left made it far from The Selkie. Priory, as she'd heard was common among most major cities, was unkind to women left unaccompanied. Millicent protected the girls while they were under her roof, but if her property scorned her by turning their backs on her, the wrath of the Madame could be felt for a thousand miles.

Nox didn't know where to go, but she didn't want to stay here. She didn't know if she could truly leave, but at the very least, she had to get out of this office. She stood, holding her robe closer to her sides.

She found her voice again, utterly disgusted, "What is the point of this—of a creature like this? Why would I do this? Why would something be created to murder?"

Millicent nodded thoughtfully, still looking down at the book, "Yes, the murder is something we can work on. But look, my dear."

The vanilla-scented woman rounded her desk. Goddess, how Nox had grown to hate the smell of vanilla.

Millicent rested two hands on each of Nox's shoulders guided the young raven to an ornate glass oval on the wall, painted with two women—one with an embellished updo of curls and jewels, standing beside a truly stunning girl with shimmering brown skin and hair as dark as night. She looked at the metallic sheen of the painting for a moment. One was clearly the Madame, but the other...

Nox gasped audibly at the face that stared back at her. It was not a painting, but a mirror. The dark-haired woman within it was utterly alien. She hadn't recognized herself at all. She had never been plain, per se. Her features had always been pleasant—likable, to be sure. People had never lost their breath when they looked at her. No one had flung a hand to cover their mouth the way they had when they saw the frost-capped Amaris. But this...

Could this truly be her?

The young raven who looked back at her in the mirror was vibrating with a terrifying beauty. Her long black hair seemed to come alive, as glossy and vibrant as the star-drenched sky. Her dark eyes were the trenches at the bottom of the ocean, so deep that you could feel yourself tumbling into them. Her lips, her breasts, her hips all seemed fuller somehow. Her skin glowed with a secret fire burning just beneath its layers, setting her aflame with the allure of a secret glimmer.

She was breathless, "It makes me beautiful?"

"Oh, my dear." Millicent's voice was barely a whisper. "It makes you powerful."

13

Deliciously buzzed, a day-drunk Amaris stumbled her way from the dining room up toward her chambers. She felt the bright pop of the bubbles as they continued to warm her belly, body tingling from the ale. Ash had seen her leave and chased after her, waving off the good-natured reprimands of his friends and fellow reevers as they scolded him to leave her alone. He'd downed just as many pints as his sparring partner, even if he hadn't earned them the way she had. She'd deserved the celebration.

She'd heard him get up from the table and rolled her eyes good-naturedly, not bothering to look over her shoulder at him as she wandered off. She enjoyed the taunting from the other reevers, appreciating that they had her back, even if she didn't mind Ash's company. All of the reevers were uniquely bonded to their sparring partners, even if their particular relationship had taken on an unusual flavor.

The coppery young man's feet were quiet as he padded out of the dining room and trotted down the hall, ignoring the objections of the others to stop pestering her. They both knew she was headed to her room. Her desire to spend most of her time alone in her quarters was logical. While the rest of the reevers had relatively small accommodations in the keep, hers was big enough that she never felt like leaving her sacred space.

"M'lady," he jogged up to her, offering his bent elbow. She leased an airy chuckled and accepted it. His muscles were firm beneath her hands. She always enjoyed his presence.

"Any bruises?"

"These days? Always. If you don't stop kicking my ass, I'm going to have to find a new sparring partner."

"But then how will you ever get better?" she winked.

Amaris rested her head on his shoulder briefly as they walked, vision swimming from the alcohol in the afternoon sun that lit the hallway. He beamed down at her, his bright, ember features glowing from the beer in his belly and the girl at his side. The endorphins from the morning exercise hadn't hurt, either.

"Are you studying today?" He asked, his question heavy with ulterior motives.

She lifted her head and looked at him suspiciously. She didn't miss a beat. "Are you asking if I'm looking for lessons on the male anatomy?"

He grinned, delighted. "As always, I'd love to be your willing subject for experimentation."

She gave him a shove, releasing his arm. She bit down a laugh, refusing to give him the satisfaction. "You're something of a bastard."

"That I am, but one of these days you might just say yes."

"A man can dream, I suppose."

He feigned a bow, "I live to fight another day." Hands in his pockets, jolly from the drinks and the exchange, Ash sauntered off down the hall. She could have sworn he was whistling.

Amaris shut the door behind her and found herself giggling rather stupidly, even as she shook her head, clearing away any feelings that arose from his advances. She liked the attention, she enjoyed his energy, and she loved how high his spirits remained as she knocked him to the ground time after time. In their years at the keep, she'd watched Ash as he'd gone from months of disappointment in pummeling a weakling, to the pride and respect of watching his partner blossom into a one of the reev's deadliest champions. He'd been an excellent sport.

She peeled off her clothes and walked naked across her bedroom to the bathing room, leaving a trail of sweat-damp things on the floor. While she was treated exactly like a male reever in nearly every way that mattered, they had allowed her to keep one of the only chambers with an adjoining bathing room, just as she had her first few nights in the keep. She sank into the waters of her bath, soaking away any aches from the day's practice. She kneaded her tender muscles under the warm, soapy water.

The silvery reever dipped her head below the bath's surface and submerged herself entirely, running her fingers through her hair as the bathwater washed off the sweat, dirt and grime. When she broke the bath's surface, she looked into the mirror she had mounted on the opposite wall. She'd found the reflective piece in the fortress in a stock room nearly two years ago and, though she'd inquired, none of the men claimed to have needed it. There were other mirrors scattered around the keep, but this one now belonged exclusively to her. She smiled at the young woman who looked at her in the mirror, loving the muscles, the bruises, and the prominent pink scars that marked her stance for her own freedom. One across her eye, and the other from her collar bone to her breast.

She would never be able to thank the goddess enough for the way Odrin had been sent into her life like the divine intervention of holy lore. The father-figure may as well have been the All Mother, arriving in flesh when needed most. He'd appeared in the hour of her need. Odrin had rescued her and brought her to a life of family, of strength, and of fortitude. Thanks in large part to the reever and the intervention of his healing tonic, the scars from her fateful morning at Farleigh had healed as beautiful, clean lines. They were little more than pink tattoos to mark her otherwise frosted features.

She blew a few bubbles in the water and thought absently of Ash, their exchange still fresh on her mind. Her sparring partner was dauntless with his endless, teasing offers to take her to bed. He'd had no trouble bedding many of the enthusiastic young women of Stone in his treks down the mountain for nights in the tavern, as being both a faeling and an elite guardian had offered him a hero's reputation amongst the locals. His conquests had emboldened him, turning him into an incorrigible flirt. His amiable advances had made beating him in the ring all the more satisfying. Nothing was quite as satisfying as rejecting a man and then kicking his ass.

Though she'd never tell him, she did have to admit to a small thrill that shot through her when her mind went to his arm around her neck, choking her out from behind, his hard body pressed into hers.

Why not take him to bed?

She continued to scrub at her body, bubbles swirling around her as she played with the idea. She wasn't saving herself any longer—not as the matrons had hidden her away, keeping her safe and untouched like the finest of decorative, porcelain teacups. Perhaps a roll in the sheets would be something worth experiencing just to do it and be done with it. It would be the final straw in breaking the efforts the matrons had taken to trap her behind tempered glass.

Whether or not to take Ash up on his offers one of these days was a question she had asked herself on more than one occasion. He was impishly handsome, roughly her age, and her physical match in nearly every way. She was, of course, extremely fond of him, and had definitely found her hands wandering to the thought of the two of them together on more than one occasion.

She knew why she hadn't said yes.

Amaris understood why she would continue to rebuff his advances, as amusing as they were. It stemmed from a deep, unspoken agreement between herself and the keep. They shared blood in their oath for a reason. They were family.

Amaris was a young woman brought into Uaimh Reev under the expectations that she would behave and compose herself like any other reever. They were meant to see her as a brother in arms. The men of all ages had grown to respect her skill and she knew that they would fight beside one another in an unbroken trust, holding each other's backs to the death if ever the situation arose.

In those ways, she didn't want to disappoint her brothers by reminding them that she was a woman. While Amaris had always been beautiful in a way that had made her stand out from those around her— and though her scars had somehow found a way to enhance her beauty, making it bold and wild—the reevers had perpetually found her appearance to be the least interesting thing about her. They admired her tenacity, her stamina, her skill, her memory, her wit, and her unwavering spirit. Her first year had been filled with bets over whether or not she'd give up and run off in the night, but she'd never given the men the satisfaction. Not only had she stuck it out, but she'd lived and thrived long enough in the reev to watch their hearts fully open to her as one of their own.

She supposed she also struggled with what it would mean to Ash if they were to truly tangle, even if that thought were secondary. Would it impact the way he saw her, or the way they trained? Could sex be worth the complications it might bring?

Unlike some of the lesser religions of the old gods, the goddess expected nothing by way of celibacy. Despite their affiliations with the church as the All Mother's sword, reevers were no saints. Many had taken lovers that they would see in their travels. Some, including Odrin, had married and started families, living out their service and keeping up with their training on the ground, away from the keep. She was even quite certain that one of her brothers had a male lover in Stone who he spoke fondly of, carefully avoiding pronouns when speaking of the man around Grem. But his identity and proclivities hadn't made him look for sex within the keep's walls amongst his reever brethren any more than hers should. Perhaps it's why Ash found it fun to flirt, as he, too, knew the unspoken agreements to keep the hewn reev as an escape from the world below with its entanglements. Knowing they shouldn't, knowing they couldn't... Well, maybe that was half of the fun.

The bubbles had popped and the water had started to cool, telling her she'd been in the bath for long enough. Whatever questions she had could be dealt with on the bed, amidst a mid-afternoon catnap.

She toweled off from the soapy waters and changed into loose-fitting clothing. The ivory girl braided her wet hair with deft fingers. She hadn't truly intended to sleep, but the alcohol convinced her that laying down was for the best, if only for a moment. The buzz in her belly lured her to the bed, tempting her to curl into a ball. Between the pleasant hum of the ale, the exhaustion of the afternoon's exercises, the joy of the victory, and the glowing, internal chemistry of the exchange that had gone unrealized between her and her sparring partner, she was tugged beneath the dark waves of rest before she realized what was happening.

Amaris couldn't typically perceive when she was dreaming, but as the scent of cinnamon and plums filled her nose, some piece of her knew she must be asleep. This was no perfume. The decadent smell was all-encompassing. Forbidden. A memory she'd hidden away. This scent was the sort of trigger that tugged at the box she kept locked within herself, a pain and past that she refused to open in the light of day.

She struggled against the urge to open her eyes, knowing it couldn't be real. The internal debate raged within her as she felt the press of skin, the sweet scent of familiarity; a cloud of love and family and hope surrounding her. Her eyes fluttered open as she decided she didn't care. It felt real. Goddess, it felt so achingly real.

She wasn't resting on the cotton pillows of the keep. Instead, her cheek pale was pressed into soft, tanned skin as the anticipatory titillation from her the way her fingers had wandered in the bath carried her on its waves into a pleasantly charged dream. She allowed her eyes to remain closed even in sleep as she inhaled, breathing in the scent that had been too painful to remember. She hadn't allowed herself to think of its owner. She'd done her best to cage all memories of the girl who had held her, enveloping her in the spice that swirled around her now.

"I've missed you," the one who owned the plum scent spoke. Her voice was low. It was a dark, sweet sound that Amaris hadn't heard in years anywhere but her sleep, though even the dreams were painful. The sentence was punctuated with the gentle kiss of soft lips into her hair, nearly against her temple. Amaris exhaled slowly as she absorbed the sensation. This was not a friendly kiss. This was not the familial kiss of a sister or a childhood companion.

There was something so distinct, so intimate about the way the lips had brushed against her.

Her breath hitched a bit, feeling her heart rate increase at the press of the girl's mouth against her hair. A silvery spike of nervous excitement tingled down her spine, rousing her from her dream-like state. Amaris inhaled again, allowing the dark spices to consume her as she nuzzled against the exposed skin of Nox's collarbones, sternum, and the pillow of her chest.

The reever permitted her eyes to flutter open so she could turn her face to see the dark-haired girl who possessed such a lovely voice. Part of her wish she hadn't.

Amaris knew what Nox looked like. She had been her best friend for years. She had been her only family. She had been the source material for many of the portrait drawings she'd done under the supervision of the matrons. She'd seen her face more times than she could count. Even still, she'd done her best to quiet her gaze when it had wandered. Amaris had regarded Nox's features, pausing her eyes and her treacherous heart when it had suggested a want for more. She quieted the voice, damning it for its thoughts.

She had known that Nox was lovely. She had known that the girl possessed curves and pleasant features, but she'd rejected any urge to truly absorb them. In her dream, however, she allowed herself the gradual prowl of her grazing eyes.

Her heart cracked. She knew for the second time that she must be dreaming, for everything they saw was different. Nox's dark eyes were brighter, somehow. It was as if they had taken on an incredible, doe-like quality. Her cheeks had pinked against her tan skin. Her hair was longer and glossier, so much so that the black had taken on a rainbow's iridescence. Her lips were the full, plump shade of ripe blackberries. Even her teeth seemed whiter. She looked more beautiful, more powerful, more ethereal. It was all evidence of a dream. Something about her was darker and lovelier, if not purely predatory.

"You look different," was all Amaris said. She felt sad at the thought. So many years had passed that her mind had drifted, forgetting Nox's features. She knew this young woman, she knew her better than anyone in the world, and everything she saw off, somehow. Too pretty. Too glowing. Too different. Her mind must be filling in gaps with new qualities, forgetting the friend who'd loved her altogether.

Nox smiled, but the twitch of her lips did not reach her eyes. Her hand moved tenderly among Amaris's locks, stroking her pearly hair. "Time will do that."

The reever's eyes flitted around the room, but she felt no urgency to leave. They appeared to be in Farleigh, but they were not in the multi-cot dormitories of which she had become so familiar. They reclined together in one lone, large bed that rested against the far wall of the dorm room. There were no noises of children or echoes of company in the hall. They seemed to be utterly alone, the privacy as nerve-wracking as it was intimate. The sheets were not the scratchy, cheap starchy linens of the orphanage, but a soft, organic cotton that felt extravagant against her legs. Her nightdress was lovelier than anything she'd had the pleasure of owning. Its straps barely more than threads as it seemed to hold itself together on mere prayers rather than fabric.

Misremembering her felt like a betrayal. It was painful. Dreams were meant to be a reprieve, but in a way, this was too lovely to be more than a nightmare. The hurt she felt threatened to unleash everything she worked so hard to keep under lock and key.

"I don't want to miss you anymore," Amaris said, voice thick with emotion.

Nox arched her brow curiously. "There are two ways you can stop missing me."

"How?"

Her voice was soft, almost cooing as she closed her large, dark eyes slowly, then opened them again. "You can forget about me, though I hope you won't, because I could never let you go." She ran her fingers down the silvery strands of hair once more. "Or, you can wait, and I will come find you. I'm going to find you, Amaris." Her fingers moved from where they'd been in Amaris's hair and gently cupped the side of her face, one thumb tracing softly down the length of her most prominent scar. "You look different too, you know. What a lovely scar."

She swallowed, echoing the sentiment, "Time will do that."

Amaris raised her body from where it had rested so comfortably against the soft curves of her childhood friend. She had been fifteen the last time she'd truly curled against Nox. She had been weak, unmarred, and naïve. Now she was a scarred, war-ready adult. So much had changed. She felt a knife through her heart as she eyed the dark-haired girl beside her. Amaris rested against the backboard and twisted her torso to look at her, but her eyes did more than look.

She'd intended to take in the face of an old friend. Instead, she felt her violet eyes grazing over the edge of Nox's jaw, following the curve that drew a line from her ears to her bare shoulders. She shouldn't let her eyes dip, she told herself, but she did it anyway. Amaris's gaze dropped to the sharp collar bone and the thin collar of the silken nightdress that rested just barely covering the peaks of her breasts. Her gentle lines curved in an hourglass as her waist released its arc in a lovely, wide hip. The reever's eyes lifted to Nox's face again, but quickly realized that she was not meeting the girl's dark gaze. Nox's lips were parted against her quiet breath.

Amaris leaned her body toward the raven-haired beauty, but she was not closing the distance between them for an embrace. An ache in her belly clutched at her, lower and more primal than hunger. It was like thirst. It was curiosity and questions and yearning tingling against her lips and tongue. She felt an unfamiliar need tug at her as she looked at Nox. Maybe it was because she'd fallen asleep after Ash's invitation to come to bed and the unrealized anticipation she'd built alone in the warm waters of her bath. Maybe it was something else entirely. All she knew was that she wanted to be closer.

"I've missed you too," was all Amaris could say.

It was true. She'd missed her more than she allowed herself to believe. She could never let it go, or forget, or move on. It was a memory too painful to explore. Nox's face was one that conjured too much hurt, too much confusion. In the real world, Amaris had needed to seal the suction-cupped tentacles of her vicious emotions, clamping them into a locked safe inside of her so that she could function. In some other, imagined world, the girls had successfully run away together and escaped into the forest. In that world, the Madame had never found them. There'd been no reevers, no matrons, and no distance to part them. In another world, they'd be in the same bed tonight instead of the ivory girl's dreams.

Nox dragged a slow finger from Amaris's forearm to her elbow, up her arm. The gentle scrape of her fingernail was hot and cold all at once, raising goose flesh on her arm and sending shivers down Amaris's back. It caused her stomach to clench and her throat to constrict. Her breathing trembled, staggering as she exhaled. She was conflicted. Part of her wished Nox would stop, wished that she wouldn't stoke the fire and exacerbate this unrequited want. The other part of her silently pleaded that she wouldn't.

The finger drew its path over her shoulder, tracing the figure along the lines of her neck, her jaw, and landing on her chin. Amaris's heart rate increased as she stopped breathing. She'd watched Nox's finger with a shy, confused anxiety at first as it had navigated between her wrist and elbow, but as it crept along the lines of her throat, she'd felt her eyes drift to a close and a soft sound, almost a moan, escape her lips. When the finger made it to the space beneath her chin, Nox had flexed her index finger inward so that a single knuckled tucked itself beneath Amaris's chin, lifting her face so that the reever would open her eyes once more.

She understood the intent behind the lifted chin, and she obeyed. How could she feel so deliciously powerless in her own dream? So vulnerable, so uncertain, so consumed with incomprehensible craving? Maybe it was that her subconscious knew that, between the two of them, Nox would always be the leader. The young woman knew the steps to the dance and guided them forward, Amaris all too willing to follow the music only they could hear.

Amaris's frosted lashes lifted again, her lilac irises touching the depth of Nox's gaze. She willed herself to breathe as Nox lowered her body closer, but the reever couldn't seem to remember how to summon air to her lungs. She'd forgotten how to inhale. Her pale lips parted as adrenaline surged through her. Her heart flitted like the pitter-patter of rain falling in one thousand places all at once as anticipation coursed through her.

Nox paused barely an inch above her mouth, allowing their breath to intermingle. As one breathed out, the other breathed in, junipers melded into plums, fresh winter into cardamom, cinnamon and saffron as tense, warm air exchanged between them. The electric charge that passed between them was as intoxicating as any drink that had ever entered her system. Her eyes closed again, feeling herself lean forward with longing. Nox's mouth was so close. She wanted Nox to close the minute gap. She wanted the girl's soft mouth on her own. She felt with the sharp inhalation of her breath that if it didn't happen soon, she'd suffocate under her own craving. Nox's mouth was so near, so she could taste every spice. Her scent, her hair, her soft, supple frame pressed into Amaris as the space between them closed.

The rapping of knuckles drew her attention from her dream as if she had been held under water, only now yanked above the surface by her hair. Her air caught in her throat as her eyes drifted over Nox's shoulder to the door beyond. She wanted them to go away. She wanted the room to belong only to them. The sound grew sharper and sharper as Nox began to ripple. The ripple increased as the fabric of the dream tore at the seams.

A louder knock came, and the door was pushed open before she could answer. The entrance to the room in Farleigh bled into that of her bedchamber in the fortress. Amaris blinked awake, struggling to distinguish imagination from reality as she jolted into an upright position. Her heart thundered from a flood of emotions. Her body felt strange. Her mind raced.

Amaris cursed violently in both surprise and confusion as she pressed herself up, eyes wide. She pressed herself up as she determined that she was, in fact, in Uaimh Reev, and not at the orphanage. She couldn't see her face, but was quite confident that the reddened lines of fabric had carved tell-tale grooves of her nap into her features. She swallowed hard against the lump in her throat but found herself in need of water, the same way her body felt in need of a different brand of quenching.

The door began to open before she'd called out to acknowledge whoever visited. This was precisely why she never loitered in her room in various states of undress. The boys knew nothing of privacy.

"Sorry! Were you sleeping?" Such a friendly, harmless question.

Malik and Brel let themselves in, Brel with a pastry in each hand and Malik with a glass of water and a smile. Brel offered her a pastry and climbed up onto her bed, intending the other freshly baked good for himself. The child was almost thirteen now and had finally grown comfortable spending time with her. They'd become pals in their time together, and she was quite confident that she was the child's very best friend. She wanted to yell at them, but knew nothing was their fault. It had only been a dream, after all.

She did her best to smile at them, wiping sleep from her eyes.

Malik set the water on her desk, "Still drunk?"

She shrugged, wondering if it had been the alcohol that had made her dream so vivid. It was a non-answer, but he didn't seem to mind.

"I thought as much! We can't have you hungover for our rematch tomorrow. When I beat you, it has to be fair and square. I don't know that I saw you drinking any water between your beers. As for the kid here," Malik ruffled the boy's hair, "Brel needed an extra hand so he could bring one for you and the other for himself. It would have been *nice* if someone had brought *me* a pastry."

Feeling herself grow more awake with every moment that passed, she finished shaking dreams from her mind. She made a conscious note to check in with reality. Nox was not in Uaimh Reev. Amaris was not in Farleigh. Two of her reever brethren were in her room, and they needed her attention far more than any demand of her subconscious, no matter how alluring. Amaris smiled at the boys, rolling her eyes at their fussing and selected the pastry in favor of the glass of water. The blond young man let himself out with a happy trot.

Amaris had kept a bestiary tome by her bed, as studying the dark creatures of the world had become a favorite fascination of hers since her arrival at the reev. There was a baseline knowledge required of all of the reevers regarding monsters and demons, but she'd developed a rather particular obsession with learning everything there was to know about the continent's beasts.

Brel had sat on her bed to spend some time in companionable silence. She'd learned how to talk to him and hold daily conversations, even though his parents' actions had prevented him from verbally responding.

She grabbed for the tome and turned her book to Brel. She did what she could to involve him in normal friendly exchanges, and as this was a hobby of hers, she'd hoped it would prove to be something over which they might bond. Amaris slid a small, mostly-blank notebook that she'd kept on her desk to the space beside him on the bed. She'd never had an opportunity to feel particularly maternal before she'd met Brel. Still, in her years of knowing him, all she wanted was to offer him a happy, comfortable life in whatever small ways she was able.

"Have you ever seen any of the creatures in this book?" Amaris held the bestiary up, showing the boy some of the more frightening pictures.

He wiped the pastry crumbs on his pants. She'd offered it to him to flip through, but he hadn't needed to look at the pictures. Without hesitating, he wrote, "Yes."

Her eyes widened at that. He'd been so young when he'd arrived, and she didn't think he ever left the reev. She spoke her questions, and he penned his answers. She flipped through pages and began to gesture while asking, "Which one?"

He took the book from her and flipped to a picture of a vageth. It was a canine with amphibious features, the smooth skin of a salamander.

She stared at the jutting shoulders and sharpened talons of the creature. It had the typical, large eyes of a predator on the front, then three, smaller, beady eyes decorating the outside so that it might have the advantage of vision on all sides. "Can you tell me the story?"

He considered it for a moment before writing, "When Corsoran took me from my village to this keep, we saw three vageth in the woods."

Amaris frowned at the brevity of his story. She knew two things two be true. The first was that she had never met a man named Corsoran. The second was that the blood of the vageth contained a poison that made infected wounds impossible to heal, with or without healing tonic.

"Do you know what happened to him?" she asked a bit quietly, not sure if she wanted the boy to relive any of his traumas.

He scribbled in his notebook for a moment until a few sentences were formed. "He'd beheaded all three, but was scratched deeply in the fight. By the time he got us back to Uaimh Reev, the injury was too severe."

A reever could have survived a bite or scratch from a vageth if they'd avoided contact with its blood in the wound. As any good reever, he'd undoubtedly separated and buried the severed parts to prevent the demon from reanimation. She wondered if it had been his thoroughness that had gotten him killed.

Her heart held so much heaviness for the boy. "I'm so sorry, Brel."

"I'm not," he wrote. At her confused expression, he continued his penmanship in the space below his initial sentence. "He brought me here to be with my real family. I only knew Corsoran for three days. I barely have any memories of my parents or village before him. I've known everyone at this keep for nine years. I will forever be grateful to him, but I will never be sorry that I was brought here, or let myself feel sorry about the events that led me here. I'll be a reever someday. I'll have more brothers than anyone in my village might have had."

"And a sister," she smiled.

He shook his head and wrote, "You'll be my brother, too."

Amaris had learned that sometimes when she was at a loss for words, it was best not to speak at all. She hugged him, and he tightened his arms around her in return. He was not yet old enough to feel embarrassed by her displays of familial love, and she hoped he'd always stay that way. She wondered how often the young boy received parental affection in the castle. It wasn't right for a child to grow up without hugs or gentleness. While everyone in the keep was exceedingly kind to the boy, she hoped he was getting the full and happy life he deserved.

After all, every child deserved unconditional love from their family for exactly who they were, not for who they hoped their child might be.

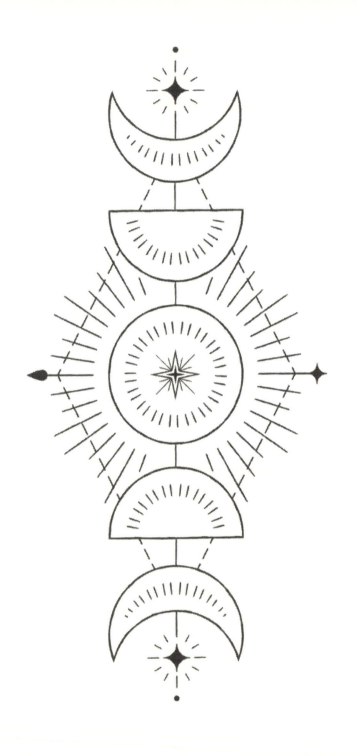

-PART THREE-

The Many Faces of Demons

14

Amaris arrived at the ring the following day, ready to start their run. Instead, Samael was holding a meeting against the early colors of morning. She was one of the first to arrive, though Odrin, Malik and Ash, and two of the middle-aged reevers had beaten her to the gathering. It would be a warm day, but the air was still pleasantly cool in the first hours of dawn. A light breeze moved her hair around her shoulders and she reached behind her head to begin tying it back as she approached. Samael was already speaking.

"I'm sending five of you down the mountain today, and I'd like you to leave as soon as you've had breakfast. I'll need Grem and Odrin to go north into Raascot, which I can explain in more detail once Grem arrives. Malik, Ash and Amaris, you'll be going to Aubade. I need you to take an audience with the southern queen."

Amaris caught the words of Samael's dispatch as she arrived, speaking the question on everyone's mind. She'd stayed on her feet while the others sat on staggered steps of the ring, crossing her arms with curiosity. "We're traveling together? Aren't reevers normally dispatched alone?"

Samael nodded at the girl's inquiry, "Sending you out in teams has just as much to do with the distance as it does the task at hand. You're all needed to meet with the continent's regencies, and I think Amaris might be particularly silver-tongued in getting the queen to listen to our cause."

Samael barely let his eyes linger long enough to convey the levity of his meaning.

No one knew what she was, or what she could do. She wasn't even sure she knew herself.

For years, Samael had kept her secret. No one in the keep had learned of her gift, and she had been exceedingly careful so as never to wield it. Even Ash only knew he had been paired with her for their ages—not for any influences of persuasion to which he might be a bit more immune than a full-fledged human. Perhaps that was why all three of them needed to go to Aubade. Ash could keep her in check should she need to begin barking orders to the humans around her. Similarly, Malik and his open, honest features would provide an excellent human buffer for any suspicion two non-humans might draw.

"The south has been accusing the north of sending their forces into its lands for years, but now we've gathered enough intel to learn that the queen plans to act on it. There's a very good chance that she is one bad day away from genocide of any northern fae or Raascot peoples found south of the mountains."

"And Grem and I are to go to the king to see if he is indeed intentionally sending his forces southward?" Odrin's gruff voice clarified. His eyes flashed briefly to Amaris, and she wondered if he wished they were traveling together. He'd been her rescuer, her teacher, her father for years. They hadn't spent any time away since he'd rescued her from Farleigh.

"Indeed. As you know, one of our men has been on an intelligence mission in Raascot, just outside of Gwydir, for the last decade. He has acted as an ambassador and held the peace in the north for a long time, checking in semi-regularly with his letters. He sent a message by raven insisting on an in-person meeting to explain his findings."

Ash looked deeply displeased, and made no effort to conceal it with his tone, "As it's my father in Gwydir, shouldn't I be going north?"

Samael was sympathetic, but unwavering. "I need you on this southbound mission. I also need you to have confidence in my reasons for entrusting you to accompany this party to the queen's city."

Ash looked profoundly unhappy with Samael's response, but said nothing more. Malik was too excited for the somber occasion, but she knew he'd been on relatively few missions and was eager to wet his sword again.

"We are the stronghold for the continent."

Ash laughed at their mighty stronghold, one dozen men in a castle once meant to hold hundreds, "There's twelve of us."

"Thirteen, now." Amaris amended, smiling.

So she was to get to Aubade and—what—command the queen not to kill people? It wasn't a particularly elegant plan, especially when her comrades didn't even comprehend the bare bones of it, but she trusted that Samael had known when he met her that she might be needed for just such a time. Maybe while she was at it she'd crown herself queen and begin her life of luxury.

Odrin had done his best to allow her full independence, particularly seeing as how Amaris was a full reever and more than capable of handling whatever responsibilities the title required. Still, in their moments before departure, he'd run through the list of items with her like a father might for his daughter. How many healing tonics had she packed? What was her weapon count? Did she have wools for the cold nights? Did she remember that most body heat was lost through the ground overnight? Had the kitchen given them enough dried foods that traveled well? Did she have enough coin to buy nights at the inn if she was injured or the weather was sour? Did she remember that the church was obligated to both fund and to shelter the reevers whenever they saw them, as they'd long been the firm sword of what was right and good, keeping peace through a constructive hand in a way that was free of the politics of the land? Finally, Odrin had insisted that she take Cobb. The dappled gelding hadn't really been his horse, after all.

Grem and Odrin saddled two of the broken-in pack horses that had served the keep for many years. Malik and Ash chose the mounts more for riding than for supplies, as the three of them had further to go and a shorter window of time to get there if the queen was coiled to strike at any given moment. While Samael and the others bid them farewell from the keep, the two traveling parties wouldn't split until they reached the bottom of the mountain.

This was not the daily trail run from the back of the ring, but required them to cross the bridge and begin the long descent toward Stone.

Descending the mountain took on an entirely new flavor when she knew she wasn't about to turn around and run back up again. Every pebble, every step, every gust of wind from the valley below seemed to echo nervous, excited energy. Grem grumbled about his headache for half of the trip down their mountain's steep slopes and how the summer sun was a hangover's worst enemy. Amaris recalled her first time walking up the mountain, shoes filled with own blood, picking her footing in the dead of night so long ago. The trip down the mountain in the morning light was much quicker than her climb up by moonlight had been.

The steep trail began to level out as they rejoined the tree line and made their way onto the continent. The path that had connected them to the fortress let off just outside of Stone, stopping near a crop of pine trees and concealed by the backside of a hill from the prying eyes of nearby people.

The groups said their parting words at the trail's base, with Odrin hemming a bit as they meant to leave. Amaris decided to close the gap for the both of them and threw her arms around the wonderful, good-hearted, bearded man who had been the only father she'd ever known. She tightened her arms around his neck.

"Thank you," she said, chest tight with emotion, "for everything."

He seemed caught off guard, and eventually lowered one arm into an awkward half-hug. He smelled of tobacco and leather and freedom. They were scents she would miss, not knowing when she'd see her father again. The crinkles in his eyes and calluses on his hands were the familiar features of the one who had saved her on the worst day of her life. The comfort of his presence felt like home. An embrace may not have been a natural instinct for the elder reever, but when Amaris pulled away she could see how full his heart was. She had learned from her time at the keep that Odrin had once had another family. She knew that it was a brief time in his life filled with love and sliced brutally short with the edge of a sword. She was his family now, and hoped that having her in his life healed some small part of a wound too unspeakable to discuss, just as he had done for her.

The time had come. She was a true reever, and ready for her first dispatch.

They didn't look over their shoulders as they mounted their horses. Amaris patted Cobb on the neck. She'd visited the docile horse in the stable now and again but hadn't had reason to ride him in nearly three years, until now. Brel had attended to the horses and other reevers had exercised them when they'd gone into villages or on missions, but Amaris hadn't had cause to step foot outside of the keep for anything other than her daily runs in a long, long time.

As Cobb was a good, broken-in horse, he needed very little

guidance or correction. This was fortunate as Ash and Malik soon learned that, while Amaris had grown up in proximity to horses in their stable at Farleigh, she'd only learned how to ride side-saddle as a proper lady. When she'd arrived at the fortress, her time with Odrin had been on the back of the saddle and she'd been offered very little guidance.

"Heels down, keep a straight line, shoulders back, stomach in—"

"Goddess dammit, Malik, I'm trying to ride a horse not learn how to do a ballroom dance! I've got it!" Even as she insisted she had it, her jerk made Cobb veer slightly from the path. He stumbled into the grass beyond the road and she struggled to get her mount in line with the others. THe boys did their best to conceal their smiles. She was glad they'd walked their horses down the mountain path so that Odrin didn't have to watch her embarrass herself.

"Are you going to let me finish?"

She grumbled something hateful as he kept his horse straight, looking at her with a bemused expression.

"Soft hands. That's all I was going to say. Keep your hands relaxed as they hold the reins unless you actually want your horse to turn. And just be conscious of how you use your seat. Since you're armed, if you twist wrong your sword might tap his hip and spook him. But mostly, the hands thing. Watch your hands."

It didn't take long for her to get the hang of it as they urged their horses between walking and trotting throughout most of the first day. After much trial and error, they were ready to stop for the night.

The ground beneath the road to the City of Aubade was pressed into parallel lines from the carriages that needed to make their way to and from the royal city to the villages of the continent. The reevers hadn't crossed many travelers on the road. No matter how empty the route that connected the kingdoms may have seemed, they didn't dare risk being stumbled upon in the night as they slept.

Perhaps it was just because it was her first dispatch, Amaris thought she might be too excited to sleep. She hadn't wanted to stop for the night, but the boys had been right to urge them from the road.

The three led their horses off of the trail and into the woods, finding a clearing tightly enclosed with trees to shelter them from prying eyes. They tethered their mounts with long enough leads to allow the horses to graze and set off to scout the immediate area for any signs of animal habitation or creatures that they might not want to disturb. They knew better than to light a fire after sundown, and fortunately the warmth of the season was enough of a blanket as the three camped below the stars. The day's travel had weighed down on them, pressing them into sleep within a few hours after the sun had set.

Amaris opened her eyes.

The world was windless and utterly still. The night had cooled, and with it hung the fresh scents of the forest and its living vegetation. Through the light of the moon, she could see the slumbering shapes of Malik and Ash only a few feet away. The horses were as still as statues. Had they heard something too?

She strained her ears but couldn't make out any sounds. She didn't hear the nocturnal hooting of owls, nor evidence of rodents foraging through the leaves, or even the flitting of insects. She didn't hear the trees, though she could see a slight breeze rub their leaves together. She was wrong. This was not a windless night. Why couldn't she hear the wind? It was far too quiet. Her heart quickened against the confusing realization, wondering if she'd fallen sick and lost the gift for hearing.

She brought her fingers to her ears, pressing her thumb and middle finger together to hear the gentle, papery sound of skin on skin. It was so quiet, no one else would hear, but it was enough to let her know she had not gone deaf in the night. Something else was happening. She hadn't been awoken by sound, but by its sudden absence.

Her gut told her to reach for her weapons.

Amaris's dagger had never left the strap on her leg, not even in sleep. Her sword and bow were lying neatly beside her, put to rest within arm's reach. Unwilling to break the pressing silence, she slowly rose to a crouch, fingers wrapping around the limb of her bow. She took one muted step away from the blanket on which she'd slept, then another. She followed an unknown sense as it angled her toward the trees, one silent motion at a time.

All reevers knew how to be stealthy, trained in the arts of moving between breaths and keeping to the shadows. Their training exercises in ambush had ranged from fun games of hide and seek to the night-darkened slinking around the keep that had resulted in broken bones and light stabbing. Their covert nature of handling disruptions within the continent's kingdoms was part of what had led less educated villagers into thinking of them as clandestine assassins, rather than the silent peacekeepers of the realms they cunningly served. While nearly any reever would have known how to conceal the sound of their feet in the brush, Amaris's small size and lightweight agility had graced her with her feline movements.

She shot another glance to her sleeping companions and momentarily debated waking them. If she shook them from their sleep for the disturbance of a squirrel, she knew she'd never hear the end of it. She couldn't justify waking them because it was too quiet. Similarly, if there was something more sinister in the forest, perhaps the sounds of them stirring would invite attack.

Reevers were typically dispatched alone, after all. She did not require their aid.

Silent as a shadow, she slipped from the clearing where Ash and Malik continued to sleep into the gloom of the trees. Her lilac eyes had never given her any advantage for seeing in the dark, despite Samael's insistence that she must possess some gifts of sight. While a supernatural advantage would have been advantageous, she had spent years training to fight and stalk in the shade as well as in the sun.

Amaris picked her steps carefully, moving through the thicket between the trees. She avoided fallen leaves, stepping around dried branches and avoiding the tugging fingers of thorny weeds to remain as imperceptible as whatever it was she currently sought. The pitter-patter of her heart was the loudest thing in the forest. It was a coward's sound, she cursed to herself.

Despite hearing nothing, something tugged her forward. Her instincts insisted that she was headed in the right direction. She followed that intuition, trusting whatever unknown impulse was guiding her toward the night's disturbance. The instinct told her not only that she was going in the right direction, but also that she was closing in on whatever she'd sensed. She cursed her thrumming heart yet again for betraying the anxiety she felt as she drew closer and closer to the unknown.

There was something brighter ahead. It was a break in the trees.

The moonlight seemed to wash the space ahead as if silver had been poured into a fishbowl and filled to the brim. It was no grassy meadow, but a clearing of bright, reflective water. It must be what was giving the space such a luminescent glow. The tree trunks encircling it were lit by the bright moon, acting as walls for the small bowl of light in the otherwise darkened forest.

Her feet stopped of their own accord. Her senses spoke to her once more, and she listened.

Amaris paused as the tree line ended just before the small pond. She'd been able to spot the small break in the forest from a few paces off, and had been careful to choose her steps so that she would not be given away by any sudden lack of tree cover. The silver light bathing the small clearing revealed everything, as the moonbeams didn't need to battle through a leafy canopy to illuminate what lay below. Her eyes scoured the small clearing from the hiding place where she'd stopped.

Why had her instincts led her here?

The smallest movement caught her eye.

The water of the pond was nearly still, but not quite. Something disturbed it, creating a ripple in the surface and preventing the glass-like reflection of the night sky that the body of water should have had for such a still night. She scanned the shores, following the tiny, silent waves to where a large, dark rock blotted out the light of the moon. The sphere of ripples seemingly emanating from the rock itself. Her eyes were focused on the rock as something—a branch?—extended from it.

The rock was strange; its offshoot even stranger.

Her lips parted against the urge to inhale sharply in surprise as she realized she was seeing no rock, but something living. The extension was not a bough, but the thing's arm. She blinked at what she was witnessing as she followed the arm to its end as a hand was filling a canteen with water from the pond. The rock shifted to reveal that it was no solid shape, but a wingspan. The creature's wings had created the illusion of a solid figure while sheltering the form of a man beneath it. The glint of the moonlight was slowly revealing the enormous, crow-like feathered wings of whoever knelt at the pond.

Inhaling slowly to stifle her fear, Amaris reached for her weapon and, silent as death, nocked an arrow. She found herself wishing she'd spent more time on the archery range and less time on swordplay now that her life might very well depend on her ability to make her target. If she shot her arrow, she'd have only one chance. If she missed, the creature would be at her in a moment.

Amaris reached into her chest, willing her heart to still as she quietly stretched the bow's string, angling for the head of the demon before her. Her damned fingers shook a bit, but she fought down her tremble. She pressed the arrow's fletching against her cheek, keeping the string taut, as she took her aim for the creature's chest. The moment before release, she felt something cold on her neck.

The chilled shape moved slightly. She was acutely aware of the precariousness of life as the sharp edge of steel was pressed into her throat. She swallowed.

She hadn't heard the second man approach. She hadn't heard anything at all. Rather than keep his dagger arm extended, the man in the forest moved so quickly that she had no time to think as one strong arm pinned her to his hardened body. She was rendered unable to twist free or grab for her weapons. He held her firmly with one arm while his free hand continued to clutch a knife to her jugular. One well-placed nick and she was dead.

Amaris had gone from ready to take down an enemy with an arrow to utterly powerless in the breadth of a second. She didn't even have the time necessary to experience panic. She was barely able to process the change as power had shifted before she realized she'd been rendered utterly helpless. She went rigid, unable to react. She still held her bow aloft, but releasing her arrow would be assured destruction. The moment her hand let go, her throat would be slit.

"Put it down," he hissed into her ear with low, dark authority, flooding her with adrenaline and the scent of leather and pepper. His lips had nearly grazed her hair as he spoke. The assailant's breath on her ear sent a chill down her spine.

She raced through her options, feeling time freeze as she called to her training. The stranger was too close for her to throw a punch, especially as both of her hands had been occupied with the bow. If she created the noise necessary to wrestle away, the demon who crouched at the pond would surely be upon them in a second, giving her not one enemy, but two. She couldn't fight.

Her heart thundered under her breast as she slowly complied, lowering the bow.

The other demon continued filling his waterskin, completely

unaware as to what transpired in the trees. He didn't look up from its place near the pond.

"There's a good girl," her assailant murmured somewhat dismissively, as if speaking to himself more than her in the same dark voice. He wrapped a large hand around the knife on her leg to pluck her remaining weapon from her grasp. He urged her forward with a step and Amaris was forced into the clearing with the man still at her back, making themselves fully vulnerable as they abandoned the cover of the trees and moved toward the lip of the water. The demon looked up at them then, wingspan flaring behind him.

She fought the urge to scrunch her face in fear. If she was about to die, she would die with pride.

Her eyes twitched in a wince in preparation for leathery skin, for jagged teeth, for a ridged spine, but instead, she saw... a man. She saw a fae with dark hair, dressed in black leathers. She'd been expecting horrible, amphibious features, but instead stood before a male who looked like he might as well have been a fallen angel. His darkened wings were not the membranous stretches of bat-like skin from her bestiary tomes, but resembled the tales of the seraphim and their unearthly beauty. The man who'd been kneeling at the water's edge folded his wings behind him cautiously as he approached Amaris and her unnamed captor. She still hadn't been able to see who held her, but her chin remained defiantly lifted and she arched her back away to keep from touching him.

One swift motion changed that.

The captor twisted her to look at him. Her hackles raised as she realized her back was to the one she'd thought a demon, but she forced herself to look the man in the eye. She was with not one fae, but two. The only full-blooded fae she'd seen before this moment had been Samael, and aside from the slender arch of his ears and too-large eyes, this man looked nothing like him.

"I'll thank you not to hunt my men," he said, though once again, something about his voice sounded like he wasn't truly speaking to her. The assailant spoke to hear the sound of his own voice, grumbling with blackened agitation.

The reever's lips parted slightly. She could see him then as she faced him in the moonlight. His black hair hung to his shoulders, as dark as night. His tanned skin and sharpened canines held a vague feeling of familiarity. The shadow of his wings blotted out the view of the trees behind him, creating an obsidian halo around his face. He was beautiful. Truly, powerfully, extraordinarily beautiful. Her heart felt as though it were already bleeding in anticipation of her death, as she was sure that no training had prepared her for this battle.

She had never been more terrified in her life.

Amaris took a half-step away from him, but the backward step only brought her closer to the one who'd been at the water's edge. She pivoted sideways, a night-haired man now flanking her on either side. She had her hands raised as if to create a barrier, enforcing the boundaries so that neither of them would take a step closer.

The one who'd held her still had her weapon. She was defenseless, save for her fists and borderline feral will to survive.

The demon with the waterskin spoke not to her, but beyond her. His voice was gentle as he addressed the one who'd held the knife to her throat. "I'm sure she was just afraid."

The captor snarled, "If I hadn't been there, you would have an arrow through your head."

"But I don't, do I," the winged man replied, shouldering his canteen. He looked at Amaris and took a step. It wasn't a move to invade her space, but one to put himself closer to his companion. She noticed with a somewhat furrowed brow that the positioning was meant to make her more comfortable. The closer they were to one another, the less trapped between the two of them she'd feel.

The captor narrowed his eyes at his companion, "Does she look like an innocent village girl to you?"

They took her in then, eyeing her tunic with the supportive leather around her midsection meant to offer extra protecting against blades. They saw her riding leathers, the holster where her dagger was sheathed, and the large scars tearing at angles down her cheek and a second sliding down below the line where her shirt cut off, allowing the imagination to discern how deep the old wound descended.

"Who is she, and what is she doing stocked to the hilt with weapons in the middle of the night?" The captor gestured to the hand that still held the dagger he'd stolen. She wondered why they didn't ask her directly and bristled with offense. The longer they spoke, the more she felt her fear replaced with anger. She didn't understand this particular brand of insult, but the fae were acting like she wasn't there. She could speak for herself.

Amaris burbled over with an infuriated question. "Shouldn't I be asking you that? I protect the people from creatures of the dark that mean to sneak in and destroy them."

He smirked slightly, but it was barely one of amusement. His smile tugged as something else seemed to be flickering behind his eyes.

"Will you be doing any destroying tonight, Zaccai?"

"I hadn't planned on it, General, but I suppose we can see where the night takes us."

They were mocking her. He extended her stolen dagger back to her, hilt first. He was giving her the knife back? As he extended it to her, he paused, something akin to shock on his face. His body went rigid, peering at her—no, *into* her. She reached for the dagger, when the snap of a twig had them whirling. As he extended his hand, his expression changed.

"Wait." The one who'd been called General lifted a hand. He was choosing to ignore whatever approached to ask a pressing question. It was as if he was considering her for the first time that night, soaking in every stitch of her features. Whatever emotion or thought had flickered behind his eyes burned intently before had clicked into place as he stared at her. "Can you—"

"Drop!" came the familiar voice of a reever as Ash barked the command from the tree line. Heloosed an arrow. Amaris flattened herself against the ground in a second, but she wasn't the only one who seized the warning. In the moment it took her to get out of the line of fire, Zaccai had grabbed for the general's attention and they'd darted into the air, then dove back down into the trees with the inhuman speed of a bird of prey. Ash sprinted out from the tree line to her, grabbing her by the shoulders and hoisting her to her feet. The pond was still once more. Her eyes remained fixed over Ash's shoulders on the space above the forest to where the fae had disappeared.

"Are you hurt?" he demanded.

She shook him off with growing irritation as she continued to stare at the sky where the fae had gone, "I'm fine."

His face was still painted with contempt, "Did they take you?"

"No, I thought I sensed something in the woods. I followed that sense here."

"Why didn't you wake me?" His voice was breathless, angry. His flame-red hair, normally bound in a knot, was wild and loose from sleep. The sound of Malik's jogging was crashing through the underbrush, breaking into the clearing to meet them. The commotion had him running for his companions, not caring how much noise he made.

She made no attempt to conceal her irritation. "I am just as competent a warrior as either of you. Reevers are meant to be perfectly capable alone." She looked to Ash, then to Malik from where he'd run into the clearing at the pond's edge. "I don't need your accompaniment when inspecting threats. Besides, if I had investigated the sound and found a mouse, you would have accused me of being a paranoid woman."

He scowled at her, lowering the bow he'd continued to angrily grip at the ready. "I hope you don't seriously believe that of me."

The golden-haired Malik was looking between his friends, eyes bewildered. "Is someone going to tell me what happened?"

"Amaris went off to confront a demon, apparently." Ash was furious.

"It wasn't a demon!" Amaris held the dagger she'd been offered with one hand, the other open with emphasis. The moonlight glinted against the knife's steel, illuminating the pale intensity of her expression.

"Is now the best time to call the humanoid monsters by their right and proper name?" Ash's temper flared. "Are we fighting over semantics?"

"Listen! I woke up to… Well, to a lack of sound." She explained that the absence of noise was what had stirred her, and how she'd followed that sense to the clearing. Their faces had been skeptical at the beginning of her story, but it was decided that the winged men must have been using dampening magic to conceal themselves.

Malik considered this. "You shouldn't be able to sense a dampener. That's the entire point of its power."

Ash shook his head, "Thank goddess she did. What sick, dark magic. Ag'imni shouldn't be able to wield additional abilities. It would have to be stolen. Did they have any object? A ward? They're semi-intelligent, but I've never heard of them using tools…" he shuddered violently. "Goddess dammit. For all we know, they'd been tracking us for just that purpose."

This didn't resonate as true with Amaris. "I'm telling you, they weren't demons. I think they were just refilling their waterskins. If anything, I feel they were using their damper to avoid detection from people like us."

Malik smiled then, "That's before they met Ayla here. Who knew our oak tree could sense the forest of her namesake."

Amaris felt her temper like an iron poker that had been left in the flame. It burned so hot she was ready to let it scald anyone who touched her. Not only were they refusing to hear her, but doubling down on calling her the clumsy-footed nickname was an insult added to injury. She hadn't been an oak tree in training for years, but the name had stuck. Maybe it wasn't such an offense to be the sturdy queen of the arbors, but she was in no mood to let it slide. Her arms uncrossed themselves so she could return her dagger to its sheath against her thigh.

"One of them was called Zaccai. Does that name mean anything to you?"

The men shook their heads, unsure of its origin.

"Ag'imni can speak, but I don't know of them having names. I suppose we don't know enough about them to consider their family structure, but I'm quite certain they're nameless." Malik was frowning.

"I'm telling you what I heard," Amaris insisted.

She was angry, and there would be no changing it tonight. There would be no more sleeping for the rest of the night, so the reevers returned to their camp and repacked their horses. They made haste to exit the woods, putting as much space as possible between them and those in the forest.

The men asked her a few more questions about her encounter, but she only gave clipped responses. They'd brushed her off so fully she couldn't bring herself to say more. The depth to which they'd offended her with their dismissive refusal to believe what she'd seen was a hot, angry coal in her heart, but that wasn't the only peculiar sensation she felt. Something about the interaction with the winged fae had stirred in her, like a kernel stuck in her tooth that she couldn't get out no matter how much her tongue pushed. Something wasn't right, but she couldn't place why, nor could she leave it alone and forget about it.

The first thing that she had emphasized to her companions was that the demon had been not a monstrous creature, but a fae man. Ash had told her on no uncertain terms she had been mistaken, given that they'd all read the same bestiary and knew the creatures inside and out. He'd seen the creatures for himself, and his faeling blood had given him an advantage in the dark over her lilac eyes.

They knew of the night creatures and dark fae from their texts. They'd studied the ag'drurath and their hell-hewn wings, bodies slender and black like serpents, talons that could slice through armor, teeth that would shred and swallow your horse in one bite. What they'd seen had been the humanoid counterparts to the snake-like dragon—the ag'imni—commanders of their serpent familiars. Reevers knew all of the descriptions regarding the unspeakable things they did to fill their stomachs on fae and men alike, their soulless bodies, and their blackened eyes. Whatever she had seen had been the night doubtlessly playing tricks on her. Malik had been too late to the clearing to witness the events, but Ash knew precisely what he'd seen.

She didn't press the issue further, firm in what she had seen. The men fell into silence, allowing only the sound of their mounts, the saddlebags, the hooves, the whinnying and chuffing of the horses to accompany them. The black sky lightened to the deep gray of a stormy sea, then indigo, then lavender, and soon the sun was up over the horizon, warming the land. While they continued their westward journey, her tongue kept pressing on the kernel, pushing her to understand the encounter. Her mind would not rest.

15

Nox wasn't able to sleep, nor was she really trying. Her mind flitted rapidly from one thought to the next, an amalgamation of sounds and ideas and plans and memories. She couldn't relax, couldn't sleep, couldn't rest. Her mind felt like tavern music where six musicians all playing different instruments and clashing songs insisted on playing over one another, each vying for her attention. She tossed fitfully between her silken sheets, turning her pillow to find a cooler side. Her heart burned with hatred for the north and its kingdom. The vengeance she felt knowing they held Amaris was the spite that kept her warm at night.

Her eyes were open as they burned into the dark of the wall, thinking of what the duke had said. Yelagin. Forces were being dispatched to Yelagin.

Her mind hadn't relaxed in more than two years. Millicent had told her everything. During the year that Nox had spent behind the bar, she had considered herself lucky to be insignificant enough that the lady of the house barely spoke to her. Once Millicent had seen her for what she was and deemed her a worthy protégé, the Madame had opened up and let her in, filling in all of the gaps. A barmaid–an orphaned whore–hadn't been worth sharing the weight of her secrets, but someone being groomed to lead beside her, on the other hand… She had fallen victim to the Law of Recency when it came to her feelings regarding the Madame. Perhaps it had been the familiarity of their now-regular interactions. Yet, the informality of their relationship had begun to erode even her most awful memories of Millicent, leaving begrudging companionship in its place.

The Madame trusted her with talks of the politics of the kingdom, with the rumors of unrest, with the corruption of the church and wicked places like Farleigh. They'd spent months fostering their connection before Nox had finally loosened her lips to ask what had happened the fateful morning the Madame had taken her in the carriage to Priory. She'd heard the commotion from the far side of the manor, and then before she knew what had happened, Amaris was gone and she was being ushered into the glossy, black coach.

The truth of the morning had been worse than anything she'd allowed herself to imagine.

Millicent had been mournful to have to inform her of just how terrible the events had been in the courtyard. She'd hung the curled ringlets of her head in pity for the dark-haired girl as she told her that she had been standing on the cobblestones in front of Farleigh that morning as the silver teenager had sprinted out of the house intent on escaping to the woods. Amaris had run, not wanting to go with her. Millicent had paused sadly, commenting on how she'd traded an unfamiliar devil for the one she could have known. The assassin had seen a vulnerable girl running for the woods and abducted her.

The women in the courtyard had been helpless to stop it as the villain had swept her up amidst her cries.

Millicent had shrieked for the matrons to do something, horrified that they had let such a man in their walls, but the agent of Raascot had urged his horse into a gallop and sprinted toward his northern borders. Millicent had sworn never to deal with Farleigh again after that, knowing now that they let men take advantage of the young women they were sworn to protect. At The Selkie, the women were empowered. It was a place where men and the blood of their bulges was merely a tool for money, or even more importantly, for information. The stupidity of the brutish sex was little more than a weapon for the cunnings of women.

Hate had settled like a stone in her stomach.

Nox began to see the world for what it was. She understood the divisions between the sexes, and accepted places like The Selkie as the spy dens they really were. What better way to lure men in than to make them feel powerful, to lead them to a place where they thought they had the upper hand? How empty their heads, how blackened their hearts to think they were the ones with agency. The women who worked in the salon were underestimated, and the ability to hide in plain sight had been their truest strength.

She blinked against her dry eyes, realizing she'd been staring too long at the shadowed wall beyond her curtains. The Selkie stayed active until the third bell after midnight, which would have turned anyone into a nocturnal creature. Their sleep schedules had been reversed, allowing the girls to sleep well into the early hours of afternoon before working the floor again during the evening.

Having fed that night on the Duke of Henares, she continued to hum with energy.

Nox rolled onto her side, tossing once more as her eyes soaking in the sight of the gauzy curtains that hung around her large bed. The raven-haired beauty lived in the finest room now, nearly as beautiful as Millicent's itself. Her years at The Selkie had seen a meteoric rise in her importance. She'd begun as a barmaid in a room in the basements, then graduated to a small room on the ground floor. Now her rooms reflected the brothel royalty she'd become.

Her performance was merely that—a manipulation of the weak-willed and undeserving. She slammed her fists against the sheets in the dark night and huffed, giving up on sleep altogether. The cool side of the pillow would not be enough to soothe her tonight. Nox sat up and lit her bedside candle. She left the comfort of her sheets, walking over to the desk that rested beneath her window. She had taken to sleeping naked, preferring the silk on her skin, but she wrapped a cashmere blanket around herself as she sank into the chair at the cluttered table.

She rested her elbows on the desk and let her fingers sink into her hair, propping up her head as she stared at piles of loose-leaf pages all filled with cramped writing, diagrams, plots, drawings and conspiracies.

Her desk was covered in notes of all of the information she had been gathering. Yelagin, the duke had said. Queen Moirai was demanding the duke's forces go northeast to the lakeside town of Yelagin. Well, they had been his troops before tonight. They were her troops now. Nox felt a satisfied grin when she thought of the lordling's slackened face and the puppet he'd become. Perhaps she was a demon, but she was a damn good one.

Where else had the north been infiltrating, and what was their intent? How could she get her hands on someone high enough in their ranks to know where Amaris had been held for the past three years, and if she was even alive? She may not have known the best path forward, but she most definitely understood her end game.

A recurrent nightmare haunted her with such thoroughness that she saw it every time she closed her eyes. She saw Amaris, helpless and scared, being taken by an assassin. A man who thought he could take whatever he wanted, as men did.

Nox closed her eyes against the thought of a vulnerable, snowflake girl being held against her will. Life at the mill had been hard enough. She had not deserved to suffer such a terrible fate. Despite going years without so much as a whisper of the silver young woman, Nox felt in her heart that she would know if Amaris's spirit had left the earth. She believed in their connection the same way that the devout believed in the All Mother. She could feel the tug between them. It was a tethering bond that she knew would snap her in two if it were severed by death.

If Farleigh had been any testament to how the world saw Amaris, then surely the northerners would keep her alive, even if only for their own sick pleasure. She knew more than enough from her time at the pleasure house about the twisted, broken desires of men.

She heard a soft sound in the hall the moment before it came on her knob. She knew who it would be. The sound of her feet on the rug, the gentle way she twisted the handle, the ease in which she opened the door with every ounce of stealth.

The door opened quietly behind her and she looked over to where Emily was sliding in, clicking it closed as quietly as she could. Emily wrapped her blanket around her shoulders against the chill. The supple, strawberry girl approached Nox where she sat and put an arm around her loosely, kissing her temple.

The ginger kept her voice low in respect of the late hour, not wanting to wake anyone else in the house as she said, "I saw your candlelight."

"You should be asleep."

Emily kissed the side of her face, then her neck. Nox felt her tension ebb slightly as she allowed the intimacy, exhaling as the small pleasure pulled her mind away. Emily slid her hands slowly down Nox's arms. She murmured into her throat, "I couldn't sleep."

"I can never sleep," Nox admitted, closing her eyes against her insomnia.

Nox's heart would never belong to the freckled girl, and Emily knew it. Still, the nights were long and cold, the men who visited their chambers were sources of income, secrets and power—never that of love.

"I can help you sleep," Emily whispered. "Let me help you unwind."

Nox's eyes drifted up to meet the girl. Emily was offering more than sex, and she knew it. Every time they connected, it was a bid to prove that she could fill the void in Nox's heart. She would make a wonderful partner. She was pretty and clever and compassionate. She'd had endless patience for Nox's guarded heart, her cagey answers, her wayward emotions. Nox didn't know much of what the male patrons thought of her performance, but she was particularly skilled whenever they were together. She was right. She did know how to help Nox unravel from the tight coils of the day.

Nox's brows pinch, and she sighed. Emily ignored the weak attempt at protest entirely.

"Come on," the freckles ran down her arm, over her hand, even over the fingers that interlaced through Nox's now.

Emily pulled the raven-haired girl back into her bed and Nox obliged, abandoning her notes for the night. She dipped to blow out the candle at the bedside. Emily slid in first, lifting the covers for the other. They tucked themselves between the silk of the sheets, Nox dropping the cashmere blanket to the floor before crawling in.

Emily sighed at the heaviness Nox carried, and guilt tugged at her. She didn't want any of this to be a burden that her friend, her lover, her partner under the roof of The Selkie shouldered. Life in the pleasure house didn't require new hardships, concerns or worries. Emily carried enough without absorbing Nox's troubles. Yet, her empathy insisted upon it.

She kissed her deeply on the mouth, attempting to draw her mind away from the pain that plagued her. Her mouth tugged her here, into their present. She used one hand to draw long, sensual lines up Nox's side. Nox sighed, feeling the effectiveness of the distraction. There was nothing more Nox could do for tonight by scouring notes and studying maps. Her mission would still await her in the morning. She allowed the door to her mind to shut, opening the one that belonged to her body alone. She let go of her troubles, choosing instead to use the hands that had clutched her worries and use them to wrap an arm around Emily. Nox flipped her onto her back, appreciating the understanding face that looked up at her. Nox lowered her mouth slowly with her lips twitching upward in a smile, allowing herself a little fun, and a promised release for the night.

☽ ☽ ☽ ☾ ● ☾ ☾ ☾ ☾

Millicent was pacing behind her desk, face flushed with fury.

Nox was decidedly bored by the woman's unimaginative brand of fruitless anger. She inspected her nails, pushing on her cuticles while she allowed the woman her rather predictable outburst.

The Madame was going to wear the carpet bare if she continued to march so fruitlessly in the small, lavish space. Nox stood, unimpressed, using her attention to pick phantom strings of fabric from the silken wrap around her shoulders. It irritated Millicent further that Nox was not taking her more seriously. Agitation was an unbecoming emotion on the woman's face. It carved lines into her, betraying her age.

"I never meant for you to be the one to go to Yelagin," she said with clear exasperation. "Send his men and stay here, where we can continue gathering our forces."

"Our forces?" Nox narrowed her eyes ever so slightly, looking up from her fingernails. She was markedly disinterested in the exchange. She relaxed her back against the wall of the Madame's office, marveling at how she'd once found this space intimidating. Millicent's anger did nothing for her now.

"The forces you need! You'll need manpower if you intend to march north of the border! What do you have now, a duke and his men? A few merchants and their money? Why would you be so reckless! You can have it all! The man power is at your fingertips! Stay here until we've convinced the Captain of the Guard to visit. I'm already sorting it out to send Emily to lure him to The Selkie. She was meant to go out later this week!"

Emily had been an excellent lure, but Nox wasn't comfortable sending the girl into danger more often than necessary. This was not her fight, and it wasn't fair to continue using her. She knew that Emily would go whenever asked, particularly as Nox was involved, but the strawberry girl was fully human. She had nothing but her wits and prayers to protect her when she went out into the world to aid in their agenda.

Her answer was calm, "I don't need the Captain of the Guard. What I need is information."

Millicent froze in her steps but nearly shook with rage. She looked like she might flip her desk. The Madame forced herself into stillness, which was clearly an unusual practice for the mercurial woman. Her nostrils flared until she'd dragged in enough air to calm herself and find an authoritative tone. "You are being foolish. You're letting your love blind you."

Nox was in no mood for Millicent's temper. She had once feared the woman many years ago. Millicent had never been cruel to the girls at The Selkie, but she wasn't exactly a joy as an employer, either. The first year behind the bar, Nox had done her best to stay on the woman's good side. After Nox discovered her gift—or her curse—Millicent helped her to cultivate and master it. For the first few months, the Madame had been a steadying force—one may have even called her a mentor. As Nox learned more about the politics between the north and the south and the truth of Amaris's ensnaring, their plan had begun to take shape. Millicent helped her in her hunt to gather intel on her northern enemy. They learned the weak points in Queen Moirai's army and the best ways to access her troops. In turn, Millicent benefited directly from the array of puppets she gathered around the kingdom.

Of course, Nox and Queen Moirai had a common enemy in Raascot. She saw her actions as in line with the royal highness's own wishes, even if the queen might not see the unsanctioned vigilante efforts so kindly. Hopefully, if all went according to plan, the intercalation would remain undetected. What Moirai didn't know wouldn't hurt her. But Nox would be damned if the southern queen advanced on her plans to invade the north and left Amaris imprisoned by an oversight. Amaris was an orphan without a name, as Nox had been. Who would risk their forces for a nobody? If anyone were going to liberate the moonlit girl, it would have to be her.

"The Captain of the Guard isn't going anywhere," Nox said coolly. "Once I return from Yelagin, there will be nothing but time to accrue the needed men."

"You can't go to Yelagin!"

"Can't?"

Millicent's office had felt so grand the first time she was in it. Now she saw it for what it was: expensive trinkets of a hoarder, and nothing but manifestations of Millicent's greed. She felt that greed now in her insistence that Nox stay. It was no surprise that Millicent would want more. She always wanted more. More men, more forces, more titles, more power, it would never be enough no matter how long Nox stayed in Priory.

Nox was no idiot. She had been completely aware from the very beginning that the Madame was using her abilities as a succubus for her own, power-hungry objectives. She knew that Millicent's help was not altruistic, and that the Madame would do nothing if it didn't serve her. She would have remained a no-named servant to The Selkie if she hadn't proven herself so valuable.

Their begrudging allyship was one of mutual benefit. If they had the support of the council of nobility throughout Farehold, Queen

Moirai might consider Millicent for her court advisor. A position of prominence in the castle was the Madame's endgame. Millicent had proven herself a shrewd businesswoman in Priory, building a small empire with her riches and spy network of girls, hidden in full view as the city's most elite pleasure house. The southern queen would never consider an audience with a Madame, of course. A monarch would never openly associate with someone of disrepute like Millicent, but if the weight of every male title-holder in the south put the woman's name up for advisor, Queen Moirai would have cause to look twice at the Madame.

Together, Millicent would gain power, and Nox would find Amaris.

Nox had no need for titles, nor care for what Millicent chose to do with power that came her way. As long as they were bonded by a common goal of amassing their forces so that she could be reunited with Amaris, the Madame's ulterior motives were not Nox's concern. She'd protected the girl from infancy. She'd taken her place at the brothel. She'd be damned if she gave up on her now. Not when she had the power to make a difference.

Millicent provided her protégé with a number of effective allies in their games of chess. The bartender, the lutist, the girls who worked the floor, the lures who would wander into the world to draw in the men, they were all cut in on the profits reaped. When Nox took someone up to her room, she didn't simply receive payment for the hour—she took everything.

They didn't know the details of Nox's dark power, though she was quite certain they suspected she wasn't entirely human. Men would go up to her rooms excited for a tumble, and descend the stairs fully ready to hand over their homes, lands, and lives. The Selkie had more money than it knew what to do with. The succubus kept up her life as a courtesan so the men would wander into her bed, finding themselves beholden to her power. Not only was it an endless supply of fresh prey as she absorbed soul after soul, but Millicent was endlessly willing to clean up after her botched missions. Besides, remaining at The Selkie came with the added benefits of the luxurious lifestyles and afforded Nox the freedom she desired.

She was wealthy, she was beautiful beyond reason, she was quite literally vibrating with power, and yet she was utterly empty without her starlight. She was a night with no moon.

Millicent pursed her mouth into a tight line. "I'm sorry, but you're being too shortsighted, and I simply have to forbid it." Millicent threw up her hands.

Nox sucked in a lip. It was perhaps the least visible way she could bite back a retort. She knew Millicent well enough to understand how this argument would play out. What was this discussion but another game of chess? The best thing to do would be to let the Madame feel she had won the exchange, and then leave in the morning. If she sent word for the Duke of Henares, he'd have a horse and armed escorts waiting for her by first light. She would ride out ahead of the troops before the infiltrating Raascot men in Yelagin were spooked by word of their arrival.

"Perhaps you're right," Nox agreed slowly, doing her best to make a show of her reluctance to accept the truth.

The Madame's brows collected in the middle. "Yes, I... I'm not trying to prevent you from your goals. You know we want the same thing," she continued cautiously, "I'm just trying to help you get what you want in the most responsible way."

"I know you want what's best," Nox dipped her head.

Millicent was still poised for a verbal fight, and seemed slightly surprised, if not then quickly flooded with relief that Nox was able to see her wisdom. She hadn't realized how tightly she'd been clutching the back of her chair from where she stood until her white-knuckled grip eased, blood returning to her fingers.

"Good," the Madame nodded skeptically. "That's that, then."

That was that.

Emily was up before the twilight hours, helping The Selkie's most prized possession as she packed. She wanted to offer to ride with her to Yelagin, but knew before even asking that Nox would never entertain the idea. The freckled girl understood many things. She knew how useless it would be to beg Nox to stay, and how heartbroken she'd be to have the young woman look her in the eyes and tell her that, though she'd enjoyed Emily's intimacy and appreciated her companionship, she would go to the ends of the earth to save Amaris. She didn't need to hear what she already knew.

Her eyelashes were the same light strawberry as her hair. They'd fluttered to a close as she convinced herself not to cry. She begged herself not to want. She bartered and pleaded and bargained with her heart to let Nox go, but it would not. She was in the worst kind of love, the one that would never be returned. She knew it, and yet, she couldn't leave.

Her eyes squeezed shut all the more tightly as memories flooded in and out.

Emily and her sister had watched the two of them together for nearly fifteen years within the walls of the mill. The pair had always been off in their little worlds, black and white against the earth and all its inhabitants. The other children at Farleigh may as well have not existed for all they were worth to those two. Everyone had their reasons for being spiteful toward Amaris and Nox. Most hated the silver girl for her special treatment, others despised Nox for how the Matron Agnes preferred her, babying her, choosing her. The children had disliked them, considering them as outsiders, as preferential, as set apart. The tallest flower is the first to be cut, after all.

Emily had felt just as much displeasure when she looked at them, but never for the reasons of her peers. Why should Nox give her love so intensely, so chaotically, to a girl who was too clueless to love her back? Oh, Amaris loved Nox to be sure, but it was clear that their intimate barrier had never been crossed. They had failed to develop beyond friends to young lovers while at Farleigh. What a waste of time and attention it had been, watching Nox day after day as she had eyes for no one else.

Emily had her younger sister to keep her company, and the two of them kept their ginger heads low and their hands busy at Farleigh. They did their chores, stayed quiet, shared their meals, and planned for an escape that would never come. They'd flown under the radar of the matrons and the other orphans for years, but their bond wasn't the same. What Nox and Amaris had was infuriating.

And then a curse and a blessing had struck. Emily was bought for The Selkie. As much as she wanted to hate her station, Nox had been brought to her side six months later. The barrier had come down slowly, gradually, but now she had her. She had her in her arms. She had her in her bed. She had her softness, her body, her moans and gasps and flavor.

Yet here Nox was, thousands of miles from the silver girl who had never kissed her the way Emily had, who had never touched her, never made love to her, never her made her cry out or see the goddess or feel as Emily had, and Nox still chose Amaris over her time and time again. There was nothing she could do but be patient, and hope, and wait. She hadn't pressed the issue, knowing that when the beauty had breathed her name in bed, her heart had been with another. She'd wanted to fool herself into believing that one day, with enough time and space, things might change. She couldn't bring herself to hear the rejecting words. She didn't deserve the heartbreak that would follow if Nox voiced what the freckled girl already knew to be true.

"Are you sure you don't want company?" Emily hated herself for asking.

"It'll be a hard road," Nox shook her head, squeezing Emily's hand.

"I could make it easier."

"Em...." Nox's brows were the most expressive part of her face.

Emily searched her eyes, allowing her pained expression to say everything she couldn't. Emily looked away, hiding the pink shame of rejection that doubtlessly colored her cheeks in the dark of the night.

Nox was a lot of things, but she never lied to the women with whom she shared her bed. "Emily, I don't know what I'll find there..."

Emily moved away and grabbed Nox's traveling cloak, hating herself for helping her. Turning her back had given her the excuse she needed to take a stilling breath, refusing to let herself cry.

"I know," Emily said, facing her to look once more.

Nox was telling her that perhaps she'd return and everything would be the same between them. Maybe she'd gain nothing, and nothing would change regarding their life at The Selkie and the relationship between them. But perhaps she'd learn everything, and she'd never return. She couldn't give false promises. She couldn't tell Emily she'd be back. She couldn't tell her everything would be okay, or that she'd return for her, or that they'd be fine.

Nox wouldn't lie, and Emily didn't want to hear the truth.

She fought the impulse to say something, the desire to pull her close, to kiss her deeply, to convince her of what she felt for her, but Nox's mind was already on the road. She brushed a peck against Emily's cheek and whispered some promise to be safe along with a quiet apology for the Madame's certain impending wrath. She disappeared down the hall.

Emily watched from the third-story window of The Selkie as Nox navigated out of the pleasure house and left the brothel behind her, walking swiftly down the lawn, and mounting a night-black horse, matching the hair of its rider. She'd called for the Duke of Henares to send a horse and escorts, and he'd delivered without question. Two men on similarly dark horses flanked her as she urged her steed into a trot, putting as much distance between herself and the pleasure house before the citizens of Priory began to stir. The sky had scarcely begun to show hints of gray when their horses turned a corner down the cobbled streets, and Emily could see them no longer.

16

Each night they stopped, Malik, Ash and Amaris would forgo the continental route that connected the kingdoms and reroute themselves into the woods, seeking shelter to camp for the night away from wayward travelers. Her anger had ebbed and the tension they'd experienced had dissipated with time, mostly due to the ivory reever's reluctance to say anything more on the subject.

They had passed plenty of farmers with their wheelbarrows, or carts laden with whatever might be intended to bring back to their village for market. There had been at least a few carriages over the last several days, doubtlessly pulling some wealthy something-or-other to whatever destination the silver-spooned society members deemed worthy of their presence. At one point, a white and gold carriage had passed them while heading in the opposite direction. She'd suppressed as a shudder as she thought of the bishop who'd visited Farleigh each month. Each time he'd arrived at their orphanage, it had been a sign that it was time to be weak, to make herself small, to hide. She was not that person anymore.

Amaris supposed Ash would have drawn stares wherever he went. Half-faced and with hair as red as dying embers, he was not only beautiful, but had the tell-tale ears of the fair folk. His golden skin was not very common in the southern kingdom, as the citizens of Farehold favored the pale skin and rosy cheeks of golden-haired mothers and highland sons. Bronzed skin tones were far more common north of the border.

Malik, as amiable as ever, would most definitely have drawn smiles from the passers-by if he'd been traveling alone. He had a face that could fit in anywhere. His easy aurora was disarming to even the most suspicious of folk. The other two had sent him into towns alone on more than one occasion to fetch dinner or supplies when they needed to be in and out without raising an eyebrow regarding their whereabouts. It was a long journey from Uaimh Reev to Aubade, and they couldn't tolerate the suspicious glances and guarded citizens with each and every stop.

The maidens always seemed to favor Malik, which was just as fun for Ash and Amaris to watch as it was uncomfortable for Malik to experience. The way his cheeks flushed, humbly shying away from the attention, only made him more attractive to the village girls and their giggles. There was nothing quite like the strong, muscled shoulders of a man who didn't carry the weight of his own ego.

While the boys may have drawn attention on their own as reevers on solo dispatch, Amaris's presence made discretion nearly impossible.

After the first day of drawing gaping stares, she'd kept her hood up even in the heat of summer's mid-day sun. She grumbled with discomfort as sweat dripped down her sternum on the front of her shirt and slicked her hair. The shadow cast down over her brows and eyelashes hid her prominent features. Cobb, ever the mount, seemed unbothered no matter how many farmers skidded to a stop in front of him or horses were steered wide of the road to avoid them. Cobb's reliable calm always drew affectionate, appreciative strokes from his rider. The sweet, gray beast didn't have two thoughts in his head to rub

284

together. She didn't care. She'd met Cobb on the day of her liberation, and would always love him deeply.

Malik and Ash didn't possess emotional ties to their mounts the way Amaris had. Their steeds were some mix between whatever black moorland Fell Pony had sired most of the mounts in Stone, and the tawny New Forest pony who had been at the keep for the last twenty years, allowed to live and be with her foals. Cobb had been a gelding stray, and since he didn't upset the New Forest, she didn't bother him.

She'd visited Cobb a few times in the stables, but hadn't ever possessed the particular fondness for horses or wild creatures that she'd sometimes see in her peers at Farleigh. She was much more comfortable obsessing over monsters, dragons, demons and ghouls. Amaris would choose the chance to see a vageth over a horseback ride any day. That being the case, she'd done very little to involve herself with the reev and its stables.

When Amaris had asked the boys of their mounts' names, the young men had informed her they were on mares Nine and Fourteen.

"Your mare's name is Nine?"

Ash had shrugged, "Naming can be deeply meaningful, or it can be perfunctory. This one, of course, has the deeply meaningful title of being the ninth horse born to its mother."

Nine, Fourteen and Cobb were pleasant road companions and trustworthy horses. She'd have to see if she could do something about the colt and filly naming process when she returned to Uaimh Reev.

By nightfall, they were pulling off the road and away from prying eyes once more. Horses tethered, they still had some time to find dinner. There was leftover bread from the previous village, and if they could catch a rabbit, the hot, gamey sandwiches would be a nice break from whatever hard, sharp white cheese and apples they'd acquired from the last village. While she normally loved cheese, this one was dry and crumbled in a way that made her think she'd rather skip a meal altogether than suffer through another block of the stuff.

Malik insisted he didn't mind the cheese, but she was sure he only said that because he'd been the one to purchase it. Instead, they split their hunt three ways in search of game, both for efficiency and for safety in case one was to fire an arrow. Enough reevers died at the hands of beasts and men. They didn't need another in their dwindling league falling to friendly fire over a rabbit.

While the men hunted for their supper, Amaris had made a habit over the last several nights of walking into the forest and then stilling herself. She searched for the inexplicable intuition she had felt the night she'd been led to the pond. There had been an instinct that she hadn't been able to justify. It had been something silent but potent within her, and she clawed for it, begging it to reactivate. Many uneventful hours, camps and slumbers had passed between the night she had met the demon general, but no matter how long into the night she lay awake or how hard she strained her ears for alertness, she'd felt nothing.

Ash had teased her over the last few days for being a lousy huntress when she had repeatedly returned back to the camp empty-handed, but her attention had been elsewhere. She'd rather the boys think she was terrible at collecting game than know the truth. She wasn't ready to hear their disapproval if she explained she was searching for the winged fae. What had happened that night at the pond? How could she learn to understand it?

The winged men certainly hadn't seemed like demons. Zaccai's wings had been feathered, not like the membranous, bat-like wings of the twisted beasts in her tomes. He was not the monstrosity of the ag'imni. Even though Ash insisted an ag'imni was what they'd seen in the clearing, she couldn't understand how, where he had seen a gargoyle, she had seen a beautiful dark fae. Ash had told her that night that her eyes had been playing tricks on her in the moonlight. He'd insisted that her weak eyes had no gift for sight in the dark. She'd been annoyed once more at his dismissal. That obnoxious, desperate feeling for relief plagued her following the twists of the incident. The unrelenting sensation akin to the kernel in her tooth gnawed at her whenever she thought of the exchange.

Amaris had stayed in the forest, stilling herself until after the sun had set while the others hunted for dinner. She'd focused on her breathing while listening, absorbing the sounds around her. Nothing had tugged on her senses. She gave up, feeling both frustrated and disappointed for the second, then third, now fourth night in a row. When she returned to camp, the rabbit had already been cooked and mostly consumed, though they'd saved her a piece as they'd snuffed out the flame. Regardless of how the three had tried to move forward with their dispatch, the silver reever had become quietly consumed with the need to seek out the strange fae she'd discovered once more. When they met again, she would uncover what had been stumbled upon once before by happenstance. She would be ready. Amaris forced herself to stay awake in the late hours as her companions fell into comfortable sleep on the forest floor, pinching herself, chewing the inside of her cheek, or biting her lip anytime she felt herself grow tired. Eventually, the gentle rising and falling of their chests sounded along with the comforting depth of their sleep.

Amaris ignored the men, eyes trained on the trees. As she stared into the woods, she felt for the first time in days that something was staring back.

She swallowed, listening to the instinct that told her she was not alone.

Amaris sat up, straining her eyes against the darkness. She didn't make any move toward the woods, but watched intently, waiting for a sign, or a familiar absence of noise. She looked for the flicker of wings or the reflective flash of swords that the men would have holstered. She scanned the forest around her, looking for any hint of movement.

Then she saw it. It was the flick of a shadow. It was the slight, unnatural extension of darkness from one of the trees.

She rose from where she sat, going into a crouch. If she was about to encounter the pair she'd met several nights ago, she meant to show them she didn't intend to harm them. She wanted to speak, not fight. She had questions that required answers. Amaris flattened her palms to reveal that they grasped no weapons.

The shape moved closer. It was about the height of a man. The half-moon glow didn't show the face of a person, and she screwed her eyes as intensely as she could against the dark. Something was wrong.

A cold breeze snaked through their campsite, raising goosebumps on her arms and the back of her neck. She tasted an inexplicable anxiety, like the tang of metal, in the back of her mouth. The chill was not normal for the season. Her senses switched from curiosity to fight or flight as the cold began to permeate the campsite. The sensation slithered down her spine, and she knew she was not about to face any mortal. The shadow hadn't moved closer, nor had she stood from her crouched position but as the reek of rotting flesh filled her nostrils, she knew she had to make a move.

Amaris lowered her hand with tar-like slowness to reach for her sword. If she could keep the creature from stirring before she was armed, she might just have a chance at defense. As she wrapped her fingers around the hilt, the monster drifted out from its space between the trees and she saw it fully. Her brain took a second to connect the monstrosity before her eyes with the horrible pictures, the lore, and bestiaries she'd studied. She had seen this face sketched in the tomes at the fortress and heard the war stories of reevers who had faced it and lived to tell the tale. She was looking into the face of a nightmare embodied.

She was staring at the slackened, inhumane, corpse-like face, the sunken eyes, the reeking smoke-like tendrils of the beseul.

Her weapon's hilt. Her fingers flexed against the metal, readying herself for action. It was time to make her move. Amaris cried out. Her sound was not in fear, but one intended to alert her companions while she sprang into action. She'd barely had a moment to react, but knew she couldn't allow them to be caught unaware, slaughtered in their sleep. The men jerked from their sleeping state, their limbs a disoriented flailing for weapons without knowing how or why.

She had to create time for them to mobilize while buying herself time to survive.

Giving the others the split-second chance to get on their feet, she took off into the forest, the smoke-like corpse tearing from the trees and covering the space of the campsite as the beseul glued itself to her heels in pursuit. She ran through the forest with the outright panicked sprint of someone who knew death was licking her heels.

Amaris tried to think of what she knew of the beseul, but was so focused trying to avoid fallen logs, dodge trees, navigate shadows. Her brain struggled to split into two tasks, knowing her life depended on splitting instinct and knowledge. She recalled the creature sizzled in sunlight, forcing it to be a monster of the night, but unless she planned to keep her sprinting pace for the next six hours, the wafting, animated corpse would have its teeth upon her long before the break of dawn.

She couldn't think of anything that would help her. All she knew was that she wasn't fast enough. She wasn't running hard enough. She wasn't agile, or lithe, or strong enough to survive this attack. No matter how hard she pushed, she felt the stench in her nostrils flare, the smoke crawl up closer, the cold bite into the skin of her back. She could not outrun it.

She demanded herself to dodge the trees. The voice within her cried for her to move faster. She needed to watch her feet! Breathe, breathe, *breathe*! She cursed inwardly, obscenities cracking like hail against glass as her feet hit the branches, the leaves, the rocks underfoot.

She pushed herself to run, run, run *faster!* The obscenities continued to spill, one word over the other as if her feet did not belong to her, they were separate entities that she commanded not to trip. Her inner narrative was a mix of incomplete thoughts, demands, curses, terrified prayers, scrambled desperations, and panic. There was so much panic. Her thoughts were scattered demands, jumbled anxieties, and a desperate search for a plan.

Amaris didn't know where she was running, just that she was pulling the unholy entity away from camp, away from her friends. She couldn't confront the monster in the forest while it was on top of her. Amaris's feet carried her faster than she'd ever gone before, her strong muscles forcing her into a full-out sprint. She called on years of hardened calves and thighs as she'd powered her way up and down the mountain at the reev for such a time as this. This is why they'd forced the reevers to run up and down the mountain. This is why they trained. They ran to survive. They ran to live. They ran for exactly this moment.

She was terrified.

The beseul's speed was not that of man or fae; it was the speed of shadow and time. She gagged on its scent as the creature closed on her. She could barely dodge branches, allowing them to whip at her face, tearing at her clothes, her skin, whipping against her in sharp, painful stings as she barreled forward. She knew her face was being torn to ribbons. Her eyes stung from the lashes of twigs. Amaris had intended to loop back to camp so that the three of them could take on the creature once they'd gotten to their feet and gathered their weapons, but as its putrid, unholy wail sounded at her back, the foul stench of carrion filling her nostrils, she knew she couldn't turn. She was choking on the horrible odor of death, fleeing the chilled reach of the beast for her life. Amaris was buying not minutes, but seconds between her and the beseul.

Pain. Pain from her muscles, her lungs, from the thin branches that whipped her, from the inexplicable cold of the icy death that pressed into the skin of her back. She knew only panic, fear, and pain.

Amaris spotted what she hadn't realized she'd been looking for. She urged herself further, exerting the last of her reserves of stamina, pushing herself to her limit. She saw the open space in the forest where the dull silver glow of the half-moon illuminated grass rather than shrubs, and barreled for it. An opening. This was her only chance. Each leap over fallen logs and snag of brambles threatened to slow her, but she just needed enough space to maneuver without careening headlong into a tree. The monster was so close to her now that she could feel its chilled tendrils burning her as if ice itself had been pressed against the raw skin of her calves, her shoulders, the back of her neck, a liquid smoke on her heels.

Either she succeeded, or she was seconds from having her jugular torn by a demon.

She had only heartbeats to make her move. In the few seconds it took her to burst from the trees she dove—not fell, truly *dove*—plunging into the grass below and rolling to her back, her sword coming up in an arc as the beseul, too close to stop, practically flew on top of her. She cried out, the sound of an involuntary yelp tearing through her throat as her sword met its mark. The dead-winter chill of its half phantasmic form grazed the space above her.

It was the maneuver she had hoped for. Inertia had carried the beast of nightmares over her, inches from her sliding body as her sword made contact on some serpentine spine beneath its death-scented shadows. She felt the crunch of bone and the creature careened to the side, pummeled from its trajectory by her blow. The strike had not killed it. No, it didn't even look wounded as it flew to the side, hit the ground, and then rose, howling with the force of a legion of demons as it loosed its blood-thirsty cry into the forest. Years of training had Amaris acting on instinct, back on her feet and ready with her defensive position.

The reever had used the only ploy in her disposal. She didn't know what to do now except face it head on. If she was going to die, she would go down swinging. She blazoned her sword at her side, egging it on as she danced on the balls of her feet so it would make the next move, tensed for impact. The creature lunged for her, but was knocked from its course by something. Rather, someone?

She stopped herself in the middle of a leap, unsure as to where her sword should land. Amaris forced her muscles to freeze in their descending arc.

Something new was in the forest. Her breath caught as she jerked her blade away at the last second. Someone had come for her. Panting a groan from the exertion, the man—Ash? No, it was neither of her companions—a black-haired man threw his own sword into play and Amaris leapt to the side, flanking the creature without a second thought.

A flare of black, feathered wings blocked out her view of the moon. With the deafening beat of wings and rumble of thunder, a third party slammed into the earth, raising a long, silver rapier overhead and slashing it toward the beseul, throwing the power of three deadly warriors at the ghoul. Now triangulated between the three of them, the gossamer terror was outnumbered.

She didn't have time to appreciate the magnificence of their entrance or the relief that crashed over her.

The first man took the finishing blow in the brief second it had taken the beseul to assess its opponents, severing the creature's head from its body. The blow sent its loose, corpse-like face spiraling for the earth with a final, wet scream. Its mouth continued gaping as its head disconnected from its body, continuously animated in spite of its decapitation. The battle was over nearly as soon as it had begun.

The icy shock only known to those who survived battle pressed down on her then. She'd studied the beasts. She knew of demons. She knew that she was supposed to separate their heads from their bodies—that demons couldn't truly be killed. Now that Amaris faced it in the moment, she felt paralyzed. She didn't know what to do, what to say, who to thank, or how to move in order to do what had to be done.

Her entire body trembled with cold, with adrenaline, and with the confusion of exertion that had been stopped in the midst of a fight.

The three heaved for air, eyeing each other in the wake of their victory. Amaris had outrun death itself and doubled over, pulling oxygen into her lungs from the flight. The blackened, stinking blood of the beseul stained the earth between them. The reever opened her mouth to speak when a cry erupted. For the briefest of moments she jumped in her own skin, terrified the noise had come from the beseul, but no—the noise had been from the trees.

They hadn't had ten seconds of relief before a new threat descended upon them.

With the crash of breaking branches, pounded dirt and the grunt of a hero's battlecry, Malik thundered from the forest with Ash fast on his heels. Malik body-checked the winged soldier, catching him off guard in his post-slaying pause, wrestling him to the ground. Of course it would be the other reevers. She had cried out to alert them to the beseul and then taken off into the forest with death on her heels, running for her very life. Their training had taken over as they'd pursued the nightmare, destined to eliminate the threat.

She didn't understand why they didn't stop when they saw that they weren't facing the beseul. Confusion, anger, horror and exhaustion tore through her in equal pulls, the fingers of each emotion clawing at her from the inside out. She's already survived so much–suffered so much in such a short length of time. She couldn't make sense of the chaos as it unfolded.

The scene had erupted into mayhem. Ash crossed blades with the dark-haired general who had twisted his position just in time to throw up a defensive sword, the red-headed reever moving with the agility of the fae as he swung again and again. The motion of the clash had happened so fast, Amaris could barely see her friend wince as Malik had taken a dagger to the shoulder and rolled away as if it had been a bee sting.

Amaris watched in something between dread and disbelief. The beast had been slain and pandemonium had ensued with such immediacy she could scarcely find her voice.

"No!" she shouted, recoiling from the anarchy that had erupted. No one heard her. Nothing stopped. She didn't know what to do, how to help, how to intervene. The moon sang down on them, casting an incongruent pearly glow over the bloodlust on their faces.

The men brawled, poised to kill whatever had thundered through their campsite and torn them from their sleep. The silver moon continued glinting in time with the clang of their weapons, washing the clearing in the sight of their battle with its white glow. Her hands were raised in helpless alarm. She'd already expended too much energy, she'd fought, she'd ran, she'd clawed for her life and didn't know if she had the physical strength to beat Ash and Malik in sparring. Amaris knew she was going to have to fling her body into the fight if she had any hope of stopping the carnage as it unfolded.

"Please," she begged again, but her voice was weak.

The dark general seemed to have found his footing and began to advance on Ash, using his wings to thrust himself forward with one powerful beat. Standing in the blood of the fallen beseul, she threw herself between Ash and the man with her arms outstretched. In the time it took for her to raise her hands, she saw the one called Zaccai fall, the weight of Malik's foot pinning a single wing beneath him in an awkward bend. His weapon clattering to his side as he twisted for his wing. He raised a hand to stop the imminent killing blow. This was it. The general made a lunge to protect his man just as Amaris screamed.

"Malik, stop!" Her voice was the loudest thing in the forest.

As if the world had stilled, he did as he was told, frozen in time. Malik's sword had been in the throes of full descent. Now his arms were rigid above his head. His breath caught in his throat. His green eyes widened as he found himself trapped mid-action, unable to complete the arc of his sword. Malik was a statue trapped in an incomplete battle cry.

"Drop your weapon!"

Malik's hand opened in a horrible, forced obedience, blade clattering to the ground. His emerald eyes were caught in the wild terror like that of a caged animal. The reever slowly lowered his open hands, fear and revulsion coursing through him. He had always been so kind, so affable. Right now the golden man looked like he might scream. Amaris had never, not even for a moment, felt hatred from her friend before now.

He burned with pure, unadulterated betrayal.

Ash was staring at the events unfold with open-mouthed disgust. The winged general skidded back, ignoring the reevers and moving for his fallen man. The general offered his hand and helped Zaccai off his back, moving him quickly to his feet. The silence that resounded between them was so much thicker than the sounds of battle that had echoed through the woods only moments before.

Hurt and confusion flashed between her companions. The winged fae remained tense, ready to fight. She continued panting, face painted with pain. The first one to make a noise was the snarl of her copper friend, his voice scratched with some raw emotion.

"They're demons, Ayla!" Ash's words came out hoarse and feral.

Her eyes were pleading as she fought against his loathing. Her words and her body language alike begged them to hear her. "No, that's the demon," She pointed to the still-gaping head of the beseul, the viscosity of its black blood sticking in web-like tendrils as it dripped from its severed head to the ground. She could barely find her words, voice thick with her emotion. She couldn't stand the way he was looking at her. "They saved me from it. The creature would have taken me."

She saw it in their faces: this was insanity. If their eyes were to be believed, Amaris's actions spit in the face of everything for which the reevers fought and believed. They had trained with her. They had accepted her. They had loved her. They trained against magical imbalance, against evil, against the forces that thwarted the world and sent the continent into chaos. And the first moment they were dispatched onto the road, she had turned on them. They had been wrong to let a witch in their walls.

"*We* were here to save you!" Malik insisted, the injury in his voice so much thicker than whatever wound he had taken to his shoulder. She felt an invisible knife twist in her heart as she scanned his face. What was he feeling at that moment? The panic she had caused with her single command was something she had never seen in a man. How could she have betrayed them like this?

"They're ag'imni, Ayla." Ash sounded like he might cry. She understood what he was asking: how could the girl he'd sparred with, the one he'd fought side by side with, the one he'd trusted, have chosen the demons over her brethren.

"She can see us." The man's voice was low, looking at his similarly winged friend. "She can see us," he said again.

"The demon is slain," Amaris felt desperate, ignoring the winged fae as she focused on the reevers. "I need you to believe me."

"How can I?" Malik's voice was heavy with his distrust. Nothing remained of the friendly, honey-sweet tone she'd grown to love from him. She'd never seen him hurt like this. She'd never seen him angry. She should have never been responsible for causing injury to such a pure human, and yet, she was the source of his pain.

How could he trust her, indeed.

296

She hated her power, but she'd needed it. Still, her gut twisted. What dark ability had she just used against him? What hypnotic evil had this she wielded when her friend was poised to strike, brainwashing him as an unwilling servant to bend to her will? She could feel them ask themselves: how had such a poisonous serpent been living in their keep, under their care for so long without anyone realizing the dangers that had slept mere feet from them? How could they have let her in, have trusted her, have allowed her to live and train and join them as family?

Her heart was clawing at her from within its ribbed cage. Malik's kind, happy face was so broken. She wished for a moonless night so she wouldn't have to see their expression, but instead the silvers revealed everything. She couldn't even look at Ash, desperate for the human reever to forgive her. There was no hiding.

"They aren't here to hurt us," she emphasized. "Can't you see that? Have they made any move to attack? The only thing they've hurt is the beseul. They saved me."

"I have a dagger to the shoulder that says otherwise." His voice was low and bitter.

"It was a defensive wound," she raised her hands with a desperate attempt to placate. How could she make this right? How could she make them see?

The fae stayed silent, watching Amaris as she pleaded their case. They had made no move to attack, but they did seem prepared to flee if the situation between the reevers soured.

She needed to speak to the winged men who had caused so much turmoil in her life. She had questions, and deserved answers. She blamed them for all of this. She blamed them for the wound in Malik's shoulder and the pain on his face. She blamed them for the thick anguish in Ash's voice. She had so much to ask, so much to say. Nothing was going to happen here while she watched the hearts of her friends shatter before her.

"Go."

The command was to the reevers.

Ash and Malik stared at her with utter repulsion. There were no words to describe the way they looked at her. No one had ever communicated such vitriol in one look as she the one she felt boring into her in that moment. Her heart split, bleeding onto the ground around her as it emptied. They were her family. They were her brothers. She was angry, and confused, and desperate, and had no idea what to do. There was no clear path.

If she didn't get answers from the dark fae, this would have all been for nothing.

Ash went to Malik, grabbing his friend's fallen sword. The golden reever had already been obediently limping away, a human slave to her curse of persuasion. Ash stared at Amaris over his shoulder as they disappeared into the forest. As long as she lived, she knew that look would haunt her. She would beg for their forgiveness soon. She would do whatever it took to prove that she did not stand against them. She was one of them. She loved them. For now, she needed answers.

She was finally alone with the dark fae.

☽ ☽ ☽ ☽ ● ● ☾ ☾ ☾

Ash had never punched another reever outside of the sparring ring, but now seemed like as good a time as any to start. He was furious. He was shocked. He was hurt. He wanted to shout at her for her betrayal. He'd never been so angry at his sparring partner. He'd never been this angry at *anyone* in the entirety of his young life. He wanted to tie her to a tree and abandon her in the woods to be eaten by the next beseul who found her. He wasn't entirely positive he wouldn't kill her.

Not only had she chosen demons, but she'd yielded an unforgivable witchcraft against Malik. A magic she'd kept secret, kept *hidden* all this time. His heart was black as he burned with his disgust. To think he'd trusted her. To think he'd fought with her. To think he'd... no. He stopped himself from wherever his mind had tempted to wander.

They needed to create space between themselves and their white-haired witch before they said or did something they'd regret. They took off for the city, ready to put a bitter space between themselves and the one they left in the woods.

Yelagin was the halfway point between their far-off mountain home in the keep and the royal city of Aubade. Ash and Malik needed to put some distance between themselves and the events of the night. As mad as they were, they couldn't fully leave Amaris behind. She was their brother in arms, and even if she was a mutinous, hateful witch, her place in the stocks should be for the reevers to decide as a whole. Desiring a hot bath and a night on a mattress while his shoulder healed, the men urged Nine and Fourteen into the city below, treachery clouding their hearts. It was rare for the atmosphere to hang like heavy tar between the two genial young men.

He'd caught the smooth scar on his palm as he'd gripped the horn of Nine's saddle and knew that her blood ran through him, just like every reever before him. They were joined, whether or not she was a witch, no matter how much he hated her.

Unlike the thatch-roofed villages and farm towns centered around churches or fields, Yelagin was a sprawling city on the shores of a long, deep lake hidden behind the hills that nestled it. While this rolling landscape wasn't comparable to the gargantuan peaks and ranges that scraped the clouds in Stone and the reev, the terrain here rose and fell around Yelagin, concealing it completely with the elevation changes of its bluffs until you crested the hills and found yourself above the city itself. From their vantage point, they could take in the smokestacks and glowing windows from the metalsmiths, taverns, shops and buildings belonging to the city. Docks lined with the fishing boats that trolled the lake stretched like black extensions of the city itself, carving paths into the reflective surface of the water. Even from their distant stance on the hillside, they caught whiffs of the unpleasant smells that wafted up from overcrowding.

The boys hadn't spoken much after returning to their camp, packing their horses, and leaving Amaris behind. They left her pack, her things, and her gray mount for her to find whenever she returned. Ash had scribbled a note and left it on her blanket.

We'll see you in Yelagin, you traitorous bastard.

It seemed to get the point across. They were angry, and they did not forgive her, but they also would not disown her. Not yet, anyway.

The reevers let themselves into a tavern near the edge of the city closest to the water. It had taken a moment to shake off their cloaks and settle at a table, but the other patrons seemed to give them and their foul dispositions a rather wide berth. They shared their pints in silence, drinking in the sour ale, allowing the taphouse's commotion to drown out the turmoil of their thoughts. Jeering, heat, merriment, smells of fire, bodies, food, laughter, music, sex—it was all the senseless background noise of civilians who never left the safety of their city. How could the naïve residents know what evils dwelled in their forests, or what witches lived among them, masquerading as their friends, their family, their lovers. None of them would sleep, toast, or gamble with the weight of unholy powers anchoring them to the bottom of the sea.

To be sure, the reevers were in a foul mood.

Malik left the table to inquire about a room for the night. He needed somewhere to lie while the tonic worked its way through his blood stream and his shoulder healed. The injury had been relatively shallow, but it was to his right side—his sword hand—and he couldn't risk any damage to the tissue.

While Malik found the innkeeper, Ash scanned the faces of the patrons. The faeling's character was normally amiable and open to townsfolk when he traveled. He'd done quite well with the ladies when he'd wandered into towns, more than happy to use his ears as an ice-breaker and see where the night took them. This night was different. He felt sickened at the sight of their simple faces as they went about their merry, superficial lives. What must it be like to have your greatest worry be the springtime taxation, or whether or not they'd received an invite to a mayoral dinner party. He admitted he might be feeling a little bit biased by his own bitterness as he drained his ale. Ash intended to shoot back as many as possible tonight. He was on a mission to get as shitfaced as the innkeeper would allow before he was cut off.

The young man set the pint down as the barmaid approached.

He glanced up to order another drink, but it wasn't the barmaid at all. He looked into the twinkling eyes of the single most beautiful woman he'd ever seen. He straightened a bit, clearly surprised as he looked at the oddity standing at his table. She seemed to glow from some unseen inner flame. Her bottomless eyes were utterly mesmerizing, and she was looking right down at him. She leaned onto the table, pressing her palms onto its wooden surface. A cinnamon smell overpowered the honest auroras of stews and breads that had filled his nose only moments before.

"Hello," she smiled, teeth glinting. "May I sit?"

Ash was baffled, and his amber eyes betrayed his surprise. He'd done fine with women before, but he had been radiating acidic energy from the moment he'd stepped into the alehouse that night. There was no reason anyone should have wanted to come within three table's lengths of his bitter company.

"I'm sorry, m'lady, I don't think I'm particularly good company tonight," he offered as both apology and an attempt at dismissal.

She made a somewhat amused face at that, "I'd rather a man be honest with his emotions than feigning pleasure while concealing pain. Would you share your table with a lady? Maybe I can make your bad day better."

Making some unintelligible gesture in an attempt to recover, he motioned his hands in front of him. He'd meant to tell her to be his guest, but there was nothing charming or elegant about the way he'd reacted. Doing his best to compose himself, he asked, "May I buy you a drink?"

"You may," she grinned, delighted. She eased from where she'd been standing and leaned onto the table, seated directly across from Ash.

The young woman clasped her delicate, bronze hands in front of herself. Apart from himself and Samael, he hadn't seen many people with her particular coloration. The lovely tanned skin would have made her stand out in the tavern by itself, but the woman was a testament to the goddess's eye for beauty, as she was a masterpiece. Her glossy black hair seemed to shine like wet ink. Her teeth were white and flashed with unnatural allure each time she smiled. Her charm was in part to what seemed to be an effortless, winsome smile.

His eyes grazed from her hair, the rouge of her cheeks, her soft mouth, her elegant throat, to the curious coat she still wore. It had been too warm of a day for the royal blue cloak she had dawned. The girl unclamped it at the neck, draping it on the chair behind her. When she removed it, it was clear why she'd been covering up. Her dress left astonishingly little to the imagination, plunging and hugging deliciously around her shape.

"Are you from Yelagin?" she asked.

Ash had forgotten the common tongue. All thoughts had vacated his mind as he did his best not to gape at her. He wasn't convinced he'd ever known how to speak. He'd only had one pint, but was feeling terribly drunk by the shock of her presence. The reever shook his head, doing his best to keep his eyes on her face. Maybe the All Mother had seen what a terrible night he'd had and taken pity on him, sending him a silk-wrapped present. The thought, however foolish, warmed him.

302

He managed to strike what he hoped was a casual tone as he answered, "Just passing through, I'm afraid. Are you a local?"

She feigned offense, bringing one hand to brush her chest as she pointed to herself. The brush of her fingertips as they grazed the space below her collarbone served more than one purpose, truly testing his resolve to retain eye contact.

"Of this landlocked town?" She tossed her hair easily to one side. "Oh, I could never settle somewhere so far from the sea. Where's the sense of freedom in that?"

She was a coastal girl, then. He supposed there were probably people in the far southern isles with dark hair and bronze skin. That would make more logical sense than if the girl's complexion was of Raascot, but he found his mind distracted from thoughts of her lineage. He could have sworn she was leaning in so as to press her breasts together, which made discerning her origins rather challenging. How absurd that a woman of this stature would have to do more than glance at a man to have him at her beck and call. In fact, it was a bit *too* absurd.

Ash kept his voice casual, but a guarded caution had crept into his features. He'd more or less shaken his initial confusion, though her presence was still immensely distracting. The woman was art. "How fortunate that two travelers' paths should cross, then."

The barmaid had brought another ale for him, and a glass of red wine for the lady. He slid her several pennies, and two extra as a tip. They raised their drinks in toast.

The barmaid cut in, "It's only silver if you're wanting a room for the night as well."

The dark-haired girl raised a conspiratorial eyebrow, amused at whatever foregone conclusion was being implied.

"Your friend said you were the one with the coin purse." The barmaid seemed a bit frazzled at the night's crowd, but waved a hand to where Malik watched from the bar. He raised two fingers in a mock salute as Ash spotted him. Malik must have seen the lovely young woman take a seat at their table and taken his cue to make himself scarce, ever the valiant wingman despite his injury.

Ash produced a silver and the barmaid went on her way, presumably handing a room key off to Malik.

"And staying at this inn as well?" The woman's lips twitched up slightly, eyelashes lowering as she looked into her wine, then back up at Ash. "Fortune smiles upon us. My room is just upstairs."

Was she inviting him into her bed? Ash hadn't bathed in nine days, and had been scowling at the world for the hour leading up to arrival. There was no way this creature wanted his company tonight. Feeling a twinge of something that may have been an irritation for letting himself believe she could have been interested, he course-corrected by asking her, "Is there anything I can help you with, ma'am?"

Her smile was unchanging, ever the picture of grace, but something nearly reptilian had twitched in her eye at his question. This was not a woman used to men rebuffing her advances.

She kept her tone unbothered, bordering on flirtatious. "Tell me about yourself, traveler. Are you also from the coast?"

He shook his head, returning to his ale. "That's where I'm headed. I'm from up north, just into the mountains."

"The north, you say." She smiled easily. Once again, there was something within her smile. It was a glint behind her dark eyes that he couldn't quite place, though he felt quite sure that whatever he saw was something untamed and predatory. "That must be why such a handsome young man is armed to the teeth. Who would think one gentleman would need so many bows and blades? Treacherous roads, I hear."

"It's just the one bow, miss. But you can never have too many blades."

"Mmm." She seemed to consider it, drinking deeply from her red wine. Its reddish-purple nearly matched the ripened blackberry shade of her lips. She was beautiful—perhaps even the most radiant woman he'd ever seen. But there was a sinister edge to her beauty. Something he couldn't quite put his finger on, like a word on the tip of his tongue. The jovial sounds of the alehouse didn't match their exchange. The music was too bright and the laughter too loud for the rising suspicion he shouldered.

The men at the tables around him were eyeing him enviously. What did the red demi-fae boy have to offer a woman like that? Perhaps she was a thrill-seeker, he told himself, as occasionally women would see the arch of his ears and seek him out, having lain with one of his kind. It was hard not to notice the stares she drew from those around her. He knew once he left, the men would be swarming the table. Perhaps it was time to let them have their shot.

The reever was ready for a bath and a good night's sleep. Ash exhaled, looking for his exit. Maybe Malik would give him a few minutes to himself in the room while he thought of the beautiful body hidden just below the curtain of her generously revealing dress. He had no doubt that making love to her would be the most spectacular event of any man's life. She had the hungry look of a true maneater, after all.

Ash had more ale in his pint that he'd intended to drink downstairs in the tavern, but perhaps he could take it in his room. It didn't seem like the sort of establishment that would care too much about whether or not he carried his pint up the stairs. The need to depart seemed more pressing than finishing his beverage. He looked to Malik, who seemed just as bewildered as the men around him.

The golden reever had watched Ash go home with many a girl in the village of Stone, usually as he'd stayed behind to salute appreciatively and continue playing his card games with the villagers. It clearly baffled him that Ash appeared to be doing his best to shake the raven sitting across from him.

Malik motioned his hands in a baffled shrug and moved his mouth, silently asking a single question from across the tavern. "*What the hell?*"

There was no way to explain it to his friend. It was a feeling. A distant one, but an odd one to be sure. Maybe it was because he was angry with Amaris. Maybe it was because a beseul had torn through their camp, and their white-haired friend had betrayed them, and the ale was too expensive and too sour. But it didn't feel like that. It felt like something else entirely as his body shifted away from the dark-haired beauty.

"I wish you a safe journey on your roads, miss." Ash began to stand, but she clamped a hand down on his, perhaps too eagerly.

"Are you going to make me finish my drink alone?" She asked, running her thumb softly over the top of his closed hand. "Don't leave a lady unaccompanied in a place like this."

The surge of emotions he felt was powerful. Her cinnamon scent seemed to pulse, growing stronger with each moment that passed. Her contact was electric, weakening his resolve.

Two wolves fought within him. One distinctly male wolf clawed at him to take her to bed, to rip her clothes off, to ravage every inch of her. He'd love nothing more than to pin this stunning creature to the wall of the inn, or take her on the table right here while the patrons watched and cheered. The second wolf stood its ground. It was the cautious, lone wolf dressed for survival. It bit back the desire, nipping at the throb in his manhood, urging him to keep his wits about him.

The first wolf was loud, but the second wolf was powerful.

Out of politeness, he sat.

"Tell a girl about the north, would you?" Her voice was sweet. She had an incredible charm about her, almost as if it were a physical aura shimmering around her. There was something so distinct about her, almost as if he could taste her very presence like a ripe, dark fruit. She continued talking, "I've never made it much further into the continent than here. It seems like a dreadfully long way to the mountains. I'd love to hear more."

He nodded, doing his best to comply as he watched the wolves fight, curious who would win. "It is quite the journey, and not one for anyone who fears heights, I'm afraid."

She looked impressed. "You're on a mountain itself, then?"

"I am."

"And what is the name of your city?"

Hundreds of years ago, when the reevers were welcomed as guardians and respected for the peace they brought to the kingdoms, Uaimh Reev had been a household name. He would have told the girl of the reev and she surely would have been delighted to have been sharing a drink with a guardian. Over the years, as their kind grew fewer and the continent more suspicious, it had proven pertinent to keep to the shadows. On the best days, people thought of them as assassins. On the worst days, they were equivocated to nothing more than hired swords. Samael had said the past fifty years had been the most challenging to live among the humans.

Ash opted for a deflection. "I'm not sure the northern names would hold much meaning to anyone from outside of the area."

"Try me," she pressed. Was her brow arched with curiosity, or something more hostile? It was the second wolf again, clamping its jaws down into his flesh to draw him to awareness.

"I'd rather hear more about you, miss," he replied.

Her frustration was unmistakable this time, but only for a moment. It took the young woman a beat to steady herself. She took another drink of her dark, rich wine while eyeing the taproom and its patrons, its music, its tables and scents and sights while she seemed to regroup her thoughts. She didn't lower the glass from her lips, still looking away. Clearly, he'd rattled her more than he'd intended. The young woman took a drink yet again.

Finally she'd summoned the casual air to say, "You're too kind. Men don't often ask much about me. What can I say? I'm a simple girl. The most exciting part of my day would be hearing about your adventures in the north."

"I doubt that very much."

She sucked on her teeth and he finally recognized the look behind her eyes. He'd seen it on more than one occasion, whether crossing blades or beating back talons. It had taken a while to place given the distraction of her night-black hair, her painted mouth, her tanned, glowing skin and otherworldly beauty. The dress was simply the cherry on top, an invitation meant to bait her prey. She had the distinct look of someone who was going to kill him.

17

Amaris didn't know how to feel, save for confusion, anger, and that she was certainly not to blame for the horrible way everything had gone. Her world had fallen apart, and she was confident it was not her fault. She'd lived her reevers for years and never had to use her dark gift until these crows had flapped their stupid wings into her life.

"First you hold a knife to my throat, and now you—"

"Rescue you?" The general, Amaris had learned, was a fae man called Gadriel. He raised a single brow, challenging her. Though she hadn't yet gathered enough information to be sure, she was already quite sure she might hate him.

The southern kingdom had taken to calling his breed of fae "dark fae" long ago, mostly to call attention to powers that were more familiar with nightlife. The bird-like wings of his companion and the nocturnal eyes that allowed them to see in the dark were just the most apparent features that set them apart as residents of Raascot. Northern fae had a variety of other gifts that emerged just like those of the fae people in the southern continent, though the dark gifts often took on a more ominous edge.

Magics were slippery when choosing how they'd manifest. Unlike height, hair color and eyes, abilities had no clear-cut inheritance when passed from parent to child. Rather than replicating their abilities, powers seemed to share common themes. While a fae mother may have the gift of healing, she could have a child who could make plants grow. Their skills may have been different, but the uniting energy was one of health and life.

It was the same with the small magics that could emerge among humans with distant magical ties, though very little was understood about how their recessive powers manifested irrespective of human lineage.

Pleasant gifts, like the ability to make things grow, to shield, or to grant wonderful things like luck upon others often were affiliated with light. The few fae who remained in the south were often found with powers of empathy and its respective ability to soothe the distress of others. Some fae were blessed by the goddess with the tailoring traits of being able to fabricate anything from manufactured objects to physical appearance. Other lighted gifts were those that blessed crops, multiplied food, or manifested water.

Despite fae rarely being able to intentionally breed desirable magical features or characteristics, the fae of the north had found a dominant trait in their wings. There were other magics that had grown more popular north of the border that Amaris carefully avoided. She wasn't sure that she was ready for the fallout of the answers to her questions.

Dark fae, Gadriel had said, were no friends of the 'demons' as she called them, despite what the primitive superstitions and prejudices among townspeople in the southern parts and the rumors they'd spread about the northern kingdom. The dark fae had as many common enemies in the vageth, the ag'drurath, and the beseuls, like the one they had cut and buried as any other human or fae on the continent. Beasts were harbingers of no natural master, regardless of their side of the border.

The three hadn't moved from their small glen for a long while since Ash and Malik had departed. Zaccai had gotten to work shoving the monster's disembodied head under the earth, as was tradition, while the other two remained locked in a speechless stalemate. It had been fifteen minutes of tentative placations before the stench of the slain monster and black blood around them pushed their conversation toward Cobb and where her companions had initially made their camp for the night. Though she hated herself for it, Amaris was relieved the reevers were gone upon her return. She didn't have the energy to verbally battle with Ash or Malik right now. These dark fae before here were the kernel she had needed to dislodge for so long. These were the answers she needed.

"Have you been following me?" Amaris asked.

She turned her back on them and busied herself with flint and kindling while she waited for an answer. The girl lit a fire, perhaps only because it gave her hands something familiar and comforting to do, given the circumstances. They'd been intentional to avoid fires at night, but it seemed as though the worst thing in the nearby woods had been slain, and that the general and his winged companion were just as terrifying as anything else that might come for them if attracted to the light of their flame.

"We hadn't intended to," Zaccai answered for them both. "We're joining a few others over the hill in Yelagin. Then, after that night by the pond..."

"I could tell you saw us," Gadriel finished.

"Of course I can see you," she bit, her voice as sour as her mood.

Her words were angry. She knew she should be grateful that they had intervened, but what had it cost her? Amaris felt comfortable enough that she no longer needed to directly face them. They owed her answers, but they didn't seem to pose immediate bodily harm. The night air wasn't particularly cold, nor were they in true need of a flame, but she warmed her hands by the fire just for the comfort of the mundane action.

"No," Zaccai corrected, running a hand through his hair as he looked for his words. "You see us for who we are. The others see... something else. How do I..." His words drifted off as he looked between Gadriel and back to Amaris. "I'm sorry, it's been so long since we've spoken to anyone south of the border. You saw the way your companions reacted, didn't you?"

Amaris narrowed her eyes slightly as she evaluated them. "You're enchanting people to see you as monsters? What sort of defense is that?"

Gadriel shook his head to disagree with a matter-of-fact response, "This is not our doing. Cai is pretty beastly and wins no favors with the ladies—"

"I do just fine, thank you very much."

The smoke rising from the fire was comforting, but the flame wouldn't warm her heart. She couldn't explain what she felt, but there seemed to be a glass shard jutting from her most important organ. She'd spent three years cultivating community and family, and in mere moments she'd lost them. Amaris took a half-step closer to the flame, willing it to melt the frost that clung to the wound in her chest. It felt distinctly human, even if no one sitting around its warmth could claim to truly be one. Ash and Malik may blame her for her treachery, but it was Gadriel and Zaccai who had destroyed her life with the fell swoop of two sets of wings.

The arrival of the dark fae had thrown an undeniably terrible wrench into her life.

Zaccai spoke again, shrugging, "One day, it just happened. We were fine, and then suddenly, we weren't. For the last twenty-some years, there seems to be a curse on the border. It doesn't matter how we cross into the southern kingdom, how high we fly, how far around we

312

deign to go, once we cross the border into Farehold, it happens."

Their words were illogical. Her brows collected as her lower lip rose in disbelief. "When you cross the border, you look like monsters?"

Gadriel corrected, "No, when we cross the borders, we are *perceived* as monsters."

"Then why cross the border?" Amaris felt irritated. She had so many more questions she wanted to ask. She didn't just want to know why they'd bother to cross the border if it held such a curse, but also why they'd go so far as to put her in this position. She wanted to know why they'd used their demon faces to turn her friends against her. She needed to know why they'd followed her. Why hadn't they stayed behind their border and stayed far, far away from her? Instead, she allowed her original question to spread thickly between them, its weight hanging in the air.

They exchanged looks. Zaccai offered, "This spell hasn't put a stop to things that have to get done on the continent, it's just made it substantially harder to accomplish them."

Gadriel scowled at the ground, "We've lost more men than I can count."

The silver reever returned to the fire, if only to keep herself from making more enemies. Her heart was not particularly given over to kindness at the moment. Amaris was tempted to make a comment about how they must not be great spies or warriors if they're picked off like flies, but thought better of it. As soon as she'd seen the beseul, she had herself possessed the single need to end its wretched life, if only for her own survival. When Ash and Malik saw these winged fae— particularly given the rude awakening that had startled them from their sleep with the ice of carrion and death—they must have felt the same. She gritted her teeth, doing her best to reach for something like sympathy.

"How often does this happen—" she gestured between them across

313

the orange of the campfire, looking from one man to the other. "How often can people perceive you?"

Cai had been speaking for most of the night, but Gadriel looked at her very seriously for a moment, holding her eyes as he answered.

"Never."

"Never?"

Gadriel crossed his arms and leaned back into his explanation. His husky voice still sent the same chill of low, dark authority she'd felt in her ear when he'd held the blade to her neck, even if his words were amicable. "Relations between the kingdoms have been strained for the last two hundred years, but there has always been an open route of communication and the cordial politicking expected from neighboring kingdoms. As was said, roughly two decades ago, this curse hit the border. At least, that's the most we know of it. No one has been able to see us, nor hear our words in the common tongue. Whatever this perception spell is, it has a death-grip on its people."

Cai made a face, but said no more.

Amaris allowed a small, appreciative sound as she considered his information. Finally, she responded with, "Well... that's pretty shit if you ask me."

Zaccai, who'd been swigging from his waterskin, almost choked.

Gadriel laughed, his teeth reflecting the light of the fire with his crooked grin. It was a genuinely amused smile, "Yes, I'd say it's pretty shit."

Wiping his mouth with the back of his hand, Cai looked to her and said, "This is where you come in. We've never had someone south of the border who could intercede on our behalf. Gad and I have been talking about it for the last several days, ever since you saw us in the woods. We can't get near anyone without having arrows or spears or torches and pitchforks—"

"Yes, I get it, the things for demons." Amaris raised her hands in conclusion. "You want me to be the demon whisperer."

"Well, that's rather rude."

She shrugged her shoulders, "Listen, I'm sure you're both perfectly lovely. Most women love having their missions disrupted and their friends abandon them in the middle of the night because demons were stalking them. Thanks for the beseul, by the way. But however noble your spying cause for infiltration of these lands may be, you saw how my companions reacted. I love those men. I've trained with them for years. They are my family. We would die in battle together if the occasion called for it. And now I am a—what was the word?" She held up the slip of paper Ash had scrawled. "That's right, a *traitorous bastard.*"

Gadriel began to move around one end of the campfire, unable to stay fully still. She didn't seem to understand the weight of this exchange. "I sympathize with your position."

"Do you?" she asked, making no attempt to conceal the contempt in her lilac eyes, "Because I did not ask to be hunted for days by two winged assailants. I certainly didn't request the company of anyone who would further alienate me. Look at me. I don't exactly fit in. The reevers were the only family—"

"You're a reever?" The general's face lit at the word.

She paused, feeling a protective flare for her family. She slowly answered in a cautious affirmative.

"That's great!" The man called Zaccai looked like he might hug her, which was not the sort of reaction anyone had given her to such a word. "We've lived with a reever in Gwydir for nearly ten years! The reevers have helped out Raascot for hundreds of years. He's quite instrumental in our monster control."

Gadriel looked to him as if to stop him from saying more.

Amaris considered his reaction. It effectively halted her oncoming tirade about how they could fly off and mind their own business. "Is your reever red of hair?"

"That's the one!"

She was almost sorry for them. "Yes, it's his son who tried to kill you tonight."

Gadriel smiled again, "Ah, well, that's unfortunate. I'm sure Elil would be disappointed that we didn't make a better first impression, though I can't say I'm surprised. The man is rather singularly focused on his mission. The apple must not fall far from the tree."

Amaris realized had never asked Ash of his father's name. She wondered if that made her a bad friend. Perhaps she could excuse her poor manners as an orphan, surrounded by other discarded children of dead or unwanted heritages, for failing to instruct herself on the polite ways of inquiring of lineages.

"Perhaps I can help you," she started. They seemed to glitter at her words, but she needed to mitigate their excitement before they got ahead of themselves, "But I don't want to."

Zaccai was looking to his general while the warm, orange fire popped between them. The reddish firelight caught the black feathering of their wings in a way that made them seem more like the fabled phoenix than the crows they were. Gadriel's face made it clear that, as a general, he was far more familiar with obedience. A defiant, silver girl was a bit outside of his comfort zone.

The general leveled his gaze once more, unsure as to her sense of where her humor and impropriety intermingled. "Are you serious?"

"I find you disrespectful, invasive, and suspicious." She crossed her arms firmly. "Why would I help northern spies? Especially ones who make me look like a traitor to my brothers? But even if I did want to help—and believe me, I do not—I'm on dispatch at the moment. My companions and I need to seek an audience with Queen Moirai."

"Regarding?"

Her initial reaction was to tell him it was none of his business.

316

Then, she considered the coincidence. On the one hand, no one was entitled to the knowledge of her dispatch aside from her, Ash and Malik. On the other hand, she was open to believing in a world where accidental happenings might be mutually beneficial. It didn't seem useful to withhold this particular set of knowledge, nor could she see a disadvantage in sharing it. Amaris chewed on her annoyance for a moment and made the decision to tell them.

"Well, *you*, I suppose. Two other reevers who left Uaimh Reev were dispatched into Raascot to investigate why your king is sending his men south of the border. They need to learn why spies have been reported throughout Farehold, and learn to confirm or disband rumors of infiltration of the southern borders. Meanwhile, I'm meant to find answers as to why the queen is ordering the slaughter of all northerners in her territory, and perhaps ask her to stop. Though, now that I know northerners share a striking resemblance to ag'imni, I can't say I blame her."

"And they're sending a bear-mauled reever girl because of the witch power you exercised in the glen? This sounds like a flawless plan. Who's the seat of power in Uaimh Reev, is it still Samael? I may have to have a word with him."

"First of all," she sunk her weight into her hip, tightening the grip of her crossed arms, "This bear mauling is of my own infliction, though that's a story for another day. I realize upon saying it that it doesn't sound like it helps my cause. But, second of all, I'm no witch."

"You're right," Gadriel eyed her dryly, "You're absolutely delightful."

She narrowed her eyes. "Though, yes, I suppose your conclusion is about right all the same. Still, who the hell are you? Why are you here? I've learned what I needed to know: you're Raascot fae. I don't see a particular benefit in prolonging this exchange."

It appeared that when she'd commanded Malik to stop his death blow, everyone had seen her power for what it was. She wondered if she'd be welcome back in the reev once Samael learned she'd used it on Malik. Perhaps once she pleaded her case, the others would understand.

Gadriel clapped his hands together suddenly. "That's it!"

She had been prepared to head for Cobb when she looked at the general. "What's it?"

The other two looked at him expectantly, the dancing flames filling the campsite with the warmth of its crackle. "You need me."

"I'm quite certain I do not."

Gadriel's eyes were wicked with delight. "Believe me, you do. You need to get to the queen to tell her to stop killing northerners with your persuasive sorcery? Excellent, I couldn't love a plan more. Coincidentally I, too, would like her to stop killing us. What do you say, Cai, want to be conscripted swords-for-hire to a surly, white-haired witch girl?"

Zaccai grinned, "I haven't heard a better plan in quite a while."

Amaris scowled, "I told you, I'm not a witch. I don't think I see much of an advantage in accepting your demonic help."

"Fine, you're not a witch. What are you going by these days? Enchanter? Conjurer? Magician?" He was goading her into further reaction. She refused to take the bait.

"Your abilities are..." Zaccai searched for a word.

"I'm not a witch!"

"That's not what I was going to say," he corrected. "They're just very powerful. You saved my life when your friend would have killed me. I've never seen a power like it."

Amaris had already endured enough of the conversation, and began to gather her things. She understood Zaccai was attempting both to thank and compliment her, but she didn't have the space in her heart for his words. She hadn't gotten any rest that night, and if she hoped to rejoin her companions and convince them to trust her despite the presence of these northern barbarians, she didn't know if she could do it while sleep-deprived.

"You work out what to call me while I make my way to the city," she muttered, shearing her weapons and draping her bow over her shoulder. "Two ag'imni couldn't possibly follow me into its streets anyway. Think of the children."

Gadriel was not amused.

"See? Not so nice, is it."

Zaccai raised his hands reassuringly. He seemed pleasant enough, but Amaris was not interested in his olive branch. "This will give us time to talk to the others at the outpost in Yelagin. Once they know what a resource we have in this wi—um, this girl. This reever, I mean—they'll want to help as well. I'm sure of it. They're going to be so thrilled to learn about you."

"I don't think I want demons talking about me."

"We're not—" Gadriel bit back annoyance, overcoming whatever agitation he felt with her to breathe through his nose. She felt a spike of pleasure at his agitation. If he truly was a general, he was used to obedience. Her lone pleasure of the evening would not be giving this man whatever it was he felt entitled to.

"Gad, she's—"

"I know." He cut off his friend with a sharp, silencing look. Gadriel finally cooled enough to say, "You're going to need our help, whether or not you understand as much at the moment."

She untethered Cobb and made a few steps to lead him out of the forest, the brambles and thickets crunching beneath his weight. He'd been marvelously unbothered by the tumultuous events of the evening. "Great, I'm sure an army of the damned is exactly what I need to have Queen Moirai opening me with welcome arms."

While she began to lead Cobb away, Gadriel chided her. "Go, see if you can salvage what's left of your friendship. Let me know when you manage to relieve yourself from that attitude and see my offer to help for the asset that it is."

Zaccai wasn't nearly as sour as his general. "For what it's worth, I'm pretty sure I'd find it in my heart to forgive you if it were me. We'll meet you on the other side of the city within the next few days. If you're anywhere near the road, we'll be able to find you."

"Don't bother," she called.

Gadriel took a few quick steps to close the gap between them and grabbed her hands as Cai finished speaking. "Wait, witchling—"

"Stop it, demon!"

He ignored her, his rough hand chafing her forearm with his grip. She looked down at where his hand encircled her arm, then back up at him, feeling a spike of heat at the closeness of his body and the intensity of his gaze. "You've saved us, and I don't even know your name."

She motioned to shake off the clamp of his rough hand, but he resisted, holding her to him. She barely kept the scowl from her face as she answered.

"Amaris."

He seemed to chew on the name with a bit of a smirk, as if appreciating a dark, private joke. When he finally spoke, it was a whisper. "Of course it is."

Amaris had made it into town just after the two o'clock bell. After the adrenaline had worn off from her fight with the beseul, she was left with the heaviness of the way Malik had looked at her, the disgust that Ash had felt for her, and the weight of the sleep she so desperately needed on her eyelids. The boys hadn't said where they'd be staying, because, of course, they hadn't known the layout of Yelagin or its establishments. She'd hoped that their oath could carry the weight between them in moments like these where their faith in her had faltered.

She was relieved to see Nine and Fourteen tied to a post with a few other road-weary horses on the first tavern at the edge of the water just as she began to enter the town. She edged Cobb toward the familiar beasts and began to dismount, when the tavern door swung open. She jolted in her saddle at the sudden rush of bodies and noises, pulling the reins tightly as she stopped Cobb short of the chaos. Ash and Malik were spilling out into the street clutching their belongings, the cries of angry men and screams of a barmaid following close behind them. Ash saw her the moment he hit the pavement.

"Go, go!"

Amaris blinked rapidly at the sight, then urged Cobb forward, cantering over the hill and away from the furious mob. The boys were on their horses behind her within moments, their horses urged into gallops as threats to never return and vulgar curses from the mouths of the men chased them past the city. They slowed their horses further down the road when Amaris widened her eyes and whirled to them from where she sat in her saddle.

Her eyes were wide as she twisted in the saddle, "What the hell was *that?*"

Malik, who had been smiling from their harebrained escape, seemed to remember that he was angry at her. "I should be asking you the same!"

Ash decided for the three of them, "Let's talk about it in the morning after we've had some sleep." The glower in his voice made Amaris's gut twist. She wasn't sure she wanted to hear what conclusion they might reach in the morning.

"You still want to sleep after that?" Malik was aghast.

Amaris chastised them, "It's a big city, surely word won't have traveled as to what sorry bastards you are if we make it to the other side of the lake. Besides, you're hurt."

"Takes a sorry bastard to know one." Ash tossed it at Amaris, and she was glad for it. The anger she could handle. Antagonistic exchanges were so much better than the icy indifference she had feared. Instead, the banter told her that no matter how long his temper might last—and surely, it would burn for a day, a week, a year—when it passed, the men would forgive her.

As they took the wide road around the outskirts of the town, avoiding as much of Yelagin as possible, Amaris asked, "Are you going to tell me what you did to the poor citizens of Yelagin?"

"I'm pretty sure I was almost eaten by a witch. Speaking of witches, are you going to explain to us what sort of black fucking magic you've been hiding?"

"I wish people would stop calling me that."

"It's what you are," Ash said darkly. No, it was clear he had not moved on, and had not forgiven her.

She looked at his silhouette in the moonlight and felt the dagger that had been used to connect their palms, their blood, as it was driven into her heart. It twisted within her as she felt herself losing them. She suspected it was the very same dagger he envisioned plunged into his back. They were going to leave her, and she would deserve it.

It was a long three-mile semi-loop on horseback around the edge of the city before they were comfortable reentering the outskirts of Yelagin. They felt confident that if they checked in to the tavern now and left first thing in the morning, they'd be long gone before word had spread of their blacklisting. As they rode, Amaris told them about her persuasion, and how she hadn't known about it until her meeting at the reev, nor had she ever used it since. She informed them that Samael not only knew, but had saved her power for just such an occasion as this. This was why she needed to speak to the queen. She assured them that the road would be long enough to give them all the time they needed to tell stories of demons and whatever enchantress had nearly eaten Ash, or whatever nonsense he claimed.

There were two rooms at the inn that they'd found. Given his pierced shoulder, Malik would get his own room, taking up as much space on the bed as he needed. Soon they were off the streets and under the roof of the inn, settling for the night. The communal bathing room was at the end of the hall, and they took turns washing the endless days of travel from their bodies. Malik went first, tending to his wound and taking his time with the healing tonic. Amaris had offered to help him while he sat shirtless and bloodied, but he'd nearly kicked her out and made her wait her turn in the bathing room.

Amaris was the last to use the bathing room, using a pressed bar of homemade soap smelling like milk, almonds, and honey in her hair and all over her body. It felt so good to wash the road away. For a moment, under the water, with the comforting scents of nuts and sugar, she could forget about her mission to see the queen, forget about Ash and Malik considering her a traitor, forget about the dark fae begging for an intercessor, and most importantly, forget about her evil witch's power.

She was fae, she reminded herself. Samael told her that she wasn't fully human himself. She clung to the wisdom he had instilled in her on their first meeting as a source of comfort as she dipped beneath the warm waters of the bath: a power is no more good or evil than the one wielding it.

It was so late by the time she finished in the bath that she was confident not even the innkeeper was awake. Amaris hadn't bothered to redress, walking down the communal hallway of the inn wearing nothing but a towel. Her white hair dripped honey-scented puddles in her wake. She was exhausted physically and emotionally, and all she wanted was to feel loved. The knife that had stabbed her heart at their rejection was a wound that needed healing. Its pain was just as pressing as the knife Malik had taken to the shoulder.

She could have lost everything tonight. She had no family, until they'd taken her in. No people, until she'd become one of them. Who was she without the reevers?

Rejection's sharp sting made her think she might fear abandonment more greatly than death. The dagger within her twisted again as she remembered the hurt, the betrayal, the disgust in their eyes. She needed so desperately to have the knife pulled out—to tell her that everything was okay. She needed to feel whole again.

She opened the door to a wet-haired Ash who had looked poised to continue their argument, but halted himself when he saw her, mouth open for the fight. He was clean, and had dressed into clothes for sleep. The anger had evaporated from his face at her wanton state of undress. She closed the door behind her and leaned against it, her eye contact with the golden-eyed man unbroken.

"What are you doing?"

She said nothing as she looked at him, wondering if he could see the knife that pierced her heart, and whether or not he would be the one to fix it.

"Ayla," he took a cautionary step toward her, almost as if he were warning her to stop, but she didn't. She couldn't. She'd suffered too greatly, she'd had too much taken from her in her eighteen years on earth. She wouldn't let herself lose anyone else.

Her lavender irises locked onto his as she felt the gentle drip of milk, almonds and honey continue to pool on the floor around her from where the bath had washed away the night. She could replace the dagger with something good, something fun, something he'd wanted, something they'd teased and flirted with and danced around for years.

Amaris brought her hand to where the towel wrapped around the space beneath her arms and began to unwind it. She dropped the towel completely, bare before him as she leaned against the door.

It was an invitation he'd wanted for a long, long time.

Ash didn't need further encouragement. Whatever arguments he'd been ready to have were gone. He closed the space between them in a flash, pressing his body into hers, his mouth on hers. It wasn't the gentle kiss of a lover, but the hard, anger-tinted kiss of a man who had thought she might die tonight. He gripped her to him, the contrast of his rough, tan hands against her soft, milk skin heightening her arousal. She kissed him back with equal ferocity, desperate for the healing closeness. She gasped as endorphins and dopamine swirled into the wound, moaning lightly at the alchemy of pain's transformation into pleasure.

He put a hand beneath each of her thighs, hoisting her naked body up against the wall. Her back hit the wall with a thud as she pressed into him. She wrapped her legs around him and reveled in   how it spurred him on. Every touch, every movement, every brush of lips or flex of each muscle heightened as he pinned her against the door.

They weren't close enough. She needed more. Amaris wanted to pull the reever into the pain, into the fear of rejection, into the sense of abandonment and use his body, his love, his hands, his mouth as a promise, a bandage, a sense of forgiveness. She dug her nails into his back, arching her spine as she succeeded in bringing him. His body pressed into hers, air rushing out of her lungs. Her movement left her throat exposed, inhaling sharply at the sensation.

"Take me to bed," she breathed against his cheek.

He growled in response, a positively animal sound at the opportunity.

Ash carried her across the room, tossing her thin, white body onto the bed. He tugged his shirt over his head in one swift movement. She propped herself up on her elbows, watching. He moved on top of her with an intensity she only saw in him when they were sparring in the ring. Amaris wrapped her legs around him once more from where she'd remained prone, attempting to flip him as she would if they were in hand-to-hand combat, but he resisted the flip, asserting his place on top. She leaned into the pressure, wanting him to crush her. The more she felt Ash, the less she could feel anything else. Amaris felt him throb against her skin and felt so ready to let him in. She craved the fullness of it, the forgiveness, the love and understanding and absolution she'd feel if he were inside of her. Her heat, her thirst was pounding down her veins. She wanted—no *needed*   the intimacy—to feel accepted, to feel enveloped.

She arched her hips to meet his and the motion seemed to bring him back into his body.

Something changed in him, as if waking himself from a spell. The impulsivity fell from Ash like raindrops off of a roof. Frozen in his stance, his features transitioned from fierce, to contemplative, to soft. A muscle in his jaw throbbed as he eyed her. The copper reever looked down at her, the fury of his passion turning into a different emotion as he drank her in.

He closed his eyes as he exhaled slowly, unmoving. It was clear it had taken him a great force of will to stop himself. "Why are you doing this?"

She swallowed, feeling the nerves of rejection even more profoundly now that she was vulnerable. "No, don't stop," she reached for him again, hoping to recapture the magic of the moment. It had been working. They'd been connecting. They'd been healing. "Please, I want... I don't want to lose you. I—"

He opened his honey-colored eyes again and his brows knit with a deep sadness.

The moment rushed between them, snipping the taut cord of tension that had drawn them into this intimate, vulnerable embrace. The strand of this moment fell on either side of them. As the energy shifted, she relaxed the grip she'd had around him with her thighs, sinking down into the bed once more. Her lavender eyes looked up to touch his, but he looked away. He remained poised above her while she waited for him to speak the thought that had hung itself on his shoulders.

He was quiet as he said, "You're not going to lose me. You're not going to lose the reevers. It's me who thought I was going to lose *you* tonight."

"Ash, I–"

He lowered himself slowly to the space next to her. Despite Amaris remaining fully naked, he draped an arm around her midsection, turning her to face him. She tried to bring her knees up to her chest, wanting to curl into a ball. When he brought his hand to touch her face, she felt the tears that she didn't know she had been holding back. The weight of everything crashed through her. She wouldn't be forgetting. No, not tonight.

"We're angry because we care. Don't you know that by now?"

She turned her chin away, shame burning through her. She understood why she'd thought this was what she needed and wanted in order to restore their intimacy, but her miscalculation made her sick. She wished she could turn back time. She wouldn't drop her towel. She wouldn't betray Malik in the forest. She would never have met the demons in the woods who'd caused so much turmoil in her life.

"Stop that," he chided softly, pulling her into a hug. "You're a witch and a bastard. Just let me be angry. But you don't have to do, or be anything other than what you are. Except for the witchcraft. Maybe don't do that one anymore."

She couldn't look at him. "I… I'm sorry."

"Oh, please don't be. I've wanted to see you naked for years."

She laughed through the discomfort, feeling the rush as the tension cracked between them. She smiled into his chest. "Fuck you."

"You sure did try."

"*You're* the bastard."

"Always will be."

Instead of pushing it away, she would face it. The sorrow, the humiliation, the pressure, the fear of abandonment poured out of her in hot, salty tears. He tucked her close to him and held her while she cried. After the single tear shed on her first day at Uaimh Reev, she had never let herself show weakness around any of the men. Years of tears spilled out, shaking her shoulders. The orphanage, the Madame, Nox, all of it crashed over her like the ocean's waves until she had no more water left in her sea. The desperation she'd felt in the moments she'd thought the reevers had left her had been paralyzing. She had gone mad with the need to be loved by the only family she'd truly known.

But they were family. Not by birth, but by rite, oath, and choice. What they had was stronger and deeper and more important than heritage. It couldn't be broken by a mistake, or a perceived treachery, or a fool-hearty attempt to use sex as a bandage. Ash didn't release her, holding her as her tears broke. She wasn't sure if that made things better or worse, other suspecting that it prolonged the crying process. A few ragged inhalations and exhalations punctured the noise of his calming shushes. And eventually, between the shushes, the tears, and the warmth of skin, they fell asleep.

Morning light filtered in through the window, catching the dust in the air like ten thousand specks of gold.

She was the first one awake, stirring from a much-needed, dreamless rest. Staring at the still-naked faeling in her bed now, a deep guilt itched her behind the ear. She fully understood what had possessed her to desire intimacy the night before, but this hadn't been a union she'd truly wanted, and even in the heat of their embrace, he'd known it. Their flirtation and friendship had been an affable source of joy, of inspiration, and of kinship. She did love him, though not in the way a woman might love a man when standing naked before him and wrapping her legs around his waist.

She'd have to put the embarrassment of this misstep into the airtight box inside her if she had any chance of forgetting and moving on from her botched attempt at seduction. She tested the container to ensure that it had room to hold yet another traumatic experience, and then slipped the night inside, securing the chains behind it. She wouldn't think of it again.

Ash slept heavily beside her, uncovered. He looked so peaceful. The reever was one year her senior. He had been lean and sinewy when they'd met three years prior. His chest, arms and back had filled out beautifully, matching the firm, strong legs that had carried him up and down the mountain. They were not the muscles of an overgrown brute, but the functional body of a man of action. His hair had dried in the night in wavy, coppery locks around his face. He slept so silently, he may have been dead if she hadn't been slumbering beside them night after night in the forest, knowing he never snored.

There was a friendly love in her heart that wanted her to press a kiss to his coppery hair while he slept, but no. Their chapter had closed. They were brothers in arms. That was the only love she wished to foster.

Amaris slipped out from beneath the covers, hoping this would never be spoken of again—though he was right, he had made no secret of wanting to see her naked for years. In the end, perhaps they'd both been done a small favor.

She allowed him his sleep, redressing silently. He didn't stir as she let herself tip-toe down the hall and into the tavern below where bread and eggs were being served. Malik was already awake, sitting at a table by the window. Warm, morning sunlight lit his features, creating a halo against his golden hair. There were no other patrons in the dining room at this early hour, only a friendly-looking innkeeper picking his way quietly around the room as he set up for the day with a broom and a dustpan. Malik's eyes were on the road beyond the windowpane, scanning. He saw her walk in and smiled. Perhaps a bath, a night on a proper bed, and a healing tonic had been all he'd needed to forgive her. His heart had always been a bit too pure for this world.

"So, about last night. Should I go first, or do you want to?" She slid into the seat across from him. Tea and a breakfast plate were set before her moments later, the innkeeper appearing happy to be working in the quiet hours of the morning before most patrons awoke. The man tittered off with a rag and his chores, leaving them be.

Malik shrugged, "I'll go first, though I'm not sure that I have much to tell. We were at the tavern—room already paid for. I was watching some night-haired girl with these gorgeous coal-black eyes try to get Ash into bed. The woman was a goddess. Honestly, I don't know what happened. I would have sold my soul to have taken her for a tumble."

She found it to be quite the piece of information. Apparently, two women had tried unsuccessfully to get Ash into bed that night. She was in good company.

"Well, I guess I'm glad you made it out with your soul," she rolled her eyes.

He shoveled a few forkfuls of egg into his mouth and took a long sip of his tea to wash it down. The breakfast had been over-salted, but it was hot, and better than the cold, dried goods they ate on the road. "Like I said, I really don't know what happened. It was after the second time he'd tried to get up from the table. I can't quite explain it, but the girl lost her damn mind. It was so bizarre. First, they were flirting. The next thing you know she was screaming at Ash, and by the way he stumbled backward, the other patrons thought he'd done something truly terrible to her. Isn't insanity the curse of all beautiful women?"

"I don't know. I'll have to ask the next one I see." Amaris smiled, picking at the warm center of her bread. "Did you find out what the girl was looking for? Or why on earth she thought Ash had anything to do with it?"

Malik shrugged, "Your guess is as good as mine. Maybe it was a case of mistaken identity."

"Does he look a lot like his father? Maybe she knew him."

He didn't know. "She did seem to single him out because he looks like he's from the north. I suppose that could be it. Or maybe she had a thing for would-be assassins. Maybe I should make an effort to display my blades a little more prominently next time I'm drinking. One of life's great mysteries, I guess. Honestly, sometimes the crazy ones are better lays."

Amaris tossed her half-eaten bread at him. "You're disgusting."

He laughed, emerald eyes twinkling with their delight.

She beamed back at him, feeling the healing wound of whatever had been broken between them. She also knew Malik well enough to know he was a perfect gentleman with the women, no matter how foul his mouth was this morning.

"Your turn."

Her smile faded slightly.

"Malik, I just wanted to say how sorry I am."

She had already explained persuasion in broad strokes while on the ride around Yelagin as they'd found a new inn. As it had been well past the two o'clock bell, and given the chaos of their escape from the first establishment, they hadn't gone into detail. They'd just wanted to get off the road.

Now, she told him everything. She explained that Samael had known, and it's why she had been partnered with Ash. She also explained it was the reason the three of them had been sent to a unit to speak with the human queen of Farehold.

He offered a dismissive half-shrug. "That's what I get for being human, I suppose."

She didn't know what to say to that. Was it better to be fae in this world? Long life was their most coveted trait. Youth, beauty, gifts that manifested themselves in various ways throughout the bloodlines were a source of envy, even of hatred from the humans. But was it such a gift worthy of contempt? Was it a blessing to watch your family, your friends, your schoolmates and the townsfolk around you grow old and sick and have their minds lost to the ravages of time? What gift is it to be forced to relive heartbreak on an endless cycle until you become so cruel, cold and desensitized that you cannot love, cannot be vulnerable. Perhaps the humans should pity the fae instead.

She thought that if she could choose her fate, she would have elected to have been human, born with a small magic. If she could be human with the ability to heal, to summon wind, to manipulate water then she could experience the favors of fate without the cruelties of time. Her mind wandered to Brel and thoughts of his human parents, terrified of his gift. Perhaps there was no one born under the All Mother's preferential treatment. Everyone suffered in their own ways once they entered this earth.

Movement in the room's corner drew her eyes to the red hair, now neatly pulled into a knot once more, of her friend. Ash eyed her cautiously as he crossed the room toward them, checking her face for signs of regret or shame from the night before, but she held none. Nothing had changed between them, and by the time he slid into his chair, he knew it. While he took his turn on the bread and eggs, she began to explain her encounter with the ag'imni.

"They're fae," she whispered.

Ash looked up from his forkful of eggs, but continued chewing, allowing her to speak.

"There's some sort of enchantment at the border—that's what they said, anyway. For nearly two decades, when dark fae pass from Raascot into Farehold, they're perceived as the demonic things you saw last night. They were just men, two fae men, only as evil and grotesque as myself or Ash or Samael."

Malik chuckled, "I guess that's her way of telling you she thinks you're ugly."

The men exchanged elbows, allowing her to continue.

"I don't know why, but I didn't see ag'imni when they were speaking to me. I saw them for who they were."

Ash considered this. His eyebrows slowly lifted as he processed the information in real time. "Here we've been wondering why your night vision was so terrible for a faeling. Maybe this is your gift of sight. Amaris, perhaps you can see through enchantments."

They both considered the purple irises looking back at them. Amaris tucked a strand of milky hair behind her ear and continued. "I made a judgment call last night, and I need the both of you to support my decision."

Malik gave her a dry raise of his eyebrows. "Yes, we were there. You made the call to brainwash your favorite friend and spare the demons."

"I'm pretty sure I'm her favorite friend."

"You definitely aren't. Amaris, which one of us do you like better?"

She winced, ignoring them and their ill-timed humor, "Okay, so I made a few judgment calls last night. I told them of our mission." The boys stiffened briefly at that piece of information, but Amaris continued. "Samael instructed us to find out why the queen has a vendetta against the north, and to see if we can't persuade her to stop the killings of men or fae from Raascot. It seemed pertinent to tell the dark fae that my mission, in so many words, is to save their lives while on this side of the border. Also, I like Malik better."

"Told you."

They weren't thrilled that she'd made the decision without them, but they saw the wisdom in her choice. Her companions nodded, ready to accept her rationale—Malik was particularly agreeable since he'd been established as the favorite. Their dispatch wasn't exactly of utmost secrecy, and it would only grant them more allies if the dark fae knew that the mission was to find amnesty for them. Besides, what was the harm of one or two fewer demons in the woods who needed to be slain?

Ash finished his final swallow and drained his teacup. "The question, then, is how are we supposed to know if we come across a real ag'imni? Swinging first and asking questions later seems like a bad policy for prospective allies."

"I guess you'll have to keep me around," Amaris smiled.

"Oh," Malik amended, "and what is your punishment if you ever use that on me again? Can I hang you from a tree by your thumbs?"

The boys took their time discussing various methods of suitable torture while she finished her breakfast. While most of their ideas revolved around particularly cruel and unusual ways for her to apologize, they landed on using a hot iron brand to say "I'm sorry, Malik" across her forehead.

"For what it's worth, I *am* sorry."

"Tell it to the iron brand."

While their night at the inn hadn't been an eight-hour slumber of down pillows and crackling fires that one might have hoped, it was certainly refreshing for them to have taken a break, however brief, from cold nights on the ground with insects and wild hares as their only company. The baths and hot meals had done them a world of wonder. Even the horses seemed to have enjoyed their night in the stables with fresh straw and the bag of oats mounted on the walls of their stalls. It didn't take long to saddle their steeds. Soon Cobb, Nine and Fourteen were carrying them up the hill out of Yelagin, the road to Aubade stretched out before them.

18

"Do you know what the most dangerous force in this world is?" Millicent clasped her hands in front of her, resting her elbows on her desk. The ornate walls of her office populated the space behind her. Today she wore all black, including a small black hat atop her pinned hair, and her ever-present inky gloves.

Emily had been invited into the Madame's office many times before and had become familiar with the choking cloud of vanilla perfume that filled her lungs every time she'd sat in this chair. In the past, she had sat in this chair to discuss clients, techniques and procedurals. In more recent visits, she and the Madame had gone over Emily's instructions for how to target and lure the Duke of Henares to The Selkie, or her upcoming plan to bait the Captain of the Guard for a visit to Priory. The duke hadn't been her first act as bait, but it had unquestioningly been her most successful. The power of suggestion was so much more effective, she had learned, when the target believed the idea to be his own decision. Now she sat across from Millicent, shifting uncomfortably at the woman's change in energy.

Millicent raked her eyes over the girl before her, from her

strawberry hair down every freckled inch of her curves. Emily felt the threat in the stare, and had no idea what she was meant to do.

"Death?" Emily offered, heart rate increasing. She didn't know why she was here, but she had a distinctly sick feeling about it.

"Oh, not a bad guess at all. Yes, death can be an effective motivator. But, no, death motivates only from fear. The brave and the foolish alike do not fear death, at least not as they should." Millicent leaned forward onto her elbows, bending in closer to the girl. "Money is also quite powerful, of course. A man with no title can still buy the lands, the forces, the wine and women and the obedience of others. Though money, like death, is motivated by selfishness. Selfishness can be predictable. It has its limits."

Millicent stood from her chair, leaning on the edge of her desk. Emily remained seated, her unease growing as the woman in black continued to speak. "Knowledge has kept universities running, it has kept politics flowing, it has aided in the ebbs and flows of kingdoms. Yes, knowledge is certainly important." She took a few steps around the desk, now on the same side as Emily. The choking vanilla cloud intensified. They were within an arm's reach of each other. Millicent shifted her hip, perching on the edge of the desk, looking down at the young woman as she leaned against the piece of furniture. Emily wished the wooden desk had stayed between them. There was no reason for them to be this close unless she were in some sort of trouble.

The woman continued talking, but she was only speaking to herself. "Power for power's sake is preferential, as it requires little effort aside from being born a crowned prince, but who among us outside of the royal family can claim true power in and of itself? Even the royals probably have limits, as they're not the goddess herself."

Emily looked up helplessly.

"No? No guesses?"

Emily shook her head, desperately wishing this lesson would end so she could leave.

Millicent began to slowly tug at the sleeve of her left glove as she answered her question with an air of resolution. "Love, my dear, is the most dangerous power we know. Men will lay down their lives for the love of their country. Mothers will throw themselves into the teeth of wolves to save their babes. Kings will ride into battle to fight for love. It's why I knew The Selkie would be such a success. No little girl dreams of owning a pleasure house for its own account, you see, but to sell synthetic love? To market an opportunity to taste love, even in its most bastardized form, if just for a minute? Well, it has made this the most established line of business in all of the lands since the beginning of history. You, my dear, are a proud member of the oldest profession in the world for a reason."

Emily's astonished gape was one of terrified revulsion as the glove was pulled away. She didn't fully comprehend what she was seeing at first as the glove moved from the elbow to the wrist, exposing the Madame's hand entirely. She was left staring at the gray, amphibious hand that slithered down Millicent's arm, ending in blackened, razor-sharp talons. "Unrequited love will keep Nox collecting the men I need in her desperation to ride north for the object of her affection, and love will drive those very men to her doorstep—*my* doorstep—in droves. But do you know the one thing I will not allow love to do?"

Instantly petrified, Emily shrank away, eyes peeled open in shock as she shifted as far in her chair as she could possibly go.

Millicent placed the reptilian on Emily's bare throat, and the girl immediately felt herself go sick. The limp muscles of a terrible fever, the shakes of illness, the weakness of death consumed her. Her mouth opened, desiring to scream, but only the feeling of dust escaped her lips. She tried to writhe, to fight. She was powerless.

"I own love. I trade and barter and profit in love. Love works for *me*. Love will *not* defy me. It will *not* aid in my most prized tool's disobedience and escape from Priory when I need her here. It will not offer her comfort or confidence or strength when I need her angry. I need her to be hungry. I need Nox, and Emily—you stupid, foolish cow—you and your love will *not* stand between me and my victory."

Emily was withering. She knew she was dying. She felt the void as it sucked her dry. She looked at her hands as she tried to get them to rise, to beat against the Madame, but what she saw was alien. Her hands were dehydrated, paper-thin features belonging to an elderly grandmother. She couldn't fight. She couldn't scream. She couldn't run. She couldn't move.

Millicent towered down on her, eyes flashing with her power and burning with anger. She tightened the grip of that shriveled, monstrous arm on Emily's throat and leaned in close as she said, "Your love has no place here, and it is your love that has killed you."

The light dimmed from Emily's eyes, snuffed out like a candle under a douter. Millicent released the decrepit cadaver and watched the ancient remains of what had once been a beautiful, freckle-faced girl as they slumped to the floor. She pulled her black glove over her hand once more, concealing the evidence of her deathly power. With a huff akin to annoyance, Millicent strode from the room to send word for a morgue attendant. This bedraggled elderly woman with a mind ravaged by dementia had wandered off the streets and into her townhouse, confused, Millicent would explain. The benevolent Madame had brought her inside to offer her charity when the woman drew her last breath, the poor thing.

When Emily was not on the floor of the salon that night, Millicent had shrugged, aghast that another one of her girls would run away after all she's done for them. Ungrateful girls who didn't realize how good they had it under her roof often thought they'd be better off on the cruel streets of Priory. The others who worked the salon floor speculated that she had gone after Nox, and Millicent swore that she would do whatever it took to bring them home safely.

19

Nox was incensed. She had never lost control like that. How had that man—that idiotic, red-haired, dagger-covered mercenary—resisted her charms? This was her power! This was what she possessed! This was what she did!

She'd been rattled the moment she'd seen him, but she had still seen the path forward in their game of chess. Perhaps her opening hadn't been the simple forward pawn she'd intended. He'd sensed her eagerness.

She had felt utterly stonewalled as turn after turn she had sensed him pulling away, the young man making it clear time after time he'd wanted to leave their exchange. She paced the suite at the inn on the outskirts of Yelagin, nearly overturning the table with her rage. That fool, that *imbecile* had so publicly displayed his weapons, nearly identical to the ones she had seen on the assassin years ago in Farleigh. After learning that the northern assassin had abducted Amaris, she had reached into her memory and written down everything she had known about the man. She'd made a thorough record of height, his hair color, his clothes. She drew the swords and daggers and crossbow in sketches on the papers of her desk over and over. She sketched his face, burning it into her mind. She'd flitted in and out of seven taverns in Yelagin that evening and there it had been: a nearly identical sword, slung onto the back of the tell-tale bronzed skin of a northerner.

She'd nearly stopped breathing.

It had taken her a full minute to compose herself before she slipped into character. She would need to use everything she possessed to get the answers she needed from the northerner.

She slid out her pawn as an opening move, and he'd responded with one of his own, cautiously guarding the conversation. Her interactions with men had always been a game of chess, and she was a world-class player. She'd never lost a match, and when she finally did, it had failed spectacularly. Her round with the coppery mercenary had been a two-move checkmate, and she had not come out the victor. Their exchange had been a textbook execution of The Fool's Mate. It was the single, worst opening in the game.

That's what she was. A fool.

So what if the boy's complexion matched her own? She would not go north of the border for camaraderie, but with a vengeance. What had the north done for her but bred her mother with its demons, abandoned her at a child mill, and spirited away with the only person in this world she had ever loved? What would a band of assassins have done with a girl so fragile?

She felt like she was going to be sick. How had she let the man get away, and how could she find him again? Her reaction had revealed her hand, and he had fled. Why hadn't she taken a horse and followed? Why hadn't she screamed that the young man had stolen from her, or sent someone else after him? Why hadn't she kept her wits about her? She'd been too hysteric to think rationally. She'd run this race for so long and here she was, tripping at the finish line. Nox had simply let her knees go weak, sinking to the floor of the tavern as he'd wormed away from the grip she'd had on his tunic. The surrounding men, eager to defend her honor, had taken off after him, hurling their curses and threats while she'd remained slumped on the ground.

She hadn't just lost; she'd failed.

Surely, he had returned to whatever Raascot men of his had been in Yelagin and alerted them to her hunt. She had been careful not to use any specifics, like her name, or even Amaris's, lest she risk spooking them into discarding the problem. If she had been able to get the young man back to her room, she would already know everything. He should have been hers. He was within her grasp. She had sat across from the answers she'd needed. She had touched his hand. She had been so close to everything she'd burned to know.

She hadn't just failed herself, she'd failed Amaris.

He should have been a husk of a man at this very moment. He should be slack-jawed, consumed with love, willing to take her north and give her anything she might need. Had she been able to pin the assassin beneath her in her chambers, she would know where in Raascot Amaris was being held. She would know how to get there, the conditions of the girl's life in the north, and what it would take to infiltrate and conduct a rescue mission with a northern escort to guide her way. Whether Amaris was tortured in a prison cell or happily married to a damned northern farmer, the point remained that she had been taken. Nox rarely let herself consider the latter option.

What if, after all of these years of pining and planning, Amaris had found some kind of joy and peace amidst the northerners? What if her snowflake had fallen prey to the hypnotic lures of captor-bonding and had made a life for herself amidst the people of Raascot? What would she do if she stormed Gwydir and found the girl living contentedly as a courtier or exotic princess of the snow? She would still need to see it for herself. Regardless of the outcome, she needed to look upon Amaris and know that she was safe, that she was happy.

And if it were the alternative? If they'd hurt her? There would be no hell prepared for the mangled bodies she'd send into its fiery, sulfur pits. Nox had but one talent at her disposal. Her succubus power was meant to work in the night; it was a skill for behind closed doors, for the influence of time with a victim who was in her clutches one-on-one. And if she used it well, one capability was all she needed.

She couldn't bring herself to return to Priory just yet. It had been more than a week of travel by horseback to get to these lakeside knolls, and to have faced a defeat so swiftly was utterly demoralizing. Tonight, she would rest. Tomorrow, she would flex her seduction and work the men of Yelagin until she found at least one morsel of information to have made her travels worthwhile.

Nox had never been one to rise with the sun. As the years went on, she preferred to stir later and later. Especially now that she was both a lady and creature of the night, she would sleep until noon if circumstances allowed. She had paid for three nights at the inn upon arrival and had tipped handsomely for her privacy. No one disturbed her as she rested well into the late morning. The sun was bright and in her face through the suite's window when she blinked her eyes open through a curtain of thick, black lashes.

Today she opted for a more subdued approach to finessing the fine people of Yelagin. While nothing she owned could be considered particularly modest, the emerald dress she selected scooped to display her collarbones and hint at her cleavage without exposing her entire upper body quite as dramatically as she had the night before. Her attire wasn't the layers of fabrics worn by most proper ladies, but a long skirt with a rather daring slit up to her thigh was the best she could do. Her blue cloak would help conceal her body from the additional attention, as it had the night before, until she had locked in a potential source of information. The cloak was a rather flowy scrap of fabric appropriate for the summer temperatures, and though it was unusual to wear a cloak in the middle of the day, doing so shouldn't draw too many strange looks.

The innkeeper had desperately wished he could have been more helpful to her when she explained that the redheaded gentleman had lifted a very precious heirloom of hers while trying to sweet-talk her over drinks last night. The man apologized profusely for not knowing more about the boy or the blond mercenary with whom he traveled. He swore he'd ask the barmaid as soon as she came in to work if she had any more information on the miscreants, and that he'd send word to Nox right away if any news filtered through the chain of innkeepers regarding the thief. When she'd inquired about Raascot's presence in the town, she had been reassured on no uncertain terms that no one from the neighboring kingdom had set foot in his tavern for decades.

Nox made stops not just at the taprooms, but also chatted with any shopkeeper, vendor, or young boy who ran through the square. Most of what she heard was superstitious nonsense. The news consisted mostly of the gossip of superstitious peasants who bemoaned how their once-safe woods were now home to demons and monsters of all varieties. She didn't doubt that a pig or two had been killed by something like a vageth, and their education had only offered them what little vocabulary they'd had access to describe the incident.

One elderly cobbler informed her in a hushed voice that a customer not two weeks back had a daughter go missing, and when they found her, the blood had been drained from her body. Nox wasn't familiar with too many blood-drinking creatures in the bestiary aside from sustrons. Many a thief who sought to kill the creature for the cloaking power of its scent would wind up in its clutches instead. She'd even heard a story from a regular at The Selkie of a peasant boy who had kept a sustron chained in a stone root cellar, stealing its blood so that he could spy on the naked maidens of the village. She had discerned it for the hopeful folktale told by the aspiring voyeurism of men who wanted to see tits for free. What a fateful irony that a creature with blood so useful to humans would find the humans' blood equally delectable. She thanked the cobbler for sharing his story, though the tales of the bloodless maiden were not helpful to Nox or her search.

Frustrated, she took a seat near the water fountain. She was beginning to hate Yelagin more with every second that passed. She could smell the lake everywhere she went. Whether she was smelling seaweed, fish, or algae, she didn't know, but it didn't have the same exciting salt and brine of the sea. She'd learned nothing. She'd embarrassed herself. She was exhausted and irritated.

She extended her palm to let her fingers dangle into the water and shuddered, stopping just short of breaking the surface. She wondered what sort of bacteria and illness lurked in the inconspicuous waters of the fountain, and withdrew her hand. The only water she trusted was that of a hot, soapy bath she'd drawn for herself.

Nox continued sitting on the edge of the town square's fountain. Her feet were tired, and her spirits just as damp. Enough townspeople milled by that she was able to stop someone now and again interrogate them. She was just asking some awe-struck teenage boy about any sight of tanned-skin peoples like those of the north when a young girl approached from the side and tapped her on the shoulder. Nox turned curiously to address the child, who appeared to be a child no more than five years of age. Her hands were clasped behind her as she rocked back and forth on her feet.

"There are demons, you know. My mama says they come from the north."

Nox smiled kindly. She felt her heart soften, despite the wave after wave of frustration that had been drowning her ever since her failure the night before. It was a nice break from the parade of male faces to speak to the little girl. "What's your name?"

"I'm Tess." The child's grin was proud despite missing its two front teeth. She was small for her age, with gorgeous dark hair nearly as long as she was tall. It had been set in a braid, but the exuberance of childhood had scattered much of the loose ends from what had surely once been neatly plaited hair into a muss of tendrils around her face. While Tess's hair was as black as soot, her face was as fair and milky as the common folk of Farehold.

Nox felt a tinge of something like sadness as she regarded the girl. She felt the inexplicable urge to pull the little one into her lap and cuddle her deeply, but out of common decency, she resisted. She knew it wouldn't be appropriate, and would most definitely frighten the child.

"I'm sure your mother is a very smart woman. I know she'll keep you safe from any demons." She didn't feel the need to hurry the little girl away. Her life had sorely lacked human conversations with women and girls who weren't her colleagues or employers, or ones who lacked ulterior motives. It had been so long since she'd had an exchange with anyone that was simply two normal people just talking.

"The demons don't hurt us," Tess said with confidence.

"Oh?" Nox was amused. "Do you have charms at your house? Wards etched into the doorway?" She had seen several runes scratched into the tops and sides of the frames of homes as she'd wandered about Yelagin earlier that day. She wasn't sure what sort of iron grip the demonic lore had over this city, but she supposed it had something to do with how isolated they were. Yelagin was very far from the castle and from the buzz of civilization. It was even further from the university, where one would probably learn just how useless those runes were for the creatures in the forest. She didn't know much about the art of magical manufacturing, but greatly doubted that the doorways had been crafted by someone trained and gifted to actually create something effective.

"No, but when they meet in our barn, they never bother us. Mama has said they're not bad, and to leave them alone."

Nox's lips parted. She was struck with genuine surprise. No one in the town square was listening, but she still found herself lowering her voice, counting the burble of the water fountain to cover her words. "The demons meet in your barn?"

The little girl smiled, delighted to have shared her confidential information. "Mama says we're not supposed to tell people about it. It's a special secret."

Nox nodded slowly, choosing her next words carefully. She hoped she didn't look as nervous as she felt. "Your mother sounds quite intelligent, indeed. I'd very much like to learn from her. Do you think she would teach me about demons?"

The little girl considered this. The plump cheeks of her youth colored with the smile when she decided that yes, she would take Nox to meet her mama. Her tiny, fair fingers slipped into Nox's palm as Tess led her by the hand to a stall nearby within sight of the town square. They stopped beneath the shade of the vendor's stall, out of the sun.

"Papa," Tess chirped for his attention, "I made a friend."

The thin middle-aged man turned and nearly fainted at the sight of the woman holding his daughter's hand. He struggled for words, flustered as he greeted her. He picked up his cap and ran a hand through what remained of his thinning, sweat-slicked hair.

Nox tried to balance her smile, needing it to be both charming and yet the inoffensive greeting of a woman who did not seek to ruin his marriage. It took some effort to hold back the blaze of her glamor as she looked at the man. "Your daughter has invited me for dinner. Do you suppose you have room for a traveler at your table tonight?"

Tess's mother was less than thrilled to have a dinner guest, to say the least. The woman did very little to conceal the loathsome look she gave her husband, and Nox had no doubt that the man would spend the week sleeping in the henhouse. She couldn't say she blamed the woman for either her cold greeting or for the disappointment she felt in her weak-willed husband. The woman was right to feel both.

There were four of them at the farmhouse on the outskirts of Yelagin. Tess and her family lived in a home that sat just on the lake's edge. Nox had fetched her own glossy black mount from the inn and followed Tess and her father as they returned to the farm, grateful that her blue cloak was long enough to conceal the trap for the lusts of men she hid underneath. Her outfit would have won her no favors with the lady of this farm. Perhaps if the woman had been in a more favorable mood, she would have offered to take the cloak from Nox, thus forcing her to expose her rather inappropriate dress. Fortunately, no such offer was extended.

Tess had proudly declared to her mother that the woman was to teach Nox about demons, but the young woman laughed the testament away, waving a genteel hand. She dismissed the statement as good-naturedly as she could. "Your daughter is so precious. When she chatted with me in the square, she set me to missing my own little sister so dearly. I've been on the road for some time, you see. I haven't seen her in ages. When little Tess asked me for dinner, I couldn't remember the last time I'd had a home-cooked meal. I hope it's not too much of a bother?"

Nox did her best to telepathically communicate with the woman, *"I am not a threat. I am not interested in your husband. I wish you no ill will."* And while her tone and posture meant those things in earnest, the lady of the home was too shrewd to fall for it completely. The truth was, the lady's instincts were correct. She was right to distrust the young woman who'd crossed her threshold, and Nox had respect for the woman's intuition. Nox *had* come here with ulterior motives, and she wouldn't fault the lady for her acute perceptiveness. Nevertheless, she needed to find a way to make it through dinner without being thrown from the farmhouse, and at this rate, she wasn't sure if she'd make it through the next twenty minutes.

The husband knew his mistake the moment he saw his wife's face. He'd unlaced his boots and taken off his hat and slumped into his seat at the table. The man's weak attempt of, "There's more than enough chicken to go around," only earned him a scowl.

The lady of the farm was not ugly by any means, nor did she have the lines marked by permanent frowns or a life of discontent. Her face was one meant for openness, for tenderness and easy smiles. Tess had inherited her black hair from her mother, whose hair was in a crown of braids common to the dairymaids Nox had often met in villages around Farehold. Perhaps it was specifically *because* she could sense that the normally receptive, neighborly woman had her guards up that confirmed her suspicion that something atypical for the provincial life of farmers was afoot here. This was far more than any petty distaste or insecurity over a beautiful stranger. Nox wouldn't insult the woman's character by assuming her attitude was one of jealousy. What was this cautious woman concealing?

She hadn't even been invited to sit down. She continued to idly by the door, waiting for the formal offer. The door had been shut behind her, and she now let her eyes graze over the humble house for clues.

The family kept a lovely home. It wasn't extravagant by any means, but the gentle touches of humble artworks hung from the stone walls, the warm fire, and the way the legs of the farmhouse table had been carved into beautiful curvatures were marvelous. The honest smell of the country, coupled with the abundant presence of books made it the kind of place Nox would have loved to have lived. In another life, she could envision herself here, waking up to a glass of tea by the window, looking out as the sun came up over the lake. She could picture herself waiting for Amaris to finish her book just there on the stuffed sofa, or see the life they'd lead tending chickens and selling eggs in Yelagin's square. She imagined their shared conspiratorial smiles as the townsfolk made comments about what very good friends the two maidens must have been to share a home and to have never taken husbands. She was sure she'd learn to love the smell of the lake if she shared this home with Amaris. It was ridiculous to let the daydream cross her mind, no matter how fleeting.

"What's your name, then?" The woman asked.

"I'm Ginny." Nox offered her hand.

The woman accepted it, obviously trying to fight off the outright glower of suspicion.

"Theresa." The woman said in response. Ah, so little Tess had been named after her mother. Unlike the precocious little girl, Theresa was not one for chatting that evening.

"Take a seat, Ginny. It's time to eat."

The woman gave truncated responses to nearly every question, no matter how innocent or unrelated to matters outside of country life. At one point, Theresa's husband had made some half-hearted comment akin to "*Come then, be nice,*" but the withering look he'd received in response had told him all he needed to know of what he was to get from her stance for the rest of the meal.

Theresa's hostility was so thinly veiled that it had almost become amusing. It had taken on a life and flavor of its own, almost like a tangy, metallic sting in the back of her throat. She found herself twitching against a smile at each new way the woman rebuked her.

The sun had set on the farmstead as Theresa ladled their plates with braised radishes, chicken, and hot, sweet bread accompanied by little pads of freshly churned butter. Dinner was hardly off of their plates before the hostess clapped her knees. She looked first to her husband and child before turning to Nox.

"Alright then, *Ginny*, I'd hate for you to get stuck on the roads back to town too late into the night. Much safer if you make your way back before it gets too terribly dark, miss." She emphasized the name as if she knew it had been a lie. Nox was impressed. Should she ever find herself in a position to recruit interrogators or spies, she'd put Theresa's steel-trap of a mind on the top of her list.

"The sun's already set, Mama." Tess said informatively. "Dark is dark. It can't get more dark than dark."

Her husband began to say something about a guest room, but thought better of it and muttered away his own interjection, pushing around the food he'd barely touched. With his slumped shoulders and thin hair, the farmer seemed so dejected. Nox nearly pitied him, but couldn't quite bring herself to the emotion. No one had coerced the man into bringing a strange, stunning woman back to his house, but he had seen her beauty and been flattered at the attention. She used that knowledge to keep firm in her path, unwilling to allow herself whatever small guilt ached in her belly. His shortcomings were not her fault.

"Yes, but Miss Ginny has to get going. I'm sure her travel companions are waiting for her."

She hadn't mentioned any travel companions. Perhaps the woman was using the opportunity to clarify that she didn't care what lies needed to be spun, it was time to say goodnight. Nox was torn between the next right move. On the one hand, she could indeed motion for sanctuary, claiming she was scared of the roads at night and would love to stay with them. On the other hand, she could leave now and return after they'd gone to sleep. The possibilities played out in her mind as she finished what was left of her water. If she stayed here, she had no doubt that Theresa would not sleep a wink. Whatever the lady was hiding, it was a secret too guarded to allow the intrusion of a stranger's sneaking about in the night. Nox wondered at the husband who sat dejected at their table. If he had felt as strongly about the secret, would he have allowed her to come? Was there a possibility that he didn't know what went on in his barn?

Indeed, for all Nox believed of men, she was entirely willing to accept that this farmer woke in the morning to tend to his farm, sold his goods in the market, and slept soundly at night. Tess may have only stumbled upon the secret with the playfulness and the innocence of a child hiding or wandering out past her bedtime. Yes, it was easy to believe that the man of the house knew nothing and hid nothing. These were Theresa's private dealings, and hers alone. But why?

Nox did her best to beam with the innocence of a country maiden as she took her cue to depart. "I can't thank you enough for your hospitality. The food was truly delicious, and spending time with your family made my heart so full. You're right though, I'd hate to stay out too late. I don't want the innkeeper thinking any girl under his roof has reason to be out much past bedtime."

Theresa nearly choked on her relief, standing to all but push Nox out the door. "You're so welcome, Ginny. It was lovely to have a new friend for dinner. Do stop by anytime you travel through Yelagin. You'll always be welcome here."

The words were right, but the tone was comically off-kilter. She was positive that Theresa would nail boards to the front door if she ever saw the young woman on her sooty horse come their way again.

Despite Theresa's unfriendliness, Nox knelt for the little girl. She felt a genuine surge of love once more and longed to squeeze the little one too tightly until her eyes popped out. She wrapped her arms around Tess in a big hug, and put her whole heart into the embrace. She clutched the sweet child, soaking up every ounce of the innocence that was so rare in her life. In another world, one where Nox had been blessed with the ability to give rather than take, she would have granted Tess a beautiful life, full of luck, love and fortune. Instead, she merely squeezed the little girl's shoulders as she pulled away. "Be good, and listen to your mum, okay?"

The mister and missus waved her away at the doorway as she took the black horse the duke had given her and urged it into a walk toward Yelagin. Once she was certain the door had closed and Theresa was no doubt yelling at her husband, Nox urged the horse off the road, into the trees. Her beast protested slightly with a whinny, acting the part of a temperamental primadonna. It jerked and to show its disapproval as it was forced from its comfortable path on the well-trodden road to the brambles of the underbrush.

"Oh, hush. As if your life is so hard." She rolled her eyes at the horse.

The horse seemed to object to this as well, chuffing grumpily as she dismounted. She leashed its reins to a tree and began to slowly pick her way through the forest back toward the farmhouse.

She had been a lady of the night for years now, making her exceedingly comfortable with the late hour. Sleep was the furthest thing from her mind. If Millicent and her damned tome of monsters were to believe, she might very well be a creature of the night as well. And if demons truly were meeting in the barn, perhaps they'd welcome their long-lost succubus kin with welcome talons. She nearly snorted at the absurdity of the mental image it conjured.

Her eyes had always adjusted well to the dark. Perhaps it was the goddess's humorous gift to her namesake, or maybe it was a blessed curse from whatever had sired her. They didn't strain as she watched the candlelights in Theresa's house blink out for the night. The absence of their orange glow made it easier for her to monitor the silhouettes of the home, the henhouse, the hills in the distance, and of course, the silvered outline of the barn as the light of the half-moon lit its frame. Or perhaps it wasn't quite a half-moon, as its shape waned ever so slightly from its monthly bisection as it rose behind the barn.

As she waited, she uncovered a very dull truth. One thing no one had told her about espionage was that it was dreadfully boring. There was no excitement that the spying heroes of novels and ballads had led her to believe. There was no thrill from the deception as she watched the barn. Her mind wandered—not to Amaris, but to the girls in the salon. She thought of troops she needed to gather. She thought of the toffee-haired Duke of Henares and of oxytocin and power and of the bluish-white glow that every soul had as it left the body. Her mind wandered to her childhood days at Farleigh, to the teachings of the church, to the bullies she'd met and the peers she'd hated. She thought of Emily, and something like regret drew her attention.

This is where her wandering mind would land. She ruminated on the freckled girl. Her feelings of care were profound. Emily was beautiful, patient and kind. Emily understood Nox in a way that others couldn't hope to fathom. She had been compassionate as Nox had poured over her plans for the north. She had endured Nox's heartache over Amaris, even on the nights she'd cried into her pillow with tears over another woman. The strawberry girl was truly too good for the way Nox treated her. Emily had been worthy of a life filled with emotional diamonds and jewels from her lover, and was being given crumbs and scraps of a shredded heart instead. Emily deserved a better life than the one offered, whether by her, or by the cruel realities of the world within The Selkie. Nox offered only pain to someone who deserved a life of pleasure.

The memory of her freckled face was just starting to fade when Nox saw the distinct flash of blackened, bat-like wings.

20

Over the past few years, Nox had come to think of herself as brave. She rarely, if ever, met an opponent she couldn't tackle. The matrons and the Madame had favored her. The townsfolk had opened doors for her wherever she went. Men had swooned at her feet, handing over their mortal lives for a chance to be with her. As she sidled along the edge of the barn, painted in its shadow, she couldn't hear anything inside over the furious thundering of her own heart. She willed her knees to bend, her feet to move. She pleaded with her gut to find some courage, but she couldn't help from damning herself as a coward. She'd never make it inside the building if she couldn't stop trembling.

She realized that, no, she had never been brave. She was strong, resilient, and clever, but she was not courageous. Before now, Nox had simply lacked the opportunity to be truly afraid.

The barn was traditional in its structure. The lower level was meant to house animals, with an upper loft intended to store their hay. The two enormous doors on the front of the barn were meant to open and close for cattle and horses, both of which had been closed for the night. A human-sized door on the barn's side that divided into two parts, top and bottom, was the entrance she angled for. She knew it to be common for barns to have such a division on their doors in case farmers might need to toss in food or check on the animals without risking a lamb too small and nimble to grab, or a flock of chickens rushing out at your feet. Nox reached the handle of the door, and each movement took her every drop of strength. If the rusted handle let out even the smallest sound, she was relatively sure she'd faint. How heroic.

Nox had to muster every ounce of fortitude she possessed to grip the handle in her clammy palm. She rallied any bravery inside of her as she opened the door with painful slowness. Unfortunately, only the top division opened.

"Fucking goddess damned piece of—" she felt quite confident that opening this door was the most frightening thing that anyone had ever done in the history of the continent, and it was outright offensive that she'd have to summon the courage to do it not once, but twice. Her string of obscenities was contained to the quietest of unhinged whispers as she tantrumed. She rallied her nerves to go again.

"Come on, you spineless jellyfish," she cursed herself under her breath. It took a few rallying movements to summon another bout of courage.

The bottom half containing its own separate latch remained just inside for a farmer to open or close once the top had been freed. She rolled her eyes against the ringing in her ears, somehow both terrified and irritated with herself for her reaction as she continued the process of maneuvering her way into the barn. Perhaps it was laughable that turning a handle was the most terrifying moment of her life, but when she considered the gnashing of teeth and beady eyes that might await her on the other side, Nox knew her survival depended on her silence.

When she'd managed to finally open the door she could hear the low sound of something that may have been voices. The noises within the barn hadn't paused or stilled when she'd released her door, assuring her she hadn't yet been detected. It took her far too long for her to move the iron latch, terrified that the lock would make a clang or reveal her to the things above once released, but once again she was able to make progress without exposing herself.

She didn't mind the strong wave of hay and animal smells that hit her as she slipped into the barn. There was an honest, bucolic reassurance carried on the scent of farm life. The homeyness was comforting, which was a feeling she needed if she were to make forward progress tonight. Choosing her steps carefully, she closed the top half of the door, but left the bottom half ajar should she need to make a quick escape. She didn't need the light of the moon seeping in and alerting them to the intrusion any more than necessary.

Nox crept closer to a ladder that she was just barely able to make out in the center of the barn. A horse in one of the stalls, obscured by the dark of the night, made a shuddering noise, perhaps shaking a fly from its skin. The sound caused her to pause, but the voices above continued, unbothered. There was something odd about the way they were talking. She wasn't close enough to understand what it was, but the voices were something distinctly unlike the common tongue.

An omnilinguist had once visited The Selkie. While some humans were born with the small magics of palm reading, of fire, of scrying or of stone, this young man had been invited to hold an audience with the queen for his gift of gab. He'd been eighteen—nearly a man in his own right—before he knew he'd even been born with such a magic, as he hadn't done much traveling before taking work on a ship. Everywhere they docked, whether the remote southern isles, the hot sand shores of the Tarkhany Desert, or even across the Long Sea, he'd understood and spoken with anyone he'd met without ever having met their people nor studied their words. It didn't take long for word to spread of his gift. It was a delightful power, to be sure. While some magics terrified simple folk and villagers, there were few ways the power of language could frighten the citizens of the continent. The proud man had just concluded his meeting with the monarch when he'd marched directly to the best brothel on the coast to celebrate his honorific title as the court's translator.

It had been comparatively exciting to hear from someone directly who dealt with the queen rather than rumors or cityfolk's opinions of the lordlings. The omnilinguist claimed Moirai was a sharp and suspicious woman, wary of all who entered her throne room. After her daughter, Princess Daphne, had passed, she had sequestered herself to rule as Queen Regent while the young crowned prince grew to maturity. Once probed with enough drink to loosen his omnilingual lips, he'd described Moirai as a paranoid old witch and declared himself ready to serve the young king whenever he ascended the throne. Nox had smiled at that, always finding new ways to be amused at the pliability of men. What wouldn't they say in the company of women, those whom they underestimated so profoundly?

No matter how much coin he'd offered, Nox had refused to go up the stairs with him the night of his visit. At the time, she had not yet managed to sleep with a man without killing him, and this man of many tongues would have been a shame to murder. She hadn't particularly liked him, but she had seen the potential for usefulness in keeping him alive. She made some laughing, vague reference to her moon time of the month as an excuse, but promised that if he were to return to The Selkie, she'd give him the ride of his life. Now that she'd mastered her curse, she'd love the chance to add the queen's omnilinguist to her harem of puppets.

She knew, however, that she did not possess such a gift for speech. Two of the men she'd killed in her journey of mastery over her feeding frenzy had been from foreign lands. The sea-fresh faces of the foreigners sailors had been safe practice marks, Millicent had said, as they were too far from home for the families to come looking for them.

The Madame had always applauded Nox for her effort, reassuring her of her progress whenever she had to clean up a body. Hers and the Madame's companionship was not a virtuous one, but she had been grateful for Millicent's assistance and encouragement in those early days.

She thought of this now as she listened to the voices above. While she knew in the pits of her stomach that the sounds were not those vowels and consonants of the common tongue, somehow she found herself comprehending their words. Their male voices carried well enough as they floated down through the barn.

"I'm telling you, she saw us. Gadriel can confirm."

Nox positioned herself behind the ladder. She had gone as close as she dared before the demons in the loft might spy her. The dullest murk of moonlight filtered from the upper windows of the barn's loft down into the lower levels. She kept herself hidden from sight of whoever, or whatever, sat atop in the hay.

"He's telling the truth," the one they'd referred to as Gadriel responded. "I don't know how it's possible, but she saw us. Truly saw us, and wasn't afraid. If it weren't for her gift of sight, her companions would have killed us."

"What do we do with this information? Could she be–" A third voice gave its rough response, sentencing slicing down the middle as he'd stopped abruptly in the middle of his thought.

Nox absorbed their words, but felt as if the sounds were coming out in monstrous shrieks. There was something inhuman and beastly about what her ears heard, yet deeply sentient regarding what her mind understood. Perhaps if Millicent were correct, and she were part demon, it was her demon half now that found itself able to comprehend the shrieks and gnashing teeth of the damned, no matter how her human ears attempted to block it out. The contradictory noises horrified her, but she pressed herself into the ladder so she might continue to listen.

They pushed each other for plans and seemed determined to head southwest toward Aubade. If they were going southwest, she could leave and intercept them closer to home where she had the safety of reinforcements. She could have the troops of Henares rallied the moment she arrived. What good would she be now, caught in a legion of demons alone on a lakeside?

"I'll leave another letter for Theresa telling her we're headed south, but to leave our outpost in Yelagin available for retreat," the first voice had responded.

That explained how they were communicating with her, but not why such a shrewd woman would accept the unholy scribbles of demons as any form of command. Perhaps they had threatened her or her children. She didn't know much about demons, though nothing she'd read on the ag'imni had led her to believe them to be very intelligent. The bloodthirsty humanoids were rumored to have some gifts of speech, but only for the purpose of lies and fears. These voices seemed like the astute plans of men, not the serpentine whispers of the damned. Her head swam with questions of the farm woman, but she pushed them aside to listen.

"How does she expect us to help?" The third voice again. From the sounds of shuffled weight, there seemed to be more than three. How many additional diabolical presences were loitering overhead in the hay? She had wasted all of her fear outside when she'd worked up the courage to slink into the barn. Now she was determined to absorb every moment that information disseminated from the loft above.

"She didn't ask for our help. We offered it." The only name she'd learned, Gadriel, had insisted. "This is the chance we've been looking for. I'm telling you, this is the one. She's southwest bound on the regency's road as we speak."

The first voice chimed in with cautious optimism, "She travels with companions, but I don't believe they'll pose a threat to us. At least, I have high hopes."

A new voice now, a fourth guttural and bitter voice responded. "I have too many dead men to trust your beliefs, Cai. How many years will it take for you to see the bodies of your friends and countrymen before you stop hoping for the best in these people."

Cai was the first voice, then. She had two names to work with now. She'd remember them for her ledger when she made it back to The Selkie. Nox was sure she'd think of nothing else for the entirety of the nine days she was to spend on the road back to Priory, pushing her horse within an inch of its life on the hard ride home.

"I need you to trust me." It was Gadriel speaking. "I don't know if we'll survive. I've never guaranteed our safety. But we all know why we're here. The king has not stopped searching in over twenty years, nor has he shown any sign that he intends to stop. How many men will be sent across the border to die at Farehold's hands? How many of your brothers will you see filled with arrows? For the king, that number has no limit until he finds what he's looking for. This girl is the first time in twenty years I've held even the smallest of hope that we might end the carnage. I'm telling you, she's the one."

"Damn the mad king, and damn his useless fucking plot to lead us all to our graves." the fourth voice said angrily.

No one responded to this, but the silence that followed was not a comfortable one. The sounds of night loomed about them. A few horses shifted their weight in their stalls, filling the quiet. The summer sounds of nighttime insects and nocturnal birds made a dull, comforting chorus beyond the barn's wooden doors. The demons above seemed to shift their weight, troubled by the treasonous tone of the fourth man, before Gadriel offered his final words.

"He is our king. That's the last word on his charge. This is the order, from here on out. We know how to stay alive, how to cling to the shadows. Travel by night and avoid the villages, but follow the girl to Aubade. Keep her safe. Our only hope rests on her meeting with the queen."

"How will we recognize this *savior*?" The fourth voice was bitter, something of sarcasm in his listless question.

"She fits the description," Gadriel said quietly.

"She's hard to miss," Cai responded. His voice was the cheeriest of the bunch. "She's traveling with two men, one half-fae. The girl herself is as white as the moon."

Nox felt her soul leave her body.

No human or fae on the continent fit that description—no one, save for one. A sound like the ringing vibrations of her own blood clouded her ears as she clung to consciousness so she could hear their next words. She reached for the ladder, feeling splinters bite into her fingertips as her vision swam. They were still talking, but she could scarcely hear their words.

"Look for her white hair," Cai continued, voice a controlled excitement, "and if you're close enough, her eyes are as purple as lilacs in the spring. Though, come to think of it, she might be traveling with her hood up to hide her features for exactly that reason. If she's concealed, keep an eye for her companions. We met her human and her fire-haired faeling in the woods. The fae boy may have some Raascot blood, so he shouldn't be too difficult to spot."

Though she knew she needed to remain concealed, both hands were gripping the ladder for dear life. If she fell to her back, they'd be alerted by the thump of her lifeless body. The ringing in her ears grew louder, drowning out the voices that had suddenly stilled. A horse whinnied, but something about the sound felt far away. Where blackness had been, suddenly stars began to swim in her vision, coloring her sight with their light. This was not the detachment that called to her as a friend. This was darkness at her door, threatening to take her against her will. She felt drunk, as if wine swam through her head. Nox began to sway, and knew with certainty that no matter how tightly she gripped the ladder, she would faint.

She fought against the black that swam before her eyes, but void would win this battle. She took a ragged breath in as she began to fall. The last image as she drew in a final moment of consciousness was the monstrous face of an ag'imni staring down at her.

Straw and manure were the first things to enter her consciousness. The smell of animals and wood were in her nostrils before her eyes dared to flutter. She raised herself to her elbows, straw clinging to her hair and her cloak. The quiet was pressing. When no sounds of voices or stirrings of demons moved above her, she knew the barn had been abandoned. She brushed away a piece of straw sticking to her face and forced herself into a sitting position. The creatures were gone and she was alone. All things considered, she was lucky to be leaving with her life. She should have been torn to ribbons after they'd discovered her. She should be a gory shell of entrails, left for Theresa and her husband to discover in the morning. Instead, she was about to walk out of the barn, unscathed and armed with knowledge—even if she had failed rather spectacularly at her first attempt at espionage.

It took a moment to find her feet, but she found blood returning to her limbs. Nox slipped out of the half-door and latched it behind her on shaky legs. She hadn't been unconscious for long, as the moon had made markedly little progress across the sky. She continued picking pieces of straw from her hair and her cloak as she made her way amidst the shadows across the farmyard into the trees. The horse was extraordinarily impatient as she mounted it and urged it onto the road. It was a decidedly unfriendly beast, and perhaps if her wits ever returned to her, she'd ask the duke for a new steed.

They had been talking about Amaris.

The demons had been talking about Amaris.

How many ways could she turn the revelation over in her head? She was in a barn filled with ag'imni discussing Amaris.

She rolled it around from the front of her brain to the back. She said it out loud a time or three. It would make more sense to convince herself that she had hallucinated the entire encounter than to believe that four damned creatures of hell had been discussing the white hair and lavender eyes of her Amaris.

That hadn't been the only information they'd shared. She made herself focus, desperately wishing she'd had a pen and paper. Amaris was heading to Aubade. Amaris was not alone. Amaris could see them. What did that mean, she could see them? They were not invisible; she had seen their membranous, stretched skin of the bat-like wings as a demonic entity had entered the barn's upper window. She had seen the gargoyle's face as it had peered down at her. What else had she heard? There had been more; she knew there had been more.

There had been four voices, yes, that much she was certain. She'd learned two of their names. They were talking about Amaris. She was traveling south with… what had they said? She was traveling southwest toward Aubade to meet with the queen. She had two male companions. One was fae. One was fae? Had there been another word used to describe him?

Yes, she realized. One was a fire-haired fae. That's how the beast had described him. Nox had been sharing drinks only one night ago with Amaris's ruddy, faeling friend. Not her captor. Not her enemy. Her riding companion. She had been across the table from Amaris's friend. She had grabbed the hand of Amaris's friend.

What else had they said? Nox felt strongly that there had been one more piece to the puzzle, but all she could hear was the voice inside herself shouting *"Amaris is alive! Amaris is here, in Farehold! Amaris is heading south! She's alive, she's alive, she's alive!"* Whatever the demons had said, they had clearly wanted to ally with her. She knew she'd fight on the side of the ag'imni if they were truly Amaris's allies. But that couldn't be true. The ag'imni were creatures of nightmares. They were damnation personified, clawing their way up from the earth, escaped abominations who had wriggled free from the goddess's hell. In what conceivable plot could Amaris be the champion of hell?

The sooty horse was happy to keep to the road, moving forward of its own volition while she was left to her thoughts. It carried her far from the farmhouse and the forest and its trees, keeping the freshwater lake on her right hand side all the while. The road led straight into town, right to the first inn on Yelagin's outskirts, nestled on the edge of the lake. Nox dismounted numbly, leading the horse to the orange glow of the inn where the blessed release of sleep and perhaps several tankards of ale awaited her. If her head weren't so foggy, she'd press herself to ride out now in the dead of night, with or without the duke's armed escorts. But no, a few hours of rest would do her a world of good while she sorted through all that had been said.

She was nearing the inn's stables, swinging her horse wide to avoid the annoying blockade of another patron's glossy, black carriage. A sharp voice preened to her from the shadow looming against the carriage's side.

"Isn't it the oldest lesson in the book? You tell a strong-willed woman not to do something, and it's the first thing they do. I do take full blame for that one, my dear."

Nox skidded to a halt in front of Millicent.

21

"How—"

"Yes, yes, I travel rather fast. This is something you know of me, darling. Don't be dull."

Nox gaped at the Madame in her black dress, the color of shadow. She was mere arms lengths from the light and safety of the inn. Nox gripped the reins of her horse, in a true state of shock for the second time in one night. She'd thought she'd gone numb, but she could still feel the leather of her horse's reins, still smell the animal's sweat and the leather of its saddle, still feel the chill down her spine from the Madame's voice. She was present, and once more, she was not. This is how she'd learned to survive. She'd found a common retreat in the ability to stay present while wandering far, far away. Seeing the Millicent had been her final straw as she felt the tether that kept her in her own body snap, whipping in the wind like a rope on the docks amidst a storm. She was so taxed, physically and emotionally. Her head and heart whirred with too much force for her to process the woman before her.

"Climb in, please. I haven't got all night."

Millicent opened the door to the carriage and beckoned her forward.

Nox shook her head mutely. She was positive she did not want to go anywhere with the Madame. She pulled her horse closer, but it was not a loving animal. It resented the movement and tugged its long snout away from her, making her feel even more vulnerable than she had before.

"Traitor," she whispered to the horse.

The Madame arched a curious brow as Nox fidgeted with her inky black mount. "Would you like to return the horse to its master? I can certainly leash it with the others. We don't have to leave your beast behind, if that's the issue."

"Millicent…" she exhaled the Madame's name, too deadened from the night's turmoil to form the words she needed. She was a shell.

"You act like you haven't ridden with me before. It's childish, dear, really. We'll be back before the morning. You can sleep in your own bed tonight."

"My bed?" She repeated, uncomprehending.

What were her options? She was powerless against Millicent as far as succubae were concerned. Her charms held nothing except the sweet song of likable favoritism with most of the world's female parties, save for the guarded Theresa and the shrewd dislike of the wary. If she dashed into the inn, then what? Perhaps the innkeeper would shelter her from the Madame for a moment, so she could… start a new life in Yelagin? That wasn't in the cards for her, particularly as she knew that Amaris was already more than a day's ride southwest toward Aubade. Priory was just another stop along the way to the castle. What was the point in resisting if it were indeed the most effective means of getting her where she needed to go?

Nox found her words long enough to ask, "You can fast travel?"

"Me? No, dear. This carriage, however, was the most marvelous trinket I picked up when I studied at the university. I'll tell you all about it some time—marvelous chapter of my life, it was. My manufacturing professor was something of an inventor, always fabricating this from that. Very compelling man. He was ever so reluctant to part with it. You and I both know that women have our ways of being persuasive, through one method or another." Millicent leered at the memory, flashing her teeth at some distant man from her past.

The young raven moved forward in a daze, knowing only that she did indeed wish to go southwest. Amaris was headed southwest. Her room was there at The Selkie, her notes were on her desk, and Emily would be waiting for her there. She felt a pain somewhere below her ribs at that. How would she find the words to break Emily's heart once she told her Amaris was close? Nox handed the horse's reins to Millicent, though the awful midnight animal put up quite the protest. She didn't care whether or not it came with them to Priory or if it was set free to roam the hills of Yelagin, but the action seemed like the only way she could consciously force her body to move. The chestnut horses bound to the Madame's carriage were equally unpleasant creatures and did not care one bit for the additional companionship.

Nox crawled into the carriage feeling utterly disembodied as she did so. The void was so comforting as it called to her. She had a familiar friend in darkness. Detachment knew her name, and begged her to visit now. It cooed softly in her ear, telling her that she didn't have to feel any of this. She didn't have to be present. She could slide into the empty space between things as she had with the bishop, as she had so many times before. She didn't have to be strong. She didn't have to fight. She could retreat to the vacant place within herself where no one could harm her.

Her legs moved her forward while her mind dissociated into replaying the events from the night. She was focused on envisioning Amaris and her riding partners, on remembering the words of the ag'imni, on combing through her thoughts to remember what else it was they had said.

"Let's get you home."

Nox must have fallen asleep, though she didn't know how. She hadn't remembered resting her head or closing her eyes, yet when she opened them again, the glows of Priory were scarcely one mile away. She was choking on the sickly, familiar scent of the Madame's vanilla perfume.

Millicent's carriage was perhaps the most interesting piece of magic she'd ever thought possible. Nox had never heard of such devices that allowed the map before you to fold just as if it were no more than a piece of paper, with one destination meeting its opposite in the through the crease as they poked through locations. It wasn't the only magic item she'd seen. The Madame had shown her a spelled quill once, claiming it was able to write its letters and have them appear on papers anywhere on the goddess's earth, so long as the recipient had its matching feathered counterpart. Nox had heard stories from men at The Selkie about spelled objects, but it had been hard to tell fact from fiction when they spoke of such things while intoxicated and in the presence of beautiful women. The Madame had also told tales of coming close to owning an enchanted mirror once, claiming it reflected one's possibilities rather than their present, and she seemed a bit more reliable source on such things than the bragging of drunken patrons.

Nox recalled a day more than three years ago when she'd opened her eyes and been in nearly the exact same spot, watching as the carriage approached Priory. Could it go anywhere in the world? Or was it tethered to exits predetermined by its enchantment? If she stole such a device, could it take her to Amaris?

"Did you learn much on your travels?" Millicent's cadence was odd.

Anger would have been easier to understand, but something about this restrained attempt at friendliness was inexplicably chilling. Nox considered what to tell the Madame. She knew precisely what she wanted to say. She could inform Millicent that yes, she'd learned that Amaris was alive, and that she would no longer be acting as a pawn in the Madame's game to amass forces. She wanted to say that she wouldn't be helping her in her quest for puppet title-holders any longer. She wanted to wish the woman and her elaborate curls luck on their mission for dominations and damnation before bidding her adieu, but she said none of this. Millicent was not a reasonable person. They had been accomplices over the last few years, thinly bound by common needs for their mutual ulterior motives. They were not friends.

Come with me instead, the darkness within her beckoned.

She shook her head, answering the void while ignoring the Madame.

Millicent considered her expectantly while awaiting a response, and Nox thought of the enchanted mirror and its possibilities. The happiest possible future would show her a vision where she immediately reunited with Amaris, aiding her in her apparent quest to speak to the queen. This future probably included more demons than one might hope, but if the ag'imni were to be believed, it was a possibility. One future would perhaps display the possibility of her liberating the other girls at The Selkie and rallying them to her cause, or taking the reins to the carriage and urging the trotting horses into a gallop toward her friend. She'd love to see a possible future where she opened the door and kicked the Madame out in a swift motion, watching her jewel-toned dress and elaborate curls roll on the ground as she sped away. In the most probable future, the one she felt quite certain the carriage was taking her to now, Millicent would surely keep her under lock and key at The Selkie, ensuring nothing allowed the precious succubus to slip away again. Millicent needed her puppeteering ability far more desperately than Nox needed the Madame. The possibilities were contingent on what happened next. What would a mirror that reflected the present reveal?

The shadows inside herself told her to just let go. They urged her to release her grip, to release her fear. They promised she would be safe if she sank into herself and allowed herself to float away.

"No," she said quietly to the shadows.

"What was that, dear?"

Nox looked up to Millicent. She would not allow herself to detach. She would not disassociate. She would stand up for herself. "I said no."

"No, you didn't learn anything interesting?"

She could not allow them to get to The Selkie. She couldn't yield to the seductive temptation of letting herself go along, unfeeling, dissociated from the world. No. She would not go. Not to the brothel, and not into the dark.

"Let me out," Nox said, reaching for the latched handle to the carriage door as its horses plodded forward outside the enclosed cab's walls. She'd been tempted by the numb release for so long between her faint in the barn and her surprise at encountering the Madame that her lips barely worked. Still, she found the words she needed as she began to move.

Millicent's surprise was tangible. She intercepted the girl, her painted mouth opened in a startled gasp. The Madame attempted to subdue Nox's movements, treating her with outstretched like one might a drunken companion who insisted on swimming in the river after a night at the alehouse.

"Are you mad, girl?" the woman's eyes blinked rapidly in horror.

Nox began to muster her fighting spirit, saying it again, louder this time with insistence. Maybe she had gone a little mad. The darkness no longer called to her. It was not her friend. She had to stay lucid. She had to find strength. She'd seen demons and learned that Amaris was practically within arm's reach, but she'd never find her moonlit girl if she allowed herself to disassociate, she'd never see Amaris again if Millicent got what she wanted.

"Let me out!" She wriggled, freeing one arm from Millicent's restraint. Millicent made more attempts to contain her, using her body to block the exit to the carriage as she grappled to restrict Nox's flailing arms. Millicent's eyes bulged, not dissimilar to a dying fish as the scene unfolded. She had never snapped like this. It was as if she were wrangling a crazed animal rather than a human woman.

Nox grew more rabid with every moment that passed, each heartbeat an increase in her ferocity, consumed with the singular need for exit.

"Let me out!" She screamed, grabbing a handful of the Madame's hair as she yanked her to the side, battling for her life, her survival, her freedom. "Let me out, let me *out!*"

She had gone feral with the singular need. She was tearing at Millicent, willing to rip the woman to shreds if it would get her out. She'd found every drop of her warrior's heart and she would not allow herself to be locked up in The Selkie again. The Madame had her teeth set in a grit and was releasing a snarl in protest as she fought back, every motion an effort to contain the crazed young woman.

If she could just open the door enough, Nox would roll onto the road and begin running. Even if they both tumbled out onto the ground together, carriage in motion, she would twist herself free and run until she made it to the woods. She would hide, she would intercept Amaris, but she would not go back to the pleasure house. She would not enter the gilded, silk-tufted jail cell that awaited her.

"Stop!" Millicent shrieked like a banshee in the midst of the disaster, but there would be no stopping. She would sooner have them both die here having scratched one another's throats to ribbons than be locked away. She was so close to Amaris, there was no coercion or command that would confine her to the tawdry cave and be Millicent's puppeteer for one moment longer.

With barbarian effort, Millicent managed to rip a glove free from her hand and grab for Nox's bare wrist with the steeled cinching of a manacle. The inertia from Nox's movements, propelling her forward only moments prior, crashed into her like the ocean's waves breaking against a cliff. The thrust that was meant to send her flying past Millicent and out of the carriage exploded instead within her. Her motion landed her in a crumpled pile on the coach's floor. Millicent had released Nox's wrist nearly as soon as she'd grabbed it, but the effect had been immediate.

The fight was over.

Nox was instantly still. She was limp, silent and lifeless, her dark hair in tendrils covering her face and neck.

Gloves now covering her fingers and forearms once more, the Madame, badly scratched and hair torn from its updo, knelt nervously over the slumped girl. She quickly put Nox's head on her lap in the tight space of the carriage's floor where only feet had been meant to rest, brushing the night-black hair from her face with indelicate motions. Millicent felt for a pulse, slapping Nox several times in quick, successive taps. The Madame's voice was panicked.

"No, no. Nox. No." Millicent kept trying to swallow through her surging fear.

Nox remained unresponsive.

"Come on, you're okay. Wake up. You're okay."

The girl did not awaken.

Deep within her chest her heart, though substantially slowed, continued to beat. Her once-lustrous skin was now ashen of hue. Millicent had the distinct look of desperation as she did several more rapid taps against Nox's face, but the pallor of her cheeks declared the grave illness she had fallen into with the morbid announcement of funeral trumpets.

"Wake up," Millicent urged, voice hitching with desperation. "It was just a touch. It was the quickest touch. You're okay, Nox. I need you to wake up. You're going to be okay. Please wake up."

But Nox, all but lost to the world, did not open her eyes.

22

"This seems as good a place to camp as any," Malik said, leading their horses to the sounds of running water. The last two days had been blissfully uneventful given their chaos in Yelagin. Encountering demons, being betrayed by Amaris's hidden power, and being chased from a tavern had been enough excitement for one journey. The boys hadn't attempted to hide their gratitude that they had not seen the ag'imni in several nights. Now it was time to stop for the night and relax against the peaceful serenity of fresh water.

The river they discovered was fast, but not treacherous. Its chilled, crystal-clear waters were shallow enough to wade into without fear of being swept off one's footing. The horses enjoyed it nearly as much as the reevers. Both man and beast splashed into its waters, dunking themselves against the heat of the road and washing the dirt from their faces. Cobb's snout dripped from the exuberant way he continued to dip his whole nose into the river to drink.

The line of trees stopped a few arms' lengths away from the banks of the river, allowing grass and stones to stretch between the bending trunks and the rippling water. They took idle turns kneeling on the gentle slope of the bank and filled their waterskins, each disappearing from the group for stretches at a time to rinse the grime of travel from their bodies. While Malik warned them that the babbling of the river's current might drown out sounds they needed to hear from the forest, his caution was overruled by the other two. The lure of clean, fresh water took precedence over better judgment. They decided to sleep along its banks for the night.

The three had laid out their blankets and were gnawing off bites of salted meats with the watery light of the moon illuminating the river's surface before them. A dark shape shot above them, blotting out the stars. The reevers noticed immediately, eyes trained on the sky. The shadow like that of a large bird passed overhead once, then twice. The dark figure felt terribly foreboding against the indigo of the late hour. Ash set his sorry dinner down and reached for his bow, gripping its limb.

"Do you see that?" He asked cautiously.

Amaris spoke quietly, "I think that's the dark fae."

"And they're ominously circling as a greeting?" Malik's voice was ripe with distrust. The man was not a coward, nor would anyone believe the title if it were ascribed to him. His worry came from his education, training, and instincts when it led to battle. He knew fear for what it was: an intuition that kept champions alive when an enemy approached.

"If I had to guess, I'd think they're doing it *so* we see them. That way they won't startle us when they land." She continued eating her meat, not entirely convinced at her own argument. She was not particularly pleased with the fae's arrival, either, but if she could stay relaxed, perhaps it would convince the others to stay calm as well. Ash did not release his grip on his bow, and Malik left his fingers on the hilt of his sword in solidarity. They eyed the large, dark bird as it swooped lower itself below the tree line on the same side of the river. All was quiet for several minutes as the three listened, but little could be heard over the gentle burble of the stream. When the first sounds of movement through the underbrush hit their ears, everyone was on their feet.

"Amaris?" a voice called out.

She breathed a sigh of relief that it had not been a night creature, but the men at her sides had their hackles up. Palpable dread stretched between the men. Their eyes remained screwed onto the shaded space between the trees, disregarding how her posture had relaxed. She grazed over the tensed reevers and realized they'd need a bit more reassurance than she'd thought.

"Don't worry," Amaris whispered to the reevers, but turned her voice and shouted into the woods so that the Raascot men could hear, "They aren't monsters, just the very persistent, obnoxious bird-fae who don't know where they aren't wanted."

Ash whipped his voice at her, body still angled for the trees. "That is no screech of fae."

She scrunched her face apologetically. She lifted and lowered one shoulder in a shrug as she said, "From what I understand, you can't hear them for how they sound. The curse affects all facets of perception. I can't imagine what noises you're hearing, and I'm sorry for that, but he just called my name."

Malik gawked, turning his head while his sword remained raised in front guard. "That's how your name sounds in *demon*? It's good to know we'll be able to properly address you in hell."

Amaris ignored him and called into the forest, "I hear you. My friends won't hurt you—probably. Just walk in slowly so you don't spook their gentle sensibilities. And if you're particularly annoying, I'll be sure to tell them that you're going to drink our blood and let them attack."

Malik's jaw clenched in irritation. The tendons in Ash's forearm were taut from how tightly he held his bow, refusing to lower his weapon. They wanted to trust Amaris, but they would not do well to fully lower their guard and be caught unprepared against a true enemy. Several moments dripped with tangible anxiety as they waited, eyes trained on the dark spaces between the trees. Finally, Malik released out a long, low breath as four ag'imni stepped out from the shadows of the forest.

What ensued was the most delightfully uncomfortable campfire shared in the whole of recorded history. Amaris knew it was wrong to chuckle. She knew that empathy was demanded of her and that both parties of men must be going through their own personal brands of torment. That being said, the absurdity was perhaps the single funniest thing she'd ever been privy to, and she savored every delicious moment of it. If this moment had a flavor, it would have been orange slices covered in chocolate. If it had been an animal, it would have been a puppy so ugly that it was cute once more. As a holiday, it would have been a birthday party where everyone arrived with gift-wrapped coal just for giggles. These things were delectable for those with a very specific palate, but most definitely not universally acceptable for common sensibilities.

As it turned out, Amaris loved chocolate oranges and ugly puppies and the idea of gift-wrapping coal, and she *really* loved the comedic discomfort of this campfire. She was having a positively delightful time.

Their seven bodies had formed a horseshoe around the crackling fire. As has always been true, it was generally unwise to light fires at night and risk attracting unwanted attention. That being said, they were without a doubt the seven strongest and most terrifying things in the forest. As the only one who could successfully translate between the reevers and the Raascot fae, Amaris took on the role of deeply reluctant hostess. She assigned the men tasks just to give them something to do so they didn't sit and stare at each other. Amaris ordered the Raascot fae to gather wood and kindling, and had the reevers use their flint to

light and foster a warm fire. She then told the men of Raascot to take a
seat on one side, the river to their left, and the men of Uaimh Reev to
take a seat to the opposite, the river to their right.

"She's really bossy," Malik frowned apologetically at the demons.

"Oh, it's good to know it's not just toward us," Gadriel responded.

Ash and Malik cringed, but tried to remain polite. "What did he
say?"

"He said that I'm delightful and that you should be grateful to have
me."

Gadriel gave her a withering look as she continued coordinating
their evening.

At one point, Amaris was the one who left to collect more
firewood. She was quite sure that no one had moved a muscle in her
absence, everyone too rigid with discomfort to risk speaking or shifting.

She sat precisely in the middle at the top of the horseshoe as the
intercession for the two groups of men and folded her hands over her
legs. "You're a chatty bunch tonight, aren't you," she mumbled to
herself. She would be the first to admit that she was taking entirely too
much pleasure in their distress.

They deserved their bitter medicine—both the reevers and the
Raascot fae alike. Their intersection in her life had nearly cost her
everything.

The dark fae tried to keep their conversation to a minimum for the
first while, since every time they opened their mouths, Malik and Ash
seemed to be performing a two-man act in displays of wincing, disgust
and the stoic bravery to conceal their very obvious discomfort. Amaris
knew that, in theory, her friends were being very courageous. She
understood that they must be seeing and hearing something from which
nightmares were made. Even knowing that to be the truth, the boys had
to be witnessing four demons just… sitting there. Surely, Ash and
Malik saw ag'imni relaxing around a campfire, hissing and snarling in

the language of the damned with the charming ease of scary monsters at a tea party. The ridiculousness of picturing an ag'imni warming itself by firelight while it chatted politely with its companions was enough to fill her belly with smiles. She wished she could see the disturbing comedy through her reever brother's perspective, if only for a moment.

On the other side, it was clear the dark fae had not been those close to southerners in decades. While Ash and Malik flexed and tensed, the men of Raascot shifted uncomfortably, self-conscious at their effect on the others. Amaris could hardly contain her own grin of amusement, though she did try. She'd never taken herself for someone who delighted in the pain of others, but she wished she could bottle the humor that she alone experienced on this night and take sips of it in the months and years to come.

The goddess would probably punish her for finding her amusement in their misfortune.

"Stop laughing," Malik scolded at one point.

"You'd laugh too if you saw what I saw!"

While she knew Gadriel and Zaccai, the other two were introduced as Silvanus and Uriah. She did her best to serve as interpreter and aquatint the two parties. Ash and Malik were easy enough for the dark fae to recognize, but Ash mumbled something about the four creatures needing to stay in their assigned seats or their names wouldn't matter, as all ag'imni looked exactly alike. He did seem to be making an attempt at acceptance. When enough time had passed with no one being maimed, eaten or hunted, the reevers appeared genuinely convinced that everything Amaris had said was the truth. They knew enough from their bestiaries to know that monsters did not sit for civil conversation. The beasts before them were simply enchanted fae; little more than men under a perception curse. While that didn't make it any easier on the eyes or ears, they would find a way to deal with the reality.

Malik, in a triumph of bravery, stretched his arm over the fire barrier between them and offered some of his salted meat to the slick, gray creature nearest him. Cai looked startled by the gesture but stood to receive the cured, meaty olive branch. The transaction was the icebreaker they needed, as the men breathed out a collective sigh of relief, relaxing their tension ever so slightly.

"Do you have a plan to get in to see the queen?" Gadriel asked of the group. It was the first time anyone from either side had made an attempt to speak to the opposite party.

Amaris took it upon herself to translate to the reevers, answering, "I planned to wing it. No pun intended."

Several of them seemed to flex and flare their wings unconsciously in response.

"I don't think we can help you get into the city—at least, not during the daytime."

"Then it's a good thing I didn't ask for your help in entering the city, is it?"

"Could you at least try to be pleasant?"

She chewed her meat for a moment, considering it. "No."

Ash frowned, "What are they saying?"

"They want to be even more problematically involved in our lives than they already are."

Gadriel ignored her response. He had spent hundreds of years serving as a respected general in Raascot, and the goddess's humor had forced him to collaborate with a headstrong, disrespectful witch. He pretended she hadn't said anything as he answered. "If you can travel by night and try to call an audience with her majesty after the sun is down, we'll have your back to the best of our abilities."

Amaris frowned. "I do think there's something we haven't considered. While we know the queen was ordering the killing of northern men, often the simple folk are just as responsible as Moirai's armed troops for hunting you, correct? The citizens of Farehold are not slaughtering fae; they're killing what they believe to be demonic abominations. How would my persuasion change that? I mean, if I saw what Ash and Malik saw, I'd kill you too. Come to think of it, I still might."

It was Zaccai's turn to speak. "I think you need to give us a little more credit. A pitchfork flung by a spooked farmer isn't what's taking us down." His lips twitched in a half-smile, "I don't doubt any reever's ability to face us in battle–you'd make a formidable opponent. But you've had plenty of opportunities to kill us. Admit it, you're our friend."

"I most certainly am not."

Gadriel arched an eyebrow at Zaccai, "Are you sure you want her as a friend?"

Amaris's eyes narrowed.

One of the new companions, a brutish, unpleasant man who'd been called Silvanus spoke. "Queen Moirai—goddess curse her to hell—knows what she's doing. She's sending orders knowing where we are, and what her troops are to be on the lookout for."

Gadriel this time, "It could never be an open battle with a fight like this unless she marched north and came to us. We exist in small pockets throughout the south. We travel by night, and our unifying gift is flight. Moirai can't send any true warband to take us out in her kingdom. What she has done for the last twenty years is ensure that wherever she has a duke or lord who serves her anywhere in Farehold, his men are conscripted to hunt us. Her troops are readied with weapons meant for us and us alone. They're given intel on our outposts. While townsfolk might take a swing or loose an arrow, her men have been equipped with metallic, shredding arrows specifically fabricated for our wings."

It took Amaris a moment to relay the information to the reevers who had been straining the muscles in their necks and faces as if they might, through some miracle of the All Mother, be able to comprehend what was being said. The perception curse allowed nothing through its cracks to be heard except for the grating of monsters.

"I'm sorry," Malik said apologetically, "but your demons sound like they're cutting knives on plates with their vocal cords. You don't hear it at all?"

She frowned, "True ag'imni are said to be able to speak—even if it's only for mischief or fear-mongering. All the texts say so. The fact that these crows can't be understood at all is a testament to the thoroughness of this curse. Whoever created it had no intention of allowing anyone from Raascot to be seen or heard south of the border, ever again."

"We're not crows."

"Hush. I'm not talking to you."

Gadriel made a face to make it clear to the entire party that he'd never been so openly disrespected in his life. If she wasn't mistaken, his men seemed to enjoy the exchange. Zaccai was making no attempt to conceal his delight. That being said, none of the men from Raascot appeared to appreciate Amaris's comparison to crows, though she did have a point.

Malik's frown deepened, "So they weren't even made into real ag'imni. Just… demons."

Ash spoke, looking at Amaris, and then to the creatures. "If we are to work together, I need to know what Grem and Odrin were sent to find out. Our reevers are in Raascot seeking an audience with your king because if the reevers are to have any hope of keeping the peace, we need to understand his motives. Why are you here? Why risk your lives to infiltrate Farehold at all of these outposts? What does Ceres want?"

There was a tension that needed no translation, as the pause that stretched between them transcended linguistic barriers.

The happy burbles of the stream filled the responding quiet. The dark fae seemed to fight an uncomfortable internal battle. The men looked to Gadriel, their general, as their spokesperson. Amaris had offered the purpose of her dispatch many nights ago, but they had yet to reveal theirs.

It was clear that whether or not they would be honest rested solely on the shoulders of the general. After far too much time had passed, Gadriel exhaled slowly and looked at Amaris.

"King Ceres believes he has a son."

Ash and Malik looked expectantly at Amaris for the translation, but her brows were knit together in a study of Gadriel's face. Her interpretation came out as a reiterated question, asking them for an explanation. "The king has a son?" She could see Ash and Malik discuss this information while she continued to search the general's expression.

Maybe it wasn't that they had expected him to reveal this information, but his men continued to trade looks. Zaccai's eyes briefly touched hers, but quickly looked away, allowing the general to continue to speak for them. She felt a strange pinch of discomfort for the first time that night, but didn't know why.

"We've been searching for the child since it was born. Something about its birth seemed to set off the curse."

She tested the words carefully, rolling them back and forth in her mouth, repeating herself as she worked out the material. "The king has a son, and his child is the reason for your curse in Farehold. The king has an heir in Farehold. The curse is a result of his heir?"

Cai shrugged, still not meeting her eyes. "It would seem that way. The curse is about twenty years old, so we expect the heir should be in his twenties, if he lives at all."

Uriah, who hadn't spoken all night, was quiet. "If the son had died, the curse would have broken."

"We don't know that the curse and the heir are related," grumbled Silvanus.

"If they aren't, then that's one hell of an unfortunate coincidence,"

Amaris mused.

"What else do we know?" Malik asked. He looked at the creatures, but kept his question on Amaris. "Why would his son be in Farehold and not in Raascot? Was it a stolen baby? Is this a witch's dealings?"

Gadriel was the only one who maintained unwavering eye contact while the other fae looked into the fire. "The king believes it to be hidden somewhere in the southern kingdom. It would seem that this curse is a way to prevent him from ever being reunited with the heir to his throne."

Amaris conveyed the message.

Malik's mouth was downturned. Gadriel had side-stepped several parts of his question. The reever didn't know if the evasive answer had been by design. "What of the mother?"

"We don't think she lives. The king had made it sound like she passed long ago. He's…" Gadriel searched for the correct word. "King Ceres has been a bit difficult for some time. We haven't uncovered much, but we do have a lead as to how we might find out."

"Difficult how?" Amaris prodded.

"Being reunited with his child is the only thing he cares about. Occasionally, his obsession seems to cause Ceres to stand in his own way."

"I'm listening," Malik prompted, hoping Amaris would continue.

"By this time tomorrow, we could be at the Temple of the All Mother."

Amaris made a face, "And what, pray for answers? I didn't take ag'imni to be so religious."

It was a taunt, and even though the dark fae's expressions ranged from flashed teeth to scowls, their anger was playful enough. Perhaps after all these years, it was validating to hear the words from the voice of a southern girl. They'd undoubtedly come to understand how they were perceived, and yet she was not afraid. She did her best to empathize with whatever relief they must be experiencing to finally feel seen after so much time.

Cai was smiling a bit hopefully, "We haven't been able to ask the priestesses our questions. We've tried writing letters that have been left at the temple's door, but for some unknowable reason, the priestess doesn't seem to want to put the great secrets of the universe down on paper, so we've never gotten a response. We have reason to believe they have an item of great power that could help us find the Raascot's heir."

The hour was getting late. The northern fae may have been nocturnal, but the reevers had not had the necessary time to adapt to such a sleep schedule. They made a plan to begin the transition into night life so that the winged men could better aid them in their mission, but for now, they needed to rest. They made a plan to reconvene the following night at the Temple of the All Mother. Zaccai informed them that if they followed the river, they would find the temple over the edge of its waterfall.

Uriah, who hadn't spoken much that night, made himself quietly useful and smothered the fire as they stood. The Raascot fae would be patrolling the forests while the reevers slept. As they were saying their parting words, a question plagued Amaris.

Amaris inhaled sharply, face pinched in a question. The fae paused to hear her. "One more thing, before you go." She tilted her head to the side as she looked to Gadriel. "How does the king know it's a boy?"

It took them nearly a full day to find the temple. It was for the safety and sanctity of the priestess's and their sanctuary that the temple was far from the main road, discouraging travel for all but the devout. This would have made it difficult to find even if they'd been traveling through conventional methods, but the reevers were following the river. Unlike the easily traveled road that bisected the continent, the river wound in tight, snake-like coils. The woods on either side of its banks made it difficult to cut a more direct path with their horses, so they hugged the twists and turns, almost definitely doubling their travel time. Hours had passed without the hope of any progress until their ears picked up the distant, tell-tale thunder of a waterfall. Ash was the first to hear it, motioning the others forward. The faeling rushed ahead and made it to an overlook, skidding to a halt at what he saw.

They had most definitely located the Temple of the All Mother. Reaching it would be a separate feat entirely.

The Raascot men had failed to mention that the waterfall's pool at which the temple sat was no gentle slope, but the bottom of a rock face far too sheer to climb. Their initial assessment told them there was no straightforward route to descend. Though they'd met the river's edge and found the waterfall near what the evening sun told them would have been the six o'clock bell, it took the reevers several hours to navigate the trees, pick their steps along climbable slopes, and create paths wide and safe enough for them to lead their horses down to the temple's glen. By the time they had tied their horses, they were in the twilight hours of dusk.

What they saw took their breath away.

Amaris remembered hearing a pearl of wisdom once spoken that one shouldn't use words too big for their occasion. The proverb, one of the few lessons that resonated with her throughout the years, had delineated that one was not to say 'infinitely' when they meant 'very', lest they run the risk of having no words left when they needed to describe something truly infinite. Amaris thought of this bit of wisdom now as she beheld the Temple of the All Mother.

Few things in life inspired a sense of awe, not in its true sense. It's easy enough for a child to capture a beetle in his fingers and refer to its jeweled shell as awesome. A young lover might claim that he is in awe of his partner's beauty. A lady of the house might express awe at the turnout for her dinner party or the behavior of its guests. None of these circumstances are worthy of genuine awe.

New mothers may have absorbed the pure droplets of awe when they looked into the eyes of the life that had grown inside them, basking in the wonder of their birthed creation. The first man to discover the sea may have basked in it when he stood on the shores, unable to comprehend the blue horizons that bisected the worlds of water and sky. Nox may have been flooded with it the night she had crept on bare feet to see a baby made of starlight on the orphanage floor. And Amaris knew she felt it now.

The Temple of the All mother was no church, nor was it any common temple. The sacred space belonging to the goddess and her high priestess practically hummed with the intrinsic magic of the goddess's power. The forest of their day's trek through the summer sun had been a mix of rough boxelders and oaks to maples and buckthorns. Their shins had been scratched and torn by weeds, brambles and the snagged by the underbrush. As they approached the temple, the woods surrounding this holy place had changed slowly but completely, as if each step they'd taken had brought them closer to a better, lovelier world.

The trees lining the temple's glen were made of papery, silver-white bark, gently quivering in the breeze. The vegetation underfoot dwindled until they walked only on soft, cool grass. The twisted brown trunks had grown lesser and lesser as they'd drawn nearer to the temple, slowly replaced with the consistency of aspens, birches and willows. She knew their leaves to be green, but it was a blue-green, bordering on silver as they rippled from the wind and flashed their underbellies, rubbing together with the whispers of a haunting forest song. Their wooded scent was both mellow and fragrant, refreshing and filling. The waterfall tumbled from the cliff, but it was not the jagged, looming cliffs like those found near Stone. This river had ended in a seemingly obsidian lip, scooping inward to hollow out the hill below it in a dark, shallow cave. The water fell, free of the interruption of rock, plunging its bridal-white mist into the pool below—a basin that seemed unnaturally clear and still for a body that was receiving tumbling water from above. All of these elements of beauty and wonder were before one even considered the temple itself.

"Oh my goddess," Malik whispered, voice hushed in reverence.

"I didn't know such a place existed," Amaris's lips parted in wonder.

Ash said nothing, posture honorifically stiff as he stared at the building before them.

Amaris looked to one brother, then the other. She'd never seen their cheery faces so slack-jawed. There would be no witty quips, no banter, no commentary about the Temple of the All Mother. For once, they were both gloriously silent. They'd stayed at the tree line, standing amidst the shadows of the aspens. Something about the space seemed nearly ominous in its glory, as if their grubby, world-weary presence would be an insult to the art of the goddess's temple.

The Temple of the All Mother was hewn from the cream-smooth of white, marble stone. Enormous, unbroken pillars connected the floor to the lofted ceiling. Its height, width and length were that of a glorious cathedral. The roof of the temple towered nearly to the lip of the cliff, though far enough back that neither crowded the other. The marble glimmered with shimmering gold flecks that appeared to be embedded within the milky rock itself. Steps led up into a wide-open entrance, one with no doors or hinges or locks, allowing them to see directly into the temple's innermost places. The size of the temple, the beauty of the waterfall, the stillness of the forest was nothing compared to why the enormous temple required such a space, for even from where the three reevers gaped hundreds of yards from the entrance, they could see what rose from the center of the temple.

Growing in the middle of the pristine temple was what appeared to be the ancient, twisted, expanse of a tree living. The tree had few leaves, but its knotted arms wove throughout the temple, lit by some ethereal light that seemed to glow from both above and below. It wove its way upward and outward, filling much of the temple.

"What do we do?" Ash asked, breaking his silence.

Amaris shook her head. She had no answers. She knew they were meant to wait for the fae, as it had been Gadriel and Zaccai who had suggested that the temple would be where they found information of great importance. She felt like no amount of time would be long enough. She would never feel ready to cross the glen and mount the steps. She would never feel worthy of setting foot anywhere near the tree, older and more beautiful than time itself.

Yes, Amaris was certain, this was what it meant to feel awe.

There are few times in life that Amaris had been truly unaware of the passage of time, but as their feet felt glued to the bluish mossy grass underfoot, so soft it may have been plush carpeting, she and her companions may have stared for ten minutes or one thousand years. She would have stayed in that spot, soaking in the temple and its glen, its aspens, its moonlit pool, the lavender sky overhead and the incredible tree in awe and wonder for the rest of her life. Only the sound of a demon could have torn them from their reverie.

Though the sun had not quite set, the sky was purple enough to have emboldened the dark fae to travel. She heard the general before she saw him. His voice was hushed so as not to startle Amaris or her companions. Gadriel approached her and stood at her side. Perhaps they'd used whatever dampening wards had enabled them to stay hidden on their first encounter, because he had been utterly silent until he was upon them. Ash and Malik stiffened at the horrid contrast of the amphibious, humanoid monster in such a hallowed place, but said nothing.

"We couldn't have prepared you. No words do it justice," Gadriel said quietly.

It felt wrong—*sinful*, even—to enter this temple with any motive other than that of prostrating oneself before the All Mother. Last night she had mocked them by asking if they had gone to the temple to worship. While she had never been a religious girl, she could imagine no other purpose to enter this temple.

"What do you need me to do?" Her voice was so quiet she felt as if the quaking aspens might have whisked her breath away. For once, she held no irritation as she looked at Gadriel. The surroundings seemed to have a similarly calming effect on the general. Their eyes touched briefly as he assessed the silver girl in the glen. She belonged. Her moonbeam features were as ethereal as the marble pillars, the weeping willows, and the otherworldly tree itself.

From across the glen, a voice called to them.

A woman had spoken.

"Step out of the forest," she said.

The musical sound of the call was so beautiful, so serene. Her sudden presence did not alarm them, but tugged at the recurrent sense of true, unadulterated awe. Amaris had not seen the woman before, though now that she looked she cannot imagine how anyone could have missed her. The woman was as onyx as Amaris was white. Her skin glistened with its depth, something richer than night. While the Raascot fae tended to be bronze, this woman was the true, dark, resonant browns of the whispered beauty of the Tarkhany Desert. They were known for their gorgeous depth of skin, but she knew that even in the desert, this woman would have towered as a goddess of beauty among the rest. Perhaps this woman *was* the goddess. Her long black hair, in thick, elegant braids independently fused together, was clasped up in a golden band. Her dress was marbled like the temple around her.

She told them to come forward.

Gadriel had not lingered behind as she might have expected. The Raascot men tried so hard to stay concealed, that she hadn't anticipated him following her into the temple. Zaccai seemed to be close at his opposite shoulder, the reevers on her other side. What a motley group of five they were, dirty, travel-weary, human, fae, and ag'imni, approaching the most magnificent place on the continent. They stopped when they arrived at the base of the steps, looking up at the priestess where she stood.

The priestess regarded the winged Raascot fae, but she did not seem afraid. Her face was nearly impassive, containing perhaps a touch of curiosity. She moved with the slightest hint of the tilt of her head as she looked at them.

Her voice was not loud, unkind, or excited. It, like her expression, was almost entirely blank. The serene priestess simply *was*.

"Why do you seek the Temple of the All Mother?" she asked.

The reevers took a nearly imperceptible step backward, as if urging Amaris to speak. The moon-faced girl looked to the dark fae, then to the priestess. She wished she had something grand or eloquent to say. She didn't feel like this was a place where any words could do justice to its splendor. She struggled and came up short, but Amaris did her best to summon reverence and make her words important.

"We..." she twisted her mouth, looking over her shoulder to her reevers, then to the fae. Amaris lifted her eyes to the priestess and tried again. "We seek knowledge, and believe the answers we need may live here at the temple," she said finally.

The priestess nearly seemed to smile at that. "Live," she mused quietly.

Amaris had chosen her words either very well, or very poorly. She couldn't discern which.

The woman extended an elegant hand. Moonlight reflected off of her arm, silhouetting her as she held her palm still in a beckon. "You are welcome here, child." Then with taciturn serenity, she added, "Men may not enter the temple."

She didn't need to look to them again to know that they would not press the issue. She would enter alone.

As children, the matriarchal religion had always won small favors with both Amaris and Nox for this reason alone. The bishop who had visited Farleigh—a man of the cloth—was the lackey sent ever on the road in services to the All Mother. The only role in their faith that suited males who opted to worship the goddess were those outside the sacred temples. Bishops may lead in lessons in their town churches, but they had no place in the presence of the All Mother herself.

Men of the cloth existed throughout the kingdom. They could worship through the upholding of The Virtues and ensuring the All Mother's graces were valued in her outposts of charity across Farehold on the hardships of travel, beyond the walls of the All Mother's home. Perhaps this is how the All Mother was worshiped in other kingdoms as well, but she had no way of knowing. Amaris knew that the love for the goddess was felt in other lands, but could not speak to their practices. She hoped men were kept from the sacred temples in Raascot, Sulgrave, Tarkhany and the Etal Isles alike.

Amaris took slow, solemn steps toward the priestess, following the woman as she led the ivory girl into the temple. Amaris was vaguely aware that there were other rooms, other pillars, other shadows and alcoves and perhaps things to be seen, but she could see only the tree that served as the temple's heart.

"Wow," she'd murmured, not aware she'd made the sound out loud.

"The goddess is beautiful," the priestess said knowingly, not shaming Amaris for the child-like way in which she absorbed the tree. It was not brown like an oak or white like the birch. There was a grayishness to the way its large drunk rose at an angle, twisting back with its arms intertwined and outstretched to the heavens.

Amaris felt herself catch moments after they'd passed. Had she heard that correctly?

"The tree is the goddess?"

The unreadable priestess sounded lightly pleased and somewhat amused, her mouth the ghost of a smile. "Yes. No. What have the worlds called our All Mother? She is the Tree of Life. She is Bodhi, Genesis, and Yggdrasil. She is here with us now, and in the worlds between. She is our All Mother. From her, all living things come."

Amaris had never considered herself slow of wit, but these words, though intelligible on their own, made no sense to her when combined by the priestess's lips. The names held no meaning, no knowledge.

"There is more than one tree?" She attempted.

"The All Mother will not limit herself to one body. A single body can be cut down, destroyed. A single name can be forgotten in the wind. But what of a forest? What of the earth? Can all tongues forget 'tree' even in its absence? Ideas surpass the bounds of worlds. Her concept is everlasting. It is transcendent. That is the All Mother."

Perhaps Farleigh had not offered the most rigorous theological education. She knew of the All Mother to have no face. She knew of the goddess's graces, her virtues, her joys and charities. She had learned the prayers and recited them in her lessons. There had been no mention in her studies of a tree.

The symbol of the All Mother that she'd seen emblazoned in iron in churches of Farehold or even the one that had been welded to her orphanage filled her mind with a sudden, sharp comprehension.

The symbol was simple and recognizable. It consisted of two parallel lines running vertically, and an up-turned horseshoe that intersected the lines about one-third of the way down. It could be made with three strokes of the quill, and was easy to embroider into cloth or hang in homes of believers. As she reflected on it now, she had been looking at a tree. The two lines were its trunk, the horseshoe its branches.

Amaris extended a hand as if to press her palm to the source of life itself, though she was several scores of arms' lengths from the trunk of the great, twisted life that expanded before her. She held her hand aloft, no intention of truly pressing her fingers to its wood.

"I was never taught that we worshiped a tree."

For the second time, the priestess displayed emotion. This was the downward turn of her lips, the puckering of her brow. It was a combined displeasure; maybe it was sadness, maybe frustration.

"She is, and she isn't." The woman said, looking first to Amaris, then to the tree. "She is here, and She is all. Why should she not manifest in a place where those who wish to revere her may worship."

Though the woman's riddles were beautiful, Amaris did not find them particularly helpful. Perhaps she'd make a note to live a more virtuous life and actually read the theological tomes. In the meantime, she had questions.

"I need to ask you for answers."

"I expect so."

"What can you tell me about the curse on the land?"

The priestess offered the ghost of a smile yet again. "Me? I can tell you nothing."

There was an impropriety with which the priestess answered. Holy woman or no, Amaris felt as though she was being intentionally difficult.

"What can you tell me?"

"I can tell you many things."

She pursed her lips, "Will you share them with me?"

"What would you like shared?"

The reever's fingers flexed and relaxed once more at her side as she fought frustration. Answers were only as valuable as their questions. Amaris sighed, "How can I learn about the curse on this land?"

This phrasing appeared satisfactory. The woman looked to the tree, then to Amaris once more. Her face had been a nearly unreadable mask through the duration of their visit, yet there was some emotion in the distance behind her eyes that the reever almost recognized. She scrutinized the priestess while the woman spoke.

"Magic is energy," she said. "It is neither created, nor destroyed. It exists before it takes shape, and maintains its presence after it is uttered. If you find the orb of its physical shape, there too you will find your answers."

"Do you have the orb?"

"I do not."

She stopped herself from asking the priestess if there was *anything* helpful about the woman. Amaris prevented herself from the insult, knowing it for the disrespect that it was. Even in her agitation, the woman's presence was calming, returning her to her senses.

If the priestess frustrated her, perhaps she should focus instead on the tree. What had the woman called it? Bodhi? Genesis? Yggdrasil? The tree absorbed her attention. As she asked her next question, she realized the tree had seemed to pulse every time she spoke.

"Where can I find the orb?"

Again, her question earned little reaction. Perhaps the priestess, lost to the reverie of her worship, was so far gone from this mortal world that she had little connection to the emotions of the living. She did almost look too magical to be human. Her dress looked like the pillars and marbles had offered some of their milk and gold to be sewn into an elegant, flowing fabric. Her arms were bare, save for an elaborately engraved cuff on her upper arm. She was as much art as she was human.

"It is held where all magic's secrets are held. You will find it there."

Amaris's fingers flexed for the second time. Why couldn't she contain her irritation? What was agitating her so greatly that she found herself unable to quell her emotions? Maybe it had something to do with that curious, unidentifiable emotion that the priestess had. Perhaps this woman didn't realize the importance of the mission, and that's why she felt no requirement for helpfulness. The woman was communicating to her that she was concealing something, while simultaneously telling her that whatever she hid was to remain that way.

That was it, she realized. The distant flicker in the priestess's eyes were the shrouded defenses of secrecy. The look in the back of her gaze was like a wall covered in beautiful, flowering vines, guarding all that she would not share. She knew more than she was saying.

Amaris took a stilling breath, begging her temper to ebb.

"And where is all magic held?"

Why couldn't the priestess give her a name and address like any sentient creature would understand she desired? How hard would it be to say, "Amaris, the orb you seek is on the top shelf of a peddler's stall in whatever such city", or "the orb is a traveling ball of magic on such and such a ship, currently docked at such and such a harbor." Instead, the priestess merely smiled at the tree, ignoring the little reever entirely. The white-haired young woman's presence may as well have been the dull gleam of a fae light for all the attention she was paid.

Amaris drank in the woman's appearance one last time. No pointed ears. No enlarged irises. No extended canines. Her ethereal beauty notwithstanding, she was not fae. Hoping her next action would not damn her to hell, Amaris gave a command.

"Tell me where to find the orb."

The priestess considered her now, amused.

She did not answer Amaris, nor did the holy woman scold her. Instead, she laughed. Her voice was the music of tinkling bells, the sound of the quaking aspens whose leaves had trembled and descanted in the glen. The unrecognizable secrecy was there, but there was also something a bit like pride. Yes, the woman looked distinctly proud. Not of herself, but of Amaris.

Her face mellowed into a soft, human smile. The gentleness was almost maternal as she eyed the reever kindly for the first time that night. She took her time soaking in the reever's appearance, appreciating every strand of moonlit hair, the swan-white skin, the orchid eyes, and lithe stature. Amaris remained still, allowing herself to be studied. Nothing about their interaction had been familiar to any conversation she'd had with man, fae, reever, matron, demon or the like, so why should this careful examination be any more usual than the rest of their exchange?

The priestess began to raise a hand as if to touch her, and she felt herself flinch in surprise. The woman seemed to return to her senses, allowing the smile to fade as she allowed serenity to descend upon her once more.

Rather than give her any sort of answer, the priestess offered a question.

"Why is it that those who walk this earth need such finite limits to understand the world around them? The binary ways of fae and men are trivial to the All Mother. I hear your words for what they are: a gift from the goddess's tongue. Humans are meant to bow before your will. That is your blessing."

She blinked in surprise, lips parting as she wordlessly attempted to make sense of what had happened.

Three words pinged back and forth in Amaris's mind, like a billiard ball on a tavern table clanging its way toward a hole. They strung together to form a single, humorless, rhetorical question. It was one of chagrin, of appreciation, agitation, blurred attention and befuddlement.

She did not voice her unamused words as the thought simply, *"What the hell?"*

The words the woman had said were understandable as just that: words. But their meaning? The priestess was not fae. How could she imply that she was not human? What 'other' existed under the sun that her education had failed to instruct upon? Was it not taught, or just not known? And of that, was it unknown, or merely misunderstood? Why precisely did her curse of persuasion fail to land when she swung for its mark? How—and rather, why—would the priestess think to call such an ability a gift of the goddess?

"I'm sorry," she said finally.

And she truly was, but only because her attempt at persuasion had failed. Perhaps the command would have been justifiable if it had led to something useful. With the priestess laughing at her attempted flex of power, she felt only shame. She was a small, dirty, pitiful thing in an enormous, pristine, sacred space. She did not deserve to be here.

"You use what you have in the only ways you know. The goddess will wield it for you at the fullness of time," she said. The priestess waved it away as if it hadn't offended her in the slightest.

The woman began walking in long, elegant strides. Her footsteps were quiet, not the authoritative clatter of heels that one might expect from a woman at court, but the muted movements of the pressing silence in the temple. It was a silence that was, and wasn't. For though there was no sound, it was not stifling. The air glowed with life.

"Can you tell me anything I need to know?" She watched again as each time she spoke, the tree pulsed ever so slightly. She nearly tripped on her own feet as she followed the priestess around the tree, attention so focused on the effect her words had on the tree. "My friends seek King Ceres's son. It's why they're here from Raascot."

The priestess continued her slow, stately circling of the tree. She did not look at Amaris, only at the twisting limbs of her goddess.

"I know why your men come from Raascot."

Amaris followed, brows knit. "Can you see them? The dark fae?"

"Ag'imni do not wait politely at the feet of my temple. True demons have not bothered entering these holy woods for one thousand years, since their unholy birth in the wilds. I know men and fae when I see them, and I know an enchantment even if I cannot perceive what it conceals."

What a beautiful, political way of always responding while never answering. Perhaps in Amaris's second life, she would sit upon a throne in the courts and remember the lessons learned here, authoritatively speaking to the questions of the people while revealing nothing. It was effective for the priestess, and mind-numbing for Amaris.

"Can you—or will you—tell me where the king's son is?"

The woman paused. She tilted her chin to look ever so slightly over her shoulder, not facing Amaris as she spoke her solemn response. "The king has no son."

"He has spent twenty years believing something to the contrary."

"Yes, he has."

Was this priestess a friend, or an intentional obstacle? With each obtuse question and indiscernible answer, the woman felt more and more like a foe. Amaris flexed her jaw as she briefly considered the consequences of her soul. Would she be damned to hell if she threw her shoe at the back of the holy woman's head? She had thought she had learned patience amidst a childhood of hiding in Farleigh and her years of training in Uaimh Reev. When the matrons had tucked her away, she knew the bishops would leave, or the market day would end. When the mountain runs and sparring had daunted her, she knew a day would come when her practice would pay off. When she asked this priestess questions, she knew that the woman held a library of answers within her mind, and stonewalled any attempts to access its trove. Patience in this temple may offer her nothing. Still, the night was young, and frustration was an unbecoming emotion.

Amaris reached into her heart and stilled herself, ready for the riddles. Perhaps the visit to the temple would not be succinct, but she would not let it be cut short by the immaturity of her own disquietude.

"Does the king have an heir?"

"He does," she responded, continuing to circle the tree.

"Why is the king certain it's a son?"

"His beloved gave unto him a son."

"He sired a son?"

"He did not," she did not look back as she continued their volleys.

"A son was born from the one he loved?"

"A son was the result of their union."

"But King Ceres has no son."

"The king does not."

What a fruitless game. Together they were the ouroboros, a snake eating its own tale of infinite futility. Each step, a question deflected. Each movement around the tree, a frustrating non-answer. The king had a son. The king didn't have a son. Both seemed equally true and equally false. The line of questioning was getting her nowhere, so she shifted her questions to a matter of geography, following the priestess one step at a time as they circled the tree.

"Do you know where the heir is?"

"I do not."

"How can I find out?"

The priestess came to a full stop. They had finished their resolution, ending with the trunk of the tree exactly where they had begun. She brought her hands together, pressing her fingertips lightly in front of her as if in a relaxed, gentle prayer. "May I ask you a question instead?"

Amaris blinked. Perhaps this would be a refreshing change of pace from their spinning evasion. "Yes."

The priestess had spent so long staring at the tree that Amaris felt herself shrink under the weight of her gaze, "Why do you seek to aid the kingdoms?"

"I'm a reever," she responded. "We've taken an oath for magical balance, and this curse is an obvious imbalance in magic. I was trained at Uaimh Reev—"

The priestess moved her head once, a cut to the side. It was the most elegant way to slash a sentence where it landed. She repeated herself, "Why do *you* seek to aid the kingdoms?"

Amaris blinked again. She found herself shrugging—raising her shoulders like a child—at the holiest woman on the continent. She had no satisfying answer. Could she say it was because of her dispatch? Was it because a knife had been held to her throat and she'd been forced into a hasty allyship with the tenacious crow-fae of Raascot? Was she helping the kingdoms because she had been an orphan with no purpose who latched on to the first meaning her life had been given?

It was all of these, and it was none of them. Her final response was a weak one, her voice tilting upward at the end as if she were asking, rather than telling. "Because it's the right thing to do?"

Following the priestess's steps, they began to walk away from the tree toward the entrance where four male silhouettes had not moved from their mark in an unknown length of time. Two reevers and two winged fae waited for her just beyond the palatial walls of the temple. Gesturing a long, elegant arm, the priestess bid her adieu with this: "When you know the answer to my question, you will have the answer to yours."

"Is that..." Amaris paused at the top of the stairs, looking out onto the glen. She looked back at the woman. "Is that everything?"

The priestess allowed herself the same softened emotion once more. "If I may... What were you named?"

"Amaris."

Her face softened for the final time that night, eyes rimming appreciatively with another in a long string of strange, conflicting, distant, unreadable emotions. The priestess turned her head before any feeling might betray her, discovering her quiet once more. The flowering garden of secrets within her would remain impenetrable. She glided away from Amaris with slow reverence, returning to where she kept watch beside her tree.

Amaris walked away from the temple, her feet carrying her of their own accord. Her legs felt numb as she descended the steps, rejoining the men. She couldn't explain why, but she felt like she wanted to cry. It was as if she were waking from a dream. Part of her felt like it had been so surreal, so bizarre that it could never have happened at all. She felt this with greater intensity as she left the smooth, holy walls and stepped amidst the shapes of men. Their exchange had come to an abrupt, dissatisfying end before she'd learned anything. Her companions flashed glances between their friend and the holy woman expectantly.

"So?" Malik was the first to speak, his voice ripe with anxious tension. His tone was hushed despite his eagerness in honor of their sacrosanct location. "Did the priestess tell you what we needed to know?"

"Yes." She answered, leading them away from the marble structure and toward the trees.

Gadriel this time, forcing his voice to control his eagerness at the debriefing. "And? What did you learn?"

"Nothing."

The men were not patient with her as she recounted her experience. However irritated she had been in the temple, their frustration compounded with a combination of testosterone and helplessness that they had not been present, nor could they do anything now. The cross-examination that ensued was not particularly pleasant. Reever and Raascot alike found themselves pacing before her, throwing up agitated gestures with questions like, *"Why didn't you ask this?"* or *"Why didn't you say that?"*

Perchance this was among the reasons men were not permitted in the temple. Sure, the paths forward seemed so obvious to the boys as they stomped through the forest, retrospectively analyzing the events that had taken place at the foot of the Tree of Life. If they had been there, maybe they would have made more demands, and perhaps they would have learned even less, been discarded even sooner. Amaris had played the priestess's game to whatever dissatisfying end it yielded. While Gadriel was furious and Ash was beside himself, Amaris felt relatively confident that she had learned something, even if she didn't know what it was. She sat between Malik and Zaccai who seemed content to watch their prospective counterparts storm about.

"She was beautiful," Malik offered. It was a comment of admiration. To look at the priestess had been to look upon art.

"She was."

"And that tree," Malik mused, more to himself than to the others.

"Have either of you heard anything about the Tree of Life?" She looked to Malik, then to Zaccai. Perhaps the men couldn't communicate effectively with each other, but that wasn't going to stop her from talking to them. "Yggdrasil? She had given it other names, mentioning that it had held many. I've never heard of such a thing."

Both of them shrugged against Amaris's question, admitting to not having been raised particularly religious on either side of their borders. Malik's parents had taken him to their village's church on the solstices of the year, always with donations and offerings to the All Mother, but he had supposed it was a practice born out of community solidarity as much as it was any sense of spiritual obligation. His mother had never made a pilgrimage to a proper temple, he'd said.

In the north, Zaccai had said that many worshiped the goddess, but his mother had raised him outside of the views of the church. His mother had believed in more tangible magics than the abstract offerings of an unseen goddess. Malik looked at her as if waiting for her to translate, but she did not. Instead, she sat in a long, pensive silence while considering the continent's faithful.

"It's a tree," she finally said.

"What's a tree?" Zaccai asked.

"The symbol of the All Mother. It's a tree."

403

They considered the iron they'd seen and it connected with them as it had with her. Three minimalistic strokes had been the goddess's sign, but they'd seemed meaningless in and of themselves. They had been lines and a curve, nothing more. Now they could see the symbol for what it was.

"It seems so obvious now," Malik said quietly, looking into the distance. His eyes peered through the shadows of the distant woods, presumably off to where the enormous plant had grown in the temple's heart. Of course the iron symbol would be born to represent something so sacred and beautiful.

Amaris considered the tangible magics, and thought only of Brel. She wondered how many humans she had met with the small magics and never known them for what they were. She then found herself wondering if those with tangible magics were considered human at all. Was sweet, young Brel and his ability to speak to fire what the superstitious folk would have called witch? What was it that caused magic to bubble up in a human lineage?

Hoping her question wouldn't be taken with offense, Amaris pressed Zaccai further. "Cai, when you say your mother was more interested in tangible magics… was she a witch?"

He shook his head, unprovoked by her question. "Both of my parents are fae. 'Witch' is usually a term ascribed to humans with the small magics—though, I've heard plenty of people use 'witch' on the fae as well if the fae has a power feared by others.

"It's not unusual to hear humans and fae alike refer to those who possess feared traits as witches. My mother herself had discovered no skills beyond that of a typical northern fae—flight, health, long life, ease of nocturnal sight—though she saw those with power for their value, not their fear. A healer, a water-speaker, a medium and a grower all held far more practical value than the goddess, at least on a day-to-day basis. Unless of course you ever meet a manifester."

"What is a manifester?"

Zaccai paused a bit too long before answering. He considered the question as if it held more weight than Amaris understood. "From what I understand, manifesting is something like dreaming, and making your dreams into a reality. You just," he snapped his fingers, "create. From what I've heard about manifesting, it's only been seen a few times over the course of history. It cannot not be used freely, quickly or lightly. It may not exist at all. Plenty of people think the idea is little more than a fairytale."

Amaris was just intelligent enough to spend every passing day feeling less and less educated on the realities of her world. The more the world opened up for her, the smaller she felt. How could she have spent fifteen years studying at Farleigh and have learned little beyond her letters, maths and recited prayers? Uaimh Reev had trained her body, developed her muscle-memory, and created a formidable warrior. In the keep, she'd learned of beasts, of tonics, of poisons and health. What did she know of the magic that flowed through the world? Why hadn't she spent her time learning about gifts, abilities, fae, witches and power? Was it so terrifying that those in Farehold needed to keep it secret, closely guarding any evidence of their skill? Was it rare enough to possess a tangible magic that it hadn't been worth educating?

She took a different approach, still speaking to Zaccai. "Do you not believe in the goddess?"

"I believe that the world is full of magic, both good and bad. Who's to say whether it is or isn't from a superior power? It seems a bit pointless, don't you think? We just have to take our days one day at a time, no matter who is or isn't watching."

The conversation should have concluded, but she had one more question. His answer may have been irrelevant, but she pondered it nonetheless. "What is a witch, do you think?"

He had an easy wisdom about him. Zaccai always seemed

thoughtful without being arrogant. He looked off as he considered her question, then answered, "Perhaps 'gift' is just the favorable term for when we see a talent we can appreciate. For the others, perhaps people needed a word like 'witch' for the magics they neither liked nor understood."

Maybe that was the thing about knowledge. What if the truth to learning was that the more you studied, the more lands you visited, the more people you met, faiths you uncovered and things you read, as more and more rocks on this earth overturned to reveal their secrets, the more you realized how profoundly little you actually knew.

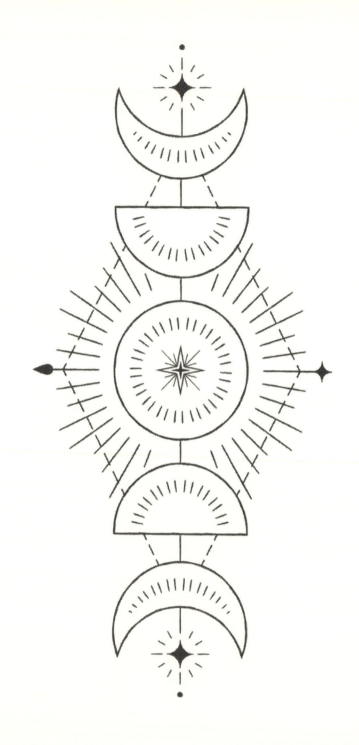

-PART FOUR-

What Must Be Done

Nox was dying.

She'd felt it for days now. She was on the silk sheets she'd sworn she'd never feel again, surrounded by the gauzy curtains she'd never intended to see. She had refused to return to The Selkie, and now it would be her tomb. She remained immobilized on the bed of her room in the brothel as girls had been filtered in and out, their faces plastered with worry. Eventually, Millicent forbade anyone from visiting her. Not only were the other young women afraid for Nox, but they also feared that whatever mysterious illness she'd contracted might be contagious. Millicent leaned into this fear as an excuse to lock them out. The only people allowed into Nox's chamber was the healer whom the Madame had summoned. Much to everyone's dismay, the healer had no answers for them. The unhelpful healer stayed under the roof of The Selkie at the coin of the Madame, if only to clean up after the soporose young woman.

Nox had been too weak to speak, trapped inside the comatose illness of her own body. Her eyes would flutter open, blinking yes or no to answer the simplest of questions. They didn't seem to understand her rapid "no" blinks anytime the vanilla cloud of the Madame drew near. The healer would dab a damp cloth to her forehead and her chapped lips, urging small dribbles of water or broth into her throat and holding her head and neck aloft so she might swallow without choking. Nox had scanned for the telltale freckles of Emily in the faces that had come and gone, but she was a shell of a woman. She'd become little more than sentient eyes caged behind a withering body.

Her supple cheeks were gaunt and sallow. Her tanned skin was chalky and clammy. Her hair seemed dull and limp. She was hardly recognizable.

Nox had nothing to do but think and sleep and think and sleep and think and sleep. Her mind dwelled on how it hadn't been until after her succubus powers had manifested that suddenly she'd 'learned' so much about the day Amaris rode off with an armed northern assassin. Millicent had told her Amaris had been abducted and led her to believe the girl was being held in the north. The lie was so elegant. So simple.

The world's best lies are composed from truths. She'd been groomed to hear such a lie. She'd been too thirsty for knowledge. Her need for answers and tangible solutions had opened her up to a beautiful deception.

The anger of her manipulation burned hotter than her fever. She hated herself for how blinded she'd been. Of course, she had been willing to gather forces with something so crafty woven into her motives. How else could the Madame have possibly convinced Nox to create her small army of puppet men? She had known that Millicent wanted the power all along, but it had been presented as a shared need for power. It was a brilliant lie, so subtle and so effective. Nox would amass the troops for a sham, and Millicent would swoop in to use what she had collected.

Nox had become a murderer of men. She had thought she was doing it for justice, for liberation, for love.

She had been the puppet.

If she'd never been purchased by the Madame, taken in the stead of the deposit paid for Amaris, she never would have been touched by a man. She would have lived her life without knowing the dark curse that lurked within her womanhood for any male who dare come near her.

Her anger grew as her mind would meditate on nothing else, trapped in a cycle composed only of: sleep, wake, think, hate, plan, repeat.

She didn't want to study the elegant etchings on the carved four-post bed. She didn't want to look at the gauzy curtains or silky pillows or ornate paintings. She didn't want to see anything of the room around her, the faces of the healer, the worried, peeping eyes of the other girls. All she wanted to do was remember, and to let her rage fester.

Nox relived the moment in the carriage over and over again, so grateful she hadn't said what had been on her mind. She had wanted to call the Madame out for her lies, to scream that she knew Amaris was alive and beholden to no captor. She knew Amaris was free and in Farehold. She knew everything. Instead, she'd tried to leave, and the evil bitch had all but killed her. How lucky she was that the woman could not hear her thoughts.

I'm going to kill you. I'm going to get better, and I'm going to watch you die.

Millicent was crazed. She had nearly run a threadbare line into the carpet of Nox's room for all of her fretting and pacing, watching the coal-dark eyes of the incapacitated young woman follow her back and forth in the room. She had muttered everything from excuses and apologies to pleas as Nox lay on the bed, motionless. Millicent was a harbinger of death, but her innate ability only seemed to pull her further from the things she craved, not bring her any closer to the power she desired. The powers of death that coursed through Millicent's gray, otherworldly hand rarely brought her a single step closer to anything resembling victory. Millicent had said it herself once to Emily: death was powerful, but its influence rested only in fear. The hand of death she possessed would have her hung by the noose sooner than it would bring her nearer to any sense of fulfillment this empty life had offered.

She needed Nox to get better. She needed the girl to see reason, to forgive her, to rejoin her team. If she could heal her, perhaps the young woman would feel indebted to her. If she could explain herself and make things right, they could work together again. All she needed to do was to keep her alive. She would not let her die.

Millicent had been a child when she'd learned of the powers of love and death and the line that severed them. Her arm had been deformed and discolored from the moment she came from the womb, but her parents had loved her all the same. The left arm did not stretch or reach or grasp as did the fat, happy hand on her right. It was not the hand itself, but the claws that tipped her nails in shiny, black talons that had her parents hiding her mutation away.

She had inherited her golden hair from her mother, and the tight ringlets of its shape from her father. They were a simple family of kind, beautiful people. Her mother had sewn her a sling in her infancy, as her mother had sewn all things in their home, from her dresses and skirts to the curtains and pillows. It kept prying eyes from ogling their otherwise healthy, happy baby so that she could live a normal life, free of judgment. No one needed to see the bizarre coloration, nor the dark, hooked barbs that protruded where healthy fingernails should have been.

Millie, they'd called her. Merry little Millie with her tenacity, her willingness of spirit, her dauntlessness in the face of adversity, was the apple of her parents' eye.

Her father had played and laughed and taught her all of the things a girl must know. He brought her to his bakery on many days to learn about flours and breads and pastries. She knew how long though needed to rest and rise and how thin to make the laminated, buttery layers of delicate desserts. She was exceedingly capable with her right hand, managing everything any other child of her age could do with two. All of her clothes were lovingly tailored to keep her left arm snuggly inside of her shirt, resting against her.

If Millie wasn't following her father to the bakery before the four o'clock morning bell, she was staying home to learn stitch work from her mother. Their home had been happy and their life had been full.

It had been her mother who decided that she should begin to exercise her left arm. The woman was wary of the talons her daughter possessed, avoiding them completely as she taught Millie to stretch and grab and hold.

Millie was given small, light objects to grasp, nothing more than quills or spools of yarn. Then she was given tasks, like to pick up and carry the knitting needles or embroidery hoops from where they rested to where her mother sat. They allowed the growing girl extraordinary independence as she began to master her arm and its movements, watching it heal and come into its shape much faster than anyone could have expected. If she left the house, she was to do so with the use of her sling. Inside the protective walls of their cottage, she could continue to practice her exercises.

She didn't recall how old she was, only the look on her mother's face when the woman lifted her eyes from a particularly intricate threading design to see the family cat dead in Millicent's lap. Millicent was looking up at the woman with the silent, screaming eyes of a confused child.

The mother had buried that cat quickly, but her parents' suspicions had begun to grow. They'd hushed her, returning her arm to its sling. Their loving eyes had been etched with fear. Their open hearts had been instilled with guarded spirits.

Now that Millie had learned how to use her left arm, she struggled to obey their simple instruction. She did not want to keep it in its sling any longer.

Her father saw it for what it was the day his beautiful, perfect, joyful child had thrown both of her arms around her mother's neck in a hug, clasping the grip of hands firmly against the back of the woman's neck, talons grazing his wife's fair, exposed skin. He had ripped Millie from his wife, throwing her to the ground. She had unleashed an unholy wail, a tantrum erupting through her pain and confusion while the man cradled his beloved wife in his arms. The woman was sick for nearly three weeks before her soul left her body to be with the All Mother.

Death was the parasitic spirit leeching on the household and everyone felt it. Millie, though a child, had understood what she was and what she possessed as she watched her mother lowered into the earth. Death gripped her and her father with a hand just as twisted and gray as the one that belonged to her.

Love had shown its face every day as the three of them had lived their contented, simple lives. Love had taught her how to bake, love had urged them to encourage their daughter to stretch herself and grow, not limited by what others perceived. Love had caused her father to throw his daughter to the ground and cradle his wife on the floor of their cottage. Love made a child kill its mother with its embrace. Love forced the man to sneak off into the night to have tailor-made gloves for the child that would run to the length of her elbow. Love protected her as the baker ardently defended her against the bishops of the church when they came for her, insisting that he had it under control. Love kept her sequester in her home as the months stretched into years, as the seed of fear planted in her father had grown into a weed, its roots deep and tangled. Love put her on a three-week carriage ride at the age of fourteen with a strange crew of west-bound men with a letter begging the university to accept her and train her so that she might find mastery over her gift. Love wrote her a farewell letter before she was able to graduate, telling her she'd always be in his heart as his spirit went to join her mother. Love broke her heart time and time again until there was nothing left but death.

Millicent knew of love and of death. Over the decades, her heart may have grown to be as grotesque as the talons at the end of her left hand, but when she saw Nox glowing with the light of her gift in her office those years ago, Millicent's own light had ignited. Love may not be something that would grace her doorsteps, but perhaps it could be something she could control and possess. Its embodiment had crossed her threshold. Nox was the perfect complement to complete her puzzle, the missing link between love, death and power. If Nox died, the bridge would die with it.

Millicent knelt at her side; her words hurried and manic. "I will heal you. You just have to feed."

There are many horrible things in this world.

There are the malicious horrors of hate, of enslavement, of torture. There are the horrors of nature, from the plagues that swept through the villages, and winters so cold that they froze whole families in their beds as they huddled for warmth, to the curses of magic decided well within or before the womb. There are the common horrors of the ravages of time, and the unspeakable horrors of the cruelties of mad kings and their violent delights.

Then there are the horrors that went on within The Selkie as a paralyzed Nox, too sick and weak to move, and a drunken man who found his way up the stairs at the behest of a Madame, unworthy of the breath on his lips closed the doors behind him.

Millicent fussed over Nox throughout the next three days, fetching her any wild thing the woman suspected she might want. Nox, who had made a remarkable recovery from death's door, had not left her rooms. Chocolates and a ginger-colored puppy with curled fur and paintings of the landscapes near Farleigh and friends from the salon were all sent up to her, all turned away—all except for a single, dusted truffle, though one piece of candy would hardly be missed. Millicent sent jewels and dresses and the doting compliments of would-be suitors, should Nox have wanted either their companionship or their life force.

Emily had not come to see her, and no one at The Selkie had heard from the freckled girl since the day Nox had ridden for Yelagin. For nearly a week, Nox treated Millicent like a phantom, refusing to acknowledge her presence. She poured over her notes and her books, scribbling furiously everything she knew about Amaris, about the demons, about Millicent and her powers, about herself and her own curse. She listed all of the enchanted objects she'd ever heard of or encountered. She wrote and recreated through her command of language every gift and magic known to men and fae and witches alike. She recorded everything she knew of the kingdoms, including every trait or possession or inclination mentioned of Queen Moirai and the crowned prince. She wrote names, places, kingdoms and objects. She drew the barn with the silhouette of a bat overhead. She drew the leering face of the ag'imni on page after page. She even drew Millicent's ungloved hand.

Why she did these things, she did not know. Her mind was a busy, violent place. Writing and drawing the thoughts drained them from the cage of her head, leeching the terrors from her body onto the papers.

Knowing that she was always one touch away from death, she decided to do whatever was necessary to survive. She stayed in the safety of her rooms, never venturing down to the lounge. She would entertain no clients, she would work at The Selkie no longer. When she left, she would not return.

By the end of the sixth day, Millicent let herself in with a quiet knock.

"I was hoping we could talk."

For nearly a week, the Madame's voice had been unrecognizable. It was not the cold preen of a bird or the authoritative demand of a Madame. It was a soft, uncertain, pleading thing. From the onset of Nox's 'mysterious illness' to her seemingly miraculous recovery, Millicent had not once spoken to her with the force or prudence that the Madame had worn like a suit of armor for years. Instead, her voice was always colored with a tinge of desperation. Nox knew three things. The first was that Millicent needed her more than she would ever need the Madame. The second was that the woman was terribly dangerous. And the third was that no matter what penance was paid or amends were attempted, Nox would see personally to the witch's death.

It had been six days since she'd blossomed aglow with health once more, and still the young woman had remained in utter silence. When Nox spoke, she was almost surprised at herself that any voice remained at all.

"What do you want, Millicent?"

The Madame was in magenta today, a color not unlike many of the silks around her room. A similar color flooded her face as she nearly slumped in relief. She sounded like she might cry as she said, "I'm just here to check on you, dear. How are you feeling?"

"Physically? I feel fine."

Millicent considered the specification, wringing her gloved hands.

"Nox, about what happened in the carriage—"

"You did what needed to be done," she kept her response matter-of-fact before turning her body away, her attention once more on her drawings.

"What?" the Madame paled.

Nox did not look up from her desk. Her words carried over her shoulder with little emotion. "I was in the middle of an episode, and I would have flung us both from a moving carriage. You stopped us the only way you knew how."

Millicent nodded, her movements jerky with extreme hesitation. It was, of course, the excuse she would have wanted to hear, no matter how hollow or false it sounded. Surely it would have been the very words the Madame would have used to plead her case in defense of her actions.

"If it's alright with you, I'm quite tired today," Nox said, still not bothering to look up.

"Of course, dear."

"But," Nox stopped her before she could exit the room, she twisted in her seat to look at the Madame. "I'll send word when I'm ready to see the Captain of the Guard."

Millicent used the excuse of the closing door to hide her baffled expression, but it was unmistakable. Let her think whatever she wanted. She didn't need to be convinced of Nox's allegiance in order to desire advancement of her plans. If Amaris was going to seek an audience with the queen, then so was she. If she happened to have the kingdom's chief executioner and head of all of Moirai's troops at her beck and call through its commander, maybe that wouldn't be such a terrible thing.

24

The road to Queen Moirai's castle ran through the heart of Priory, a sprawling city belonging to the people outside of the walled city of Aubade. Priory had been built as a port town and began along the coast, but had grown in a way that hugged the sea as it wrapped around the shores all the way to the castle. The boys wanted to stop for food, but Amaris urged them forward. She had no pleasant affiliations when she thought of this city. All she knew of Priory was that she had marred her face and run to the mercies of a would-be assassin rather than allow herself to be taken here. Now she was on Cobb's back, Nine and Fourteen at her sides with their reevers atop them, surrounded by the very city that had plagued her nightmares.

Everything on the coast looked and smelled different. The stones were an unfamiliar color, from the cobbled streets to the buildings themselves. The roofs were of reddish clay tiles, the bricks, mortar and rocks all shades of beiges and custard. Some homes that clung to the cliffs seem to be entirely white, as if the foam from the sea had splashed upward and frozen in time, creating houses and structures for the coastal residents. There was a fish, salt and brine to the air no matter where they went, and a pungency unique to large, packed cities. She had never smelled the overcrowding of people before she'd entered Yelagin, but compounded with the ocean and its odors, her senses were overwhelmed.

Cityfolk shuttered their windows like common, superstitious villagers as the three rode by. Perhaps it had less to do with their appearance and more to do with the weapons that were strapped to every space on their bodies. Each reever was equipped with sheathed swords, daggers, and wrapped with a bow across their chest. Amaris, accompanied by her ever-visible scarring, was a testament to their willingness to put those blades to use.

Nothing about Priory was particularly welcoming. The roads were narrower within the city than she liked. Most of the villages she'd entered had large grassy areas between homes, or the cobbled streets meant for wagons and markets. Unlike the farmyards and set apart homes of country villages, these townhouses melted into one another with alleys that allowed an intersecting pedestrian to get entirely too near before they were spotted. Everyone seemed to be on foot as they scuttled about Priory, few carriages, horses or carts gracing the roads. Fishermen and salesmen would push past the three with things like flat-bed crates of dead fish yet act as if the reevers were the unpleasant site, rather than their stinky, scaled corpses of dead things. The feeling of discomfort pressed down on her.

"What exactly is our plan?" Ash hissed. He kept his voice low, knowing that even if the citizens had closed their windows and slammed their doors, they'd remained pressed to the frames as any good gossip might.

Amaris was unmoved, "I've told you several times."

"We've had weeks to come up with a better plan than 'wing it'."

"Why am I the only one responsible for planning! That feels sexist if you ask me."

Malik didn't appear overly bothered, nor did he attempt to speak in hushed tones like the other two. He even deigned to wave at a woman as she scurried past them. She began to lift a hand to return the friendly gesture to the handsome young man, but thought better of it. "Not that you've asked, but my plan is to get through the walls into Aubade and then find us something to eat."

Amaris raised a hand from where it had rested on the saddle's horn. "See? A man with a plan. Thank you, Malik."

"At your service, m'lady."

Differentiating itself from the casual strides of townsfolk, a clattering of hooves was rounding a corner up ahead. The sources of the oncoming commotion hadn't yet turned into their line of vision, but the horses were moving with purpose. The three had barely begun to pull on their reins and exchange looks when the constabulary cantered into view. Six men on horseback dressed in the queen's seal urged their uniformly black mounts so as to cut off the three. The reevers weren't given the opportunity to so much as breathe a question before the Head Marshall took charge.

Clearly, they would no longer be needing a plan. Their fates seemed to have been decided without them.

A throaty, armored man boomed his command. "State your name and your business in Priory."

Their armed presence must have caused more concern among the citizens than they'd realized. Three travelers should have been able to filter in and out of the city without detection, but typical travelers wouldn't need the kind of weaponry they boasted.

Amaris stilled herself. She was sent by Samael to be the voice piece for the reevers specifically because she had the power of speech. Perhaps she could use education and kindness before flexing persuasion. Before launching into demands, she attempted diplomacy.

"We're reevers—peacekeepers from Uaimh Reev. We seek an

422

audience with Queen Moirai."

Despite having been told with the repetitive defensiveness of someone trying to convince themselves that reevers were an important and respectable stronghold for justice, the title was not received with any such reverence by this particular subsect of guards. The lawmen chuckled to themselves, and Amaris felt profoundly tired. She was exhausted from travel, emotionally drained from the trials and taxed from the weight of the responsibilities that had revealed themselves with each new passing day. She didn't have the energy to put up with their ignorant, stilted laughter.

For the last several years, she'd been disgusted by her gift. Even within the recent week, her ability had been a source of both contention and shame. However, the constabulary had caught her on a bad day. The priestess at the Temple of the All Mother had said with every bit of authority that persuasion had been a gift from the goddess for humans to bow to her will. She wasn't sure if it had been the priestess's words or her own exhaustion, but with the nonplussed expression of a woman who was weary from the world, she exchanged a look with the men before her and then said with an unimpressed calm, "You will now escort us to see the queen."

The effect was instantaneous.

Amaris was an excellent reever in her own right. She had proven herself as a talented warrior in agility, intelligence, and skill. Over the course of their dispatch, she had manifested her gifts for the power of sight, and had saved their lives on more than one occasion. However, it was for this power of persuasion that she had floated to the rank of small party's undisputed leader. They had been right to put their faith in her. They'd stepped back to let her speak with the priestess, and had done so once more with the Head Marshall.

Amaris found herself looking to Malik to see if using the ability on the other humans triggered an emotion in him, but his face was unreadable.

She sensed nerves and relief muddled into whatever amalgamation of emotion her friends were feeling as they nudged their horses onward. In immediate obedience, the marshal had simply nodded and he, with his men, had turned their horses and led the way from the long road of Priory into the city of Aubade. As they walked their horses forward, she could hear Malik under his breath, "I guess this means we aren't getting food."

It had taken no small stretch of time to get through both Priory and past the walls of Aubade to the castle at its center. Both Priory and the royal city beyond were far larger than any of them had anticipated. The constable and his men cleared an easy path for them. "We're escorting them to see the queen," was a perfectly reasonable answer no matter who of importance might ask and met with no resistance.

The guards at the walled city of Aubade would have certainly stopped the reevers, though Amaris could have probably handled them just as effortlessly. Instead, they were waved forward as the Head Marshall escorted them beyond the opened, iron gates into Aubade.

Amaris had spent years in Uaimh Reev and referred to the keep many times as a castle throughout her stay. It had been hewn from the mountain's granite—made, not built—into the side of the sheer rock. When she was little, the children of Farleigh had often thought of their stone manor as a castle, for it had been large and stately in many ways, with enough rooms and corridors and alcoves and turns that their imagination was able to conjure importance and intrigue into its walls. It wasn't until they were within Aubade's walls that it became clear she had truly never seen a castle.

If the walls surrounding the city itself hadn't been protective enough, this cream-colored citadel was a solid stronghold, built to the teeth with fortifications. The beige and yellowed stones had been rounded for uniformity, creating a brick-like appearance to the vast, thick walls and towers that covered Aubade's center. While the reev had been cold and gray, the coastal city offered warm, earthy tones to the megalith, forged from the earth, clay and rocks of the stones in its climate. As Priory had been on a lip of the coast, they'd been able to see the castle from a far-off angle, appreciating its size and shape from miles away. It had taken on a familiar, animal frame from a distance. Amaris found herself able to discern precisely what shape it was as they drew nearer.

Now that she was nearly upon it, four primary towers, countless windows in height, jutted from the angles of a rectangular backside, but a long secondary rectangle with a curved front angled its way forward, as if the castle had been created to resemble the head of a horse. The snout-like portion of the castle seemed comprised of at least five levels. From Priory's coast, she'd gathered that there had been another structure at the back of the castle looming over its cliffs. While she couldn't be sure, something circular seemed to frame the back of the castle, as if the beast were wearing a halo atop its head. She smiled to herself at the idea of the birds-eye view of the ruddy-cream, horse-faced, halo-wearing angelic fortress of Queen Moirai and its crowned prince. The southern kingdom sat within a horse's head. It was strange what idle thoughts brought one comfort in uncertain times.

There was something oddly comforting about the expanse before her, as if she found some small relief in knowing how easy it would be to slip away in a fortress so large, hiding in the castle for days or weeks or twenty years without ever being found. She and Nox had found ways to hide in Farleigh, and it had been a thimble compared to this megalith. Surely, she'd find safety in the expanse of its custard walls.

The constabulary, having completed their primary task, were held up not by security upon arrival at the castle, but by servants. The reevers may as well have been grimy street urchins at their door. The guests would certainly need to bathe, they insisted, before they could be ushered in to see Queen Moirai.

The reevers were filthy. Other than their dips in the stream, they hadn't had proper baths with soap since their night in Yelagin. Feeling rather embarrassed at the implication, the reevers dismounted and allowed their horses to be led away by flustered servants. She realized the attendants had been dressed to reflect the neutrals of the stone, as if they were merely living elements of the castle, scarcely discernible from the rocks on which it was built. Even in their simple linens, they were impeccably clean.

She hadn't thought a bath would stand between her and her dispatch, but she understood the need. Perhaps a good cleaning would give her time to calm her nerves. Amaris's heart was pounding at having come so close to completing her task. Adrenaline flooded her veins as she raked her brain for speeches and words important enough for the queen, a simple comment grounded and comforted her. Despite the severity of their situation, she could have sworn she heard Malik asking about when they might be fed.

She knew it was impolite, but she didn't care. Amaris would rather burn down the castle than be forced into a frilly dress. She argued with the personal attendant on the dress provided for her, and it was clear that her obstinance had driven the woman to the verge of tears. Amaris had not worn a dress in years and she absolutely wouldn't be forced into one now. She'd barely been old enough to transition from pants to dresses in Farleigh before she'd escaped and returned permanently to the male garb of the reevers.

"Miss, please, see reason…"

"You will find pants and a suitable shirt," Amaris said cooly, flexing her persuasion yet again. Perhaps she was abusing her gift, but she would rather brainwash every servant in the kingdom than be forced into a girdle.

The woman dipped her chin obediently and turned to find something appropriate.

She comforted herself that she was in the right. She couldn't possibly wear a proper lady's dress. What if things went poorly? What if she needed to run or fight? How was she supposed to dive or roll or crouch while wearing skirts and lace and petticoats? The personal attendant's nose had reddened in the moments before crying, clearly taking crimes against fashion very seriously. She left Amaris with two other young servants to help her bathe and wash her hair—despite her protestations that she was capable of bathing herself—and ran off. When the attendant returned, she had found an outfit worn by a court entertainer that— though hideous—did include a pair of pants that fit her small stature. At least, she wanted to call them pants. The bottoms provided resembled black jester's tights far more than the riding leathers she'd preferred.

When she asked why she couldn't wear her tunic, the stewardess informed her that her filthy road things were set to be burned. The servants stopped only upon a command from the immediate obedience of Amaris's dark power. She had grown a little more generous with her guidelines for acceptable usage regarding her gift over the last few hours, it seemed. Since she would not be wearing her tunic, she examined the outfit before her. The outfit was composed of four pieces. The first was a lovely, clean, off-the-shoulder saree blouse made of a gauzy white fabric. She examined herself in the mirror, appreciating the way the saree gathered around the smallest part of her waist, giving her thin, boyish shape the illusion of a more womanly figure. She would have preferred to have worn the white blouse its own, but unfortunately, the ensemble included both a black bustier and something that may have been a gaudy attempt at a silver, puff-sleeved jacket.

She slipped into the black tights and white blouse, but required the attendant's help in lacing up the black bustier.

"Who in the court has worn this?" Amaris asked, gasping through the effort of sucking in her lungs as they cinched her waist tighter and tighter.

The attendant stood at attention, her hands clasped before her. "The court juggler, I believe."

"Wonderful."

Of course she would be assigned the juggler's clothes. It was a fitting punishment for a woman who refused a dress. Why be taken seriously when seeking an audience with the queen? The outfit made it clear: she would be allowed no dignity in the eyes of the court.

Amaris sighed, accepting that it didn't matter. Whether she'd worn the formal, royal dresses, the grimy travel clothes, or rolled in red paint and entered the throne room naked, it wouldn't impact her dispatch. They could dress her however they liked, she still needed to complete her task. At least this would give Ash and Malik something to laugh about for the ride home. Soon they'd be finished with their mission and the whole keep would share its ale-drunk commentary about the humor of a reever in juggler's clothes before Farehold's queen.

"It will have to do," said the displeased attendant. "I did think the silver jacket was a lovely compliment to your hair, given your objections. Though if you change your mind about the dress, I have the most stunning lavender to match your eyes—"

"The juggler's attire will do just fine."

Amaris seemed to consider the extra space in the room. She remembered how isolated she'd felt in her early days in Uaimh Reev. It had been cramped, but well-loved. It was old, but clean. This bedroom space in Aubade was disgusting in its opulence. Between the abundance of furniture, the lavishness of the decorations, and the excess of the golds and jeweled features in the space, Amaris had missed a key detail. She'd been so distracted with the finery of the beds, the chaises, the tables, the windows and the bathing room that she hadn't taken stock of anything that mattered.

She stiffened as she looked around. "Where are my weapons?"

The steward who'd stood in statuesque attendance throughout Amaris's series of ridiculous requests looked horrified. She began fixing the white reever's hair as she answered, "You can't carry your weapons around the castle! What do you think this is! Honestly, child, what sort of question is that?"

"But where—"

The stewardess did not seem like a particularly strong woman, in the emotional sense of the word. Everything seemed to rim her eyes with the silver threat of tears. If it wasn't Amaris's protestations about the dress, it was her queries about the weapons.

Through choked frustration, the attendant informed her, "They'll be returned to you when you fetch your horses. Though, truly, the idea that any untested, mysterious outsider would be allowed to meet Her Majesty with daggers and swords and arrows is so preposterous that it's downright offensive." She had been combing Amaris's hair into some elaborate updo of braids and seemed to pull a little harder than necessary as she punctuated her words.

Amaris didn't even have her daggers. Is this why they had bathed her? In seeing her nakedness and combing through her hair, there was truly nothing she could hide. There was a cleverness to the seemingly perfunctory acts of the servants that she both admired and feared. She wondered if Ash and Malik had been set to the same shameful stripping and scrubbing, rendering them weaponless.

A distant memory recalled a time when Odrin had been forced to remove his weapons before he could shelter for the night in the kitchens of Farleigh. While the servant tugged brutally at her hair, she felt a surge of sympathy for Odrin at the memory. As a reever, removing your sword felt like removing a limb. Still, the knowledge that this was somewhat common practice comforted her. If the man she called her father could do it, so could she.

The door to her room opened, which annoyed her. Would there be no end to the disturbances before she met Queen Moirai? Would she have no time to process her thoughts or make a plan?

A new servant popped in her head through a crack in the door. They were informed that the queen was in the middle of a previous engagement, and she was to take dinner in her rooms until Moirai called upon her later tonight.

"My friends?"

"—are also being served in their rooms."

Amaris knew Malik would be pleased to learn they were being fed, and inquired as to the whereabouts of her companions. Though she knew they'd be in the same room in an hour or so when reunited before the queen, she hadn't been separated from the reevers more than a handful of times over the past three years. It felt unnatural. Perhaps it was more than just the unfamiliarity that was disquieting.

An anomalous instinct filled her stomach with stones, though she couldn't explain why. She ignored it, telling herself that she was falling victim to anxiety. She was afraid of doing something new, and if she were to succeed, she would need to learn to adapt. She scolded herself for dreading the unknown. Of course the castle was unfamiliar. Of course being bathed by servants and dressed by attendants was new. How would she survive in this world if she felt a surge of fear every time she faced a unique situation?

"Will you be needing anything else, miss?" The servant stepped away from her hair, finally finished with Amaris's ornate braids.

"No, I'm fine. I'll just stay and eat until I'm called upon. Thank you."

"And the dress?"

"Absolutely not."

Eventually, the attendants left her to her thoughts in her stupid clothes and her clean, freshly washed hair and skin. The ivory reever smelled sickeningly of florals, as though she'd been bathed in perfume rather than soapy water. She moved from the bed to the desk to the window, trying to find a comfortable spot to relax while she eyed the unfamiliar coastal food.

She opened the doors to her balcony, hoping some fresh air would help dissipate the overpowering scent of flowers. She couldn't even smell her food over the choking perfume.

Amaris tried to take at least a few bites of the meal, but her gut had already been stuffed with apprehension. It was truly a pity, as she hadn't seen a meal this fine in perhaps all her life. Not only had fishes and cheeses and vegetables been brought to her with beautiful plating and seasonings, but chilled fruits and hot pies and caramelized tarts and exotic wines. She was wasting a once-in-a-lifetime dining opportunity on her own fretfulness.

Amaris told herself that the fear was perfectly natural. She convinced herself that everything would be fine. Even if the queen was a nightmare and the meeting went in the worst possible direction, she had nothing to fear. Her power had emboldened her for such a time as this. This was her divine purpose. Amaris would simply command Moirai and her men to stop their bloodshed and hunting of northmen. She would command the queen to release her. She told herself her plan over and over again, using it as a meditation. She forced herself to take several more breaths, convincing herself that everything was fine. She was fine. Her plan was fine. Everything was fine.

Amaris was unable to convince herself of the pretty lies she spun. Everything did not feel fine.

The pearly reever chewed on her bread, but couldn't stay still to enjoy her meal. She returned to the grand, glass doors of her balcony, wandering outside to view the setting sun while she picked at her loaf.

It truly was a marvelous view. The sky colored magnificently on the western coast in a way she'd never seen before. The smell of salt and the ocean spray reached her even from where she stood on the balcony. The birds who dove and cawed near the cliffs were large and wild and unfamiliar in their songs, distracting her wholly. The sea was the sort of thing children scribbled with blues in their etchings without ever fully comprehending its vastness. She had been like any other peasant, uncomprehending of true infinity before she'd seen how the horizon met the blue line of the ocean. Her fingers continued to absently move her bread to her mouth, nibbling at the simplest of foods provided to her. Watching the sun change the water from gold to pink as it descended as warm sea air drifting up to her perch was a magical experience.

She felt her jaw unclench. Her muscles relaxed. Maybe it was the sound of the waves breaking, the homeiness of the bread, or the fresh air, but her tension dripped out of her as she soaked in the setting sun.

Amaris had contented herself to sit on the balcony until she was fetched by an attendant when her eyes fixed on a particularly large seabird against the dusk of the disappearing sun. It vanished entirely, leaving the last indigos of its dying light in the sky before the stars began to sparkle into existence.

She saw it again, and knew it was not a bird.

"Goddess dammit, can I not get one moment of peace."

Amaris felt a hot flash of anger, knowing her only chance at relaxation was being snatched from her. She ran back into her chamber, blowing out the room's candles to further obscure them in the shadows. Her next move was to slide a chair against the door that excited into the corridor, lodging the handle in place. Her irritation hadn't betrayed her readiness in times of need. She'd barely slid the wooden back of the chair to stop and still the handle before she heard a flutter of air and the gentle footsteps of a man. Somewhere on her balcony, Gadriel had landed as quietly as he could. His great wings folded behind him as he muted his footsteps.

"What are you doing here?" she hissed. Her room was dark, but not dark enough. If someone really wanted to spy, they'd be able to see the Raascot fae and his angelic, feathered wings—that, or the bat-like wings of a demon.

He didn't bother greeting her. Gadriel took several steps into the room before using the rushed, militant, informational voice of a general. "Silvanus hasn't reported since our night at the river. We thought we'd meet up with him after the temple, but I have a bad feeling." His words were meeting her ears in a whisper.

Amaris kept her voice low, "Your presence is going to give us away! What were you thinking!"

"Do you think I want to be here? Ask yourself, does a man who looks like an ag'imni feel particularly safe inside Moirai's castle?" Gadriel closed the space between them. He did not look kind as he grabbed her arm. She tried to jerk away, but his grasp was firm. His eyes were fixed on hers as he spoke. "Listen closely, ungrateful witchling: I need you to succeed. I'll have your back if it kills me. Oh my goddess—"

"What?" She looked around, head jerking nervously at his sudden shift in tone.

"What's that smell?"

"Go fuck yourself," she rolled her eyes. As if she weren't already suffering enough.

His anger and support were incongruous. His words clashed defiantly against his tone and posture. His fingers began to hurt her arm as his dark eyes burned into hers. Yes, she definitely hated him. She was fairly certain that she didn't want the others to die, though. "Get off me, demon," she attempted to shake him loose, but failed.

"You're stuck with me."

"And Cai? Uriah?"

The general relaxed his grip slightly, "Both instructed to hang back. You might need help in the castle or outside of its walls." He made a face, loosening his fingers slightly from where they'd remained on her forearm. "I guess I'm your man on the inside."

She was both baffled and appalled. How could a man who claimed to lead militaries have been so foolish? "I am telling you with absolute confidence that your presence is going to do more harm than good. I already have backup."

"You have your reevers, I know. But the queen and her men know Ash and Malik are here. They don't know I'm in their walls. You can never be too careful."

Amaris was nearly seething with his recklessness. How could Raascot trust him to lead troops if this was the sort of thing their general found acceptable? She tugged her arm away from his grip. At first he resisted, but by her second jerk, he released her. The stupid winged man was going to draw suspicion, and if Moirai or her counterparts saw him in the castle, the royals would never be able to trust the reevers.

She took a few steps away, moving with her back to him as she paced for the wall. "How could you even risk coming here! If the queen is hunting for dark fae across her lands—"

Gadriel didn't let her get too far. He gripped her once more, tightening his fingers around her arm until she looked at him. He cupped her face with calloused hands. This was not a lover's gentle touch, but chafed against her cheeks with rough intensity. He had never touched her like this. It was so familiar, so intimate. She raised her hands to grasp his forearms as if to pull him off of her. Her hands pushed his grip away, but Gadriel tightened his hold on her chin, staring down into her lilac eyes. She stilled, looking back into his.

"We have never had a hope like this."

Her anger, her fighting spirit, her intent paused. She stilled wholly and completely. Amaris understood everything from a place deep within herself. Her anxiety was high at the risk of her mission, and her stomach churned knowing that Gadriel was putting himself in such danger, and yet, she understood. If this was truly the first glitter of hope in decades—if it had been her in their shoes—she would have stopped at nothing to see the mission through. Hope was dangerous. Hope was reckless. Hope was essential.

Her eyes lit, realizing that his presence may come with more than a few perks. She shook her arm free once more, and this time he obliged. Amaris caught him off guard with her topical change, "Can I have one of your daggers?"

Gadriel's face tightened in disapproval, "You let them disarm you?"

"They made a very persuasive argument as to why I can't meet the royal family dressed with the ability to chop off their heads. That, and I was stripped and scrubbed naked. I didn't have much choice in the matter."

Gadriel was wearing no fewer than six blades, he informed her, though none of them were the heavy weight of a sword that might impede his flight. He winked like the perverse show-off he was as he showed her the glint of a knife strapped to his forearm, hidden up his sleeve. Fishing a lightweight throwing knife from his boot, Amaris thanked him and tucked it securely against the small curvature of her breasts just beneath the front of her tightened bodice. Even if she were searched before meeting Moirai, no one would think to check her sternum.

The general slackened his grip even further, touching her forearm lightly as he dragged a thumb over her exposed skin. It was so gentle.

"Stop touching me," she said, but her command lacked conviction. He was fae. Her persuasion did nothing for him.

She looked at him fully, ceaselessly amazed at how beautiful he was, irritating though his lovely may be. It would be so much easier to glare at him if he hadn't possessed such sharp, perfect features. Gadriel had the strongest jaw she'd ever seen, such bottomless eyes, such night-black hair. His eyes were gorgeously dark, as deep as the ocean's trenches, identical to ones she knew so well from her childhood. His dark eyes reminded her too much of Nox—everything reminded her too much of Nox. So many things about him stirred memories of the one she'd left behind. Maybe that's what kept her from stabbing him whenever he was particularly rude or difficult. This demon should count himself lucky to share any commonalities with an angel.

"Amaris?" Her name on his lips was a whisper.

She wanted to snap at him, but her tone came out more gentle than she intended as she looked back at him. "Yes?"

He looked at her intently and she waited for his words, an unfamiliar want leaning against her ears. He finally said, "You look ridiculous."

Her mental to-do list now read: persuade the queen to stop killing northerners, escape the castle, and kick Gadriel in his manhood, in that order.

She heard footsteps in the hall and turned to him to tell him to get lost, but the dark fae was already on the balcony, slipping into the shadows around the corner of its opened door. Amaris ran to remove the chair from the door just in time for it to swing open.

"Her Majesty will see you now."

25

The Madame had sent two of The Selkie's girls over the past few days to plant lures and whispers about the marvels of The Selkie, but no one had the gift of suggestion quite like Emily. Millicent had felt so sure of her action at the time, but she'd need to make note of the preservation of valuable lures for the future. Despite her attempts, it seemed none of the men in the queen's personal guard had taken their bait about wanting to trek into Priory.

While none of the working girls she'd sent into Aubade had been able to speak to the captain directly, they'd learned all about his inglorious reputation. The man was named Erasmus. He was said to be a nightmare of a leader for his men, and was often caught leaving the tavern with a new woman more nights than not. Even if the girls hadn't been particularly effective in setting snares, they'd gained more than enough for the raven in newfound knowledge alone. Nox found the information of the guard's reputation lovely—she vastly preferred a man of low moral fiber. It was unspeakably comforting to have a target in her sights with no guilt attached, let alone one for whom she could exercise unbridled contempt.

Nox was pulling on her black silk dress and grabbing her cloak. The other escorts hadn't failed her, they'd simply set the stage for its final act. Her dark eyes twinkled as she told the Madame she would be the one going tonight in their stead. She hadn't selected jewelry for her endeavor. She was ornament enough.

Why would she send rookies to do a champion's job? This was her game, after all.

Millicent was torn in three directions. In the most potent way, she wanted Nox under her roof where her beautiful raven was safe. On the other hand, she wanted the captain of the guard with an unspeakable greed. On yet third hand, she needed Nox to feel that enough of a trust had been forged between them following the events in the carriage that the succubus could openly communicate—coming and going as she pleased—particularly if it served their mutual goal.

Eramus would be the most important key in getting both Nox and Millicent close to the queen, and once again, they were united with their need for a common target. Fortunately, The Selkie's girls had not been useless. They'd come back to the salon with plenty of information regarding the captain's inner circle, his regular schedule, and his reputation. After each visit from yet another lure, Nox found herself exceedingly relieved to hear that the captain was not known for being exceedingly honorable. A chaste knight may have been a nightmarish opponent for entrapment with lust, though she trusted nothing was impossible with her wiles. Nothing, except perhaps for the fae. She'd never be able to shake the lesson she learned as the redheaded faeling had refused her in Yelagin. In hindsight, she supposed she was glad she had not killed someone who turned out to be Amaris's close friend. Nox would never again make the mistake of seduction against someone whose ears pointed in telltale betrayal of their lineage.

All things considered, she mused at the size of the world and how small it often seemed.

Her thoughts returned to Eramus. The man was said to live within the castle's walls. This was perfectly logical, as the queen would need to be able to call upon her most trusted man regardless of the hour of the day or night. Though Nox had never been inside of Castle Aubade, she didn't think she'd have much trouble buttering palms into an invitation. She'd grown rather confident in her charms. With the unification of their target, Millicent had a few more intelligent tricks than flirtation. The Madame had called upon a calligraphist to forge a letter of invitation.

Nox made a face as she lifted the letter to the light in the Madame's office, "Are you sure this looks convincing?"

"Used it myself," the calligraphist swore, solemn as a saint. "Got myself invited to a banquet. Ate the finest pies of my life and nearly bedded a courtier—well, she was married and her husband was also in attendance, so perhaps flirted with a courtier is more accurate."

Millicent ignored the forger, focusing her attention solely on Nox. They may as well have been the only two in the room. Time was running short and Nox had made it clear that she would wait no longer. "Do you know where to find him?"

Nox nodded, "The girls have seen him each evening at a tavern called The Bird and the Pony just outside of the castle."

Millicent's hands were on her hips, her eyes averted to some distant corner as her wheels turned. "If he isn't there? Your plan then?"

She wiggled her forged document in mock triumph. "I don't need a plan. I have an invitation."

"There is no banquet to crash tonight, Nox. There's no crowd to get lost in." Usually, the Madame referred to her as the more pejorative 'dear'. The usage of her name belied the jeweled woman's nerves at the night to come. The dark-haired woman had just returned from the brink of death days after an escape to Yelagin, and now she was to infiltrate the castle. Their relationship had undergone an undeniable shift that neither of them would address outright. "Perhaps we're rushing our plan. Surely there will be a masque—"

"He will be at The Bird and the Pony. There's no need to wait for an excuse."

"But if he isn't—"

Nox had no time for discussion, "If he isn't, then he isn't. Do you believe me to be clever?"

The Madame nodded, somewhat reluctantly. Nox was terribly clever. In fact, it was her cleverness that had outmatched her to the Madame. She'd found herself on more than one occasion wishing for a simpler, more naïve girl of such great, formidable, terrible power under her care. Yet it was the very same cleverness that might win them their captain, and eventually their rank in the castle.

"Then trust me when I tell you, I will not fail tonight."

Nox would not fail, nor would she return. After her feet crossed the pleasure house's threshold, she swore she'd never look back. These would be her parting moments in The Selkie. It had been the place where she had been purchased, used, discovered, and cultivated her power. If she came back, it would be to sit atop a mount outside while a fleet of men beholden to her rushed in to behead the Madame, not emerging unless they clutched her by her golden ringlets. That particular detail would have to stay concealed for now.

"Here." Millicent pushed three bejeweled hair pins into Nox's hand. All three were meant to go above the same ear, slicking the hair back on one side. The underside of each pin had been sharpened into a thin, strong blade's point. Nox felt a twinge. She hated Millicent with every fiber of her being, but the begrudging, distasteful alliance was unavoidable.

She was grateful for the covert weapons, slipping all three into the hair above one ear. They had been an excellent addition to her outfit as she was to appear alluring and unarmed in every conceivable way. They were perfectly delicate, harmless adornments with a deadly purpose.

The time for arguments had come and gone. If Emily had reappeared, she would have used this time to say her final goodbyes. Instead, Nox walked from the front doors of The Selkie rather unceremoniously. Millicent, of course, had assumed return the next morning. Nox had no such intention.

The Madame sent her in her personal glossy, black carriage, though it did not fast travel to the castle. Manifesting two horses, a woman and a carriage from thin air would draw more than a little suspicion, she supposed. She had wanted to take a horse, but saw the wisdom of avoiding the elements of wind, salt, and air so that she stayed in her most pristine condition. Tonight, she was both bait and huntress.

☽ ☽ ☽ ● ● ◖ ◖ ◖ ☾

While she had insisted to the Madame that the captain would be at his regular tavern with an air of confidence, she had been undeniably sick with unease somewhere in her lower stomach throughout the carriage ride. In three years, she had failed only one time to lure a man. She had failed once and only once. She later discovered it was only because he was no pure man at all, though she hadn't yet learned that seduction seemed to fail on fae males. Nox absentmindedly wondered if this also meant someone of full fae lineage would survive a night with her, though she wasn't morbid enough to try it just for the sake of experimentation.

The Selkie women had reported every single detail about Eramus, the Captain of the Guard. Nox had insisted upon it, plying them for information. She had the girls describe his height, his weight, the set of his eyes, the shape of his jaw, the color and length of his facial hair, the crook of his nose to her several times, drawing the man on the papers at her desk from their memories over and over until they were able to positively identify it as the spitting image of the captain. She knew him from his teeth to his toes long before meeting him. Tonight, she took no chances.

Nox was having trouble deciding what had been more terrifying: spying silently on the demons in the barn, or opening the door to The Bird and the Pony. Tonight would be her first kill as a succubus outside of the walls of The Selkie. She corrected her thought: tonight would be her first near-kill, as she did intend to keep the captain alive. It would have been preferential to hunt, feed, and capture on familiar soil, but she had to work within the conditions provided. Nox stepped out of the black carriage and didn't allow herself a moment to gather her thoughts. No stretch of time would have any impact on her bravery. If she went, it would be now or never.

The relief she felt when she pushed open the pub door to immediately see Eramus sitting like a prize-winning pig in the center of the pub, surrounded by his cronies and adoring maidens, was like a cool, refreshing bucket of cold water in the suffocating summer heat. The forged note she'd taken from the calligrapher had been a gamble at best, and a death sentence at the behest of the royal family for conspiring to infiltrate the castle at worst. She was exceedingly grateful she would not have to use the document.

The pub had been like any other. It was full of patrons and wenches and the smell of spilled beer, hot with the crackles of fire and the warmth of bodies. The roar of men seemed to ebb as she entered and faces turned to regard her. Her opening move in this match had been little more than walking through the door. Nox was aware of the effect she had on men, especially since she'd recently fed on a drunken bastard who deserved a fate worse than the death that swallowed him in her bed. The recent feeding had set her skin aglow with an unearthly beauty, making her all the more alluring. For tonight, it didn't matter to her that Millicent had sent him to her room as a sacrificial lamb to the slaughter: any man who would touch an immobilized woman shouldn't have just been killed, he should have been hung from the city square by the bloodied stump of his ripped apart manhood. Perhaps Nox would see to it that the captain implement precisely that as the new punishment as the law of the land for any man who forced himself, once she had him under her guise. The hatred fueled her, manifesting itself as the glimmer of beauty. She was glowing and she knew it. She was the perfect bait.

Nox removed her royal blue cloak, feeling greedy eyes on her as her dress worked its delectable magic. Her black, silk dress was the ultimate temptation. It had been her favorite weapon on more than one occasion. Her stunning, curve-hugging gown was a pawn in the game in its own right. The piece revealed enough to let others know that she was confident and sensual, while covering enough to make them want to see what secrets it kept beneath the contours of its fabric.

She relaxed into the knowing effectiveness of the kill rate she'd had in this dress. Hunting in the open-air like this was nothing like the task of bringing men upstairs from the salon. When patrons entered The Selkie, they knew not only precisely why they'd come, but also what rules governed their permission to stay. Her only challenge at the pleasure house had been to get the men to forget that they were at a brothel at all, convincing them to pursue her and desire to win her despite where they'd met and the role in which she lived. It was a mistake so many girls made in The Selkie. Even in a pleasure house, you couldn't make yourself seem like a sure-thing if you wanted to win a big spender. She'd learned the rules of life in a brothel enough to excel within them.

Here at the alehouse, she felt markedly more vulnerable. She had assumed that the pub would have also been an inn, and kicked herself for the assumption. Nox had realized her mistake the moment she'd crossed the threshold, but it had been too late to change course. The bar had no rooms above. There would be no simple slip upstairs when she was ready to seal the deal. The Bird and the Pony was a crowded joint, lively with its own popularity. An enthusiastic fiddle player and his female songstress entertained the crowd with drinking song after song, leading the men in familiar choruses. Everyone seemed jolly with the opportunity to join, sloshing their pints and spilling their ale as they slurred their rough, off-kilter contributions to the music. The musical pair was skilled at commanding a crowd, keeping their attentions jovial and the spirits high. The bar itself was crowded to the gills with a particular brand of rough, militant men and the maidens that were either supplied by the establishment or the young women of Aubade who were drawn to the masculine exterior of such brutish energy. Everyone had their motives, and as long as everyone in the bar was mutually benefitting, it seemed like a perfectly lovely place. She'd only wished this hadn't been her first time on unfamiliar soil. Hunting was an art, and she was a painter without a brush.

Nox eyed an open spot along the main bar, far from the tables of men and their swooning women. She draped her cloak over her arm, allowing her bare back to be seen by the patrons as she maneuvered through the pub. Nox arched her spine slightly, ensuring that she was the picture of feminine beauty she knew to be desired by their male gaze.

Nox avoided the men's eyes entirely, choosing to play coy. She knew precisely who had seen her when she walked in, and whose eyes were on her as she took her seat across the room. Men liked to think something was their idea, after all. This reliable method was the very technique that had gotten the Duke of Henares and countless others to The Selkie. Nox lifted a finger and ordered herself a glass of red wine, though the lifted finger had been unnecessary. The bartender had noticed the unfamiliar face the moment she'd entered.

She made a show of scanning the bar, pointedly ignoring the soldiers bearing the queen's crest. The men, their armor, their weapons, their sigils were meaningless to her. She was no clout chaser, interested in titles or the authority that might entice one to seduce those within the court. Instead, she looked past the guardsmen, feigning mild interest in a tawny young man of barely eighteen far across the tavern. He'd noticed her immediately and practically spit up his beer. She did feel a bit sorry for the heart attack it appeared to have given the boy as he choked on his ale, sputtering it onto the table. Hopefully, this boy and the collateral damage of his emotional confusion would be the final pawn she played before stronger moves were required of her.

Nox knew plenty of timing and the role it played in seduction.

If the fiddle player and his songstress were beginning a new song now, she estimated that it would take until the second chorus for the captain to approach her. All she had to do was graze her eyes over his, touching them briefly so that he felt an invitation, and he'd be on his feet in a moment.

She was ready. It was time to put her next piece into play.

The song lifted, rising in the notes of its first tawdry chorus. Nox began her scan, knowing very well that Eramus, along with more than one of his men, was looking in her direction. With an idle disinterest, she allowed their eyes to meet. Nox held the captain's gaze for the briefest of moments, and then she continued her scan with indifference. The bartender caught her eye with something of a knowing chuckle. He recognized her ploy, knowing she was baiting the man. Good bartenders made their living off of reading people, she supposed. If the other girls at The Selkie were to be believed, Eramus was a known hunter. Perhaps it was refreshing for the bartender to see the captain be the prey.

The first step in her job was nearly done. Her eyes abandoned the tap house altogether, ignoring the amused barkeep, the gaze of the men, the stare of eyes on her bare skin, and the envious looks of the women who wore far more appropriate clothing than she had. Nox lifted her cup, studying the wine in her glass as the first chorus ended. The second verse began, and like clockwork, the captain was standing. If she knew anything of timing, she knew he wouldn't rush to her. There was an order to this dance, as predictable and important as any waltz. His men were cheering on some good-hearted mixtures between encouragement and envy, mostly unintelligible hybrids between grunts and cheers as the captain worked his way around them. It would take him the length of the verse to acknowledge his men, pat their shoulders, accept their envy and move. Slowly, he approached—bypassing the subtlety of opening pawns, he went right to his knight on his own. By the beginning of the second chorus, he leaned against the bar, ever the picture of suave.

Eramus was just as she'd drawn him from the girl's description, except with an almost virginal quality. His hair was golden brown, cut a little shorter than most men of the age. His locks were a bit curly, hanging to his cheekbones. His eyes were a bright, sky-blue color that stood out against his hair in a nearly virginal halo. Eramus didn't possess the rakish, nearly bawdry handsomeness of her duke. Instead, he had a disarming angelic aura about him that neither of the women had quite explained when describing him to her. He asked if he could buy her a drink and she tipped her nearly-full glass to him.

Nox smiled, burying her berry-dark lips against her glass before she spoke. "I have a drink, but perhaps instead you could tell me your name?"

He twinkled wickedly. "I'm Eramus, but you can call me 'yes, sir', depending upon how the night pans out."

Years at The Selkie had been an education in acting. It was a battle not to cringe or laugh at the man who fancied himself so terribly dominant and charming. She recognized the angelic face for what it was: the beautiful coloration of a venomous snake. Disarming, attractive loveliness was how the goddess's most dangerous creations hid in plain

446

sight under the guise of beauty. After all, it was how she operated, wasn't it?

Clearly, his combination of innocent loveliness and assertive domination worked on women who favored the company of men. Nox didn't always hate men. She had found some friendly, and others tolerable, if not occasionally charming in their own way. This encounter would be a feat of thespianism.

Fortunately, she felt confident she could throw out the chess board altogether. He was making this too easy. He'd won her the match with his arrogance.

He arched a brow, smiling at her over his pint, "And what should I call you?"

"Call me yours."

One of his men had clapped him on the back as he left The Bird and Pony with his arm slung around her hourglass waist, hand touching the bareness of her lower back as he carried her blue cloak on his opposite arm. The pub had been intended for the castle's traffic as it truly was mere steps from the royal gates, but she was surprised to find them entering the enormous regal structure. She'd known the captain resided within its walls, but it was another thing entirely to be led into the castle. Did he genuinely sleep here? Did he intend to bed her on the castle grounds? In a royal bed?

Every step brought her deeper into the cream stones of Aubade and further into the depths of uncertainty. She continued to chastise herself, telling herself that her nerves were only a product of unfamiliarity. If she were to thrive in this world, she couldn't allow herself to ring the alarm bells any time she was on new grounds. Nox justified his actions, supposing it made right and proper sense for the queen to need her best men close should there be a time of need. Moirai couldn't very well be the one to ring the bell for men to awaken from their various townhomes interspersed amongst the coastal city if the castle found itself under siege. Still, it seemed unwise to be leading a strange girl into such a private space, especially if rumor was to be believed that the man took women home with regularity.

It was colder than she thought it would be. There were lanterns all around. The castle was insulated. His arm was around her. Why was she cold?

Something was wrong.

No. No, she was allowing nerves to better her. Nothing was wrong. Something being unusual didn't make it wrong. A man being atypical didn't make him bad. A situation being unfamiliar didn't make it dangerous. She was okay. This was normal. Her instincts were probably frazzled due to some base need for familiarity. She needed to quiet herself if she were to remain the cool, collected picture of confidence required.

She did her best to maintain an allure of idle chatter, and he answered in polite, bright tones. There was something stilted about their conversation that she couldn't place. Nox had facilitated many a night of chatter with drunken and sober patrons alike. Their conversation flowed as easily as the meads, ales and wines that had refilled their cups time and time again. She knew how to ask questions and how to prompt responses. With Eramus, she found herself bumping against an odd disconnect. They both seemed to be the one facilitating the flow, relying on the other to fill the void. She'd been on unfamiliar grounds in the bar, and then taken to a new second location. The unexpected change that happened even as their conversation stilted continued to set off her alarm bells.

The castle felt ominous after sundown, though she assumed it was just her own sense of alarm knowing she was on a mission of devilry. All castles were ominous by design. What use was a fortress if it felt jubilant and inviting? Nox batted away at the feeling, using her internal monologue to soothe herself time after time. She did not believe that this castle had been structured with the intent of feeling welcoming. These inner halls held no windows, only closed doors to chambers beyond and the staggered placements of haunting torchlight. The corridors wound in such a way so as to make the wanderer feel quite lost. The plush running carpet, the monotonous layout, the sameness of the cream-colored stones in the corridor all lead to a consistent feeling of déjà vu. It was unnerving, knowing she was far from an exit and too disoriented to know how to properly escape.

After their long walk, the captain stopped at one of the doors, rustling in his pouch for a key. She continued to hold his arm as if she were any excited, love-lorn maiden of the city while he fiddled with the lock. Eramus flashed her a reassuring smile that didn't feel at all reassuring. He opened a door and ushered her in.

Nox stepped inside first.

For a moment she didn't understand what she was seeing. There was no bed, nor were there windows. There were large chests, racks and shelves of… weapons. He had brought her into an armory. There was an oversized wooden table in the middle with something that appeared to be manacles embedded into each of its four corners. No, this wasn't an armory. Why were they here? Like a deer hearing a tree snap in the forest, she felt all of her senses go wild, straining against the predatory sensation that loomed down on her.

Then she heard the clink of a metallic lock sliding into place behind her.

Yes, she saw it now. She saw everything.

She'd fallen for a move that had been meant to placate her into assumed victory. She'd let her guard down in premature celebration. She'd given up their game of chess without realizing he was still playing. Not only were his pieces still in play, but Eramus had been so many steps ahead.

This was his check.

She saw the weapons on every wall. She saw the chains meant to strap and constrain. She saw the brownish smears of blood. The objects meant for entrapment, for entanglement, for torture. She saw the man who was not a man at all, but an animal. He did not crave the bodies of women for any human lust.

The stilted conversation had been that of two predators not knowing how to interact with one another. The alarms had been of two hunters fumbling to strike for the kill where they'd intended prey. She had cursed herself for her senses, and now she hated herself for ignoring her intuition. She was in grave danger.

He hadn't moved from the door. His smile had remained unchanged. It was a cruel, bizarre mask against his virginal features as it mixed with the scent of dried blood and metal.

Nox understood everything. It was so obvious to her how important the captain's innocent face had been as a lure. She understood the frequency with which he needed new women, never bringing the same one home twice. Nox doubted that anyone brought into this room was left alive, and fully comprehended why she was in a windowless room with the door locked behind them. How cruel an irony that the huntress had been the one to let herself fall victim to the teeth of a beast.

In that moment, Nox knew a few absolutes. The first was that no charm or seduction would help her now. The next was that one of them was about to die, and she certainly didn't plan on it being her.

"This is not how I go."

The steel cage of her mind clamped down around the sentence, and Nox was prepared to fight for her life. This would not be a battle of fists. He may have spent his life in preparation for steel, flesh, and his role in the guard, but she had something that he didn't. Nox had the upper hand of a player who had not revealed all of their cards.

He wanted fear.

She was nowhere near triumph, nor was she in the guaranteed

clutches of defeat. She would win; her life depended on it. There were moves to be made. She could strategize her way out of this.

"Oh, sir," she purred, referencing the submission he had mentioned at the bar. "I do love a good sadist."

Nox bit her lip and slid her hands onto the table behind her, ignoring the smudges of uncleared blood. With the perverse delights of someone sharing in bloodlust, she did a backward hop onto the table, hoisting herself up by her hands and spreading her legs open for him. She allowed her dark eyes to fix on the bright blue sapphires of his angelic face. She was the picture of lust, spurred on with excitement. This was the performance of a lifetime, and she would not fail.

The surprise was clear on his face. Good.

He was shaken from his regular pattern. Nox could see the chess board in her mind, understanding how he'd strategically put himself at every advantage. She wasn't sure that she was out of his check, as her would-be king remained carefully pinned in their match. Surely, he had expected a panicked woman, the look of shock, perhaps even a gratifying scream. Maybe he fed off of their fear the same way she fed from love. She could see the surprise, curiosity, and perhaps even disappointment as his blue eyes scraped from her to the door. No matter, it seemed, if the room itself had not rattled her, he had a few more tricks up his sleeve. The Captain of the Guard took a few steps to a cabinet, eyeing the options after opening its doors. He ignored her fully, fingering the barbarous selections it held. Perhaps this was his next step meant to unnerve and terrify. Nox forced her exterior through the power of sheer, desperate will to remain the picture of calm amusement, channeling pleasure, unfocusing her eyes from the terrible things inside. The metallic, spiked glint of a flail was the first thing she saw. There were blades, whips, and arrows. Next to the flail hung a crossbow. She had no hope if the man picked up the crossbow. She made the slightest, most sensual hitch of her breath, drawing his attention.

Another bold move. Her life depended on this victory.

Nox lifted one palm, using the index finger of her right hand to beckon him forward while her left hand began to slide up the side of her dress, slowly tugging on its slit to reveal her thigh. She kept her voice low and feral, leaning into whatever animal nature she hoped possessed him. "I like it rough," she practically moaned, her low voice a sensual whisper. Everything in her fought to keep her tone easy and aroused. She clamored for a balance, wondering what words would strike the subservience of someone who enjoyed sexual torture while still expecting to make it out alive.

Did Eramus carnally consummate his unholy sacrifices before maiming the women he brought here? The blood pounded in her ears, drowning out any hope of using her senses. The battles she fought were raging in her mind: who were these women? Did their families know that their daughters were dead? Were any left alive when he finished with them? She could smell the faintest remnant of blood in the air, no doubt from the ruddy brown smears on the table and mortar between the stones from nameless others. She couldn't let herself be afraid. She couldn't let herself picture the women. She had to focus. She was the predator. He was the prey. There was no other alternative.

Eramus seemed to decide, then. His fingers wrapped around a nine-tailed flogger and turned toward her. Not a whip. Anything but the whip. A stab in her heart, the burble of terror as she remembered the crack of the whip, the sting of her blood as it pooled around her in the courtyard of Farleigh a lifetime ago. The pain of the whip would be nothing compared to the flogger in his fingers. He took a step toward her. "Bend over."

In her mind, she could hear him as he once more echoed, "Check."

The board was not moving in her favor. All of his pieces were advantageously positioned to keep her cornered. There had to be a way out. She couldn't let him move one more piece, or he'd be the first to reach checkmate.

The room was too cold. It was too small. Her heart was beating too fast. She needed to keep up the ploy. She needed to win his favor, to sweet-talk him, to urge him into letting down his guard if she were to gain the upper hand. She needed to keep her face relaxed, her lips parted, her eyes filled with lust and excitement, no matter what she felt. The next move had to be hers.

No. No she would not turn her back on him. If he were simply a man asking for a sexual favor, bent would do the trick as well as any other. But if she were in a vulnerable position, she'd have no way of knowing if he were bending her to enter or to break her skin with the weapon he held. Floggings ripped at the flesh and broke the ribs and backs and spines of their victims if the wielder refused to stop.

The only way to get out of check was by interposing a piece between the threat and the king. Death awaited one of them at this match's conclusion. She moved her queen.

Nox spread her legs further. She bit her lip as she ran her hand up her thigh, purring her words, "Warm me up first and I'll let you do whatever you want to me.

This seemed to spark a glimmer from the man, "You'll eat those words."

"I can't wait."

He flashed his teeth in a snarl, agitated by her seductive taunt as he advanced on her.

She'd done it. She'd made the most aggressive counter-move, and it had paid off. She knew it at that moment. She had won.

Nox had only a moment to seal her victory. She licked her palm, wetting herself as she enticed him forward. He stepped toward her, taking himself out of his pants. It was not with lust that he advanced, but with the cruel monstrous need to dominate, to silence, to exert

453

power and control and force. The moment he moved for her, she locked her legs around him, unwilling to let him leave. These were the moments that separated life from death for both of them, for terribly different reasons. This was not the passionate embrace of lovers. He'd no intention of kissing her, but as he jammed himself inside of her, she smashed her mouth onto his and sucked.

Nox had known she'd won well before the captain realized he'd lost. It took less than a beat for Eramus to begin to fight as she drank him in. She could feel his panic within a single heartbeat as he seemed to understand on some primal level that he was being devoured. She clamped down harder, engorging herself with the life force of the animal in her grasp. He attempted to claw at her, pulling at her hair, pushing back, fighting with his dying heartbeats to wriggle away, but no strength remained.

"Checkmate," she panted aloud, anger, triumph, hatred, and relief surging through her as her lips broke free.

The battle was over. His life was forfeit. Nox had won.

With one kernel of life remaining, she shoved him off of her.

She needed a moment to heave in disgust as she'd done years ago after her first kill. She'd seen death. She'd met wicked, cruel, and repulsive men. She'd encountered soldiers and warriors and power-hungry military officers. This was the first time she'd met a true villain.

Eramus was a monster. She bent herself over the table while he remained trapped in whatever remained of his shell of a person-suit. Nox held her head in her hands and wasn't sure if she would scream, laugh, vomit or cry. After a time, she felt herself begin to grin, though not with joy. The smile was not one of happiness, but of vitriol. She was a force of nature; she was lightning and thunder and wind personified. She was the night. She was the monster. She was the demon in the shadows.

"How are you doing down there?" She feigned a pout as she looked at the crumpled man, her conviction returning.

Nox straightened from the table as she examined her conquest. She wiped her mouth clean of him, teeth glinting from her victory. She straightened her dress, smoothing it like a lady. A hand went to her hair, fixing it as she raked her fingers down her mane in a tender gesture. She crossed over to him and spat on him, then lowered to his face, the water of her spit resting upon his unmoving features. She stared into his baby blue eyes for a long time, allowing herself to see into the depths of the blackened soul she'd stolen. "You still in there, Eramus?"

He let out the barest whisper of a terrified moan.

"Good."

She took the tailed flogger from where it had fallen on the floor and brought it to one of the blades on the wall. Nox snipped the long strand from its flog and returned to him. Nox sighed as she began the laborious effort of shimmying the captain's pants further down his hips, revealing his testicles. She made a noise to express her displeasure before she set to work. The dark-haired victor wrapped the leather strand tightly around his scrotum and his sack, watching them grow purple instantly as they filled with blood. She knew enough from the gelded horses in Farleigh's stables to know that it would take two weeks for his manhood to fall off in its entirety, and wasn't so sure she'd let him live that long. Two weeks was too long for a man who did not deserve to draw breath. Still, castration—even a slow one—was a relatively satisfying victory. He would never, ever be removing this leather band.

"How does it feel? Nice and snug?" She feigned something like friendliness, a pout on her lips as she scanned the rapidly-fading terror in his eyes. Soon, he wouldn't feel anything. She needed him to stay awake for a bit longer. She needed his consciousness for a few more minutes.

Another defiant, ghostly groan scratched over his lips.

"Oh, I hear you, captain. It's scary to feel trapped and helpless, isn't it? Nowhere to go, no help in sight, right? That must be terrible."

She rose from her kneeling position and eyed the tools on the shelf. She was still in the lovely silk dress that showed her arms, her back, and the daring slit up her thigh. There was something particularly malevolent about someone so lovely cast against a backdrop so evil.

Nox turned to him from where she stood, smiling as if they were children on the yard at playtime. "How about I point to one, and you tell me if you've used it on a woman. Does that sound like a fun game?"

He grunted again. The sound was nearly human, presumably meant to be a cry for help.

"Ah, I see. Not so fun because you've used most of these, right? Or has it been all of them? Busy, busy boy." She decided to keep it poetic and, after considering her options, landed on the same nine-tailed flail—now with eight remaining tails, as one was tightly wrapped around his purple, rapidly dying manhood—that he'd intended for her.

Nox knelt again, grabbing his chin and feigning another pout. She painted her face with mock sympathy as she spoke, "I'm not a cruel person, Eramus. I've never tortured—not physically, anyway. Though I do suppose you and I have a thing or two in common. In a way, I use men as you use women. We both take. We're takers, you and I. The primary difference is that the men I use... well... for them it's a disembodied heaven on earth. Of course it took a few tries to get it right, and I do feel bad for the men who fell to my trial and error before I'd learned to wield my puppets. Really, I do. I'm not a killer by choice. Maybe that's our primary difference."

Nox rose and looked down her nose at where he remained slumped against the floor, his purpling bulge still visible. She nudged him with her foot, dark eyes tumultuous as storm clouds. "Don't fall asleep now. Stay with me. I have something to tell you! You see, sometimes I feel bad about who I am and what I do. It's true! Can you believe it? Occasionally I get all tangled up in things like morality... but then I meet men like you and I remember exactly why I don't need to feel *anything* about what I do. Justice can be a cruel mistress, can't it, captain?"

He breathed again and she knew with a wicked delight that he'd given up all hope. His sounds weren't those of a plea. They weren't even noises of pain. Had he already resigned? How disappointing. She continued to allow him the twinkle of consciousness he needed to stay himself for a moment longer. Somehow, she felt quite sure this was not cruelty. She was no more evil for this than she had been for discovering her heritage in the first place. In fact, if she had to ask the ghosts of the women who'd been lost to this room or their families, she'd be quite sure she'd be considered an avenging angel.

She kicked him again, "Stay awake, captain. In a bit, I'll put you in a daze. Trust me, you'll love it. But the thing is, I don't quite feel like you deserve to love anything just yet, so I just want to make sure you're still *you* for the next few minutes. You'll get to live for a few more days while I see how you might atone for your sins—and trust me, you will atone. For that reason, I think I'll leave your limbs on for now." She ran her fingers along the eight-tailed whip, enjoying the luxury of its sadistic leather against her skin. "We shouldn't waste any time, don't you think? We have a long night ahead of us before your daze begins. Is that alright with you?"

She rose with one certainty: she would never doubt herself again. Instincts were meant to keep you alive. Telling herself she had been wrong for feeling nervous, convincing herself that she had been crazy for her worry, chastising herself as insecure—ignoring her gut had almost gotten her killed. She'd protect and honor those instincts until the end of her days. For now, she'd enjoy the end of his days.

26

The image of a horse was still in her mind as Amaris pictured Castle Aubade's architecture. From the outside of the castle, the ivory reever had assumed its snout to be roughly five stories high, and now she understood the reason for its height. The horse's nose belonged to the throne room.

Moirai's throne room was a long, grandiose cathedral. Three levels of balconies had onlookers curiously watching the three reevers as they approached the thrones, with two additional pseudo-floors left solely for the light and expanse of palatial luxury. At least, there would have been light pouring in from the upper levels of skylights if it hadn't been so late before the queen had summoned them. Amaris, Malik, and Ash had scarcely had a chance to exchange two words in reunion before they were ushered into the room. She absently hoped Malik had been fed before they'd been shoved from the landing through the double doors of the monarch's room. The entrance closed behind them as the reevers were led into the magnificent, imposing space to meet with Queen Moirai. Guards stepped from their place on either side of the doors, stoically safeguarding the only exit.

"Are you ready?" Ash asked her under his breath before they took the final steps down the long, carpeted aisle to see the queen on her throne.

She nodded once. She was ready.

Enormous columns connected the floor to the vaulted ceiling. Equally large stained-glass windows lined both sides of the throne room, and Amaris was sure that during the daylight hours, the rainbow they cast must be spectacular. The only thing they could do was put one foot in front of the other. Their eyes wandered to take in the space around them, but forward progress was their only option. The three reevers were walking down an ostentatiously long, plush rug of deep burgundy, trimmed in golden thread that created a perfect runway from where they'd entered to the two imposing thrones, seats far too gaudy to feel noble, awaiting them at the end of the runner. The thrones, presumably one for the queen and one for the crowned prince, were on an elevated platform, to allow the royals to look down at anyone who approached. The entirety of the space was adorned in the gaudy reds and golds of Farehold.

It appeared that only Queen Moirai would be taking an audience with them, as the throne beside her sat empty. Amaris did her best not to move her head away from the queen, understanding enough of courtly propriety to know it to be improper. From their brief meeting in the hall, her friends had also appeared to have been dressed as fashionably as she had, and walked with as much stately reverence as they could muster. Ash and Malik flanked her, a man on each side keeping an arm's length behind. Their flanking was meant to ensure that Amaris was showcased as their speaker, as she may be the only one with the opportunity to exchange words with the queen. When she spoke, she needed to make every word count.

The reevers reached the end of the rug and all three knelt in an appropriate bow. Their lessons on poisons, monsters, and how to be one's own battle-medic hadn't exactly prepared them for decorum, but Amaris had the fortune of being educated in such ways at Farleigh. Ash and Malik followed her lead, bowing their heads with their knees bent.

As the sword-arm of the goddess, reevers served no king. This did not excuse them from observing whatever customs and mannerisms were appropriate for the kingdoms they visited.

The queen was dressed in a blood-red gown, trimmed with gold along the collar and large, gaping bell sleeves. An ornate gold belt studded with rubies hugged her waist, which may have been lovely when she was younger, but at her advanced age, it seemed misplaced. Her crown was just another accessory in her collections of crimsons and golds. The gilded circlet rested atop her curls as she frowned at the reevers.

"Your majesty—" was meant to be said in unison, but she had distinctly heard both of her companions pluralize the word. It was an odd, jarring moment that Amaris almost tried to convince herself hadn't happened. She kept her eyes lowered until the queen motioned for them to rise. The lilac-eyed reever scanned again to ensure she had not missed the crown prince. It was more likely that she had misheard her friends. She stilled her inner voice, focusing on the task at hand while Queen Moirai spoke.

"Why have you crossed the continent to call for an audience with us?" Moirai's voice tended toward the theatrical. Her voice was not kind, nor was her cadence particularly beautiful. It was the robust, irked voice of a monarch who had better things to do than to entertain the league of guardians who were best left ignored.

This was Amaris's moment. This was precisely what she had waited for throughout the weeks of travel. This is why Samael had looked at her that day in the reev and had known her persuasion was more gift than curse. Diplomacy came first, she told herself. First she would ask the queen, and then she would tell.

460

"Your majesty," her voice came out quieter than she had intended. Amaris rose to her feet, watching the reevers on either side mimic her actions as they straightened their postures. She lightly cleared her throat and summoned her courage. The moonlit reever spoke from her belly, allowing her words to carry. She locked eyes with the queen of Farehold. "Your highness, I am Amaris of Uaimh Reev, and these are my reever companions, Ash and Malik. As you know, the reev has only served to keep peace. That is why we seek an audience with you today."

The queen did not look appreciative. She was the perfect picture of inconvenienced boredom. She had dinners to eat, nobles to meet, baths to take, books to read, peasants to spit on and all manner of things she'd prefer to accomplish rather than be in the company of whatever assassins operated outside Farehold's law.

The courtiers in the balconies were not especially numerous, but the ones who did observe appeared to be listening intently. A few could be seen whispering behind laced gloves or outstretched fans. The reevers had been around for centuries, but Samael had said himself that their numbers had dwindled in the last fifty years. He had not left the keep in practically five decades. No one in this room appeared to surpass that length of time in years. She wondered how much may have changed in the dozens of years Samael had remained sequestered.

Amaris only noted the courtiers with the studiousness of the warrior she was trained to be, then blocked them out for the distractions that they were. It was not useful to dwell on her audience. The only other bodies in the throne room that mattered belonged to the fully armored soldiers, still as sentinels, holding lavishly feathered spears on either side of the twin thrones. When she spoke, it was with authority and finality. She may be a girl with no family and no title, but she was a reever. She had a right to speak on behalf of balance regardless of the monarch before her.

"We are on dispatch to inquire as to the killings of Raascot men

461

throughout Farehold."

The transition from disinterested to amused was abrupt. The queen nearly snorted at this, casting an entertained look to the empty seat beside her, then gesturing as if to the audience of courtiers. Her defensiveness was immediate. "Have any bodies been produced? Show me evidence that I have killed a single northman on my lands."

There were a few humorless chuckles from the balconies.

Amaris refused to look at the nobility lining the balconies. She kept her eyes on Moirai.

If the queen had been truly innocent, her response would have taken on a different form entirely. Her wording was telling enough. Of course no bodies could be produced if they were to be perceived as ag'imni. Moirai was incriminating herself by the moment.

Once again she reminded herself that first she would ask, then she would tell. "We are here on behalf of the reevers to request that your Majesty stand down on her orders to kill northerners found south of the border."

Moirai let out another laugh and then raised her eyebrows further. It was surprising that there had been any skin on her forehead remaining to experience the ever-arching eyebrows, but somehow they'd climbed. If she managed to be any more surprised, her brows would disappear beneath her curls and join her crown.

"What do you think?" Moirai asked the chair.

Amaris flinched at the oddity of the motion. She tried to catch Malik's attention, as the mop of his golden hair seemed a bit closer to the tilt of her chin. He did not meet her eyes.

Moirai raised a hand to her ear, as if to better hear. Amaris blinked several times in an attempt to maintain her poise. Had the queen gone mad? Surely, there would have been word if a mad queen had sat upon the throne. Even in Farehold, gossip had spread about the instability of the man who sat on Raascot's throne. How had nothing been dispersed

462

about the woman who spoke to furniture?

Raising her voice to its loudest, most regal bellow, the queen announced: "The crowned prince is quite right. He and I find it offensive that Uaimh Reev—a keep that has claimed neutrality for hundreds of years—comes into our kingdom and makes such accusations about our people and our intentions! What kind of peacekeeping is it, then, when you march into our throne room and defend the north from some offense invented by your reev! What sort of northern agenda have you truly come to press upon the good people of Farehold?"

The onlookers seemed to be murmuring their agreement.

This was bizarre for more than one reason. Amaris was too confused to make her next move. She knew she was supposed to keep her eyes on the queen, but they darted to Ash beside her. "What prince?" she breathed, barely a whisper.

His amber eyes widened with horror at her idiocy. Ash angled his head forward, using the barest of motions to gesture toward the throne. She was fumbling her dispatch and they both knew it. Amaris was botching the mission. With the intensity of his urgency, Ash mouthed, *"The crowned prince!"*

Her eyes tore from her copper friend. She stared at the empty seat for a moment longer. The queen and all of her courtiers watched Amaris expectantly. The inelegance of finding herself mute at the foot of Queen Moirai when an answer had been demanded of her was its own catastrophic failure of adherence to courtly standards. The expectant sounds of fidgeting silence of the courtiers around her pressed down on her. But she couldn't speak. Not yet.

This wasn't right.

Amaris dipped her chin again, doing her best to conceal the movement of her lips as she continued to angle her head for Ash.

"Do you see a prince?" Her question was low and hurried. She widened her eyes at him, signaling her seriousness. He blinked several times at her, perhaps thinking she'd lost her mind. He was disappointed. He was horrified. He was pleading. Why wasn't she speaking? Ash flared his nostrils, using all of his nonverbal signals to urge her to pull herself together.

Amaris couldn't pull herself together. She looked over to the remaining reever.

"Malik!" she spoke his name in a hushed cry for help.

"Talk to them!" He urged as quietly as he could.

She looked back at the queen, realization slackening her jaw. Samael's musings ran through her as he'd looked upon her purple eyes, as Gadriel's had on their second encounter. The first meeting she'd had with the leader of the reevers rang through her memory with a single sentence: "...*with those eyes, I'd love to see what gifts of sight you possess.*" The reever's mouth went dry, filling with cotton.

Her next statement came out, barely a ghost of a murmur that only her friends could hear. Her heart fell into her stomach. Her blood went cold. She felt as though she tasted pennies on her tongue.

She swallowed, "There is no prince."

Her voice was so quiet. The queen made a motion of annoyance, looking to the chair again and nodding. Moirai was conversing with a phantom. No one was there. Amaris blinked a second time, then a third.

It was all an act. Amaris had the gift of sight. She had the gift to rightly see. She heard a ringing in her ears as she stared at the empty space beside the queen. Slightly louder this time, she repeated. "There is no prince." Her voice found purchase this time, knowing she had been heard. The queen's eyes instantly tightened. The woman gripped the arms of her throne, knuckles flexing white. Perhaps her exclamation had been a mistake, but she was possessed with her realization.

"What are you doing?" Malik's voice was a hoarse, desperate rasp beside her. He could feel them losing the favor of the crown with every passing second.

"There is no prince," was all she could say, repeating herself stupidly. The pieces of the puzzle clicked together. Her heart was in her ears, her breaths were shallow. There was no prince. Everyone saw a man who was not there. They perceived something that did not exist. Everyone saw it... but her.

Why? *Why?*

"It's an illusion." Then louder, the accusation bubbling up, her hand nearly raising to point an index finger, though her fingers crumpled inward, too horrified to find the strength. She didn't have the time to do what was right and proper. She wasn't afforded the luxury of discussing things with the reevers. She locked eyes with the queen and lifted a finger. "You have the gift of illusion. You—Your majesty... the perception at the border... it's *your* curse."

The reevers at her side had gone rigid. They felt the court's tide turn against them.

Moirai blinked rapidly, gripping the handles of her throne before she barked out the single word, "Guards!"

Amaris had found her voice fully now. She was not timid. She was not anxious. She sounded demented to all onlooking, but she knew. She knew the truth and demanded that all hear her as she screamed at Moirai. "It's *your* curse! The border is your curse! You have the gift of illusion!"

The guards advanced as Amaris seemed to remember her only task, one she had failed. She'd been sent to persuade, not to reveal. She stared at Queen Moirai, the world around her melting into a tunnel as she saw only one woman's face and summoned her power. "You *will* let us go!" Amaris shouted past the bodies that closed in around her, ignoring the world and rallying her power for the Queen of Farehold.

"Guards, seize them!" the queen was on her feet, pointing. Moirai's intensity and hysteria should have betrayed her guilt before her court. She had been discovered. She had been foiled. The woman's voice was too loud, too frenzied.

The guards rushed for the reevers while Amaris continued her deranged shouts, looking the queen in the face as she willed her persuasion upon the woman, focusing all of her energy on Moirai. Her companions were helpless, knowing they could not fight. They were unarmed and outnumbered. They were in courier's clothes, weaponless and powerless. Even if they initiated hand-to-hand combat, how many trained centurions could Ash and Malik truly fight before they were overpowered? They'd counted on Amaris to persuade the queen, and in a single moment, their hopes had been dashed. The struggle beside her was little more than the sounds of grunted protest.

Her voice was more shrill than they'd ever heard. She was little more than a girl being plunged underwater, sputtering her desperate screams against the lapping surface of the waves. "Queen Moirai, you will let us go! You will set us free from this castle!" But the queen was unyielding, trembling with rage as she held her hand firm, pointing with all of the venom in the world.

The throne room had descended into colorful chaos. Courtiers were burbling their shock. Flashes of color and jewels swam from the balconies. Metallic breastplates and the tinkling of armor filled the air around them.

"Silence her!"

The guards grabbed their arms, but she remained a wild animal crying uselessly at the queen, demanding that the woman hear her commands. Her words were little more than the mad ravings of a lunatic bouncing off of the enormity of the throne room and all its finery. Courtiers continued gasping and shouting at the eruption of excitement. The reevers beside her were omitting gasps and grunts as they wormed to keep their feet on the ground. She saw none of it, heard none of it, willing herself to see only the queen. "You will let us go! You will stop killing the northerners! You will—" a thud deadened everything and stars swallowed her vision. She fell to the ground as the pommel of a sword hit her over the head and her world went black.

27

"Captain Eramus!" A voice was shouting down the hall while the sounds of doors opening and then promptly clattering shut made their way toward the succubus and her prey. Nox, still in her black silken gown, had been perched on the torture table picking at her nails, the picture of boredom. Whatever chill she'd felt in the night had long-since dissipated. It had been hours of exertion, and her muscles had warmed her body. Now she enjoyed the relaxing hours of morning as she'd eyed her accomplishment. Nox was careful to avoid the red-brown stains of the table before sitting down, not wanting to dirty her dress. She looked to her glazed captain with just her eyes, lifting her eyebrows slightly, "You ready, pet?"

Eramus had been redressed for some time, though the bulge in his pants as his purpling manhood throbbed beneath from its leather-tied death grip looked a bit improper. To the untrained eye, it looked merely as though he was having filthy thoughts unable to keep to himself. No one would expect the swelling castration to be anything more than a distinctly male blunder.

Her exercise in vigilante justice had taken all night. Once she had finished cracking down her punishments, ensuring he'd heard and felt every moment of his lessons, she had used what remained of her power to breathe into him the droplet of life she'd need for him to be under her charm. Hours had passed, and she had no doubt that, had this room possessed any windows, cheery morning light would be filtering through. She smiled at the thought of the sun shining down on her and her painful brand of divine, feminine vengeance.

Nox hadn't worried about her enchantments when she'd sent the Duke or Henares from The Selkie. The toffee young man had quite the reputation for being a lazy, debaucherous lordling. Diddling about his estate in Henares babbling like a drug-addled, love-sick puppy wouldn't draw too much suspicion as it was within his line of character to do so, relatively speaking. Nox had no doubt he'd do just fine handling himself while out of her sights. This captain, however, would require a bit more of a hands-on approach. His responsibilities were far greater and that, due to the inflexibility of his title, his margin for error was practically nonexistent. Nox would stay close to Eramus, firmly steering him until she'd used him for everything he was worth.

She inspected her nails once more for the tell-tale signs of dried blood as the panicked sounds of searching echoed down the hall. She'd been using a slender knife to remove traces of her punishment, but set it to the side as the noises drew nearer. Her nails were rather short given her romantic proclivities, but the speckles of blood and struggle had found their way beneath them nonetheless. She was unbothered as the noises grew nearer. She had nothing to fear. The mighty Captain of the Guard was at her side, after all.

Nox had assumed that she would have had the bewitched captain to escort her out of the castle this morning, but it appeared that if the commotion in the hall was any indication, they would be taking a detour. This was fine, of course. If Yelagin's demons were to be believed and Amaris had need for the queen, then Nox had no problem staying close to a royal resource. There was nowhere Eramus could go that she couldn't with him posing as her chaperone—even if it might raise more than a few eyebrows. Eramus was roughly as high-ranking and authoritative as one might get without possessing a noble title. She very much doubted anyone, save for the regents themselves, would have been able to deny him his sultry, black-haired companion.

Someone—presumably a servant, from the deference they used in their title—continued calling his name. The individual used the clanging of keys to lock and unlock every door in their corridor until finally the entrance to the sadistic armory flung open.

The eyes of the attendant standing before them darted with surprise as his gaze flitted between the captain standing loosely in the middle of the room to the woman resting against the table. Nox continued to look both relaxed and unimpressed, allowing her puppet to lead the way.

"Sorry, sir." The servant fidgeted, unsure about what, exactly, he'd walked in on. "Captain Eramus, you're urgently needed at the arena."

"Regarding?" The captain asked. She was impressed with own handiwork, as he did not sound quite like the opium-drugged lovers that often left her chambers once entranced. His tone held almost enough authority to pass as competent. She had told him, under no uncertain terms, that she wanted to know everything he knew from this moment forward. This was more than likely why he was obediently asking follow-up questions of the agitated servant.

The servant squirmed slightly from where he stood in the doorway before approaching Captain Eramus and whispering in his ear, presumably to discuss matters of utmost secrecy out of the earshot of whatever lady friend the captain had been entertaining. It was clear from the discomfort of the servant's flickering eyes that he had noticed the captain's bulge. It took a few moments for the message to be relayed before he backed away, offered a quick bow, and took off down the hall.

"So," Nox asked calmly, "what takes us to your arena?"

Amaris opened her eyes. At least, she tried. One of her lids seemed impossibly heavy, perhaps swollen from the blow she'd taken to the face as a thick memory of a sword's pommel had connected to her skull. She felt discomfort everywhere, disoriented while her eyes slowly widened to take in her surroundings. Her head throbbed as though her brain was trying to drill its way out of her skull. Her shoulders ached. She absorbed every sickening sensation of lying face-down on a cold, filthy floor. Amaris's face was pressed into the dirt and stone of the ground. She breathed in through her nose and the odors of unwashed bodies, mold, animal musk, and waste assaulted her. She still hadn't opened her eyes, nor was she sure she wanted to.

She had failed. She had barely awoken, yet she already knew with definitive certainty that when her abilities had been required of her, she had been useless. Amaris made a motion to push herself up into a seated position, but found herself unable. Her hands were restrained behind her back, bound tightly. The reever swallowed, attempting to still the throbbing in her head, and felt her tongue connect with an obstacle. A thick band of fabric was gagging her, disabling her ability for speech. Her mouth filled with saliva around the foreign object as if her body willed her to swallow the obstruction away. Despite the desperation of her situation, some part of her accepted the act. She supposed if someone tried to use powers of persuasion on her, she'd also have them gagged and rendered speechless. She was perhaps fortunate that her tongue had not been cut from its resting place in her mouth if she'd truly been suspected of persuasion. Amaris let out a muffled choke as she rolled onto one side. She bent her right knee, bringing it up to her chest to create space between her torso and the stone floor with her left leg outstretched behind her, toes rolling her onto the ball of her foot.

Using her knee as leverage, she pushed herself up and was able to get her feet underfoot.

Amaris blinked against the dismal, drab space, eyes straining as they adjusted to its dim lighting. Her lilac eyes had never done her much good in the dark, though as they adapted and filtered through the gloom, distant, covered windows allowed her to make out her surroundings. She was in a cream-bricked room—no, a cell—not with the straight four walls of a jail, but in a hall that seemed to curve ever so slightly. While three walls of her cell were made of the iron bars one might expect of a horrid dungeon, the wall that should have been the barrier to the outside was made out of wood, containing a single slit down its middle. Amaris seemed to be on the side closest to the outside world, as distant windows let in daylight from around the curved edges just beyond her range of vision. Now that her eyes had fully adjusted, she could see her companions in the cell opposite hers, still unconscious. Their cell, like hers, had its iron bars, but their far wall was that of the same cream stone of the Castle of Aubade. Why did hers have a slitted, wooden wall? The architectural design was the least of her worries at the moment.

She tried to call out through the muffle of her gag.

Ash's red hair was easy to spot. He lay faced away from her and made no movements at her sounds. Malik seemed to stir. She cried out again against her gag, watching his form tilt and shift against the custard wall of his cell. He had been in a sitting position, head slumped to his chest with his hands behind him. She made a third muffled attempt at a call and watched the emerald eyes of her golden friend flutter open. Her muted sound was one of relief as their eyes met.

Malik was quick to consciousness. As soon as he saw her, trapped and behind bars, he attempted to stand. His hands were quickly revealed to be bound as hers were, providing him with some difficulty. From what Amaris could see, neither Ash nor Malik appeared to have any fabric muzzling them as he did, though perhaps it was unnecessary for anyone who didn't continue a witch's malevolent power. She continued watching helplessly. It took Malik a moment to create leverage with his bound hands against the yellowed stones and get his feet underneath him, but soon he was standing.

"Are you alright?" Malik asked her. Despite her situation, she felt sad for him. His empathy was a bottomless well. As miserable as she felt, she knew he felt it in equal proportion in response to his helplessness at his inability to help her. He'd go to the ends of the earth to save the ones he loved, yet he was rendered powerless while he watched her, bound and gagged behind iron, separated from them. This seemed a somewhat more tragic fate. She carried the powerlessness of her own scenario, while he shouldered the burden of everyone's destitution.

Amaris nodded in answer to his question, though she had no idea if it were true. Was she alright? She was bound, gagged, and in what was most definitely in a prison separated from her brothers.

She called on her senses, focusing on what she had to do to get out. For now, she'd ignore Malik and focus on her bindings. Amaris pressed her face into the iron bar, searching for something jagged or rough to rub on her gag, but there was nothing. Though it chafed her cheek, the cloth of her gag stayed securely in her mouth, choking her lips in an open position as it remained tied tightly at the back of her head. While she searched for something—*anything*—to snag against the fabric, Malik was gently kicking Ash to a waking state. It took the groggy faeling a few moments to take in his surroundings, but he rolled to his side in a fashion similar to Amaris and was able to get on his feet.

"What happened?" Malik asked, knowing Amaris could not answer.

Drool was the only answer she could offer beyond her grunts. She waited as they tried to untie one another, but realized that, though rope bit into her wrists, her companions had the irons of chains around theirs. Their bindings had been so different, and she didn't know why. At least the men had been spared the cruelty of gags. Malik lowered himself to the ground, rolling into a sitting position as he squirmed his bound hands over his backside, down the length of his legs and managed to maneuver the shackles to his front. He helped Ash to do the same until their still-shackled hands were in front of them.

Ash gripped at the bars, staring helplessly at his silver-haired friend. Dirt was smudged across her face, covering both the cloth and her white cheek. She was still in the flat shoes, black tights and puffy silver-sleeved jacket of the court juggler. Amaris saw the fury in his eyes. The copper reever experienced a flare of anger at the final insult to their situation. Not only were they bound and jailed but their dignity had been taken as well. They were imprisoned not as proud reevers, but as clowns, mere laughing stocks for the queen.

Amaris could not wriggle her hands to the front of her body as her friends had. While they had been in relatively loose chains, her ropes did not end at her wrists, but seemed to coil their way up to her elbow, clasping her forearms together in a vice-like grip. She'd been kept separate, bound differently, and gagged. If their situation hadn't already been horrid, there was something unknowably ominous about these slight variations. They made no sense to her, but her gut told her that it couldn't be anything good.

Ash and Malik spent a moment talking hurriedly to themselves, then Ash spoke aloud.

"Ayla, just shake your head yes or no. Are you telling us that the crowned prince we saw was an illusion?"

The relief was like the cold water on her dry, gagged tongue. They understood her. They knew what she had been trying to communicate. She sagged against her alleviation, taking whatever small solace she could in its consolation. Amaris blinked rapidly, nodding with urgency in confirmation.

He tried again, "You were able to see the illusion for the same reason you can see the Raascot fae?"

Again, she nodded with enough ferocity that the very tendons of her neck might spasm. She let out a choked sob, relief at being understood.

Ash swallowed, leaning his forehead against the iron bars as he eyed the space between them, "And the last thing you had said was that if Queen Moirai has the power of illusion, it must be her gift that has cursed the border with this perception spell?"

Amaris groaned, only able to nod in encouragement. She was pressed against the bars, willing herself to be as close to her friends as possible. The reevers were three arms lengths away from one another so that even if they had each been unbound and outstretched, they still would have found themselves unable to find the human touch of comfort in reaching for one another. They were separated in a way that had been intended to leave them destitute.

"The queen couldn't be persuaded," Ash stated.

"But the queen is not fae," Malik's sentence was not a question. Moirai's traits didn't display a drop of fae blood. She had no ears, no large irises, no sharpened canines, nor even a hint of beauty in her horrid traits. His voice was contemplative, lost to his own thoughts as he said, more to himself than anyone else, "Moirai is a witch."

Ash was angry. "Why didn't you call the guards instead? Why didn't you command them? How could you not know your power did nothing to witches!"

Malik kicked the redhead, eyes flashing. His voice came out in a snarl. It was only the second time in her life she'd heard anger from Malik, and she knew that was for her benefit.

"What's done is done, you ruddy fool. She'd spent weeks prepared to give her speech to the queen and the queen alone. Do you want your last moments with her to be scolding her for not being all-knowing?"

Last moments, he had said. Malik was right. The queen would never let her live. In seeing through the monarch's illusion, Amaris knew more than perhaps anyone else in Farehold, and knowledge was a dangerous thing. There was no way she'd be permitted to make it out alive. It was through grime, tears and a soaked, filthy gag that she eyed her friends. This might be the final time she looked at them. Ash, with his flaws, his joys, his angers, his arrogant flirtation. Malik, with his goodness, his generosity, his selflessness and strength. Wet tears joined the moisture of the saliva against her gag as they tumbled from her eyes, absorbed by the cloth that bound her mouth. She leaned her forehead against the chilled bars and closed her eyes.

This was it. She'd die unable to say goodbye to her brothers. She'd pass amidst the stench of mold and filth. She'd leave the earth and join the All Mother with her arms aching against their binds, and heart throbbing against her failure.

She understood Ash wasn't truly angry with her, even if his words had said as much. He was just angry. He was angry at his helplessness, angry that he couldn't have saved them or have done more. His rage had nowhere to go, no place to fall but on the fruitlessness of *'what ifs'*. What if, indeed. What if she had known, somehow, that commanding the queen was in vain and that her attention had needed to pivot to the captors around her. What if Amaris had been born a brown-haired girl to a happy family and a safe village, never having heard of child mills or places called Farleigh. What if Raascot and Farehold had excellent relations between benevolent rulers and there was no curse. What if Moirai marched into the dungeon herself with handfuls of gold and a cooked goose for everyone. What if. They were the two most useless words in the common tongue.

There were no rhymes or reasons that made sense to Amaris as to Moirai's motives. Why would she need a prince? Why not just rule alone as she had for scores of years prior? What reason would compel her to spell for herself a perceived heir where none existed? How much power did it take for her to cast and maintain such a curse? And furthermore, what did Raascot have to do with any of it? Ash and Malik seemed to be having a conversation similar to the one brewing in her mind, but they had no yes or no questions they could ask of her. Her guess was as good as theirs, and no theory could be uttered through the fabric that gagged her. She wasn't sure that she wanted their last moments to be spent arguing. She didn't know what fruitless guesses and speculations would benefit her.

Amaris shifted from leaning her forehead against the cool bars, to her cheeks, her neck, allowing all of her exposed skin to feel the shifts of final sensations. She let the questions slide away, savoring what remained of her mortal life. What did knowledge matter if she was about to die? How would the queen do it, she wondered? Was Moirai known for any particular predilections of cruelty?

She looked within herself for a happy memory. She didn't want to die thinking of pain, of destitution, of failure. Amaris didn't want to die at all, but it seemed like she might not get much say in the matter. If she were to be killed, she wanted to die thinking of how Odrin had beamed with such pride at her swearing-in ceremony. She wanted to die remembering the first time she'd kicked Ash's ass in the ring. She wanted to die in a cloud of plums and spice as Nox held her, allowing her to feel safe and loved in her arms.

A clang came from somewhere around the curvature of the beige-stone hall.

No time in the world would have been long enough to prepare her for whatever was to come next. She didn't want to spend her life rotting in a cell, but she wasn't ready to be torn from the reevers. Ash leaned against the bars of his cell and met her eyes while they listened to the boots. Wet, helpless tears matched her own as amber melted into lilac.

He was saying a silent, heartbroken goodbye.

The heavy scrapes against stones belonging to footsteps came bouncing off of the jail's curved walls as armed guards made their way to the reevers.

Three men who didn't seem particularly interested in the reevers arrived. The faces that appeared before her were pocked, scraggly and utterly forgettable. She wouldn't commit any of her final moments to remembering their faces. The guards paused in front of the cell that held Ash and Malik. She could see the circlet of keys jangling from the waist of the man in front.

He slid a metallic tray to the boys through a slot on their cell floor. The men were being fed, even if it was a single loaf to be shared between them and a tin cup for water. The guard turned to Amaris and smiled. His teeth were yellow with a terribly greenish hue to the edges. "I'm afraid you won't be needing a meal where you're going, girl. You seem to have made a powerful enemy."

The men walked away with a dark laugh shared between them, continuing down the hall rather than returning from where they'd come. Their cruelty had been a source of amusement wherever it carried them. Their footsteps echoed for a long, long while. From the sounds it made, the hall seemed to have no end. What sort of circular jail…

It was the halo.

Amaris remembered the animal, and recalled musing at how the castle must appear from a bird's eye view. She remembered the structure behind the castle she'd seen as it had betrayed its outlines from the shores in Priory. As the reevers had approached the Castle of Aubade only one day before, Amaris had noted the structure to look like that of a horse. The throne room and surrounding space for courtiers had been its long snout. The four towers, what would have been the ears and rectangular band attaching the towers, would have comprised the horse's eyes; those were presumably reserved for the regency. There had been a circular shape on the back of the castle, visible only in snatches between the buildings as they'd ridden up because of how the castle sat on a hill. At the time, she'd thought of it as a halo. It had stirred a memory of the sparring ring in Uaimh Reev. Their cells were a part of the enormous ringlet of the circle, which would make the center… a coliseum.

They were in the dungeon of a coliseum.

The boys didn't touch their food. The presence of bread and water in their cell sent a message perhaps as chilling to them as hers was to her. Ash and Malik were meant to be kept alive to whatever awaited them, perhaps making them wish that they, too, had died with her. The men were wordless as they stared at the dirty, white-haired young woman. There was Amaris: their friend, their brother in arms, first female reever in centuries, moonlight personified, incredible warrior, faster than lightning and powerful speaker with lavender eyes able to rightly see through enchantments. She was a force crafted by the goddess herself, an entity neither Farehold nor Raascott could have predicted. And she was going to die. The guards had said as much themselves. Ash and Malik were set apart to see her die.

How long would they be left here while the queen passed her sentence? Would it be days, weeks? Perhaps Moirai meant only to allow Amaris to starve to death, her secrets dying with her. What would become of Malik and Ash? Would they be tortured to see what they knew, to see if the reevers had a plan to bring down Moirai and her deception, using their oath to stand against unholy powers?

Her dread was cut short by a new sound. Was there no reprieve from interruptions? Could they not be left alone to mourn and grieve together before Moirai had her final word? Once again it was that of footsteps, boots scraping on stone. There seemed to be only one set this time, though now that she strained her ears, she could hear two voices. One was a man's and the other, a woman. Was it the queen? No, the voice was too young, too gentile to belong to Moirai. What were they saying?

The man stepped into view first—a soldier dressed in a golden breastplate adorned by the sigil of the queen. Behind him followed a young, bronze woman with supple curves draped in black silk.

$$☽ ☽ ☽ ☽ ● ☾ ☾ ☾ ☾$$

Nox had never known weightlessness before this moment.

Her soul left her body as she saw who stood, filthy and gagged, in the jail cell before her. She couldn't breathe. Couldn't think. Couldn't move. The world evaporated away into a dizziness that may have been a dream, melting her feet into the cream-cobbled floor. She needed to stand, though she wanted to sink. She needed to run, though she wanted to collapse. She felt all of these things and more in the length it took for a muted, gagged shout to come from the lips of the prisoner.

Nox broke free from whatever had glued her to the ground, pushing past the armored shoulders of the captain so quickly that she seemed to dissolve through him as if he were nothing, flying to the white-haired girl. A primal cry-the cry of years of anguish, of longing, of love—tore from her as she fell to the floor in front of the iron bars and Amaris's name ripped its way from her throat. Amaris was pressed into the bars, the guttural screams of recognition and surprise and desperation and terror and helplessness scraping past her gag. Nox's fingers clawed through the bars and their slits, pulling her close, stroking too quickly at her hair, holding her too tightly through the bars.

"Amaris," she sobbed, the sound of the moonlit girl's name a strangled, wretched thing as Nox's shoulders heaved. She didn't even recognize the sound of her own voice. Her knees gave away and they both fell to the ground, iron between them. She couldn't even find the strength to kneel. They clutched in a salted, weeping collapse of fear and tragedy and reunion.

Tears flowed in hot, salty rivers down Amaris's face, carving wet paths through the dirt that had smudged her milky features, running over the fabric that gagged her. As soon as she'd managed to look up from her embrace, Nox tore at the gag. The fabric that held the girl's tongue still was too tight. It took her only a second to realize what she could do to help. The young woman fumbled into her inky hair, forgetting how to put her fingers into motion. She found it, fingers stilling against the object. She produced a razor-sharp hair pin, slipping it between the bars and working at the fabric that wrapped itself tightly around Amaris's face. Nox sliced the gag free and Amaris joined in the sobbing, their sounds rattling the very earth around them.

"Shh, shh," Nox pulled her into the tightest embrace she could manage through the bars that separated them. She continued stroking the girl's hair too fast, with too much built up intensity as love and the need to comfort overwhelmed her, even if Nox was the one who needed shushing, given the shudders of her tears. These were the throttled, hysterical, gagged sobs of years of separation. Any emotion that had jarred and stunned her upon initially seeing Amaris had broken into countless painful shards, now the powder of a million fragments of broken glass that tinkled around them like the falling snow. She had spent fifteen years at Farleigh protecting and comforting Amaris— dedicating her life to shielding, loving, and looking out for her snowflake. What could she do now that she played the role of the wicked whore on the wrong side of the bars? It should be her locked up, not gentle Amaris.

Nox's shushes were useless. They were more for herself than for the reever, as her shoulders shook and her sobs were louder than any other noise in the room. Amaris had never seen those dark eyes cry. She'd never seen her tremble or shake as she did now.

If this was their chance, she had to take it. Amaris spun away quickly, offering her rope-bound hands to the raven-haired girl who immediately began to cut and slice at them using the tiny blade that had been concealed within her jeweled hair pin. She broke through one coil, then another. The rope's tendrils fell away and the women were able to hold each other, grasping with the force of two entities refusing to ever let go. Their arms wrapped through the bars, each gripping at the back of the other, pressing each into themselves. Hair and clothes and skin and bodies gripped and pushed and held with unrelenting intensity. They couldn't be close enough, couldn't clutch hard enough.

Nox would never have imagined this to be their reunion. She'd dreamed of the moment they were finally together once more. She'd pictured it, she'd wished for it, she'd wanted it. Now, her love was an uncontrollable wave breaking against a cliff. In one moment they were hugging, and in the next, Nox's mouth was on Amaris's. It was not the mouth she had offered to patrons at The Selkie, as those had been born of survival and manipulation. They were not the lips given to Emily, for those kisses had been stolen, as her heart had always belonged to another. This salted, tear-soaked was a kiss meant only for Amaris. Despite the anger and pain, despite the tension and tragedy, it was somehow tender, full of all of the adoration she'd held in her heart for all of these years. Passion and hurt and separation and desperation met in the gentle, tragic connection of their lips.

"No," Nox choked against the kiss, unable to reel in her pain. "No, this can't be it." She pulled her in closer, kissing her with desperation. Their lips locked in anguish, mouths tasting of salt and plum and winter and dirt. This was not the moment they deserved.

The white-haired girl had her hands on the back of Nox's head, one knotting in her hair as she returned their kiss with all of the love and sorrow and intensity and agony of their moons and seasons apart. She held her with a passion born from the fifteen wasted years before their fateful separation. The movement was shattered only by the ragged breaths of broken sobs as heartache and waves of emotion continued to crash over them.

Nox tore from the kiss, leaning her forehead against Amaris's.

"I'm going to get you out of here," her voice was low and hurried, broken only by the ragged sobs she struggled to steady herself. Nox found her voice, whipping to the quiet centurion. Her dark eyes narrowed at the captain, "Eramus, where are the keys?"

Amaris blinked up as if noticing the captain for the first time.

Answering the darting question in Amaris's eyes, Nox mumbled from the side of her mouth, "He's with me."

Amaris noticed for a moment that her brothers were still in the opposing cell. They'd frozen in the same position that had gripped them the moment Nox had arrived. Neither had moved, as shock and confusion had plastered them to the floor. This moment was not about them. Amaris had already said her wordless goodbyes to Malik and Ash. Now was her time with Nox. If anyone could save her, it would be the one who'd protected her from the bishop, who'd taken the beatings, who'd rescued her from market and from the matrons and from the peers at Farleigh. If she had to see one final face on this earth, it should belong to Nox.

While Amaris had briefly taken stock of the shell-shocked reevers, Eramus wobbled an uncaring arm off in some distance, offering the name of a man they didn't know in the location they didn't understand. Irrespective of his words, the message was clear: there would be no key. Nox flew to the lock that held Amaris's jail cell, wriggling her hairpin into its opening, desperate to hear the freeing click of its unlock. Her hairpin snapped in her fervor. She froze. Nox stared at it, horrified.

Nox had gone rigid, petrified at her blunder. Her eyes widened in disbelief as she gaped at the broken pin lodging itself firmly into the lock. She couldn't believe it. It couldn't be possible. Amaris couldn't be trapped. She couldn't have failed.

Amaris didn't know how to pick locks, but she knew enough of the situation to understand that not only had Nox's attempt not worked, but that the lock was now jammed from the outside. Her lilac eyes had exhausted their fear. She'd emptied herself of whatever emotions one was supposed to feel. She was not angry. She was no longer crying. She lifted her purple irises to Nox's dark, panicked eyes and offered a small, comforting smile. Her pale hand returned to Nox's hair. It was her turn to comfort her friend as she stroked her long, inky locks.

Maybe she was doomed, her heart felt that over perhaps that was okay. This wasn't the worst way she could die. She was no longer gagged, alone, and separated. She wasn't desperate, unheard, and abandoned. The goddess had granted her a final miracle. Her last moments on earth had been blessed with their reunion. If she had to pass on to be with the All Mother, this was the most beautiful way she could die.

"I'm going to get you out," Nox said again. While stunning beyond words, more lovely than Amaris had ever remembered seeing the girl, her beautiful features were painted with every artistic stroke of panic and grief. Amaris may be feeling peace in her resolution, but for every passing moment of calm and acceptance the reever felt, Nox's hysteria only grew. After all this time, they were mere inches from one another the iron bars sent a clear message: they may as well have been a continent apart.

A sword composed of sound and light cut through their efforts. Its lurching noise jolted them from their moment, causing everyone in the room to flinch in surprise.

A golden, piercing beam cut into the prison, blinding everyone. Malik and Ash, who had been watching with unhinged jaws of bewilderment, raised their arms to shield their eyes. Eramus did the same, holding his hands up in front of his face like a child playing a hiding game. Nox and Amaris squinted against the bar of light as it grew wider, stretching from where the wooden wall of her cell was beginning to split open.

Her cell had was not three bars and a fourth wooden barrier. It was no wall, Amaris realized as fear twisted within her. She had been positioned against a great and terrible door into the coliseum. She should have known this is why she'd been separated from the reevers. She should have understood it the moment she'd connected the curvature of their dungeon with the shape that had attached itself to the back of the castle. Life was full of 'should haves'. Maybe they were as useless as 'what ifs'.

Nox looked distinctly unhinged. Her eyes were wild. Her hands tore for the ivory reever. Two men entered from the blinding light of day that had opened into the jail and started to drag her backwards out of her cell. Nox screamed in protest, her lovely hand reaching fruitlessly through the bars for Amaris as she struggled.

Amaris whipped her head around wildly, taking in the enormity of the coliseum with its teeming crowds of onlookers and the heat of the high noon sun, all absorbed in mere heartbeats. Her eyes swam painfully as they struggled to adjust to the change in light. She was still looking to Nox and screamed a command, eyes darting wildly between her and the reevers. "Save them!"

"I love you," Nox sobbed, gripping the bars with both hands as she became smaller and smaller in the distance. Her cries were otherworldly, ripping from a depth of suffering known to the pits of hell. She didn't even know what she was saying. Her heart ached, her tears lubricated the iron of the bars. Her fingers gripped uselessly against the metal that had separated them. "I love you," she said again as the doors began to shut.

Amaris had no words. The lights, the sounds, the enormity of it all crushed down on her. Her eyes whipped back to the Nox one last time. She had awoken in the cell with a blow to the head and a gag in her mouth. She'd worked through Moirai's powers, been reunited with

Nox, and been dragged backward into the high-noon sun of the coliseum. She was so overwhelmed she couldn't find any words known to man. She had forgotten how to think, how to feel, how to speak.

Nox hurled her final words, the last thing Amaris could hear before the doors drowned out the shouts. "Just buy time!"

That had been Nox's final plea. She had begged Amaris to buy time.

The gruff hands released her, giving her a shove away from them as they turned to leave her behind. A second door stood ajar to accept the men. Amaris dashed for it with the speed and wildness of a cat. She had been too overrun with shock, grief and fear to duck the blocking blow that came from the guard, a blow she would have dodged one million times over within the sparring ring of the reev. She flew to her back, wind knocked briefly from her lungs as the men escaped through the door and bolted it behind them.

28

The coliseum at the Castle of Aubade was ten times the size of the ring at Uaimh Reev in the most modest of estimations. The ring at the reev had been a friendly place, with granite stairs leading all the way from its top to its bottom. Anyone training could easily run from the center of the ring to the crest of its stairs and back again. Here, flattened walls nearly forty—no, fifty feet high— surrounded every inch of the coliseum, save for another large door on the opposite end and a few other latched and bolted wooden openings, presumably to cells elsewhere in the dungeon. What mastery of masonry and crazed architect had decided on this smooth, cream fishbowl for its fights? The grandeur was absurdist at best, a display of the royal family's madness at worst.

Those in attendance weren't merely the courtiers from the throne room, but the entire city seemed to buzz with excitement as they watched Amaris, child of snow and silver, stumble from her edge of the enclosure. Tens of thousands of voices and bodies screamed and roiled like insects in the stadium above. The heat of the blue, clear day felt suffocating as it reflected brightly off the sand. It was utterly disrespectful that the sun would bake down on them during a moment like this. This was not a day for cloudlessness, but an occasion that called for the goddesses's rain, thunder and wrath.

Amaris shook off her insultingly hideous juggler's jacket and dropped it to the ground, leaving herself only in the bare shoulders of her linen shirt, bustier, and black tights. She would not die in the puffy sleeves of a court entertainer. The sun was directly overhead which was something of a blessing as it did not shine into her eyes, allowing her to scan the stadium. She rotated, soaking in every detail of the enormous circular structure.

Only one, small thing accompanied her in the entirety of its great, oval sands. She was too far to clearly see what was with her on the arena's floor. If it wasn't moving, then it didn't matter. She ignored it as she continued to look for a way out.

There had to be a way to escape. She thought briefly of the dark fae. Could they save her? If she looked to the skies, might they fly in and grab her? No, there were no shadows to offer them cover. This was the hot, high-noon heat of a blistering summer day. There would be nothing to shelter them here.

Even if it weren't the broad light of day, a row of what must have been twenty marksmen lined the bottom tier of the stadium fifty feet overhead, planting their protective weapons directly in front of Queen Moira. They stood with the stillness of statues, all wearing metallic breastplates with the queen's insignia. The archers held their bows, strings drawn loosely in a ready but resting position. She could see from the glint of the sun that every one of the arrows they'd nocked were made of wing-shredding, Raascot-murdering metal. The queen was sending her a message.

Amaris stumbled further to the center as she absorbed the sounds of their cheers and jeers alike. There was no stockade, no noose. There was no executioner. Why hadn't the queen left her to rot? If her secret was so precious, why would she risk allowing Amaris to see the light of day?

Her eyes refocused on the only other thing that had joined her on the sands. In the center of the coliseum, she saw a single blade displayed upon two, rough-hewn wooden stands of twin sawhorses on the sand. She was being given a sword. Perhaps this was why she'd been tied with rope. She'd been meant to free herself before the public on this blade.

Amaris began to walk toward the sword. The garbled words of what may have been hundreds, thousands, or millions of onlookers for all it mattered created the white noise of a stream, their noise completely unintelligible and of utter disinterest to the reever. She approached the blade cautiously, examining the single, simple sword before her. She and the blade were alone on the enormous sand floor of the stadium. The crowd hummed with excitement in a way that told her she would not be alone for long.

Somehow, she was too dead inside to feel anything. She didn't feel afraid. She didn't feel excited or nervous or prepared. Nox was here. Nox had told her to buy time. The only people she'd ever loved or trusted were here. She did not feel alone.

If she had to die, it was okay to do it knowing that she was with the ones she loved.

A voice bellowed as if from everywhere and nowhere. Amaris spun, scanning the crowd until she found the shaded alcove of the queen behind her archers, accompanied by a similar performatively empty chair to the one she'd seen in the throne room. Moirai was in a stone space carved out of the stadium—a box seat just for the royal family. Any voice that loud, that bellowing should have been possessed by none but the goddess. Once Amaris spotted the southern queen, it was impossible to take her eyes off the woman. Queen Moirai wore a rich crimson gown. A matching ruby necklace gleamed upon her pale chest, and she wore a golden crown with red gems to complete the look of wealth and bloodlust. The red of her regalia was in such stark contrast to the homespun of peasants and commonfolk filling the stadium and all of its seats. The wealthy courtiers were near the queen, flanking her on various sides of the shaded box. At least a few had joined her within the carved alcove, cooling themselves with elaborate fans. A few members of the nobility flanked her box seat, sitting primly beneath what appeared to be the shade of an umbrella. They nobility were dressed in their finery for the festive occasion. Amaris watched the queen, wondering what spelled object could amplify a voice so powerfully. The way Queen Moirai's voice resonated throughout the stadium, she was surprised more people didn't cower or wince in fear.

"My people!" Moirai had begun, her crimson arms raised to greet the masses.

Amaris scarcely heard the first two words of the speech and she already felt her stomach church in disgust. The crowd did not appear to feel the same. Their returning cry was the barbaric excitement of men and women awaiting a blood sport.

Moirai addressed the crowd with the ear-splitting volume of her words as it coated every inch of the stadium, drowning the people in her voice. "For centuries, the keep of Uaimh Reev has rested on the border between Raascot and Farehold."

The mention of the northern kingdom drew curdling boos and jeers from the people. Moirai offered appropriate pause for them to sneer and yell their anger at their enemies to the north.

"For hundreds of years," she boomed, "the reevers have pretended to be our friends, our allies against dark forces. We have offered them sanctuary throughout the churches and temples of our lands, believing their lies when they spoke of peace!" Queen Moirai paused dramatically.

The woman had the citizens enraptured. They clung to her every word. Amaris was paralyzed, little more than a pillar of stone while she listened to the wicked deceptions of the illusionist queen. This was why she hadn't been left to rot in her cell. Moirai meant to make an example of the reever.

"The crown prince and I offered our magnanimity just yesterday, inviting this reever before you into our palace! And what did she do?"

The pregnant pause hushed the crowd, pressing the question down on the people.

"She revealed herself for what she is: a demon sympathizer!"

The citizens of Aubade went rabid in their stadium seats. They screamed at the blasphemy and outrage of the information shared by their queen. Men, women and children alike hurled a cacophony of insults, their voices an unreadable outpouring of incensed sounds. Vitriol rolled in from the stands, crashing against her from all sides of the coliseum like nauseating waves. Amaris had tuned them out, stilling her heart against their anger. She couldn't listen to the people. She wouldn't accept their cries. Her eyes were screwed onto Moirai alone.

The queen spoke over them, "Not only do the reevers *not* seek peace against the dark evils that plague our land, but they would have us allow demons to roam freely, eating our children, raping our women, and murdering our citizens! Is this the peacekeeper of legend, or do we see her for the witch she is!"

The sun scorched Amaris, burning her white shoulders. Her hair felt hot from the light of the sun. Sweat beaded on her forehead, dripping down from what was left of the elaborate braids atop her head. Despite the heat, she felt a bone-chilling cold leech through her body. Her pulse was weak and distant. She tried to wet her lips but found her mouth was dry. The audience may as well have been a brick wall for all the attention she gave it, her lavender eyes focused solely on crimson speck of the despicable queen.

"Good people, I give you your demon-loving reever of Uaimh Reev, enemy to the crown. Show the citizens if I am lying, reever! And strike down a demon."

491

A door opened then within the stadium. It wasn't the giant door opposite her, but a wooden cell slightly off to one side. She grabbed for the sword, holding the metal of its sun-baked hilt tightly as she looked to what was stumbling out of the dark space in the wall before the doors slammed and bolted behind him. She knew what the crowd saw the moment the shape lurched forward, its massive wings slashed to ribbons. While every citizen of Aubade shrieked at the ghastly, monstrous presence of an ag'imni, Amaris gaped in horror at the battered face of Gadriel.

29

Irrespective of the distance between them, Amaris could see the unmistakable glint of a purely evil smile on Queen Moira's face. She locked eyes with the only other person in Farehold who could see that what stood before her was a dark-haired fae man. When she tore her eyes from the queen, she was determined never to look at the crimson witch again.

"Gad," her voice called across the sands of the coliseum floor, mouth dry with sand, dehydration, and fear.

He stumbled forward, his hands still bound.

"I told you not to come," her voice was thick.

"It's a little late for that, don't you think?" He responded with a humorless emptiness. After a few more steps toward the center, he knelt on the sand.

What had they done to him? While the two primary ligaments of his dark, angelic wings remained on either side, grisly slashes had torn through their connective tissues and membranes. The blood that plastered his feathers together had dried, informing her that this had been an atrocity committed during the night. His hands were tied with rope like that of Amaris's former constraints and his left upper cheek was purpling with bruises. This was the man who had held a knife to her throat in the forest to defend his soldier. This was the general who fought for his king, knowing the risk every day. This dark fae warrior knew no fear. He had fallen to his knees before her now.

Amaris ran to him, cutting his bound hands free with the sword. The action won her no favors from the hissing crowd, but nothing she could do on the goddess's lighted earth would have pleased the queen or Aubade's deceived people.

He didn't look up. "You have to kill me."

He wasn't regretful, accusatory, or frightened. The resolution in his voice was both calm and absolute.

"Gad—" She was repulsed by his words, recoiling as the ropes fell free from his hands.

He didn't look up at her. Maybe some part of him knew it would make the task before her more difficult if she had to look into his eyes. The general offered her an olive branch to dehumanize himself, to spare her own soul. He knelt before no one. He feared nothing. Yet here he was, on his knees.

"They see a demon, and you know it. If you spare me as an ag'imni, they will kill you. You're worth so much more to this continent alive, Amaris. Do it now."

Gadriel kept his head lowered, not out of fear, but to give her a clean blow to the back of his neck. It was an act of kindness to her so that she would not have to see his face while he died.

"Gadriel—"

"Do it, Amaris." She could hear how he grit his teeth between his words. "I die, or we both die. However you slice it, I'm not making it out of here alive." His great, shredded wings sagged behind him as he spoke.

Anger surged through her. She grabbed him roughly by the arm, hoisting him inelegantly to his feet. "Shut up unless you're going to say something useful."

"Amaris—" His eyes lifted to hers, their gaze touching as he resisted.

"I said shut it. And you never call me by my right name. Don't bother starting now."

He had seen his death as the only way forward, but her rejection of his solution was final. He'd offered, and she'd slapped it away. There would be no clean end to whatever befell them. Gadriel had spent too many years training in battle to act the part of a coward. Even in his sacrificial death, he'd meant to go with pride and honor. If they were going to fight, then they were going to fight. He wouldn't prostrate himself before the crowd now that she'd made up her mind. The general had been ready to give his life for Raascot's cause, but if the child of the moon would refuse to swing her blade, then so be it. He would not show another moment of weakness.

He found a smile, "A witchling even in death."

She returned the upward twitch of her mouth, "Would you have it any other way?"

They each had their knees slightly bent, the prepared stance of warriors on a battlefield. The crowd around them was shouting, crying for something. A word was starting to form on their lips, taking on the consistency of a chant. The pockets of the chant were broken up enough that she couldn't quite hear what three syllables the people were bleating in unison.

She looked to him to see if he could understand the people any better than she could, but the general seemed to be scanning for something else entirely. An exit strategy? A weapon? A plan?

"Do you see!" Moirai roared to the people using the magnifying power of whatever spelled objected allowed her to be heard throughout the stadium. Farehold's queen had known precisely how this would play out. Amaris, who could see that there was no crowned prince, who knew of the curse at the border, who had called her out for the witch she was in front of her court, would not have swung the killing blow on the northerner for whom she'd come to the castle to intercede. Letting the ivory reever die in her cell would have let the curse's secrets die with her. Showing her ag'imni sympathies to the people would instead rally the queen's loyalists against the reevers, deepening their hatred for the north and uniting them against any hope of peace that could have come from Uaimh Reev.

"And what should we do to our enemies! What do we do with those who consort with demons!"

The chant from the audience grew louder as more and more joined in its chorus. Hundreds of people were saying the word over and over again, the same three sounds like a howling, wretched prayer to the goddess. Screams garbled out the consistency of their chants. The crowd was in bloodthirsty hysterics as the citizens of Aubade were unified by their hatred.

She looked at none of them. She saw none of them. The sun burned her shoulders and their sounds hurt her ears, but there was only her, her sword, and Gadriel. Moirai wouldn't earn the satisfaction of her attention again.

The queen continued her impassioned address to the savage crowd, "We throw them to the monsters they worship and we let hell reclaim them!"

Her sentence was punctuated by the cranking, metallic sound of gears. Wood groaned and chains strained. The audience lost its mind as the noise washed over the sand. Amaris turned her body to face its source, a blackened, rectangular shadow slowly spreading before her. The door on the far side of the stadium began to open, so large and thick that the aching screeches of the mechanisms used to pry the door apart echoed throughout the coliseum. A ripping, ear-shredding roar of a monster tore from the inky darkness as the door continued its slow, mechanical opening. The door clanked to its final opening and the reever took a backward step, fighting off the dread that threatened her.

Amaris had been numb, then angry, then resolute.

Now, as she stared into the foreboding shadows and the monstrous screams that tore through them, she felt true fear.

Gadriel and Amaris moved their feet deftly, positioning themselves side by side, slowly backing from the center of the stadium. They moved on instinct, putting as much space between themselves and the shadow as possible. Their eyes remained glued on the darkness of the enormous door's open mouth. Another thundering, unholy shriek, pierced the eardrums of everyone in the stadium, causing the two to flinch. They remained on guard as they backed up, Amaris with her blade held before her. Gadriel had no weapons, nor did he have his wings.

The sound was clear now. She comprehended the three syllables the people had been chanting the moment the black, four-legged obsidian snake tore from the dungeons. Its jaw unhinged revealing layer upon layer upon layer of needle-like teeth, jagged and wildly strewn about its horrible maw. Its serpentine neck, unnaturally long and horribly flexible, wriggled skyward as it cried its terrible, hungry call to every unholy beast of the continent. The scarred wings, nearly large enough to fill the coliseum, beat in such a forceful singular blast that it blew Gadriel and Amaris backward, nearly knocking them from their feet. They remained firm though the sharp, blowback bites of sand and dirt assaulted their skin as they winced against its force. They stared as the beast adjusted its front two feet, planting itself onto the sand and eyeing them with hunger in its demonic, soulless eyes. The crowd invoked the three syllables of its name over and over as they begged to see the justice of its wrath.

Ag'drurath.

497

30

"Any ideas?" Gadriel exhaled slowly beside her. His empty hands were raised to fight.

"Yeah," Amaris hissed, "don't die."

She remembered the hard point of metal between her breasts and fished the thin dagger Gadriel had given to her after he'd landed on her balcony from where she had stashed it in her bustier.

She passed it off to him, and even in their moments of peril, he managed sarcasm. "Perfect, I was just thinking if only I had a throwing knife—"

Another shriek from the monster cut them off.

This was why the walls were so high. How long had this demon been enslaved by the royal family? The snake was covered in the scars, lashings and wounds speaking of abuses that spanned decades, if not centuries. The horrid monster had been carved and mutilated from its eyes and legs to its wings and tail. Odrin had once told her that if she ever came across this beast, she should say her final prayers to the All Mother. Amaris knew one, and only one thing of the ag'drurath: they could not be killed.

Staying still would not serve them. They may not have had the luxury of training together, but they had the shorthand of warriors. The two sprinted for the far end of the arena as the quadrupedal serpent galloped for the center of the stadium, lurching backward against the night-dark well of its dungeon as its right hind leg caught on an iron manacle, the clamp and chains thicker and heavier than any work of rock or metalsmithing Amaris could have fathomed. Remaining pressed against the far wall offered them no safety, for the remaining distance could be closed by the black snake's neck. Its neck alone was the equivalent length of its body, and that was before one even considered the monstrous tail it possessed. The dragon beat its wings again, nearly sending the pair off of their feet with its hurricane force. The enormous dragon was a worm, serpent, demon, and monster all at once. Its shrieks were the legions of the undead, its teeth the thing of nightmares. Amaris couldn't look at it for too long or she'd lose her resolve. It may as well have been a large horse. A horse with millions of needle-like teeth. And wings. And that couldn't be killed.

"What do we do?" Gadriel asked, bracing himself against the gust. He was a general. He gave commands, not asked them—yet reevers were known for their studies of beasts and magic. If anyone would have an inkling of hope against one of the continent's demons, it would be a reever. So few of the draconic beasts existed that if you ever came upon one, your only instructions had been to say your parting prayers that your soul be accepted by the goddess.

Yes, she was the reever, but she felt a surge of incredulity. Gadriel was a leader. She should be asking *him* for battle plans. Yet whatever had led him to trust that if she killed him it would be for the good of the continent emboldened him to ask her now.

"We buy time," she grunted before abandoning him.

Amaris took off with fox-like agility and speed, hugging the edge of the stadium. The dragon's serpentine eyes followed her as she sprinted, and she sensed the beast coiling up to strike. The moment she felt the tension snap and the needle-toothed maw propel toward her, she used a move she'd perfected at the reev: she dove toward her enemy, tucking the drive into a roll and continuing her sprint toward its legs while the face of the beast careened into the wall of the coliseum. Its face hit the wall with the loud crack of thunder. The ag'drurath winced from the great force of its impact, unleashing another scream meant to melt the bones and minds of its prey with terror. There was one thing Amaris knew about being small when facing a large enemy: weight and size were as much a disadvantage as they were an asset.

It took Gadriel no time at all to understand the task at hand. Whether they wore it down, knocked it out, or simply lived to battle the beast until they could stand no longer, they would fight with every clawing breath to buy themselves precious time. The ag'drurath was still shaking off the pain of its impact with the wall as he began to assess the best way to distract the creature.

While Amaris was darting for the space near its legs, he saw the beast track her movement. It readjusted its snake-like neck head, bobbing to the music of an unheard song while it eyed her hungrily. The screaming sounds of the crowd were the music of war, composing a terrible symphony for their battle. Gadriel looked to the snake again, then to the reever. Its attention was fixed on her.

The dragon could snatch her in its needle-like teeth in a second. The ag'drurath had honed in on Amaris, its forked tongue darting past the horrible rows of jagged teeth as it tasted the air for her scent. With his slashed wings, the general could not fly, nor could he roll as Amaris had done due to their girth. One thing he could still do, though, was distract. He rushed in the opposite direction, flaring his broken, bloodied wings to draw the attention of the monster as it poised to strike for Amaris. He was vaguely aware of a piercing pain as his torn wings drew the dragon's eyes, but he shoved the excruciating sensation into a numb place within himself.

The beast turned for Gadriel, its attacking maw fixed on his outstretched wings just as Amaris swung for its leg. The blow caught it utterly unprepared. The creature screamed, eye line drawn to the pain at its front left leg. Her wound had been shallow, meant to divert rather than to maim. The black oil of its blood, stinking like the carrion from the beseul, oozed from the wound. Thin, smoke-like lines wove their way through its blackened blood, stitching the skin of the creature slowly back together where she had sliced. The action seemed only to irritate the monster as hell itself sewed it together before her eyes. The monstrous dragon flapped its great wings, succeeding in knocking Gadriel to the ground with the attack's rush of wind as the fae's own wingspan remained outstretched. The dragon's wings worked against the fae, wielding wind as its weapon.

For just the barest of moments, Gadriel was on his back.

The creature made another lunge as if to close the distance, but its concentration was snagged by the painful jerk of the chain on its back right leg. The noise it loosed from its reptilian throat in anger was a chilling, unnatural thing. The length of its enraged scream was all the time Gadriel needed to be on his feet. When he drew its eyes, she moved. They switched parts in a dance to the death.

Amaris was under the dragon's belly again, slashing at its tender part. She cried out with exertion as she swung her sword, her sound joining the screams of the crowd and wails from the beast.

Would one distract, one would wound. There was no other plan. They would buy minutes. It was all they could do as the citizens of Aubade screamed for their blood, watching a reever, an ag'imni, and a dragon battle to the death under the hot summer sun as their wicked queen grinned down at them.

The people, the queen, the season didn't matter.

Buy time. All they could do was buy time.

Time was not an easy ask when facing the ag'drurath. They didn't have the luxury of time that one might find while battling any normal beast, for the serpent's neck could swivel with the unnatural grace of something born only from the depths the goddess had cursed to her hell. Still, their plan was working. It was not a good plan, and it had no end game, but every second they bought on this earth was one more moment that they defied the queen. They would not go down as willing meals to be cursed in the infinite, pin-like fangs of the ag'drurath. The dragon swiveled its neck and looked to its stomach where Amaris still slashed.

The reever slid against the sand, kicking up a cloud of dust as she plunged her blade once more, grunting against the effort as she thrust upward into its belly a second time. The general was near the coliseum's wall. As long as she drew the dragon to the space beneath its stomach, he'd be safe for a few more moments.

Gadriel beat his wings against the hurt it caused him, finding the barest of lifts from the ground. It wasn't the flight he should have been capable of, but the general took full advantage of his opportunity. He plunged into the monster's neck, stabbing the ag'drurath's elongated throat with the throwing knife. While the pair had no hope of a killing blow, the knife made purchase, allowing Gadriel to cling to its neck while it flailed, once again drawn from Amaris to a new and more horrible attention as his sharp blade bit into its long, reptilian throat. The creature was savage as it thrashed, desperate to shake him off.

This game had no end. There was no victory here. Gadriel clung to its neck, blade embedded in its tinder skin while it writhed. She could continue to hack and slash, trading places with him for as long as they could muster their stamina.

They couldn't keep this up forever. Amaris's lungs burned. Her legs ached. Sweat and heat and dust coated her face, her hands, her throat. She knew she couldn't quit, but when she was told to buy time, she had no idea how to expend or preserve her stamina. Gadriel was hurt. People were screaming over the thrill of watching their murder. The ag'drurath was agitated, but would outlast them both. A surge of helplessness coursed through her as she eyed the monster.

Amaris looked for her next best move to draw its attention when, from the door through which the guards who had dragged her had left, out stumbled a disoriented, gold-breasted Captain of the Guard. While Gadriel kept the beast panicked in its need to shake him from its neck, the captain rushed for the creature's leg, his ornate sword raised. Amaris comprehended the sacrifice immediately.

She couldn't let the ag'drurath see the captain. Not yet.

Amaris slashed again at the belly, keeping its eyes from the soldier.

"Nox," the reever whispered the young woman's name like a prayer on her lips, knowing what she had done.

Eramus closed the gap and began hacking at the great trunk of the dragon's back right leg, just above where the chain had cuffed it to the dungeons for goddess knew how many years. The dragon shrieked unnaturally, flinging the winged fae successfully from its neck with a *thwack* as he careened into the coliseum wall. Gadriel slumped on impact. The Captain of the Guard, gilded breastplate reflecting the sunlight, continued his barbaric attempts at amputation, feeling and seeing nothing around him as he was possessed with the single-minded need to cut and slice exactly here, exactly this place, exactly now.

The dragon coiled, then striked.

The ag'drurath dove its mighty, unholy maw and had the captain in his jaws in a second. Erasmus's face and shoulders had been swallowed, disappearing into the void of its throat. The black creature raised its neck skyward, allowing gravity to aid it as its needle teeth crunched down on his breastplate. The sounds of metal and bone against teeth echoed above the cries from the people as they screamed in shock, their world turned upside down by his appearance.

The captain's sword hand continued swinging from where it remained outstretched as if, even as he died in the monster's mouth, he was still consumed with the singular need to hack. The ag'drurath focused its efforts on swallowing, several disgusting, wet crunches of steel and bone and gore echoing through the coliseum as it focused on its bloody, metallic meal. The serpent struggled to swallow him, so the man remained lodged in its mouth. As Eramus went lifeless, his sword clattered to the ground, kicking up a cloud of sand around it with its earth-bound thud.

Unwilling to let this wound heal as the demonic beast already began to show signs of whitish tendrils knitting together, Amaris ran for the back leg to continue what the captain had started. The simple sword left by the queen had been a ploy. The blade had been intended to either behead the dark fae or reveal the reever as a traitor to the crown. This sword would be the very weapon she would use to mutilate the dragon's leg and free it from its shackle. She could feel herself growing tired, but summoned her adrenaline and pushed past the fatigue. Amaris called on her years of training, ignoring the throb in her arms as she battled tendon, muscle, bone, fiber, and the constantly re-knitting, wicked tendrils that crept up through her hacks. She swung the sword in a butchering arc while Gadriel found his feet and sprinted for the captain's fallen weapon.

"Help me!" she cried out to him, but Gadriel didn't need the encouragement. He knew exactly what they were doing.

The audience in the coliseum felt the shift as the tide turned against their demonic dragon champion. Ripples of their anger and fear tore through their throats in waves, joining the sound of the reever and the fae as they hacked and battered the beast, using every second that its attention was on its meal as an opportunity to land their blows. The distracted ag'drurath continued to choke in its attempt to swallow Eramus.

It choked, then discarded the metallic body without consuming it.

The serpentine dragon relinquished its metallic meal, spitting the captain's lifeless body onto the sand with a loud, wet smack. An ocean of blood poured from his chewed, crumpled corpse. If the ag'drurath was no longer focused on Earmus, the reever's window for amputation would close. She escaped from where she had been mangling its blacked, bloodied leg and shot away from the snake. Her silver hair pulled its eyes to her movement while Gadriel slid under its belly, his turn to take a swing at the leg with the anger he held by the power and might of twenty years of his fallen men. The rage of Raascot rained down on the monster's leg as he unleashed his strength to the sound of crunching and shattering bone, relying on Amaris as she sprinted away to hold the giant, beady eyes of the serpent.

The crowd wasn't alone in feeling the tide turn. The more panicked the people became, the more hope filled the reever and the general. Renewed adrenaline surged through her as a glowing burst of energy consumed her. Their screams were a beautiful music, a shrieking wail of optimism that flooded the coliseum like a fishbowl with its magnificent, horrible song. From across the sand, her eyes touched Gadriel's in the briefest of moments as his powerful arms descended on the beast and its leg. His teeth glinted in an angry, terrible smile.

They saw their escape.

The queen, amplified by whatever enchanted magic object allowed her to be heard throughout the coliseum, was screaming to her archers. The men responded in a flurry. The archers began loosing metallic arrows aimed at the reever and the general, their weapons intent on execution. While meant to kill the warriors, these centurions had been chosen for their numbers, not their skill. Their action succeeded only in drawing the pain and fury of the ag'drurath, luring his eyes away from the dueling warriors on the ground to the men and their agonizing, metallic arrows fifty feet high. It reared onto what remained of its hind legs, slamming its front to feet into the stadium wall and arching its black neck up to its maximum height, striking for the archers. The dragon shifted its weight onto its back left leg, focusing its vengeance, its pain, its wounds and mistreatment on the men and their weapons. The centurions screamed their cowardice, scrambling from their posts. The crimson queen fell backward as she crawled on her elbows and legs to push herself as far away from the beast as her shaded alcove would allow before her back was against its stone. The ag'drurath struck successfully at one of the armed men, then a second. The first archer had been a strike to wound, the other was to consume. The archer was gobbled while his men in arms ran, terrified by the black serpent. Its attention remained fixed on the fleeing soldiers, leaving just enough time for Gadriel to land the final, mutilating chop at the demon's leg.

It was enough.

The dragon seemed to feel its liberation in the same moment that Amaris and Gadriel knew they had succeeded. The screams of the people and amplified, craven screams of the wicked queen intermingled with the legion of the serpent's demonic shrieks. It released itself from its prone position against the wall and flapped its wings once, then twice. It began to move away from the chain before its smokey tendons knit together.

"Let's go!" Gadriel scrambled for the ag'drurath, trying to pull himself from the spikes that ran along its spine. He hooked himself around a sharp, bony spine that writhed in time with its movements as he pulled himself up from the monster's tail onto its body. He reached an arm for Amaris and she jumped from the sand, grabbing his forearm while he swung her onto the creature. The serpent continued to flap its wings, searching for a lift it hadn't felt in a long, long time.

The dragon sensed its once-chained legs rise from the sand below it and it shrieked again, pumping its thunderous black wings while the audience erupted into chaos, screaming and sprinting, pushing from their seats to escape. The shoving and fleeing sent several clambering audience members over the edge, caught in the selfishness of the thrown elbows and arms around them, plummeting fifty feet into the stadium to their death, cracking and splattering against the unforgiving, packed sand. The cries of the fallen and terrors of the onlookers continued to attract the serpent so it paid no mind to the warriors who struggled to find grips and footholds on its back. The bloodbath caused by the audience's panic was a greater gore than anything the citizens of Aubade had come to witness.

Gadriel used his body to pin Amaris to the beast, clutching her tightly with one arm, shielding her with his bloodied, tattered wings while he held a blackened spine with every ounce of strength in the other arm. His foot was lodged firmly on the spine behind him, pressing them into the space for a semblance of security as the winged serpent broke free.

The dragon used its front feet to tear up the stadium wall, talons ripping apart the coliseum's stone and sending even more citizens careening to their deaths by either the force of its wings, or caught under its claws as it climbed. The queen continued screaming, her shrill, terrified cries amplified by her enchantment object, the gutless sounds of Farehold's spineless monarch filling the stadium. The body of the snake slithered up and over where she was trembling against the royal alcove cut into the stadium. The ag'drurath ripped its way to the coliseum's edge, throwing its great, black body off the back of the structure and over the cliff into the sea where the free fall could allow the monster to find the wind it needed to become truly airborne.

The great serpent shot like a blackened arrow over the city of Aubade, twisting its body away from the civilian's shores and toward the blue horizon of the ocean. It shrieked what may have been a horrible, blood-curdling scream of delight while it twisted in the sky, a tightly rotating spiral darting through the air. Gadriel clutched harder,

Amaris holding both to the fae and to the black spine that jutted out before them on their vile mount. The dark fae's wings acted like an extra pair of hands at her back, cradling her in close to him while the gravitational pull of the dragon's whirl threatened to rip them from their grip of the monster. The ag'drurath shrieked again, its cry the sounds of tin and metal and demons while simultaneously the music of freedom, joy and escape as it shot for the north, keeping the shore to its left and putting the coliseum with its captors and swords and chains as far behind it as it could.

They were free.

Nox, Ash and Malik were picking their way down the back of the coliseum, climbing down the cliff that led to the sea. The moment they'd witnessed the amputating blow to the dragon's leg, they'd run for their lives. Nox had made good on Amaris's final plea, using her hair pins to free the reevers from their cage within the dungeon.

She'd saved them.

Their escape had started the moment the doors had closed behind Amaris. The moonlit girl had been dragged backward by rough, unforgiving hands, torn from Nox's love and sobs while she'd clawed the empty air after her. As soon as the doors had closed, she wiped her tears and found the numbness required to set to work. Her tears would not serve her now.

First, she took another hairpin to their cell, working much more carefully than she had with Amaris's lock, ensuring she didn't make the same mistake twice by breaking her pin and jamming the lock. Nox had to stop twice to wipe away residual tears with the back of her hand, but by the time the two men were out and free of their shackles, Queen Moirai's initial announcements had ended. She'd finished her thundering piece about how the reevers were demon sympathizers.

They'd been forced to listen to every word of her vile lies from their shackles in the dungeon.

By the time the reevers were fully out of their cages, the ag'drurath was thundering its way into the stadium, visible through one of the small windows that had been around the corner while the three had begun their harrowing escape. The serpent was headed directly for Amaris and the ag'imni that the reever had very publicly refused to kill. Its demonic, bat-like wings had been tattered beyond repair. There was no hope for flight or escape. Nox knew that she had only moments before the serpent crushed and devoured the snowflake who stood so vulnerably in the stadium.

She wanted to cry out at the sight in the window, but something unseen within herself slapped her to attention. She couldn't freeze. She couldn't dissociate. She couldn't detach. If she wanted to save Amaris, she needed to stay fully present. She needed to act, and act *now*.

Nox reached the door that had been meant for the guards who had pulled Amaris from her cell and she lifted the wooden band blocking them in. If she could get Amaris's attention and beckon her to safety… but the dragon would never allow them to run across the stadium without a distraction. She could create that distraction.

Nox turned away from the reevers and grabbed Eramus, her dark eyes boring into his. The captain's baby-blue eyes were glazed and obedient as she gripped him.

"Eramus, listen to me! All you want in this world is to cut off the back right leg of the ag'drurath. Do you see where the chain binds it?"

"I want to cut off its right leg."

She growled, tightening her grip on the man, "No, Eramus, it's *all* you want. The only thing in this world that matters to you is the ability to cut off its leg, just above the shackle. Go there. Aim for the joint. You would gladly die if it meant cutting down the leg of the beast and freeing its foot from its binding."

"Hey!" a voice shouted, running for the door.

"Go!" Nox gave him a shove and he stumbled, disoriented, into the coliseum.

Nox finished her push as the centurions came for them. The first guard who reached them swung the wooden door closed and lowered its bolt. Nox leapt backward, creating room for the brawl. She looked for a weapon. She looked for any way to help, but the best she possibly could do at the moment was not make herself a further obstacle as the reevers took over.

Malik and Ash were just as effective in hand-to-hand combat as they were with a sword, whether or not their enemies were armed. It took a few defensive maneuvers, dodges and parries, but the reevers had disarmed the guards, knocked out their opponents, and taken their weapons in the time it had taken for Eramus to sprint for the dragon and begin to cleave at the beast's hind leg. The centurions had been little more than children playing soldier compared to the reevers and their training.

The captain was already well on his way to being devoured by the time the reevers had fully bested the guards, snatching their blades to arm themselves. Nox forced the bolt up, opening the door to call to Amaris, but the final, freeing blow had already been taken to the demon's leg. The two warriors in the pit were grabbing for the spines of the creature, and though Nox knew it was time to flee, she couldn't drag herself from her post. The gargoyle form of an ag'imni was hoisting her snowflake onto the dragon's back.

"Come on!" The redhead was shouting. The golden man tugged at her arm.

She struggled to tear her eyes from Amaris, but shook herself from her stupor. Once more she told herself: she could not go numb. She had to stay present. She had to fight.

Ash took off down the hall to clear a path. While the reever and the general swung atop the beast, Malik grabbed Nox by the wrist and dragged her roughly through the dungeon. He was right to do so, as she wasn't sure that she could ever voluntarily pull herself from the door. Opening that door to escape had been the only way she thought she could have helped Amaris.

The castle fell into complete calamity. Any guard who might have hoped to stop them was running, shouting, fleeing with the chaos as people screamed and ran from the coliseum. Pandemonium was their friend as no one else challenged them or bothered to intervene. Every man was for himself in the wild escape from the building. The three let themselves out through an exit and found themselves atop Aubade's sea cliffs with a narrow path down. Another horrid shriek from the beast overhead sent them scurrying downward, picking their steps and crawling on all fours in their rush to put as much distance between themselves and the ag'drurath as possible.

"Go!" Ash urged them forward, toward the ocean.

They ran. The three had reached the bottom of the cliff, feet practically licked by the saltwater's waves as the black dragon erupted from the coliseum into the blue sky overhead, spinning in rejoice at its freedom from enslavement. The demon had shot like an arrow as fast and as far as it could, beating its wings and pointing its reptilian neck with the wretched aerodynamics of a bat out of hell.

It left a few more shrieks in its wake as its wings carried it into the distance. It wasted no time before it became a black dot, scarcely bigger than a bird on the horizon. The sun had begun to lower, but the summer heat on the cliffs had not provided any relief from the scorching temperatures. Seaspray dotted them while they watched the dragon, immobilized as they witnessed the escape of their friend.

"Where do you think it's going?" Nox looked after it, voice hollow. Her eyes followed what she knew would be the white speck of a snowflake somewhere on its back.

"As far from Farehold as possible. If I were the ag'drurath, I'd head for the Sulgrave Mountains."

31

It had taken them five hours on foot in near silence, but the reevers, with the company of Nox, picked their way into the forest outside of Aubade as the sun began its plunge somewhere over the western sea. They'd abandoned the coast altogether in favor of the safety of the forest. She pointed themselves inland, away from the people. The frenzy that gripped the city had provided more than enough cover for three fleeing criminals, as no one looked twice at them amidst the shouts, looting, and the fleeing civilians.

The reevers had a lot more stamina for running than Nox, and eventually, her adrenaline had begun to wear off. She had scarcely made it out of the city before her legs were too wobbly to continue her retreat. The men kept her on her feet long enough to make it beyond the tree line. No one had the energy to hunt or to start a fire, but when they found a space that felt sheltered enough from the outside world. They stopped on the grass and began to remove their stolen weapons, allowing the heavy objects to clatter to the grass. Nox's delicate silken dress had been torn, shredded by the scratching fingers of the forest. She was too tired to stand. Her skin was raised in the angry red lines of welts from the branches and brambles. She clutched at her shoulders where the gooseflesh rippled down her arm, pulling her knees to her chest. The reevers, still dressed in the court's ridiculous garb, had no cloaks to offer her.

She shouldn't have been so cold in the summer, but as night descended and numbing darkness settled over her, she felt as though ice pumped through her veins. She shivered, teeth chattering.

Their tentative alliance with the raven-hair beauty was new, but they'd been together for hours as they escaped the city. They didn't truly know this stranger, but it was abundantly clear she'd known Amaris. Whatever emotional turmoil they'd faced when seeing Amaris bound and gagged, Nox had suffered ten times over. Ash stood with a bit of uncertainty over his clattered weapons as he watched the girl hug her knees to her chest. They were in truly uncharted waters.

Without waiting for an invitation, Malik sat beside her and put a warming arm around her. Though she hadn't meant to, Nox let herself cry. She hadn't realized she'd been storing a dam of tears from the moment they'd dragged Amaris away. She buried her face in her knees and her shoulders shook with her sobs.

"I'll gather the things for a fire," Ash offered somewhat helplessly.

Nox stilled for a moment, face red and puffy from her sobs. She looked up, wiping her tears with the heel of her palm. Malik's arm was still wrapped around her, protecting her from the chill of the evening, the welts of the forest, the pain of the world.

She met Ash's amber eyes, "Wait."

Ash paused, face blank.

"I wanted to say I'm sorry."

Ash's red brows knit, "For what?"

She offered the ghost of a smile, "For trying to kill you in Yelagin."

His startled look erupted in a short, terse laugh. It was the moment they'd all needed for a break in the tension. It hadn't been nearly as funny as his smile made it out to be, but the pain of the day had allowed any small relief to paint his features with a grin. "I'd say you've done enough to have made amends just fine."

He turned toward the forest with his intent to gather wood but stiffened, back tight.

Sensing his motion, the other two turned from where they'd huddled Nox had huddled for warmth, following his stare. Malik was too much of a bleeding heart to allow Nox to freeze from shock in the wake of her sorrow.

A snap from the trees drew their eyes to whatever Ash had spotted.

The shy face of a monstrous ag'imni waved at them from the underbrush. It made no attempts to advance, waiting for the reevers and the dark-haired girl to acknowledge it.

Though truly terrifying in its appearance, knowing now what they knew about the perception curse, the sight was... silly. A demon: waving.

Malik felt Nox tighten beneath his arm, her heart quickening. Her eyes darted to the fallen swords, but the men did not reach for their weapons.

The ag'imni held up a single twisted talon as if to beckon them to wait a moment and then ducked behind a tree. He reappeared with a bundle of blankets between his spindly, amphibious arms. The absurdity felt dream-like. Perhaps they'd perished in the castle, and this was the afterlife. Maybe they'd been knocked unconscious, and their nightmares and daydreams of escape and of monsters had bled into one another.

Ash extended his hands to accept the bundled offer from the ag'imni. Nox's first instinct was to be baffled at the obscene partnership, or appalled on behalf of the goddess's decency, but there was something else that nudged at her from within her ribs while she watched the exchange. She'd watched Amaris spare a demon from execution. She'd watched an ag'imni hoist her snowflake onto the dragon's back.

"For the lady," the demon shrieked, but the men winced at the shrill, grating sound.

Nox cocked her head, turning from where she sat and shaking herself out from underneath's Malik's arm to face the creature fully.

"For me?"

The ag'imni tilted its grotesque head to the side. It peered at her with the soulless, molten eyes of a demon. It looked at her with both calm and uncertainty.

"You were in Yelagin," it said. The reevers couldn't contain the way they shrank away from the noise, like silver forks squealing in high-pitched, painful tones while they grated across ceramic plates. Nox did not wince. She'd experienced too much pain today. Her heart had undergone enough trauma. She'd learned something of herself: once she'd reached a threshold for horrors, she could transcend into a particular numbness. In moments like these, it was almost helpful.

"I was," she answered honestly, "I saw a demon there, at a farm."

Ash and Malik exchanged looks.

"You can understand us," the demon said.

"I can."

Malik broke the silence, hearing only Nox's verbalizations of the exchange as they came out in what seemed to be responses to the creature's terrible noises of nails, glass, and tin against porcelain. She'd clearly heard words, regardless of what the reevers saw or perceived. "Can you see them? As dark fae?"

She shook her head. "They are ag'imni."

The ag'imni took a few steps forward, the talons on its gray-black, wolfen animal feet flexing into the ground as it moved. "I'm Zaccai," it offered.

She nodded her head. "My name is Nox. It's been suggested that I'm part demon. Do you think that's true?"

The hellish creation shook his head. "You're no more demon than I."

She smiled at the absurdity of his statement, leaning into the pleasant numbness she'd found. Her heart was capable of no more pain. Her eyes could produce no more tears. Fear was a concept, a distant memory. "That's not quite the reassurance you think it is."

Ash motioned to hand her the blanket that Zaccai had provided for the camp and she wrapped it around her shoulders, grateful. The forest may not be the best place for the silky fabrics of a seductress. One more ag'imni—an identical demon who had been cautiously loitering in the shadows—came out from where he'd been hiding. The gargoyle called Zaccai introduced the other as Uriah, though Nox mused something akin to what Ash had said the first time he'd had a formal meeting with them. If they moved, she wouldn't be able to tell them apart.

Nox smiled at a thought and tore a silken strand from the tatters of her black dress. Approaching the demon, she wrapped the soft fabric around his wrist. "Now I know you are Zaccai," she offered the monster a sad, distant smile. For that is what he was: a monster. He was terrible and dark and horrifying to behold, but as ugly as he appeared on the outside, so she felt on the inside. While he had the gnashing teeth of the ag'drurath, she had the beauty and allure of a goddess and her soul had been one of murder and deceit; her bed had been a graveyard. Any gargoyle that would offer help and warmth to a stranger was surely kinder and better than she could hope to be.

With Nox's help in translation, the reevers were able to explain what happened in the throne room with Queen Moirai. The beautiful newcomer was just as baffled as Uriah or Zaccai to learn that Moirai had been a witch. The ag'imni had let out sounds of true, unadulterated anger that even Nox shrank from when they learned that she was the reason for the curse.

The ag'imni did not stay with them that night. It was decided that they would return to Raascot where there was much to be discussed in Gwydir with their king.

"If Amaris is heading north toward Sulgrave, she'll look for the orb."

"Orb?" Nox asked. They took a moment to catch her up on the events that had occurred at the temple. It was clear from Nox's face that she needed a little more background, so they began to explain her role as a reever and status within the keep.

Once they finished their explanation, Malik agreed, "And if she's looking for the orb, what are we to do?"

"What would Samael want us to do?"

He frowned at that. "There's no peace or balance while Queen Moirai rules with her phantom prince in Farehold."

"My thoughts exactly."

A mixture of resolve and purpose tugged the corners of her mouth upward. Decades of injustice roiled through her. She thought of Millicent and the death powers of witches. She thought of Farleigh and the laws of Farehold that would allow for children to be bought and sold like cattle. She thought of her evil power, one she would never have discovered had she not been forced into a life of servitude in the lands of this southern kingdom. She thought of the royal woman who had ordered the execution of Amaris, and would never allow the moonlit girl another moment's peace while she lived.

Nox clapped her hands together, drawing their attention with her smile. "Great, we'll kill the queen. When would you like to get started?"

The plan was neither intelligent nor elegant, but that seemed to be a common theme with many of the plans that Amaris was a part of. Careful execution had never been a luxury afforded her. As Gadriel's muscles burned from the exertion of clenching and his hands grew too tired to grip the beast's spine any longer, he told Amaris that next time the beast dove for the tree line, they'd have to jump.

"Are you mad?" She'd shouted over the wind and wings into the bronzed face of the general who had clung so tightly to her while his own strength drained from his body.

"Almost definitely."

She had to yell above the sounds of wind, wings and air to be heard, "What if we don't survive the fall?"

"Then let's hope the tumble doesn't smash up that pretty face of yours when we land so you can have an open casket at your funeral."

The ag'drurath had been flying for nearly eight hours, according to the path of the sun as it descended to their left, over the sea, still discernible even behind the clustering clouds. For some time, Amaris had felt the temperature get colder. Her muscles had tensed and her teeth had chattered against the frigid air. She warmed inexplicably hours into the flight, and wasn't sure if it was because her cells had grown numb or if the dragon was giving off some unknowable heat, but it comforted her. She had allowed herself to relax, unclenching her muscles for what remained of their flight.

It seemed impossible that they'd stayed in the air for so long, but it had become clear that they couldn't wait forever for the beast to land. How could the monster not have wanted to stop after all this time? Black blood had left acrid trails for miles upon miles until there was no blood left to be seen. While neither could swear it to be true, there seemed to be a fibrous, skin-like sack beginning to cover the wound of its leg.

Perhaps flinging themselves from the animal truly was the better choice. If they waited for it to touch down, the ag'drurath would be tired and hungry. They were undoubtedly too exhausted to run any further from the serpent. It would be a sorry end to their tale if they escaped its jaws in the coliseum only to be eaten by it in a forest. Gadriel was right. Their safest bet was to leap as soon as they dipped into the tree line.

The reptilian monster seemed to be losing elevation, however gradually. What had once been dots and smudges below them seemed to color into the shapes of distantly scattered farmhouses, trees and cattle. The appearance of livestock seemed to pique the dragon's interest and it began to lower its flightpath, keeping its blackened eyes open for any sheep, cows or shepherds that had the misfortune of being outside this late into this most unfortunate, fateful evening.

The clear, blue day had grown chillier and gloomier the further north they traveled, clouds encroaching until they loomed overhead in thick, gray waves. The ag'drurath flew lower and lower, slowing every once in a while with a backward beat of its wingspan. Amaris peered up from the gap between the creature's back and Gadriel's tattered, sheltering wings. His protective body and blood-slick feathers were the only thing that seemed to be helping her cling to any body heat at this height. Amaris dared to lift her head enough to peer into the distance, spying where the dragon seemed to be angling. She could see a clearing on a mountainside maybe half a mile ahead that appeared to be dotted with sheep.

"It's going for that flock," she said over the sound of wind as it rushed by them. She pressed into his body, shouting into his ear so he could hear her.

He nodded and braved a look over the edge of the dragon to the fast-moving earth below. Gadriel's face was set. A muscle in his jaw throbbed with his decision. His mouth was hard and his gaze determined as he looked into her lilac eyes.

"When I tell you to, you need to let go of the spine and cling only to me, okay?"

Amaris didn't have the energy to be argumentative. If they were going to die, she'd rather Gadriel be responsible for their demise than her. She nodded. The plan sounded insane, but so did becoming a reever, seeing demons, betraying a queen and riding a dragon.

She didn't want to let go, but she knew they couldn't stay on its back. They could take their chances with gravity, or they could battle the serpent for a second time.

It wasn't long before the general was ready to plunge to the earth.

"Are you ready?" He shouted to her over the wind.

"I'll never be ready," she gritted her teeth, "just do it!"

He chuckled darkly, "You're brave, witchling. Get ready!"

The ag'drurath gave another backward beat of its wings, but the dark fae wanted to leap from its spine before the creature began to circle the upcoming sheep. He didn't want a reason to put the two of them in the demon's line of vision. It was now or never.

"Now!"

She released the grip on the black spike and wrapped her arms around the fae's torso, pressing herself into him while he allowed them to roll off the monster. They tumbled free, falling like dead weight toward the ground. Her stomach flew into her mouth as they blindly obeyed the laws of gravity, descending to the earth with the speed and force of two creatures prepared to die.

Gadriel opened his wings, and though shredded too greatly to allow him to take flight, the updraft caught the expanse of his wings just enough to slow their downward dive. "Hold on to me!" he commanded.

His wings closed as they hit the first tree, cocooning Amaris while they absorbed the impact of its branches. Her eyes were closed tightly as her body was tossed and battered in the dark, her head tucked under his chin, tightly against his chest as she bit her tongue to keep from crying out. She felt the brunt of its trunk, then a limb, then another, then another, before the thud of the ground sent her ears ringing, wind knocked from her lungs.

His wings unfurled and she rolled from him into the trunk of a nearby tree. The base of the tree stopped her by knocking the wind from her lungs, crunching her torso against its unmoving form. Her eyes swam as she twisted her body to see Gadriel. His crumpled body had collided into a lichen-covered boulder. He was not moving. She wheezed, unable to find air. She clawed at her chest, but air would not come. Stars spotted her vision, joining the gray clouds and swing of the overhanging canopy. She forced herself to relax, remembering several times during her first year at the reev that she had been kicked or thrown in the sparring ring and undergone the same frantic thrash for air, each time Ash would bend over her and calm her, telling her to breathe.

The air was there. It would come.

She could almost hear his voice as it echoed its command through her memory with such familiarity, "Breathe, Ayla."

Amaris closed her eyes. She calmed herself and, though it took several minutes, she worked through the initial panic and willed herself to breathe normally once more. She remained laying on her back, staring up at the space between the tops of trees, watching the gray clouds roll by as she focused on her breath. She heard the distant screech as a demon devoured nearby sheep. The calming techniques had worked. The high-pitched ringing had faded well enough for her to hear. She could breathe. She could see the trees for what they were. Amaris rolled her head to the side to look for Gadriel. The general still had not moved.

Amaris found the strength in herself to crawl to him, shaking his limp body with her scraped, bloodied hands. She lowered her cheek to his mouth and felt the barely-present heat of his breath. He was alive.

"Come on, demon. Don't you die on me."

Amaris didn't know what to do. She had been trained as a field medic at the reev for wounds, but he did not appear to be bleeding. His spine could be broken. His wings had already been irreparably cut to ribbons. He could be bleeding internally for all she knew. Amaris couldn't let herself believe any of it. She wouldn't allow herself to be consumed with such hopelessness. They'd escaped a goddess damned ag'drurath, they weren't going to die now alone in the woods with only pine needles and moss to keep them company.

"No," she argued against the empty quiet, "You aren't allowed." Amaris curled herself around him, resting her back against the rock. "You don't have permission. You can't die now. You fucking can't. Wake up, Gadriel. Wake up."

He did not.

She sat beside him well into the night, wishing they'd kept a weapon. This forest did not seem to be the ominous, beseul-filled woods near Farleigh, nor did it have the signs or sounds of vageth anywhere in sight. Then again, nothing ever seemed treacherous until it was too late—that was the trick of treachery. She wondered absently if this ag'drurath of their doing was the worst thing to ever happen to the nearby people and felt a faint scratch of remorse for unleashing hell upon them.

It wasn't a very peaceful thought, but she couldn't bring herself to care for the greater good. So what if the villagers were suffering from the serpent's needle-like teeth. If she and the fae were to die alone amongst the trees and shadows in the cold night, maybe they'd take a few sheep and villagers with them.

Amaris pulled Gadriel's head onto her lap, shuffling herself underneath him. She found her hands moving against her hair the way Nox had done for her so many times. She felt something hot and looked down at her fingers, wet with blood as they moved through his hair. A song from Farleigh wafted through her memory, one of the lullabies that the matrons used to sing. It was a haunting song about the All Mother's grace. Its slow, minor key intended as an ominous melody to be wary of crossing the goddess's goodness. It didn't seem appropriate, but she had no powers of healing or anything she could do to carry Gadriel to safety. She was too weak, and he was too heavy. All she could do was sing verse after verse of the soulful, eerie song while she touched the hair of the man who had used his body, his life, to shield her. The song stretched and swelled until it broke against a choke of the helplessness of her sorrow, its ghostly melody carrying her through her memories into her current, poignant pain.

Her singing came to a halt when she heard a twig snap. It was a footstep.

She looked up, eyes darting through the forest, but there was no moonlight. It was a cloudy night with no way to see what dangers lurked in the rocks and trees. There was no silver, there was no light. Her gift for sight did nothing for her in the dark.

Amaris had no weapon, and no way to fight. She felt helpless, exhausted and defeated. If a vageth was going to eat them, perhaps it was best she alert it to her presence so it could hurry up and get on with it. She was unwilling to leave Gadriel. She wouldn't run. She couldn't fight. Instead she let out a pathetic, "Hello?"

After a moment, she heard a quiet exchange of words. A blue lantern was lit, glowing into the faces of two or three people. Humans? Fae? She couldn't tell from where she sat on the forest floor. She wasn't sure if she should be getting up to flee. If she needed to run, she didn't want to abandon Gadriel.

No, she would not leave him. If they were going to die, they'd do it now, together.

She tried her voice again, now facing the looming figures glowing bluish with their lantern. She was so very tired. "Hello?"

They seemed to be nudging one another. It was a childish gesture, the elbows of jostling teenagers. The act disarmed her completely.

"We saw the ag'drurath and came to watch it hunt," said a distinctly female voice.

"I'm sorry, we didn't mean to spy. It's just... It's so rare to see a dragon, and..."

Amaris could not see the girl. She was hooded, her shape barely lit by the blue lantern. It was a youthful voice that seemed to carry the animation of someone several years younger than Amaris.

"I'm taking a course in draconology," said another voice in the cadence of a young man.

"A course?" Amaris repeated dumbly. What was this?

"It's technically a study of the bestiary, but I'm doing my focus in draconology. Seeing the ag'drurath was a blessing from the goddess."

The girl who'd spoken seemed to be scolding him. There was a quiet eruption as if they argued amongst each other, but she couldn't hear any of what was being said. Draconology? Course? She tried to force her mind to work as she looked after the dull gloom of the blue fae light.

Amaris was too numb from the cold, the fall, the forest to appreciate the information. Her brain worked around what they had shared. "You're students?"

They nudged each other again, and the hooded cloaks advanced. "We're not supposed to be out here." The female bravely approached and knelt near them, pulling back her hood. She looked to be barely sixteen. "We heard you singing while we were watching the ag'drurath hunt and wanted to come and see what was happening. But then when we saw you were with an ag'imni—"

One hushed her, his sound urgent and low.

It was too much. Amaris didn't care if they were students or farmers or priestesses or the evil queen's goddess damned armed guardsmen. "Please," she said, "my friend is hurt."

"It—"

"Please help us," was all Amaris said.

They exchanged looks, barely daring to look at the ag'imni in her lap. Perhaps they'd taken the time to absorb the oddity of her circumstance while they had watched her sing, for they did not seem afraid.

The girl spoke again. "Wait here."

And wait, she did. Amaris and Gadriel waited through the coldest parts of the night when Amaris's muscles became spasmed with frost, twitching and clenching against the chill. Her teeth chattered; her lips turned blue. She clung to Gadriel, who still hadn't stirred in her lap. They waited as an owl hooted, and a distant coyote seemed to call for its scavenging pack, possibly elated to find the scattered carrion of sheep left behind by the ag'drurath. She waited until the dark night began to color into an equally cold, gray morning, her fingers fading from the red of early frostbite to the unfeeling death of chill. When Amaris felt herself slipping, releasing herself to the cold, she found herself muttering a long-forgotten prayer to the goddess for both her and the fae in her lap. It was imperceptible, inaudible. She wasn't sure if she believed half of what she said. Her hands were so blue. Her body was so numb.

Her eyes saw nothing as she was loaded onto a cart, carefully placing both her and Gadriel on a flatbed wagon behind a horse. Her ears heard nothing as the group of people hissed at one another, one a matronly, scolding voice. She perceived nothing as the lights of the forest and its clouds changed to unnaturally bright overhead lights of looming, lamp-like structures, casting burning light greater than day into her unseeing eyes. Amaris let herself drift off to meet the goddess while the horses carried her and her companion closer and closer to the university.

I would love to hear from you!

Please leave your reviews of this story,

Piper CJ's debut novel, queer representation in fantasy,

and your experience on the continent of Gyrradin.

Reviews can be left on Amazon or Goodreads.

Connect with the author on Instagram: @piper_cj

via her website: pipercj.com

tag Piper CJ on TikTok (@pipercj), Twitter and Facebook

with reviews, images, and fanart to be shared, credited,

and featured on social media and website.

Use the hashtag #TNAIM to be featured

This fast-paced, heart-wrenching journey continues in The Night & Its Moon Series book two....

the Sun and its Shade

acknowledgements

Thank you to Meg, who became online friends with a weird girl drowning in imposter syndrome and encouraged me to start writing again after a ten-year hiatus. Thank you to Nikki, who has the only opinions I trust regarding my characters' emotional development and casting the necessary spells over so many scenes. Thank you to Bre who has been my Indie Author Commander (of the Normandy). And thank you to Serg, Kelley, and Sarah for reading my first drafts and making me feel like I'd created a world worth celebrating and exploring.

Thank you to me! I'm proud of myself for writing the books I always wanted to see and to read while growing up, regardless of what it cost, as all magic comes at a price. I want to thank the LGBTQ+ community for welcoming me with open arms and celebrating queer representation in fantasy. And to my little brother who spent so many evenings doing speed runs of Zelda: Ocarina of Time with me as we became nerds in our world of two.

Thank you to C.S. Lewis, who would have undoubtedly been displeased with the queer, sexual nature of my fantasy romance, but who nevertheless expanded my mind from youth and who first set me to rigorous thought and escapism. Lewis challenged my thinking and grew my expectations from youth well into the philosophical and theological reaches of adulthood. Special accreditation and citation is required to Amaris's reference of Lewis's quotation: when she is at the Temple of the All Mother in Book One, she uses the words of philosopher, theologian, and the original inspiration for my imagination with his quote:

"Don't use words too big for the subject. Don't say 'infinitely' when you mean 'very' otherwise you'll have no words left to describe something truly infinite."

Made in the USA
Middletown, DE
16 February 2022

61242192R00321